Praise for *Ballistics*

'Beautifully observed'

'Forest fires are raging, to match the fiery passions of a hard-nosed, hard-boiled, basically hard cast . . . Packs a manly punch'
Daily Mail

'A lean and powerful book about quiet, emotional people. It animates a world that any smalltown North American could identify in a moment, yet it transcends this environment to evoke something universal'
Guardian

'*Ballistics* is a profound and haunting novel that won't let you alone'
Spectator

'Flinty coming-of-age story . . . Wilson can make a simile and a verb out of pretty much anything . . . Description is the gift he is keenest to cultivate – rightly'
New Statesman

'A hot shot of a novel . . . Panoramic drama and epic scope'
Tatler

'Well-written, confident, and often compelling . . . Engaging'
List

'An unusual and assured novel that dives into the hinterland of human sadness, and the ways masculinity finds or fails to deal with it'
Sydney Morning Herald

'One of the great pleasures of the novel is the way it surprises at every turn. None of these twists feels forced, however: each is grounded in realistically drawn, vital characters who behave as human emotions and frustrations dictate, rather than conforming to the expectations of the reader . . . It is a harrowing, often brutal read, but it is also emotionally potent and resonant. Simply put, it's one of the finest novels of the year'
Georgia Straight

A NOTE ON THE AUTHOR

D. W. WILSON was born and raised in the small towns of the Kootenay Valley, British Columbia. He is the recipient of the University of East Anglia's inaugural Man Booker Prize Scholarship – the most prestigious award available to students in the MA programme. His stories have appeared in literary magazines across Canada, Ireland and the United Kingdom, and 'The Dead Roads' won the BBC National Short Story Award in 2011. *Once You Break a Knuckle*, his debut short story collection, was published by Bloomsbury in 2012. It was shortlisted for the Dylan Thomas Prize. *Ballistics* was a finalist for the 2013 Amazon.ca First Novel Award, and has been longlisted for both the 2013 Dylan Thomas Pize and The Desmond Elliot Prize. D. W. Wilson lives in Cambridge.

ballistics

D. W. WILSON

BLOOMSBURY

LONDON · NEW DELHI · NEW YORK · SYDNEY

First published in Great Britain 2013
This paperback edition published 2014

Copyright © D. W. Wilson 2013

The right of D. W. Wilson to be identified as the author of this work has been
asserted by him in accordance with the Copyright, Designs and Patents Act 1988

The excerpt from F. R. Scott's "A Villanelle for Our Time", which opens this
book, is used (gratefully) with the permission of William Toye, literary executor
for the estate of F. R. Scott

Bloomsbury Publishing Plc
50 Bedford Square
London
WC1B 3DP

Bloomsbury is a trademark of Bloomsbury Publishing Plc

www.bloomsbury.com

Bloomsbury Publishing, London, New Delhi, New York and Sydney
A CIP catalogue record for this book is available from the British Library

ISBN 978 1 4088 3378 0

10 9 8 7 6 5 4 3 2 1

Printed and bound in Great Britain by CPI Group (UK) Ltd, Croydon CR0 4YY

MIX
Paper from
responsible sources
FSC® C020471

FOR LOON

This is the faith from which we start:
Men shall know commonwealth again

F.R. SCOTT, "A VILLANELLE FOR OUR TIME"

ONE

Empedocles:
Having seen a small part of life, swift to die,
a man rises and drifts like smoke,
persuaded only of what he has happened upon
as he is borne away.

On a Friday evening in September, some time ago, a friend of mine spilled a bottle of lager across her lap and slurred her curiosity about how it all began, that summer I spent in a scour across the Kootenays. She doodled her finger through the caramel froth yeasting on the surface of her thighs. I thought about getting her a paper towel, but I thought about a lot of things. We were taking potshots at empty beer cans with my grandfather's .22 calibre, and I'd lost my aim to nerves and thoughts and the restlessness that endures when adventures come to an uncertain close. I touched a scar on my cheek, about as long as a pocket knife, and wondered a moment after the dead and the gone.

1

How it all began—that's a good question. That's a philosophical question. It's like asking when a bullet starts
toward the beer can. Is it at the moment slug exits muzzle?
When I lean on the trigger? Somewhere among those hours
spent checking and rechecking the chamber? It could be the
munitions line, or the semi-trailer hauling cartridges down
Highway 1, or the clerk at the hardware store who retrieves
the carton from the glass. It could be strictly mechanical—
hammer strikes casing, spark, ignition, *trajectory*—but over
seventy parts make up the firing mechanism of a bolt-action
rifle, even more if you count the bones of the human hand,
the arm, the muscles and nerves and the synapses each themselves firing. And then, getting really philosophical, there's
the Gunsmith's Paradox: to reach its target, a bullet must
first travel halfway, and to travel halfway it must first travel a
quarter, an eighth, a sixteenth, smaller and smaller, such that
it will never reach its destination, such that it won't even start
to move. This means nobody can ever be shot. This means no
journey can ever end.

How it all began? Well, I can trace Gramps' defects all the
way to his childhood: shrapnel he blocked with his sternum
when he was seven, the result of a dud artillery round on a
beach not slingshot range from home; a welding arc that
dashed across his chest while he tempted his body's conduc-
tivity in the rain; smoke inhalation, steam scalds, stress levels,
and a consistent blood-alcohol for all those years strapped
inside a Nomex jacket with *Volunteer Fire* stencilled across
the shoulders. That's his history, but if I were to pinpoint the
moment when everything Began, capital *B*, the summer my

family's past came knocking, I say this: at eighty-two years old, Gramps had his heart attack.

IT WAS A POORLY VENTILATED evening in May, the kind that encourages a man to splay himself along a loveseat and wear musked-up muscle shirts from his childhood. Gramps' house offered little in the way of airflow, so we'd wedged the storm-door with a Gore-Tex boot and unshuttered the windows, and something like a breeze tickled my pits and the skin on my topmost ribs. Earlier, Gramps had salvaged a blastworn indus-trial fan from his storeroom, but I lacked the technical savvy to revive a guttered servo, and Gramps lacked the sobriety. We'd settled onto the furniture in his den to suffer through UFC exhibition matches as we waited for the approaching dark.

I'd only been in the valley a few days, having fled from an impending thesis and some girlfriend drama that for many months has been only a few bubbles shy of boil-over. It was to be the last visit before my indoctrination: a PhD in phil-osophy. Back east, my *significant other*, Darby—who I'd dated and not married for the better part of a decade—had taken to long nights at the university's gym, training for handball, of all things; each night, calling her, I listened to the unan-swered telephone and marvelled at the gap between us. There are a number of things a handball player can do late into the night, but only one of them involves the sport so named.

Gramps went to the kitchen and banged open his fridge and I heard him grab a pair of bottled beer. Outside, the dusk light glanced off neighbouring roofs. Years ago, Gramps strung a mosquito net abreast the exterior window because brown birds tended to get drunk on the gemstone berries that grow on a nearby tree, and they'd kamikaze into the glass. One day he found a family of those birds piled at the house's foundation, and when he lifted them in his palm their necks lolled like tongues.

Pillow clouds swirled above the Rockies, and I smelled the pinprick sensation of lightning on the horizon. The sky had turned the colour of clay. Woodsmoke loitered in the air like breath—it clung to clothes and furniture, a scent like chimney filth, or hiking trips along riverbeds, or the charcoal that remains on a campground after the campers have moved on. The province was in flames. Folks in the Interior had fled their homes and each morning I woke expecting to see the town ablaze. Earlier in the month, the Parks had declared Fire Warning Red and everybody—locals and tourists, blue-collars and rednecks, cops' sons, preachers' boys, parlour philosophers, even the old, haggard men who huddle under the pinstripe tarp that sags off the bakery—doused their camping pits and boiled their hotdogs and darted amid traffic to stamp out cigarettes left to smoulder in the heat.

Gramps set the two open beer on the coffee table and his maimed dog, Puck—an eleven-year-old butter-coloured English mastiff—lumbered from behind a pony wall. On the television, two long-limbed Muay Thai fighters lilted in half moons around each other, gloved hands at temples, knees drawing like longbows. Then one of those stick-men split-kicked forward, sailfish-fast, and Gramps made this noise like *ununghf* and when I looked over the old bastard had gone scarecrow. He lurched sideways and one hand clawed for the end table but fanned it, hauled a circa 1970 lamp down atop him, shade like a hot-air balloon. I knew a thing or two about emergency first aid, so I launched into CPR and dialed 911 and, from the driveway, watched the paramedics green-light him for de-fib in the ambulance.

The ambulance veered behind a panelboard house and out of sight. Neighbours from yards abroad lurked in my peripherals: a pear-shaped man hiked his crotch on his verandah; two kids, young enough to be my sons (I was twenty-eight), leaned on their bikes. Through the living-room window, beyond the mosquito net, Puck stood a vigil, his big head swooping as he looked from me to the empty road and back again as if to say, *What are you waiting for?*

I rushed inside, grabbed Gramps' keys from his hunting vest, and commandeered his Ranger. It was a three-minute drive to the hospital, up a hill with a sixteen percent gradient and past a rundown hostel ripe with the stink of dope and gamey thrill-seekers. As I crested that hill, driving straight west, I was struck by a clear view of the Purcell Mountains. For a moment, under the sunset, they looked to be on fire, the treetops glowing red and orange, and it seemed I could see past them, through that shield of rock and carbon, to the very flames that ravaged the province's interior. I felt a gust of warmth in my eyes, like the dry heat from a wood stove, like a welding torch, as if from the blazes burning on the mountains' far side.

When I arrived at the hospital, a receptionist with curly hair sat behind a desk built into the wall.

My grandfather had a heart attack, I said.

Cecil West?

That's him.

She directed me to a lobby with a window overlooking the courtyard of an old folks' home. There, a double-bent man, out for an evening stroll, passed half a sandwich to a Dalmatian at his side. In the room with me, a toddler drooled on a Tonka dump truck he'd filled with alphabetized blocks. He wore a spaghetti-stained sweatshirt, and he mimicked an engine's hum as the Tonka trundled left to right, where he dumped its cache in a heap against his knee. On those frequent trips to the hospital when I was a kid, Gramps never let me handle the scarce toys laid out in waiting rooms—germ laden and smeared by hands too long unwashed, I suppose.

Then a tall woman my age, with blond hair tied in a bun and a square jaw like a boy's, stomped into the waiting room and glared down at the toddler. She wore blue jeans faded in scruffs at the thighs and a grey T-shirt cut above her triceps. I recognized her as a fling from my highschool years. Missy, she used to be called.

Where's your brother? she said to the toddler.

Went to get a Coke.

And left you here, she said, and looked right at me when she did. Alan?

Hey, Missy, I said.

She curled an arm to her hip. Nobody calls me that anymore, she said, but didn't seem upset. You alright?

Gramps had a heart attack.

Jesus.

Yeah.

Don't worry, if I remember your Gramps, he's too stubborn to die.

Thanks, I said.

She pressed the back of her wrist to her nose, and I thought I recalled her doing that in highschool.

You gonna be around long?

Just the summer. Or what's left.

She bent to scoop the toddler under her arm, pried a stray block from his pudgy hand.

Danny's a cop, she said. That's my husband.

I don't remember him.

You either, she said—a retort, but I'm not sure what she meant. She made a *gotta go* motion with her head and disappeared through the door, and I sensed that I would not see her again. Outside, in the courtyard, the double-bent man raised himself to height, Dalmatian by his side, and together they scuttled toward the care home's rear door. Gramps had told me, time and again, that he'd rather die than spend his final days locked up with a bunch of bluehairs. If he got that bad, I was to drive him to his cabin in Dunbar and there'd be a hunting accident involving a twenty-gauge shotgun— a weapon that reminded him of his days across the pond. Couldn't do it himself, he told me, else he'd get eternal damnation. At least once per visit he and I swung into his truck—an old four-by-four reeking of hides and the rusty scent of bled animals—and drove down Westside Road, past the ostrich farm, to the gravel pits where highschool kids built bonfires big as campers, and there we'd waste the day and a carton of rimfires on emptied tuna cans and paperback books Gramps had deemed uninteresting at best.

When I was finally admitted to Gramps' room, I found him upright in an aquamarine hospital gown, spotted with sticky discs and wires that relayed iridescent spikes to an ECG. Gramps' heart, I would discover later, hadn't stopped due to cholesterol or disease or blood pressure: like breathing, I guess, the heart is on a cyclical firing sequence, and his had simply misfired. Gramps shifted in bed. Deep lines drew along his cheekbones and wrinkles bundled like metal shavings in the corners of his eyes. He peeled his lips over his gums in what could have been a smile.

No flowers? he said.

I only bring flowers for good-looking girls.

I'm in a gown.

And it brings out your eyes, I said, and sat on the edge of his bed. He seemed very small beneath that sheet.

You doing okay? he said.

What kind of question is that.

I'd hate to ruin months of self-pity just by having a heart attack.

You are such a dick, I said.

He grinned, downward. But seriously, he said. You okay?

I'm okay, Gramps, I told him, with as much conviction as I could muster.

He cast his eyes to his hands, fiddled with them in his lap. I chewed a hangnail on my thumb. He looked old, too, all of a sudden—moisture filmed his irises and his cheeks sagged at an angle off his jaws, bespeckled and age-worn, and what little hair remained seemed wilted and thin, like the strands you find gummied to the tiles of a public shower. He looked, I guess, like a grandfather on his deathbed.

I'm dying, he said.

No you're not.

It's like approaching a wall.

I nudged his thigh with a fist. He flashed his teeth.

I'm not just traumatized. A guy knows when the time is up.

What'd the doctor say?

It's coming, Alan. I can feel it.

No. You can't.

I need you to do something for me, Gramps said in a drawl I didn't like. And I need you to do it without asking any of your ridiculous philosophy questions.

Then I was outside under the fluorescent lights that lit the asphalt parking lot like an ice rink, and then I was in the Ranger with its smell of Old Spice and sloshed beer and everything else my grandfather. From the radio, a monotone voice droned factoids about the burning Interior. I drove the long way around Invermere's lake, like I used to do when I was sixteen and desperate to ogle the girls whose folks had come from Calgary to spend their summer in the great, untamed wild of the Kootenay Valley. At the beach, kids half my age gathered under a streetlight. They dabbled toes in the water and sloshed vodka on their gums and I cringed at the idea that kids were now half my age. Home, I went to Gramps' bedroom, like he instructed, and inched a shoebox from beneath his bed. It was maroon and covered in dust and dog hair and inside I found a trove of sentimental items: a tarnished cap revolver with a sulphur-scorched hammer stained as though by ochre; a dehydrated poplar leaf big as my hand; at least two mouths' worth of baby teeth, some my own; a wedding band too large for any of my fingers; a silver Zippo lighter adorned with the American eagle. And there, at the bottom, I found an address with the name *Jack West* scrawled in my grandfather's blocky script. I ran my fingers along those letters and, lifting the paper from the box, felt the passing of a burden. What goes around comes around, they say, but I'm not so sure. Never really leaves, maybe.

I need you to find your dad, Gramps said to me from that hospital bed. Because I don't know how much time I've got left, and there are some things I need to say to him before I go.

Here's a story about Jack West: In '69, when he was a stupid kid, he shot me in the leg with a .22-calibre rifle—our very first introduction. Him and his old bastard Cecil had lodged the night in a copse of trees a short distance from the cabin they owned out at Dunbar. Cecil'd caught wind of a series of break-ins, and upon inspection found stuff missing: a couple old plates, fistfuls of cured elk, one or two sixers of beer. The cabins that lined the Sevenhead River were easy prey for scavenging, and though I could've foraged to keep myself alive, I had my daughter, Linnea, with me. Maybe I got cocky, too: the night Jack shot me was the first night I didn't do a full search of the bushes that ringed the cabin and its field. Same carelessness could get a man killed in war, I'll tell you that.

The moon shone full force that night and the cabin's front door was clear for thirty yards in all directions. I intended to camp just inside the entry because it was March, and chilly, and I could smell rain on the horizon—that scent like gravel that is universal across the world. I'd also whiffed the sourness rising through the collar of my shirt, and hoped to snag a bar of soap. My daughter didn't seem to care, but a guy needs to have his own standards—we can't all be bushmen, regardless what Cecil West has to say. As Linnea and I skulked through the forest I grunted warnings to watch for the tree branches and their pine needles, because I'd seen a guy lose an eye in Vietnam after he got whipped in the face by a bamboo stalk.

I crouched at the border of the tree line and did a slow, one-eighty scan, though in hindsight I can't guarantee thoroughness. If I'd really been searching I might have noticed the mud marks at the base of the cabin's door, or the footprints in the mushy earth where Cecil and Jack had earlier done an inspection. I sniffed the air, tilted my ear to the quiet, for Linnea's benefit, mostly. She was fourteen back then and unimpressed with anything I had to say. Partly, I hated myself for hauling her along, for putting her through that. I squeezed her shoulder for reassurance then exited the tree cover and bolted for the cabin's door.

Jack was fifty yards upwind. He tells me he can't remember the events that led to the gunshot—they're obscured to him, a mishmash of adrenaline and instinct, and I believe him. He was pubescent and he had a rifle in his hands, felt empowered, bigger than fourteen years old. He was no stranger to the outdoors: at school, during games of manhunt, Jack hid among the thick bushes outside the schoolyard's ringwire fence. Protocol forbade him from romping through those wilds, but Jack West was never really a kid to bend to any rules besides his father's. He liked the wilderness, and he liked to hunt, and he was not unaccustomed to firearms. He knew how to handle a gun: never maintenance a rifle with the action shut; a firearm's safety is true in name only; to avoid eyepiece gouges on your cheek, nestle the stock on the muscley part of your shoulder, right where the deltoid curls like a rope to your pectoral.

Here's what I think went down: Jack got scared. I darted from the tree line like a burglar and Jack traced me with his irons. I know the sensation of having a person in your sights, that flutter where your throat meets breastbone. Jack would never admit it, but he struggled in the shadow of his old man, so maybe he saw a chance to chin up in Cecil's eyes, a chance to have the old bastard give a father's approval. And in Jack's defence, I didn't exactly look like a guy who didn't need to be shot. My clothes were bushworn and sedimented with God knows how much mud and I was stalking toward his cabin, hunched like a guerrilla. I reached the door and jimmied a kinked nail in the lock and jostled it around, and the whole time Jack had me trained in that thumbnail space between the sights.

A .22 has about as much kick as an impatient cat. As I twitched the nail around the tumblers, the woods were quiet. I vaguely recall the sound of my own breath. Then there was a small *whump* across the valley, and the bullet snagged me in the calf.

It's blurry after that. I hit the wooden wall of the cabin and scrambled around the side for cover. The adrenaline was in me. Cecil came tear-assing around the cabin in pursuit and his gumboots left skid trails in the mud and he slid enough to touch his knuckles to the dirt. The whole time, I'm nowhere near to finding cover and I'm hearing gunfire like popcorn in my skull, as though I'm back in the jungle, so I plant my feet and kick a rock aside in case it trips me up. Fight or flight, as they say. I test the turf, the give, how much slick I have and how well my boots bite into the mud and bloodweed and parched knotgrass. And there's Cecil bearing down on me, the first goddamned Canadian I'd met since crossing the border, this maniac with a cadet's hair and a menacing way of moving forward, as if he knows how to handle himself, as if he's going to rip me a new asshole.

Get away! I barked to Linnea, and drew my hunting knife from its sheath on my thigh.

The gap closed. Cecil ditched the rifle—no time for him to reload it—and I lashed the knife. He twisted mid-lunge, deflected the blade along his ribs and cinched his elbow down on my arm in a trap straight out of some British Army textbook. I rammed my forehead into his nose and he dug his knee into my gut. We meshed together, held each other like wounded men. But flawless victories are for the Bruce Lee movies: people don't go unscathed; people don't stay calm. We're desperate and cowardly and we scramble like beasts—a man would betray his own son if it meant one more shaky breath. Cecil cracked me with his elbow and I gouged his eye with my thumb and the whole time my knife flapped useless, pinned.

We stumbled apart. I smeared blood and snot on my palm and Cecil squeezed juice from his eye.

I think you've got the wrong idea! Cecil hollered. He lifted the rifle from the ground.

You shot me.

My boy shot you.

Yeah?

Cecil levelled the rifle. I tightened my grip on the knife.

You ain't gonna shoot me with that, I told him.

That so?

You didn't reload.

Cecil ran his tongue along his teeth. He gave a nod and planted the gun's butt in the dirt. You're right, he said.

Get outta here.

This is my cabin.

Hell if I care.

Put the knife down.

Gimme the gun.

Cecil didn't move, leaned on the rifle as if breathless. You're bleeding, he said. I can help. Where'd it get you?

Calf.

Lucky. Hollowpoints. It come through?

I shook my head, felt the warmth sticky against my leg.

I have beer, and some fishing line, Cecil said. It won't be fun, or pretty, but you can strike it off your list of things to do before you die.

For a moment I didn't respond, sensed my daughter's eyes

on me, knew, whether I liked it or not, that I was at this man's mercy.

I'm Cecil, he said.

Archer, I told him.

You here from the States?

I showed him my gums, had no idea if he was a sympathizer or even where I could find one. Cecil waved a hand. Forget it. Anyone else out here with you?

I sheathed the knife. I've never been good at reading expressions, but Cecil seemed genuine, and he had the face of a guy who had seen enough bullshit. Then his son rounded the cabin and I looked upon Jack West for the first time. It's been a long road. His fingers kneaded the fabric at the hem of a bulky coat and he shuffled to Cecil's side. If I had it my way, that's how I'd remember Jack West—just some stupid, awkward kid on a chill evening in spring, when the future and all its shit were still distant, impossible things.

I WAS ON THE RUN from the US Army. Weeks before, home in Montana, I'd received a letter from Uncle Sam saying they needed me for another tour. It came with a stack of bills and a hardware flyer, and the mailman who handed it over—an old guy with watery eyes—bit down on his lip as if he had advice to give. At the top of the letter, in red block typeface, it said FINAL WARNING—so if I didn't want the military police on me like a herd of turtles then I had to skip town or re-enlist. One of the toughest calls I've ever had to make: I'm a decorated soldier, I've got a Purple Heart, a Long Service Medal, a Combat Action Badge—even back then I wasn't some dreamy college kid crafting posters to save the world.

The day that letter arrived I grabbed a bottle of my home-brewed wine and got in my pickup and drove out to the acreage where I grew up. That property was someone else's legacy by then, but my family had made the land fertile, had stripped their palms raw tearing up bloodweed, planted and cultivated the trees along the riverbanks to give the soil strength. If any ghosts haunt it, they are ghosts I'd know by name. The new owner—a good enough guy—had flattened our old house, but the landscape was unchanged. Landscapes take longer to move on; they're ponderous, they remember. Generations of my family went into the sculpting of that land: our sweat flavours the waters that feed the wellspring; acres of poplar trees have heard us fight and bleed and carry on. Us Coles are in the soil, and not just metaphorically.

My part of Montana is all prairie fields, but if you find yourself a vantage point and look west you can see the Bitterroot Mountains across the wheat and birch and horse-head pumps. When I got to the acreage I hiked to a land bridge above a small stream where I first put my hand on a girl's knee and where we scattered my dad's ashes in '59. He was a county deputy who spent the whole of his career without a promotion, and I don't think I ever saw him as happy as the day I made sergeant first class. I was twenty-seven; first thing he did was salute. So that stream was a good enough place to think things over. Neither me nor my dad had ever been men to shirk responsibility, but fleeing to the Great White North was an exercise in just that. Tough tradition to break.

But I broke it, and then I got shot in the calf, and then I was bleeding and wounded and madder than the Bible. Cecil put his shoulder under my arm and Jack tried to help but he just got in the way, so Cecil waved him to the sidelines. My adrenaline flushed. The cold got me shivering. When Linnea tells this story she says I forgot about her, went hyper-masculine, all big chests and tough words and facial hair. She's only half right at best. Cecil hobbled me forward and the whole time I was trying to think up a sane way to call my daughter from the bushes. Jack picked at the hem of his coat and Cecil barked for him to open the door, for the love of God.

Wait, I said, and then I whistled for Linnea to come out of the trees. She did so with more than a little reluctance, and then, out in the open, she fixed me with her devil's glare. It's a glare that promises retaliation at a later time, a glare of the very-unimpressed. She often looked at Jack West like that, almost by habit. I've come to miss its intensity.

Upon seeing my daughter, Cecil's forehead bunched up like a man in thought. Then he nodded to himself and pushed me through the door and into his cabin. There, he boiled water on a Coleman stove and I hiked my pant leg and cringed at the stupidity of my wound. Jack and Linnea stayed outside. When asked, Linnea says Jack was more terrified of her than of me, that he kept his distance just tugging sprigs from his coat. That's the one trait he sure as shit inherited from his dad—complete lockdown around the better sex. Things might've turned out different if he'd inherited Cecil's backwater sense of duty, but that's neither here nor there.

At Cecil's behest, I propped my wounded leg on a chair and he rolled the pants above my knee. The hollowpoint had splintered barely after piercing the fabric, and I doubt any shards cut into muscle—not that it didn't hurt like a bastard. The skin had gone seven different shades of yellow and I could see the purple blotches where a fragment went in, but I've taken worse injuries. The worst—my burned arm—flared up by the mere proximity to heat. Cecil set his saucepan of hot water nearby, dipped a rag into it, and, in a gentle, circular motion like a guy brushes his teeth, cleaned away weeks of dirt and sod and soil.

Jack, he called, and the boy poked his head through the door. Get the whiskey.

Jack shuffled to the cupboards and opened them and I watched him search, hesitate, and search again. He craned his neck around but Cecil had his head bowed near my calf. I caught the boy's eye though, knew from the way he winced that there wasn't any whiskey in the cupboard. He said as much, real timid.

What is there? Cecil said.

Jack produced a bottle of sherry and Cecil blinked twice and pulled his lips into a cringe. In a comically gruff voice, he said, What's that doing in there?

Jack brought two ceramic mugs, filled mine up, avoiding my eyes the whole time, and scuttled outside. Cecil lifted his eyebrows and indicated the needle dangling its trail of gut, and I raised my mug of sherry. Fucking ridiculous, but that's how it went down, that first evening: Cecil worked with a pool player's concentration, plucking metal from my hairy leg and closing the wounds that needed closing, and I drank sherry as if it were juice and wondered if I might just be luckier than the blessed. Occasionally, Cecil splashed sherry in his own mug and winced it down. I think we both pretended the sherry was whiskey, because, hell, it should have been. I've heard Cecil tell the story a couple times, and he always makes that change. Of course he makes that change.

So, where's home? Cecil said after a time.

Grew up in Montana, but we crossed the border from Washington.

Cecil's cheek twitched toward a smile. Woman drag you there?

Shit yes. Been there since Linnea was a girl. What are the kids doing out there, anyway?

Jack doesn't want to be in here.

Thinks I'll wring his neck?

Probably thinks *I* will.

I'll repay you for the stuff we took. I'm good for it.

Jack and Linnea came inside and sat across from each other at the table, Linnea beside me and Jack beside his bastard father. In the dull light of the oil lamp Linnea looked tired enough to die. Her dark hair was stuck to her forehead and heavy on her ears. I offered a dirty hand that could cup her entire cheek. She closed her eyes and put some weight in my palm, and though one day I'd switch seats with Jack West, right then I'm sure he watched that tenderness with more than a little jealousy.

Cecil removed a last piece of metal and pulled the last stitch tight. Then he hazarded a look under his arm, across his ribs where my knife had scraped and been pinned. He eased off his hunting vest. I didn't have the best angle, but his checkered shirt was lanced open, damp and oil-black in the lamplight.

Jack, he said, and his son perked forward. How bad am I bleeding?

Jack tugged the flaps that wreathed the cut and I saw a gash there, curved like a smile. Not too bad, Jack said.

I pushed my mug aside and leaned in and waved for the needle.

Lord knows I've been drunker for more delicate things than a few stitches, I said.

Keep sipping your girly drink, Cecil told me. Then he passed his son a fresh ski needle and a string of gut and for a second Jack just stared at it like it was a thing of great worth. Cecil tugged his shirt over his head, revealed his battered, wiry torso, his pale skin and farmer's tan. He tilted sideways so Jack could access the cut. It didn't go very deep and stretched only as long as a thumb, but it ran at an angle along his ribs, and Jack's forehead bunched as he tried to find a way to work. Cecil's skin gleamed sweaty and bruised and scratched along his upper arms and collar where my fingernails had grooved his flesh. I could feel myself similarly beaten; in the morning, both of us would be stiffer than a two-pecker goat. Jack worked silently and Cecil adopted what might be the gruffest expression I have ever seen. I slid the sherry across.

I worked in the hangars, in Britain, he said. Never saw any combat.

Marine Corps. Never been shot before. Hit with napalm, but never shot.

Don't worry about paying me back.

I'll find a way.

After Jack finished and Cecil had eased his shirt on, he said he had wireframe cots in the loft, but needed to know if I'd be able to pull myself up the ladder. I told him it'd take more than a pellet in the leg to keep me down, and he grunted like I expected him to. He glanced under his shirt, to inspect Jack's work.

It's passable, he said, and ruffled the boy's hair. Then he climbed to the loft to set things up, and I spun the sherry between my fingers and looked over at Jack.

Sorry, he said.

It's alright.

I don't even remember firing.

When the adrenaline's in you, I said.

You ever shot a person?

Then Cecil came down the ladder and jerked a thumb toward the loft. Two beds up there, he said.

You're hit too. Make the kids sleep on the wood.

Jack and me can sleep in the truck, he said. I'll visit the doctor in the morning, in case you need antibiotics. Then we'll think of something.

You a sympathizer?

Cecil put his hand on Jack's shoulder. He ran his tongue along his teeth, tested the point of a canine. I'm not a war supporter, if that's what you mean.

I'm AWOL, I said, sounding suddenly sober, even to myself. It's more serious.

You're too grey to be a draft dodger.

21

They'll court-martial me.

Like I said, we'll think of something.

I owe you, I told him, and Cecil made a motion with his shoulders I have come to understand as the only way he knows to acknowledge that he's been thanked.

LINNEA AND I SPENT the remaining hours on one of the fold-out cots in Cecil's loft. He'd given us one of his only two sleeping bags—good to minus ten, he promised—and we'd unzipped it to share like a blanket. Cecil and Jack suffered through the night in the rear of his pickup, where he kept two foamies. Even with Linnea's body heat, the chill dried my nose and breathing prickled my throat. Cold, for a March night. Linnea went right to sleep but I've never been able to just shut down, so I listened to the rhythm of her heart and watched her shoulders rise and fall. I like to think I made a pretty good dad. You won't hear me say that about my other talents, and Lord knows there aren't a lot of them, but I gave it my all. A guy has to do that, far as I figure. That's how we're judged, in the end.

Despite my best efforts, my daughter has borne the weight of my missteps. I didn't expect another war and by the time I got shipped out her mother had other things going on, so Linnea had to board with my sister and her preacher-thin husband. They put her to work at their raspberry farm, demanded she sort the fruit to earn her keep, even though I was paying them. By the end of each day Linnea's fingers were stained pink and freezing from the unheated water they spritzed over the berries—full-time on the weekends, a few hours every day. If I ever get back there, I've got a couple things to say. Linnea, bless her, never complained about it, and I'm not sure I deserve to be spared carrying that blame. The world can be so kind and so cruel all at once, and I tend to land on the receiving end of its kindness—or I'm a closet optimist—but the same cannot be said of the people close to me. Cecil's a good example, for more than a few reasons: even that first night, too much of a man to sleep under the same sleeping bag as his son. While Jack tugged the vinyl to his chin, Cecil crossed his arms and tilted his ballcap over his eyes and shivered in the dark.

That'd become something like a custom for Jack and Cecil—the two of them camping in the bed of his truck, Cecil freezing his ass so Jack might have a second blanket, a second sleeping bag, and God forbid Jack decline that offer. Those trips would culminate in a cougar-hunting trip in July 1972, right before the start of Jack's grade twelve year. They'd piled a two-man tent and a food cooler under the canopy, stocked their hiking for one helluva trek. Their destination was some-where southeast of town, because word spread about high cougar concentration in the woods there, and there was an open call on the beasts. Cecil's buddies had downed one earlier in the summer, skinned it and lynched it in a garage above a drainage pipe so the dripping blood wouldn't make more than an oil-spill splatter on the floor. Guys in the valley built their houses with those kind of specifications in mind. As long as I've known him, Cecil has never been a great hunter, but after his buddies showed him that massive swaying carcass, he'd gotten it in his head that he needed to measure up.

They didn't get a kill. By the end of the third day whatever cats had prowled those Kootenay wilds were beyond the limits of their supplies and endurance. They headed home. In the truck, Cecil banged his shotgun behind the bench and tore a beer from the yoke he kept under passenger—he still keeps a sixer there, far as I know—and Jack expected him to offer one over, but the old bastard did no such thing. They drove without talk. Sometimes he fiddled with the radio but otherwise he just slurped from his single aluminum can. They stopped at the cabin on the way home and Cecil took Jack's shitty rifle to the water's edge, stepped off the rocks so the lake lapped the soles of his army surplus boots. Jack asked him what the hell was going on, but Cecil just checked the safety and chambered a round and cushioned the stock in the nook of his shoulder. *Mind your own business*, he told Jack, who told me, and neither of us knew what to make of it. Cecil fired a bullet at a low angle into the glass surface of Dunbar Lake. The bullet skipped once and broke the surface and disappeared with a *ploop*. And Jack did what any good son would do: he sat on a piece of driftwood and waited it out, afraid more than anything that he'd somehow let his dad down.

If I had to pick one thing, I'd say this is where Cecil and I differ: I wouldn't have left Jack without explanation. For weeks the poor kid lived in anxiety, wondering about all the ways he might have messed up. It's too good-ol'-boy, I think, and borderline cruel. Maybe it's different if you're raising a son. Is the urge to lessen your kid's doubt reserved for parenting of the opposite sex? Maybe, or maybe Cecil just got some things wrong. For all his dogged insistence that men be judged by their actions, he won't acknowledge that a man can be measured by how well he has reared his offspring. It's one of the few times I've known Cecil to be inconsistent, but given how it all panned out, given it all, I'm not about to begrudge him one or two acts of self-delusion.

I WOKE EARLY and roused Linnea with a hand on her ankle. She blinked sleep from her eyes and I got her up and folded the cots into storage shape. Then I climbed downstairs for a drink of water and so I could dump a wad of American bills on Cecil's half-varnished table. My leg ached like nothing in the world and it took a while for my body to grind itself to motion. It felt like being an old man. Linnea gave me a look but I just shrugged and she shrugged right back.

When Cecil came through the door he pointed at the bills on the table.

What are those?

Payment, I said.

The leg alright?

A little bruised, I told him, and rolled up my pant leg to reveal the calf blued and blood-run like a cabbage head. Not my worst injury by far.

What's the worst?

Lit my arm on fire once, I said, and patted my bicep.

Cecil grunted, seemed to consider. Truck seats three, he said. So if you want to come into town we can say you're my cousin or something.

And the kids'll stay here?

Jack and your girl can fish off the dock.

He's not gonna shoot her, right? I said.

I'll take the gun with us.

What's the town?

Invermere. You can use my shower when we get there.

What're you getting at?

You smell like a dogshit, Cecil said, and laughed.

Linnea came over to me and I wrapped my arm around her torso. She tried to push away but I held on. Cecil sniffled and looked anywhere but at the two of us. I let her go.

I hear about guys who settle up here, I said. Don't ever go back.

I dunno about it. My fiancée might.

He scratched his neck, then shook his head at the bills on the table, so I scooped them up and shoved them into a zippered pocket above my knee.

You got skills? he said, winced. I mean, if you need work.

I'm a painter.

Good, that's good. I know a few painters.

I stood up and swung my leg forward, tested my full weight on it. Well, she won't buckle, I said, and loped through the door behind Cecil. We passed Jack, who stared at the ground. I climbed into Cecil's truck and he rolled down his window.

See if you can get a fish or two, he told Jack as the engine sputtered. And for God's sake don't shoot anyone.

Then he put the truck in gear and we hobbled over a fallen log, up a dirt road that led to the highway. It's all forest and bedrock and pine trees, the valley, snug between the Purcells to the west and the Rockies to the east, and in '69 you wouldn't have seen any clear-cuts on those mountain faces. You could climb most of the peaks too—spend a gruesome eight hours testing yourself against physics, and then relax with a vantage overlooking the whole valley. I've done that once or twice; the view is not easily challenged. Up there I could pitch a tent and live happily in the red hours of the morning with the valley and its towns below me in a well of darkness. I'd pack my sketchbook and a handful of charcoal pencils and I'd sit and draw. Sometimes I'd holler off a cliff and wait for the echo to swoop back to me. I can't explain why—simply felt compelled. Cecil'd blame it on the artist in me, but landscapes have a certain solidity, a certain, unquestionable reliability, and the echo is their earmark. It takes distance for the sound to splinter and scatter, to slow down enough for rocks to gather shards of voice and put them back together. It takes *scope*. An echo hints at a great wisdom—bluecollar wisdom. It departs and returns, departs, returns. A wisdom of reliability, I guess.

As we drove, Cecil bent his elbow out the window, gripped the wheel at its twelve-o'clock with one loose hand. He wore a blue ballcap with a bunch of burrs along the rim, a checkered T-shirt beneath his grey vest. He had his share of wrinkles around his eyes and a mouth that bent easy into a scowl but did so less often than you'd expect. No real scars to note besides a few spark burns on his chin. He looked like a high-school gym teacher.

I like the landscape here, I said.

Nice to be able to go outside. I was in London for a while— it felt like always being indoors. I don't know how city guys do it.

Different values. My wife was one.

And she isn't here.

Thank God for that.

Cecil slid one eye my way and his cheek twitched to a smile. You won't find city guys here, he said. We run them out of town.

Make a game of it, I bet.

We keep score, too.

The road wound through a gap in a canyon wall where the rock face was the colour of clay and high enough to block the morning sun. On the other side, we rolled through a tourist town called Radium that was built around natural hot springs. Its main drag had a liquor store and half a dozen hotels, each with their vacancy sign lit. Beyond that, the highway curled along the lip of a gully that stretched to the horizon. From our view I could see a lake and small crops of houses dotting the water's rim and, in the distance, the sulphury glow of lights—lanterns, houseboats, truckers grinding miles in the first hours of the day.

I could draw that, I said.

Draw it?

Keeps me out of trouble.

Better than my hobbies, Cecil said.

Used to draw people. That got me into trouble once or twice.

Used to?

After my last tour, just couldn't keep at it.

Cecil looked over at me. I don't know what to think about this war, he said.

None of us do, I told him, and stared out across the gully. I'll tell you this, though: it's our kids getting shot.

Was the same with the Nazis.

They deserved it, at least.

Were you at Normandy?

Ten years too young, I said, and patted my arm, the scar hidden there. We got bombed, our own goddamned guys.

Friendly fire isn't.

You gotta watch for it. Guys'll shoot you in the back, on purpose or not.

Probably doesn't even know he's doing it.

Tunnel vision, I said. That's human nature.

CECIL LIVED IN A heavily treed segment of town, down a steep hill, and close enough to the beach for him to claim he could see the water from his bathroom on the second floor. The road was gravel and dirt and Cecil, for years, would bitch about street taxes he never saw a cent of. *Not even new gravel*, he'd often say. The truck's tires churned rocks and pinged pebbles against the undercarriage. Boys ran amok on the street and the shoulder and the yards that lined it, cap guns in hand, yelling *bang* and *gotch your arm*, and sometimes crouching behind tree stumps or old cars or among the knotgrass that grew unchallenged in the ditches. As we drove by, Cecil gave short, blurting honks to clear them from his path. They waved and stood on the roadside as if at attention, and Cecil bobbed his head, winked, and more than once saluted.

His house was a small one with army-green siding that Cecil, colour-blind, called grey. He parked beside a cinder-block retaining wall with a dangerous lean. At the far end of the carport a stack of chopped lumber was dark with moisture. The lawn was green save a few patches of piss-puddle brown, which he blamed on neighbourhood dogs. We climbed a short flight of concrete steps to his front door, where he banged his boots together over a welcome mat, tried the doorknob and found it open, and went inside.

Nora, he called as we entered. You here?

In the kitchen.

Can you put on some coffee? he said, and turned back to me with a shrug, as though to ask if he should have added anything else. I got someone with me.

There was a pause, and then footsteps on linoleum and then his fiancée—Nora Miller—popped around the corner. She had dark red hair that framed her face and hung to her chin, a small nose with an upward turn at the tip, big eyes with eyebrows that seemed always on the verge of lifting incredulously. She glanced to me and then to Cecil and her nose scrunched up—hopefully not because I smelled *that* bad, but I may never know—and she reached for Cecil's face. Her small hand touched his chin and she pushed his head sideways and examined the scratches lining his jaw.

I take it something's going on, she said.

This is Archer, Cecil said. Archer, my fiancée, Nora.

Hello, I said.

Nice to meet you.

Archer needs to use our shower, Cecil said.

He certainly does.

I'll explain.

Nora grinned: a wide, authentic, lovely grin that showed her molars. I've always thought the prettiest smiles are the ones that show the most teeth.

Yes, you will. But let's get Archer into the shower, she said, and turned to me. We'll get you a set of Cecil's old clothes, too. Those ones—likely beyond saving.

They set me up with a pair of faded jeans and a plain navy T-shirt stamped with Smokey the Bear's sombre frown. Cecil gave me a disposable razor and a bar of soap, and that was that. I stepped under the hot water and inhaled the steam and felt as if I could scrape the dirt off my arms with a palette knife. The heat throbbed through my scarred arm, through the wrinkled skin on the bicep, but it always does that— muscle memory, or something. It seemed unfair that I'd get to wash first and not my daughter, stuck at that cabin with Jack. The soap stung the cut and I prodded the wounds, inspected the pucker and Cecil's handiwork. I'd be lying if I said it was a flawless execution, but I'd be lying if I said I cared.

I came out of that shower almost a different man. My leg even felt alright, but that was probably in my head—I always feel better after a shower. I carried my ruined clothes bundled under my arm, into the kitchen, where I found Nora with her back to me at the sink. She fiddled with a disassembled water tap. I cleared my throat and she whipped her head sideways, enough to see me in her peripherals. Just toss 'em, she said, and, with a rubber-gloved hand, gestured at a garbage can in the corner.

I did so, sat down at the table.

Thanks for the clothes.

She unstoppered the sink and the water gurgled down the drain. Cecil went into town, to see the doctor, she said, and pulled the rubber gloves off. A few bubbles of dishwater clung to her ear, but I didn't say anything. She crossed her arms

31

under her breasts, leaned on the corner where the counters met. You're in a predicament.

I figured so.

Draft dodgers are one thing. Government gives them amnesty.

I'm not a draft dodger.

That's what I'm talking about, Nora said. With her pinky, she hooked a string of hair out of her eyes and tucked it behind one ear. She had nice ears. And your daughter, too. We can say you're Cecil's army friend and your wife left you without any money.

Not that far from the truth.

That last bit was Cecil's idea.

I had a hunch.

You army guys, she said, and brushed past me out of the kitchen, and I smelled the air that breezed by in her wake—a scent of grapefruit detergent, of warm bread like someone who'd been baking all day, and something else, too: a tougher smell, like the outdoors, like axe heads and chopped wood and chimney smoke and big changes not so far around the bend.

TWO

Anaxagoras:
Men would lead quiet lives if these two words,
mine *and* thine, *were taken away.*

With Gramps' shoebox never more than arm's reach away, I phoned my girlfriend. Men, I think, typically white-flag it to their girlfriends or wives—or mothers, if all other women be *in absentia*—when the emotional shit strikes the Great Oscillator. It's a primal thing, no different than the human discomfort around snakes and arachnids or our general dislike of other people's feet. Men who confide, and trust primarily, in other men have learned to do so as a skill; just as instinct would have us pry a nail from our foot, so would it have us bewail our sorrows to the females in our lives.

That night, my girlfriend didn't answer, and I lay in bed and counted all the jocks I knew, like the guy with the triangular brainpan who directed the university's intramurals, or the gymnastics instructor who could stand for a whole hour with his arms bent right-angle to his hips, chest inflated like a ghostbuster. I figured I would one day find her in their arms. The window in my bedroom was busted like a spiderweb where my buddies once blasted it with a propane-powered potato cannon. Through the glass, a streetlamp's fossily light fell across the far wall where hung my modest collection of awards—medals for outstanding marksman, mostly, though also a certificate for first prize in a grade eight drafting contest (I snap a mean tangent), a trophy clock shaped like the state of Montana, and a brass-dipped Labatt beer can I won as part of a Barrel-Fill crew Gramps had slung together for Sam Steele Days. The Impressionable Lads, I think the team was called.

The cordless rang against my ear and my girlfriend's voicemail picked up. You've reached Darby, it chimed, way too cheery. I listened to my own breath and clacked my jaw in circles. For the first time in years I felt my small-town roots, that I could stay there, in Invermere, take welding lessons from Gramps, spend my days seven-to-three banging things together and then ten-to-one at the bar grazing elbows and buying drinks for girls I knew from highschool but had never dared proposition.

Invermere is a town where sons take after their dads and teenagers in lift-kit trucks catch air off train tracks. Winters are cold and punctuated with sudden warmth that melts all snow, and grotesque snowmen vanguard front yards, half-thawed and horror-jawed like hellions from the seventh ring of Dante's Inferno. Power lines slouch under snowfall and sully people's mountain views. Rednecks redline their Ski-Doos across the frozen lake. In summer, teenagers burn shipping flats at the gravel pits and slurp homebrew that swims with wood ether, and at least one novice drinker goes blind swallowing the pulp. Vehicles courtesy-honk at kids meandering the roads, and those kids nudge each other toward alleyways and paths beaten through strangers' yards. Houses sit back on lots. Properties are for sale by owner. Trees lay long shadows during dusk and dogs leap at fences to test the resilience of their chains.

I had only a handful of friends growing up, most of whom are either dead or married now—Will Crease and Mike Twigg; Brad Benson who vanished one summer after a devastating fallout with his old man; Joe Brooks; others who joined our group for lengths of time. In those days a kid was judged by how fast he could run and how quickly he could scale a neighbour's fence. A palisade rimmed our backyard, six feet high, and I could vault the slats and windstorm my legs overtop and disappear into a sprint upon touchdown. Parents watched me and their fences with a wary eye. One neighbour, a widow with skin that wrinkled horizontally, owned a bean-shaped pool, so she duct-taped a red warning line along the portion of fence that dropped into water. A crotchety Calgarian, whose liver eventually failed him during a Loop-the-Lake marathon, tire-ironed me off his property after I boarded his carport via a whip-like tree and a stunt out of *Indiana Jones*. Not infrequently through my boyhood, neighbours came knocking on our front door and Gramps would invite them in and sit at the kitchen table drinking coffee and talking in murmurs unintended for my ears.

I never thought untoward about any of this, but with the content of Gramps' shoebox so close and my absent dad weighing on me like a thesis, I wondered whether the neighbourhood vigil upon my boyhood was conventional prudence or something more personal, the result of a lineage I never really sought after. History, in a place like Invermere, is not easily entombed.

Our house had two storeys and jaundiced siding. In the backyard eight or so pines strained skyward, sturdy-trunked— trees from which a man could rescue his cat. Long ago, Gramps dug his own firepit, and in the evenings he lounged in a deck chair on the moist soil and just stared at the trees and the mountain peaks he could glimpse amid branches and other people's homes. The awe of a prairie boy, I guess. A previous owner had buried a vertical PVC pipe, thick as my forearm, to its mouth in the middle of the yard, and Gramps guessed the pipe was an abandoned geothermal project, a relic of the groundwater heating fad that'd swept the valley around 1970. One summer, my dad rescued a shotglass-sized bird from the deeps of that pipe by intermittently heaping sand on the creature's head. I have few memories of my father—glimpses of a moustached face, a man who flung footballs through a strung-up tire rubber, a certain scent of carbide and steel, maybe, though Gramps always smelled like an engine and it is through his stories that I know Jack West.

My dad disappeared when I was a year old. My last memory of him—if it is indeed *my* memory—is the two of us watching a house fire across the street. He had one hand tight on my small shoulder. We'd have been watching Gramps do the fireman thing, the way the old guy wrestled with a water hose, the people he might have dragged kicking from the flames. It wouldn't be the only fire that has taxed Gramps to his limits, but sometimes he talks about it when he drinks. He hated how close it came to home; *If the wind had been unlucky*, he'd always say, and shake his head. The whole time, as I watched it, my dad kept that smoky hand on my shoulder, not tight enough to hurt, but enough that I couldn't shimmy away. Likely, he pointed things out: *fire truck, Grandpa, hydrant*. If Gramps is to be believed, Jack was an alright dad for the year he stuck around. He'd have been twenty-something in that memory.

And then he was gone, like my mom before him, and Gramps never filled me in. Years ago, I found a pencil sketch of my mom in the garage, stashed in a steel-bound chest amid an unexplained hoard of charcoal landscapes. Gramps said he was holding them for a friend. The sketch—I kept it—shows my mom balanced on an uprooted log in a knee-length skirt, sleeves cut at the elbow. Beside her: a dog that resembles Puck before the trap accident. She must be seventeen in that sketch, less—hair draped on her shoulders, an exaggerated freckle the artist had dotted below her left eye in a softer, deeper carbon. The caption read *Linnea—72*, and the initials *A.C.* were scribbled in the corner.

I've inquired after my parents a couple of times: in grade two when, for a Father's Day project, I needed to know if he was more like a hunter, a golfer, or a fisherman; while Gramps and I crossed the blastland Yukon one winter when I was ten, en route to visit an ailing comrade; at the start of my teenage years, hating everything, when Gramps just told me to shut my yap and go collect dogshit. *There's not a lot to tell*, he'd grunt, or he'd thumb his canines—a nervous tic, I think—and say it didn't matter, that they'd ditched and he'd done his best, and wasn't that enough?

The other fire, the one that nearly killed Gramps, happened at the cusp of my grade eleven year. He was the only firefighter on shift, and he'd gone solo to investigate claims of smoke billowing from the upper windows of an unfinished timber-frame home. The house had a deck overlooking the vast lake and firebrick heaters suspended above, but those heaters weren't the culprit: they found traces of varnish—accelerant—and blamed the painters for ditching oily rags in a garbage bin. Gramps, while doing a quick one-two for people on the second floor, noticed angel fingers licking the ceiling and a pitch-coloured smoke that thickened around furniture like muck—signs, I guess, that firefighters notice when something really bad is about to happen. He took the nearest exit—the master bedroom's window—and the landing hospitalized him for a broken scapula and a leg that went garden-hose at the hip. He described a fire that stunk of sulphur, that lit nearby houses the colour of beryl, so intense and loud that as he clawed through soot and calcite he sensed the flames like breathing at his ear.

I didn't hear about his injury until the next day, and when I arrived at the hospital there was another man at his bedside, a heavy-shouldered guy with jagged cheeks and grey, pushbroom hair. He had morning stubble, his forehead set into the nook of his hand, a brownish moustache with its bristles freshly cut like straw. His clothes were nondescript greens, army-coloured pants, a wool coat and Gore-Tex boots. He straightened as I entered, nudged Gramps' good leg—a single, sharp motion that made the old man gurgle but not wake.

Got him on some heavy painkillers, the man said to me, unfolding from the chair. He kept his gaze on Gramps and brushed his thighs as though he'd just recovered from a fall. Then he offered a handshake with a half twist, flourish-like, so I could stare down into a tundra-scarred palm. I'm Archer, he said.

I clasped the hand, felt the pressure of his grip, the tough skin inside the thumb, like my own. I told him who I was, and we stood in each other's presence and waited for Gramps to wake from the injuries he should never have sustained. Gramps was too old, even twelve years ago, for that kind of feat and that line of work, but back then he lacked the ineffable quality that would let me label him a bluehair. It's something like stubbornness, but not merely so—an understanding of limitation and a deliberate testing thereof, maybe.

Archer bit down on his lip and lowered into the chair. I'm his emergency contact, he said after a time.

You are?

His cheek twitched at the edge of his mouth, enough to expose teeth. It might have been a smile.

Yeah. Decades of silence and then you get a call. You ever notice how people have a way of saying your name right before they tell you something bad?

Mr. West, I said, baritone, gravelly.

Archer *did* smile. Just like that, he said.

We fell into the silence that comes when you've run out of

easy things to talk about, and back then I was not so adept at small talk. A pretty nurse with hair that curled below her ears popped in and did whatever it is pretty nurses do. When she left, Archer and I made eye contact and he lifted his eyebrows as if to say, *Well?*

How do you know Gramps? I said.

He helped me get settled in the valley.

When was that?

Archer scratched a thumbnail along his jaw. I'm not sure, he said. Thirty some years.

You'd have known my dad.

He grunted, or snorted, a sharp flex in his gut. Yup, he said, and emphasized the *p*.

And my mom.

He nodded.

I don't know much about them, I said.

It's not some huge mystery, if that's what you're wondering.

I'm *just* wondering.

He glanced sideways at Gramps.

Your dad made some bad calls.

And my mom?

Must've seen it coming. It's really not my place to talk about this.

Archer sucked a deep breath that filled his gut. I thought either he and I were about to have at it or he was going to tell me more, but instead he deflated, resuming the languid, hunched-in-chair posture as his wind trilled out his nose. Eventually Gramps came to. He squinched his eyes at the light and did a survey of the room. He wriggled upward so he could sit straight and then he noticed Archer in the chair beside his bed.

It's official, Gramps said, not incredulous. I'm in Hell.

Next best thing, Archer said.

What're you doing here?

You nearly killed yourself so I showed up to your rescue.

That's unlike you, Gramps said, and he didn't smile.

Archer bulged his tongue into the gap between his teeth and lip.

I suppose so.

Gramps turned away. Archer rose, tugged the bottom of his coat like someone my age who didn't know what to do with their hands. He looked at me, then Gramps, the door, rubbed his hands together. You talk to Jack ever? he said.

That's his call.

Not sure it is, Cecil.

Gramps bit down on his lip, hard enough for the skin to turn white. What do you know about family, he hissed.

Archer combed his fingers through his short hair.

I thought maybe we were old enough to move on.

Gramps stared steadfast into the linens. Not by *years*.

Archer didn't move. His fingers picked lint from the hem of his wool coat and I saw loose fibres where that action had worn the fabric threadbare. It was nice to meet you, Alan, he said, touching his temple, and then he went out the door.

Gramps? I said after Archer had disappeared.

Go home.

Who is that guy?

Are you fucking stupid, he said, twisting so he could face me. *Go home.*

I was sixteen and not about to back down, but before I could lay into him he snapped his eyes to the sheets, his chin to his chest. Too sad to even look at, let alone argue with—like a dog who has given up playing fetch. So I did the only thing I could do: I left him to his solitude.

THE MORNING AFTER Gramps' heart attack, I woke to the sound of the cat yowling outside my bedroom door. It was six-fifty-six in the morning and the sky through my window swirled the colour of merlot. Downstairs, Puck's awkward footfalls *rat-TUM-tatt*ed along the kitchen laminate. My window shone with dew, and outside I saw the grass and asphalt slick with rime. Across the street, deer fleeced crab-apples from a neighbour's tree, a wobbly two-pointer among them, and as I watched those animals I felt a twitch in my sighting eye, the unmistakable stillness that happens when you've exhaled all your breath and the only motion in your chest is your doddering heart. Not that I've ever been much of a gamesman—Bambi effect, I guess—but I like the weight of a rifle, and not just its physical mass. I like the *weight* of a rifle. In the bathroom mirror I saw that I'd slept on the cordless and its buttons had silkscreened their schema into the skin of my pectoral. For a ridiculous second I thought it might not make a terrible tattoo.

Afterward, I spooled gunk into the cat's dish and loosed Puck into the backyard for a BM in his corner behind the trailer Gramps swindled from the fellow who sold him the truck. The address in Gramps' shoebox directed me to Cranbrook, B.C.—a city about an hour and a half's drive. Gramps' cupboards were filled with instant coffee, but I opted against that MSG-laden crud to avoid belching its acidity all the way yonder. There was a tube of Tums tucked in the Ranger's glove compartment between Gramps' bear spray and a zeta key set, but I figured there were better ways to roll up at my estranged father's house than reeking of bile and the playground flavour of chalk. So, I swiped a banana from the fruit basket and sipped orange juice from a highball glass until Puck squeezed through the deck's Swedish doors and pushed his drooly snout into my palm. I've never put much faith in portents, but it was time for me to mobilize.

In the truck, I eased out the drive and down the road and chose the rear exit out Wilder Sub. Town seemed distant to me, less hectic than a summer ought, and the sunlight that should have been overhead scattered among wireless arrays and the telephone cables and the giant pretzel sign that looms on top the bakery like a crane. Once, I'd imagined taking my girlfriend along these streets, if only so she might understand the part of me that can handle a firearm and drive stick, that gets impatient halfway through movies because the Toby— Invermere's slice of Hollywood—intermissioned all its film so the teenagers who'd come to spit-swap in its shag carpet loveseats would rise, groggy, and drop coin on pop. This—not the Toby, exactly, but *this*—is what I blame for my inability to eat sushi, my refusal to wear collared shirts except when cornered, my dogged insistence that macaroni be consumed from the pot with a wooden spoon. You can take the boy out of the small town, and all that jazz.

Cranbrook is one hundred and thirty kilometres from Invermere. Landmarks of note include the longest uninterrupted straight stretch of highway in western Canada, beating out even the Number 1 until you reach the Prairies. There's a filthy lagoon and a pulp mill that makes your car reek of cabbage. The shoulders are rumble-stripped, and they've jarred me from a dopey haze more than once. In what is one of the more mythical moments in my life, my friends and I once drove home through an evening mist filled with shapes that moved like bipeds, and though I don't believe him, to this day my friend Mike Twigg claims he saw a garden-gnome-sized man chasing our truck. To this day, too, I get nervous in the presence of fog. I've mowed down three deer on Highway 95 and not once found their remains.

The highway has always been dangerously hypnotic. It's my go-to, my place of contemplation. Some men like showers, or the pub, or a tent pitched on a mountainside; I like to drive. There is some deep, unexplored truth in the metaphor that is the Trans-Canada—how you can roadtrip along it, can set out with no plans or goals but still move inexorably toward one destination. Before I ever left Invermere, I would clear myself of highschool drama in a big, nightowl loop around Lake Windermere and up Westside Road—the ancient, unpaved two-laner where rednecks drag-race and kids lose their virginity, where there's a cliffside like a barbican above the gravel pits that is perfect for ditching a burning car. Mostly, though, there's the dirt-shod highway and the ground slipstreaming beneath you and the mineral scent of rain on the horizon. Mostly, there's enough time to get your head around things.

I'd evac'd for Invermere on a morning when the light yawned off the sunshade above the rear entry of our basement suite. Darby and I had argued through the bleeding hours over the same old crap, and it wouldn't be a gamble to suggest my fight-or-flight had triggered. I had a backpack one-strapped over my shoulder, a gym bag crammed with a week's clothes and a collection of translated Herder texts needed for the thesis. I was in the backyard, sunlight behind me like a cowboy, wearing my only summer jacket: a windbreaker emblazoned with the crest of the university's trapshooting club. I never did well at trapshooting—couldn't anticipate the proper lead—but I'd kept on because the practice times coordinated with Darby's handball team. After each session the two of us—her entire body sweat-drenched, my shoulders and back aching with recoil—would hit the campus great hall for slush puppies and specialty coffees with multisyllabic names.

Darby was leaning into the open door frame, teenager style. Her mud-brown hair hung messy at her ears and she hadn't changed from her pyjamas: checkered pants and a horrible T-shirt depicting two grizzlies chewing on human bones. She had a silver stud through her eyebrow and raw pockets above her cheeks and an athlete's build—narrow shoulders and tight legs that could longjump her deep into the goaltender's crease when she dove to score a point. She rubbed the heel of her palm into her eye, smacked her lips. I adjusted the weight of the duffle bag on my shoulder.

You don't have to go, she said. Are you sure you should go?

Instead of what, staying for more mind games?

You think you'll be better off in *Invermere*?

I got Gramps there.

She flicked a dust bunny off her wrist—dismissive.

I won't have to stay awake all night wondering who he's fucking, I told her.

Darby made a croaking noise and pressed her forehead to the door frame. She scratched a tear off her cheek with her thumbnail. I was glad to see that, glad to see her actually show an ounce of emotion. Someone once told me that you only cry about the things you care for.

Will you call me when you get there?

Sure.

I'm sorry, Alan.

I'll come back.

Will you? she said.

I didn't say: *I don't know.*

The night previous, I was at my desk in our bedroom with the house lightless save my laptop's blue. I'd built a collection of empty beer bottles atop the chicken-scrawl hard copy of my thesis. I'd strapped a reading lamp to my forehead like a miner so I could read in the darkness. As Darby stepped through the sliding door I swung my gaze in her direction and the phosphorescent LED lit her with an eerie cobalt glow I've long associated with the four-fingered aliens of science fiction. Her hair hung in whorls that wet her collar and her sports bra made a visible bump under her damp shirt. She'd taken to showers at the school, kept a locker stocked with the toiletries that once crowded our bath corners—gone were the days I would insomnia into the wee hours so the two of us might shower together before collapsing. It was two-forty-seven in the morning, and I honestly challenge anybody to find a handball team willing to train that late into the night.

Darby sashayed toward the bedroom, slowing enough to kiss my cheek. She smelled like soap and muscle and vaguely like vodka, or I only imagined it. At that point, it was hard to know. She tapped the computer screen and muttered about me getting to work. On the laptop, in bold font, I'd changed the title of my thesis to *Language and the Livestock of Things*, the most progress I'd made in a week. Darby dumped her sports bag on a wicker chair near the television and ran herself a drink of water, stood with her back to the faucet and one arm cocked on her hip. She wore blue jeans and a burgundy top that revealed a bra strap. She's as tall as my trachea but tough—once, she cracked three of my ribs with her skull, Ironmanning down a toboggan hill. She has a compact nose with a downward curl at the end, a dip at the ridge of her ocular, just shy of the eyebrow, where she blundered into a utensil drawer as a toddler. Her lips are thin but her smile reveals her molars. Some years ago a dentist botched the jacking of her wisdom teeth, and at rest her jaw, unnoticeably, favours to the right.

Darby flung the fridge door wide and flicked her hair over her shoulder. Want to order a pizza? she said.

I couldn't recall the last time she'd been so energetic in my presence. Weeks earlier, I'd clued in to her general unhappiness when she started to exclusively make chicken on her turns to cook—we alternated, and I hate chicken. We are, or perhaps were, a passive-aggressive couple: she might mince spices in the coffee grinder so my coffee would taste like cloves; sometimes, I left her favourite shirts out of loads of laundry.

Pizza? she said again. And a beer afterward, take a break from that thesis.

I gave a loose shrug. She rolled her eyes, playful, and swayed toward the bedroom. Her shirt hit the carpet in the hallway, empty arms outstretched like an invitation. She was acting like the girl who I once lay on a vinyl windbreaker and made love to atop a traincar, in a CPR compound in Aldershot. She was acting like the girl I'd begun dating years earlier, the girl who I played intramural dodge ball with, just so I could watch her pitch horizontal and land glamourlessly on the hardwood to evade incoming throws. After practices, her body would be potholed with bruises—hips, ribs, shoulders, knees—and if I touched those violet blushes she'd scrunch her nose and bite down on the soft skin of my ear.

I'd been drinking for a while. Maybe I was spoiling for a fight.

How many of you train this late? I said.

Four or five. It's mostly defensive drills.

The bedsprings wheezed. The bedside lamp clicked on, and its energy-saving fluorescent light hit the stippled wall.

Who was there?

You know.

How was the ball handling.

I heard her bang open the topmost drawer where she kept her pyjamas. That stopped being funny, she said.

48

Maybe I'm not joking.

While not busy with handball, Darby studies photography, and she has this habit, when upset, of fluttering one eye as though squinting through the optics of a camera. I can imagine her doing just that, her ratty tourist pyjamas half over her head, her breasts bra-less and pressed against the cloth. She came into the living room with her hair undone and her baggy shirt drooping past her elbows, crossed her arms and sat sideways on a kitchen chair.

Sometimes I wonder if you have feelings, she said. All you ever do is ridicule me.

No handball teams train this late.

That's a pretty general statement, Darby said.

You're even showering there. We don't shower anymore.

Jesus Christ, she said, and was already moving toward the shower before I could respond. She smacked the tourist shirt against the wall and it landed in the arms of the other one. I glimpsed her skin, the curve of her spine. She started the bathtub. The shower curtain's hooks ringletted across the bar, and I rose from my computer chair. On the fogged mirror, Darby had written *Take off your damned clothes*, but the words blotted together so it looked like *Take off your damned shoes*. I stepped into the shower behind her. Bruises scuffed her elbows and shins and hips, impact points where she'd toppled over hardwood. She rolled her shoulders under the hot water and the muscles of her collar strained. Her hair was wet and brown and she wrung it like a sink cloth.

Sorry, I said, and touched a beaten patch on her elbow.

Believe me now? she said, and pulled the curtain so she could exit the water.

I hung out in the shower until Darby left the bathroom. When I went into the bedroom I found her cocooned under our duvet, its cover embroidered with a fireman's Dalmatian. She'd sewn it herself, the duvet cover. I slid next to her, still damp. Her hair spilled around the pillows and from the edge of the bed I could touch those strands with my fingertips. Around her collar, where any shirt would normally hide it, the skin was raw and red, not skidburned but scraped as though by coarse hair. As if by stubble?

A breeze slipped through the bedroom window, the scent of cut grass. I looped one arm around her gut, where she hugged a hot water bottle. She smelled like cinnamon, or something else spicy—cardamom, maybe, who knows. It smelled good. Darby rolled onto her back and for a moment there was only an intimate, breathy space between us. We were close again, felt like lovers again. She flattened her palm on my chest, and I saw the curve of her neck and felt the warmth radiating not from the water bottle but from *her*, and even as I wondered about the state of things, her hand touched down on the hollow of my lower back, searching.

THE ADDRESS FROM Gramps' shoebox led me to a subdivision beyond the edge of Cranbrook, near a giant, flat marsh that stretched toward the mountains. I pulled Gramps' truck to the shoulder and stepped down on an asphalt street that warbled and cracked to the horizon's edge. The house was three storeys and not quite farmish, had a garage and a room built above it, a steep roof with some shingles loose so the exposed tar glistened like blood. A kiltered mailbox had its flag raised and the name COLE stencilled in black. There was a big window that overlooked the front yard, and on the far side of some cinched curtains a television flickered cerulean blue. I twirled my keys in my hand and ducked under a low branch that meandered like a drunken fist. In the distance the wind hushed among tree leaves and a car whirred along a country road. I climbed two steps to the front door and onto a welcome mat that showed a pug-faced dog in slippers, and then I rang the buzzer and thought about the things I would say to my dad.

The doorbell gonged like a grandfather clock and I heard somebody ease from a creaky chair. What was probably a cat thumped down from a high perch. It felt vaguely like the time I met Darby's father. The door in front of me had glasswork at nose level. Inside, a figure shambled forward.

The woman who opened the door looked Gramps' age, had spotty skin tight over her cheeks and wrinkles that curled upward as though she'd spent much of her life smiling. Her hair was tucked inside a net and she wore a nondescript grey dress, an overabundance of rings.

Can I help you?

I looked at the address in my hand and then again at the old woman.

I'm looking for Jack West.

I'm sorry, she said, sounding very uncertain. Jack doesn't live here.

Do you know where I could find him?

I'm afraid not, the old lady said. She fiddled with a ring on her thumb, twirled it round and round the knuckle. Why?

My name's Alan West. He's my dad.

Jesus, she said, and shuffled aside as though to let me through. In that case you should come in. My husband, Archer, is out back. I'm Nora.

I met a man named Archer, years ago. Do you know my grandfather?

We're old friends, she said.

The house smelled of cooking and though only two incandescent desk lamps glowed, I could see photographs lining the nearby walls. Portraits mostly, people I would never know, some in petticoats and others strung up on monkey bars and not even children. A hallway stretched through the house to what I presumed was the rear porch, where it terminated in a blaze of light. Just through there, Nora said, and placed one skinny hand on my bicep.

In the hallway, too, hung picture frames, great two-by-four charcoal drawings encased in glass, all landscapes. I recognized a couple of mountain peaks, a barrelwood cabin near a riverbed I knew instantly as Gramps' getaway near Dunbar. A picture toward the end of the hall—the only drawing with people in it—showed a man and a boy, each with a rifle upended in the ground, both garbed like outdoorsmen. The sketches were imperfect, but I could identify Gramps by the hunch in his shoulders and the lean that favoured his right leg. The boy had to be my dad, no more than seventeen, curly haired and with the sideways smile of a man who thinks he has the world by the nutsack. The picture of my mother, on that upturned deadwood, home amid my things, would have matched in every regard save the absent dog.

That rotten grandfather of yours put himself in the grave yet? someone barked from the porch. I pushed through a stormdoor into the light and blinked spots from my vision. Archer sat in a wheelchair, bald and meatless and with a glass of what looked like orange juice at hand. I recognized the slope of his cheeks but his moustache was gone, in its place a mottled lip red from years gone unshaved.

One foot, at least, I said, and Archer hazarded a smile.

I got a call, you know. I'm still his emergency contact. I'd have gone, he said, and turned one shaking, deathly hand outward. But, well.

I'll let him know.

Archer reached for the juice, gripped it with his thumb and his middle finger, swirled it like whiskey. Heard you ask my warden for your old man, he said. Your grandad wants to see his boy, I'm guessing?

Something like that.

Sent you to do the dirty work.

He's lazy.

Yeah he is, Archer said, and raised the skin where his eyebrow should be. He touched the glass to his lip and struggled to swallow. The muscles lining his throat spasmed and his Adam's apple bobbled and he made a sound like a groaning pipe. When only a dollop remained, he set the glass on its rim and wheezed a long breath.

I don't know where your dad is, he said, and twined his fingers in his lap. But I can send you to your mother.

He motioned to a plastic lawn chair beside him and I lowered myself into it. It was still early, past noon. I felt that I should know him more than I did. Nora shuffled onto the porch now and then to replace his glass, and though no words passed between them I sensed theirs was not a relationship where such doting was commonplace. The sun peeled through lazy clouds and warmed the porch and the nape of my neck and the foundry-pipe bones of Archer's face. Nora stood behind the mesh of the stormdoor while we talked, and she watched him like a woman waiting for a man to leave her.

—

It was Jack who first spotted the car as it inched along the road that looped the highschool sports field—a Ford Fairlane, moving at a cop's pace, as though on patrol, as though scouring the school grounds and the nearby lawns for signs of who knows what. Jack had been jogging laps on the painted turf, to build his endurance so he could match Cecil when the two of them went hunting. He wore his school track suit that day—navy blue and baggy like one of his dad's shirts, *BTSS* stencilled across the shoulders in white—and he stood out against the overcast sky like a fragment of the approaching dark. It was 1969, a day before that fateful Halloween in Invermere, B.C. On any normal afternoon, Jack wouldn't blow his lunch hour lapping the shitty field, but storm clouds had gathered below the Rockies and he figured it'd be raining like the Flood before classes let out. Cecil said a little rain never killed a guy, but Jack didn't have to take to all his old man's lessons. So he spotted the car, and he skidded to a huffing stop, planted his hands on his knees and hawked on the lime-painted grass. The car seemed to notice him, too—it idled to a halt across the ringwire fence. By now, Jack had a good view: chrome drag-racer's grille, chrome spinners, a yellow smiley face on the antenna that wobbled in the wind. Mostly unremarkable, save the paint job—you couldn't have a paint job like that in Invermere, not without it becoming gossip the first time some bonehead saw it off its wheels in your garage. Jack just stared. A Ford Fairlane, painted like a goddamned American flag.

FOLLOWING MY GUNSHOT wound in March, Linnea and I spent the nights at Cecil's cabin or on the couches in his living room when the weather ate shit. We kept our heads low those first weeks, playing endless games of Monopoly—Linnea hated every minute—and sometimes venturing forth for sundown cookouts in Cecil's backyard. Folk in the Kootenays had no trouble believing a guy was one of them so long as he knew how to work and liked a couple drinks—and I fit that bill. Good to his word, Cecil landed me a job with a painting crew called Jones & Sons, run by a guy ten years my junior, named Harold, who Cecil had some kind of long history with. Not one week through May, Linnea and I moved to a basement suite up the road from the Wests, and on our first night there Cecil packed his barbecue in his truck and hauled it over, and we sat on the grass and ate hotdogs in the shadow of my new home. The next-doors owned a pureblood retriever, and it wagged its golden tail at the cull lumber fence rimming my yard, until I lobbed a leftover wiener. One decade and two owners later, that fence would be torn down and replaced with seven-foot pickets by a man too prissy to see kids romping around his property, and the retriever would be dirt—a lanky, half-mutt pup the beast's only legacy.

Jack showed Linnea his favourite places around town, and I made her show me. She whined about it but I exercised my military what's-what. I followed her to Jack's haunts: a road bridge above the train tracks where half the town once gathered to watch a man push his brother in front of a coal train and where Jack liked to drop plastic bags full of tomato soup; a derelict fort overlooking Invermere's lake, with exposed cedar studs and polyurethane sheets hanging off the walls like skin; a jungle gym in an abandoned playground, where the old primary school used to be, with little remaining save a rope swing and a red spiral slide that reeked of ammonia and dope. Cecil figured Jack had other hideouts he didn't show Linnea. If he wanted to, Cecil said, that boy could keep out of sight for days.

With Nora's help I got Linnea set and ready to resume her education in the fall, at a tungsten-coloured highschool called Bill Thompson Secondary. Nora told me to keep my head low as far as possible without surrender, in case Uncle Sam went on the prowl, which seemed like a bit of excessive paranoia even by my standards. But she is a hard woman to deny. Deserters, she said, could be rounded up and shipped back to the States; the Canadian Forces demanded it. She folded her arms across her chest when she said so, as if daring me to raise a fuss. One night Cecil called me up because of some documentary on the CBC, about American army guys in Canada ferreting out deserters and draft dodgers and dragging their asses over the border—like bounty hunters, but without contract. *Brailers*, the show called them, which is a pretty fitting name when everything's done and said. So I took my pay in cash and paid rent with bills and did my damnedest to obscure my paper trail. Cecil joked about me changing my name—becoming Archer West, his long-lost brother—but no force on the living earth could make me do that.

Summer shot on by. Rainstorms pelted the valley with water gobs as big as beetles and lightning lit a few small forest fires that were themselves extinguished. My scarred arm throbbed for those fires, even at a distance—like finding true north, my own biological compass. A big logging company out of Alberta proposed to build a sawmill forty miles south of town, toward Cranbrook, and Cecil won the welding bid with a dirty lowball. It was the biggest job he'd ever done, and me and him made two material runs each evening for a week before the work started, driving his old Dodge with its bent fender and no exhaust pipe so he couldn't idle at a red for risk of carbon monoxide. Nora was on the nag for him to start planning their wedding, but Cecil played the sad-man card, or the busier-than-the-dickens card, or the still-need-to-talk-to-Jack card. She could've trumped him—there was no resisting her smile or that cackle of a laugh—but she chose not to. Whenever he bumbled through another excuse she hooked her arm around his neck and gave him a strong shake, like a headlock. Any woman like Nora is worth marrying on the spot, but there you go. That one act of physicality—it let him get on with his day. It made him think everything was aces and spades.

AT THE END OF OCTOBER, a few days before Jack saw the car, I asked the boss—Harold—for a week off, because my artist's eye favours the autumn light. The odds of me getting the time were alright, because as the days shortened and the winds picked up, business at Jones & Sons slowed and, like he did every winter, Harold eyed guys to cut loose. That was his strategy, and call it dirty if you want: hire a squad of assheads who could blast through an exterior job and then dump them elbows-first when the jobs moved indoors and the call for sobriety sounded.

Me and Harold were outside a duplex in this subdivision near the highschool. The sun had all but sunk behind the Purcells and the northern lights flickered on the mountain peaks. We needed to disassemble the scaffolding piece by piece and toss it into the gear van, just me and him, because the younger guys had fucked off. Their excuse: one of them tripped on an extension cord and took a dive off the second-floor balcony. He got lucky, sort of—landed in a pile of fibreglass insulation bags, but cracked his head when he bounced off the big pink pillow. The guy was nineteen and a Frenchman, named Philippe, and Harold gave it eighty-twenty that the kid had done it to get off work early. Philippe, Harold told me, liked to dance after work at the City Saloon, and probably misjudged how much the insulation would pad his fall. When next I saw that Frenchman he'd have nothing to talk about except some Yankee soldier killing his chances at the bar, some *real dick American* who had his rank stitched to his field coat and who drove a car painted red, white, and blue.

Days are getting short, Harold said to my request. I got guys jumping off decks.

He wore a fisherman's hat, splotched with latex paint, and an immaculate plaid coat that he didn't risk ruining since it once belonged to his dad. He stood a head taller than me but a shoulder thinner, had a skinny face with a heavy forehead creased like a father's. One of his canines had been knocked out in a bar fight—blindside highball glass to the gums. When deep in thought he'd pinch his tongue into that empty space. *Hal*, his buddies called him, but I never really got behind nicknames.

I'll make it up to you, I said as he passed me scaffold pipes. Rust had nearly eaten through them and in the wet October day it slicked onto my palms, as if I had some kind of tan. Those pipes had been around longer than Linnea, from the days when Harold's old man ran a framing company. I don't know the whole story, but Harold didn't like being called Hal because it sounded too much like his dad's name.

I'm not that desperate yet, he said.

Wait until you're my age, I told him, and bent down to heft one end of a platform. He grabbed the other end, and we heaved it into the back of his van, clattering over the pipes and bolts and empty metal paint cans. The inside of the van looked like a toolshed; Harold once had a system for storing all his material, but laziness and indolence had chipped his resolve. We called that van the Hog in Armour—or just the

Hog—and the running joke was to flatten beer cans and screw them to the exterior with flashing bolts.

Fuck it, he said, and belted me. But if I need a guy through the holidays?

I'm sure as shit not going anywhere.

He hooked his thumbs in his pockets, had that tongue in the space where his canine should be. My old man used to say that: *sure as shit*. You're the only other guy.

We'd have got on.

Harold snorted, and we heaved the last platform into his van. Then he tried to boot the door shut but the latch failed to catch, and the door bounced right back and nearly knocked him over.

SO I WAS OFF atop a mountain, a day out of town and soaked through the gotch, when Jack spotted the American car. He says that as it snaked toward him his head played a game of paranoia. He'd registered Nora's worry, her endless conversations over dinner, that same topic: the pretty girl and her ex-army dad who needed their protection. It was the right thing to do, Jack had been told, the Christian thing to do— but more than that, it was the *Canadian* thing to do. So, as he watched that invading car, maybe Jack felt patriotism's first pang, or maybe his young mind mapped a long, complicated trajectory to Linnea's heart. I'm inclined to believe one of those over the other. Jack didn't give Nora the time of day at the dinner table—he'd be the first to admit that—unless her conversation slipped toward my daughter. If you ask me, this is why he noticed the American car; some part of him flagged it as a threat to Linnea. And even if he daydreamed through most things Nora had to say, he paid attention to his dad. Jack studied his old man, the way Cecil scraped a fork across his plate while trying to scoop peas, the way he sucked so prominently on meat stuck between his teeth while Nora rattled off stories and concerns about those two poor refugees.

So Jack watched that American car roll to a standstill opposite the school's ringwire fence. His heart pounded out of control, which could have been the running, but with one final suck of breath he pushed himself upright and walked over, leaned into the chain-link. The Fairlane had murky windows and star-shaped stickers on the glass where normally you'd see the fifty states. Jack couldn't make out the inside, save hints of motion, of rustling through luggage or blankets. Then the driver door clicked open and a guy stepped out—buzz cut, field coat flown open to show a dirty white T-shirt, camo-patterned pants, and a leather belt with a buckle the size of a deck of cards. In his hands: a dog-tag keychain that he whirled around and around his index finger.

Hey, the guy said.

Hey, Jack said.

The guy took a bronze cigarette case from his chest pocket. He offered a smoke over but Jack declined.

I'm Crib, the guy said. He had a square face with cheekbones that dropped off fast and a jaw that could have been on an action-movie poster. Older than Jack by half a dozen years—practically a man. Around his neck, instead of dog tags, he wore an iron crab brooch, like the astrological sign, as big as the lid of a tin can. He pulled his lighter from one of his chest pockets—a Zippo, Jack remembered, with an American eagle decaled on the flat side—and sparked a flame as long as a .308 round. Crib tweaked his eyebrows up as if surprised. Jack *grinned*.

Jack, he said. Jack West. Where you from?

The States, Crib said, and winked. He blew a line of smoke in the air. Trying to scrub up some action. You?

Running, Jack said.

Good habit.

It's for hunting.

Crib puckered his lips around his cigarette, nodded as if considering what Jack had to say. Hunting—now there's a pastime I enjoy.

Crib smoked. Jack watched.

Then Crib said: Know of any parties? and Jack told him about the only party he knew, at the derelict fort on Caribou Road, overlooking the water, where he'd been planning to creep off to himself, and Crib kept nodding, deep in thought as far as Jack could tell.

Waterfront. My kinda place, he said. You going?

I need to sneak out if I do.

So sneak out! Crib said, tossing his hands into the air. Then he touched his forehead in a salute and about-faced and marched to his car. Jack watched, near to mesmerized. As Crib started the engine he lowered the window and hollered: Don't get lost in the shuffle, now.

I GOT TO INVERMERE in the early evening on Halloween night, more than a day after Jack encountered the American car. The lights were off, the door unlocked and the heat raging, but I may have been so cold even an arctic wind would've made me toasty. I dug the sketchbook from my rucksack so the damp clothes wouldn't ruin the paper. There was no sign of Linnea, but she rarely came straight home after school, and I'd grown used to her hanging out with Jack. On the kitchen table, where I'd left money so she could keep fed over the days I spent in the mountains, a note was pinned beneath the salt shaker. It said only *Back later Dad*, which wasn't exactly like her— she's the angry, silent type—but nothing terribly suspicious. I was too tired, maybe, too complacent. I wonder, sometimes, how much shit I could have prevented if I never let myself go complacent, if I never let my caution lapse. Christ, you can't be complacent in a combat zone.

Looking back, the signs were right there for me to see, the irregularities. Small things set off my alerts—I can tell when things aren't as I left them. It's like looking over my own shoulder. I'll notice a coat on a different hook, a chair tilted at a different angle from the table, the smell of cut grass even before I see an open kitchen window. That Halloween, Linnea had washed the dishes, made her bed, and hauled out the trash—had finished all the chores I'd be most likely to start expecting her home to do. She'd even spent a portion of the money on candy for the trick-or-treaters. Everything was in place, and I should have noticed that as being out of place. There was one other thing, too, which I still attribute to Jack West, because it is something like I'd do, something suitably boyish, suitably cunning. Of course I didn't notice it in my fatigue. They counted on that.

I WAS ASLEEP on the couch when Linnea barged through the door with enough noise to wake the unquiet dead. It was two-twenty-three, Halloween night. I'd passed out with a can of Kokanee on my chest, and it'd emptied to a dark V on my shirt, like a sweat stain. I sat up and rubbed my eyes with the heel of my palm.

Dad, Linnea croaked, a desperate little whisper of a sound, a sound no man wants to hear his daughter make, and like *that* I was awake and aware and my feet were carrying me at a half-bolt out the living room and into the hallway. I found her leaning on the wall. The cabbagy stink of dope hung around her. All the lights were off and I could only see her outline: shoulders hunched and arms crossed over her chest as though shivering. I fumbled toward her and got the lights turned on. She had her hair loose in front of her face, hiding it. With my nearest hand I reached out and tucked the hair behind her ear. She winced—at my touch, out of pain?

Who did this? I said, thinking, to my own shame: Jack West. Her cheek was turning blue at the edges of a circle—were those knuckle marks?—and she had finger-pad bruises up her neck, under her jaw, like she'd been groped, like some fuckhead had been feeling her up.

Jack hit him, she said, squeezing back tears. She balled her hand to a fist, made a punching motion, hazarded a smile that tested the tenderness of her cheek. Jack hit him real hard.

Who?

The American, she said. Crib.

What American? I said, and her eyes went wide—she'd kept

something from me, and I'd caught her in the act. But it wasn't the time or the place to give a lecture. Where's Jack now?

Crib beat him up, Dad—Jack ran away.

Is he okay?

I don't know.

I cupped her shoulders, lowered myself level with her. She didn't want to look at me on account of her red eyes but I didn't care if she'd been smoking a little dope—made me tolerant, that's what Vietnam did. Are you hurt? I said, as gently as my idiot army voice could muster. Are you hurt ... anywhere else?

She shook her head. We stared at each other and I felt so small.

You gotta go get Jack, she breathed.

I'm not leaving you here.

He *hit* him, Dad, she said, her voice breaking at last. He hit him for *me*.

I pulled her to me, then, let her cry against my chest. I never should've stayed gone so long out of town; should have come back down, should have expected a Halloween party. She was *that* age.

Linnea blubbered into my chest, told me I had to find Jack, that I had to, for her. If I loved her, she was saying, if I loved her I'd find Jack.

I led her into the kitchen and did the only thing I could think to: I picked up the phone to call Nora. But the phone was dead—no dial tone, just the white plastic silence and a squeak from Linnea in the background. I looked from the receiver to the room and then to my daughter, who had her

eyes cast to the floor. Without a word, she pointed to the telephone jack, the cord unplugged from the wall. Just in case
Cecil tried to call; and a gamble, a real gamble, that I wouldn't
think to call him. *Back later Dad*, the note said, so I wouldn't
phone to see if she was there.

Cecil, I said when he answered the phone, groggy. Put
Nora on.

The hell's happening, he said, but passed the phone without
a second thought.

Archer? Nora said.

Nora, Linnea's hurt over here, and Jack's gone.

What do you mean *gone*?

No, I said instantly. Not like that. He ran off.

Where to?

I can find him, but I can't leave Linnea here.

She breathed a slow breath, a calming breath. We'll head
over. Then, to Cecil: Get your fucking clothes on, man.

I set the phone into its holster and pressed my forehead to
the wall. Linnea wanted to wash off and I wanted a drink. She
slipped past me, favouring her right leg maybe, and I stared
after her until she'd shut and locked the bathroom door. I
poured myself whiskey and sat in the kitchen with only the
draining, grease-caked bulb of my range hood to keep the
place lit, and I listened to Linnea's feet creak on the enamel
tub. That's how Nora and Cecil found me. She let herself right
in. I had the whiskey under my nose, elbows on the table—
portrait of a pensive man.

Cecil had his hunting vest pulled over a plaid shirt, wore
his blue ballcap and patched woodsman pants as if ready to

track a buck. With her red hair frizzy and unkempt around her shoulders, Nora looked like a mother. She had one hand on Cecil's back, right between the shoulder blades. Linnea's in the shower, I said. You ready, old man?

What happened? he said.

There was a fight. Don't know much else.

Is Jack hurt? he said. He looked worried.

I don't know, Cecil.

Right, then.

I downed my drink and placed the glass on the counter and turned to follow Cecil out. Nora hadn't moved, and my eyes caught hers. *Thanks*, I mouthed, and her fingers brushed my knuckles as I shifted past. Outside, Cecil climbed in his truck and motioned for me to do the same, but I didn't head for passenger. He cracked his window.

Well?

I'll take my truck, I said. Split up, check his hiding places.

Oh.

Take the park, check the playground. I'll check the bridge.

Cecil lifted his ballcap straight up, mopped a hand through his hair. He's more likely to be at the park.

That's the point.

What the hell does that mean?

Better all round if you find him.

Don't give me one of your lectures, Cecil said.

Trust me on this, I said.

He screwed his mouth into a cringe. This isn't the time.

Playground, I told him again, and patted the side of his Dodge. With a curse he started her up and gunned down the street, and by the time he rounded the first bend he'd already torn a beer from the sixer under his seat. I let myself have one last look at my house, at the orange glow flickering from the kitchen and the small, frosted bathroom window. I'll probably never know exactly what went down at that beach party, at that cursed fort, exactly what was done and said. But Jack sure made an impression on my daughter. He saved her, somehow.

DURING THE MONTHS I'd been in Invermere, town council had erected a four-foot concrete barrier on each side of the road bridge, because of an oil tanker that careened off the edge when its clutch seized in third. People expected a bloody, fiery mess out of that one, but the driver crawled from the cab, doused in oil, while the engine hissed. He had to shower with dish detergent to wash himself clean. Traces of the spill remained on the tracks and the gravel—now stained gold— and the plant life, but the town couldn't afford to mop it all up and didn't really care to.

With their backs to the barrier, kids could dangle their legs over the lip and share liquor and stay out of traffic's eye. Between the barrier and the edge of the bridge, you had about four feet—enough room to walk comfortably in a line or for a young, hormonal male to test his chivalry alongside the girl who'd caught his eye. The tracks were a forty-foot drop, where deer moved in small groups among the trees. A man could survive that distance if he landed right, or if he was stubborn enough. A stubborn enough man can survive anything.

I parked on the shoulder before the bridge and began to walk the length. On the wrong side of those barriers, on a dark night like that Halloween, you'd have to nearly trip on a person to find them. I didn't want to run into Jack there, because that job belonged to Cecil. The old bastard liked to beat on his own chest, but he lost sleep over the raising of Jack. We may not go blow for blow when it comes to the details, but I'd be doing him a disservice if I said he didn't try. It would've been nice if a daughter could've happened to him, but you know what they say about spilled milk. Cecil was the kind of man who planned against his mid-life crisis. He was the kind of man who you could trust with your house keys. If I had to face down the maw of Hell, I can think of only one person I'd rather have at my side.

I went the length of the bridge without encountering Jack, crossed the road at the far end, and started back toward my truck. I gave it eighty-twenty odds that Jack had gone to the park—too much likelihood he'd run into a guy he knew at the bridge; when a kid has been humiliated, the last thing he wants is to meet up with his friends. Cecil'd have his father-son chat, maybe get in a bonding moment. Someday he'd thank me for it.

Then, halfway to my truck, a figure materialized from the darkness in front of me—the shape of a boy, wiry, with one knee bent as a rest for his arm and the other draping over the edge. I jerked to a stop and my boots scraped the road and the kid bounded to his feet, way too fast to be a fourteen-year-old. He had his fists around his face, a boxer's stance. I smelled beer, marijuana.

Who the fuck are you? the kid said.

I showed him my palms. Sorry.

He shrugged, and lowered his guard. I saw that he had a beer can in one fist. He raised it to his mouth and chugged the last, flipped the can off the edge of the bridge. I counted three seconds before it clanged against the ground. I couldn't be sure, given our distance and given the darkness, but the kid looked to be smiling. Littering, he said. No greater crime in this country.

Where you from?

Oregon, he said, stepping closer. Buzz cut, field coat, army ranks stitched to the breast. I could put two and two together—this was the American, Crib. Linnea didn't actually say he'd felt her up, but what *else* could set Jack off? He may not have been the most well-mannered boy, but he didn't waltz around throwing punches.

You don't sound Canadian, Crib said.

A lot of people tell me that.

Where you from, then?

Here.

Really! Crib said, and rested his hip against the barrier. He pursed his mouth. Not the nicest people in this town.

We do okay.

Look here, he said, and leaned in, head turned sideways, to show me a dark bruise on his cheekbone, right beside his nose. With his finger, he pulled his lip up over his teeth, wiggled a loose canine. Some idiot teenager almost knocked my tooth out.

Imagine that.

You don't sound surprised.

Locals don't take well to city boys.

The kid scratched his nose.

I'm not a city boy, he said. His face bent to a smile, but not the friendly kind—more like a baring of fangs. He pulled a brass cigarette case from his chest pocket and lit up without offering one over. Around his neck hung the iron crab brooch. He blew smoke up and over his shoulder. Name's Crib.

Archer.

He pushed away from the barrier, just over an arm's reach away, a jerky, hostile motion like a boxer dipping for an uppercut. Then he went bone-straight.

Now *that* is an interesting name, he said. He crossed one arm over his chest, brought the other up to his mouth, as if in contemplation. I can't think of very many people named Archer. What's your last name?

West.

His face had this ridiculous *who knew* look to it. He shrugged with his whole upper body, not just the shoulders. There's a new one for the list, he said.

I put my weight on the barrier, my hands in my pockets. What brings you here?

Just looking for a place to drink some beer.

I mean to the town.

He winked. Business.

Had you pegged as a cadet.

Done officer training, he said, waving his cigarette around. Diplomacy, mostly. You don't sound Canadian.

They teach you accent location in diplomacy class?

You might say I've got other training, too.

Ever do much hand-to-hand? I said, very slowly.

He ground the tip of his cigarette out on the concrete, flipped the butt off the ledge, and in a long breath let the last of the smoke go.

That sounded vaguely threatening, he said.

Then he shot forward, way faster than I'd expected. One strong fist latched onto the lapel of my shirt. He tugged, hard, and my head bobbed. I fumbled for the same grip, a fighting chance.

He flashed his teeth, white as gold. I don't like being threatened, he said.

I squared my feet, grabbed *his* lapel, curled my wrist in to secure a grip on the field coat. My soldier's grip, Cecil once called it. I could sense the strength in Crib's arm, the patient, waiting muscles, the bicep seized like a windlass. He stunk of cigarettes and beer, and like a campfire, but I had no illusions—he wasn't drunk.

No one's going to care if they find a dead American on the tracks, I said.

Those a pair of dog tags around your neck?

You bet.

They look American made.

All tags are the same.

And here I had you pegged as a painter, he said, and, fast as before, his free hand shot into the folds of his coat, where you'd keep a pistol, and I made an awkward lunge for his elbow, wondered if anyone would hear the gun go off. He danced sideways, the two of us still attached fist-to-lapel, and then he drew a set of dog tags from some hidden, inside pocket.

I got a pair, too, he said, dangling them in front of his face. He released me. I did the same.

He sat down with his back to the barrier, draped one leg over the edge. From God knows where, and God knows when, he'd produced a hip flask. Well it sure was nice talking to you, he said, and took a big gulp. I'm gonna sit here and sober up.

I only lingered a moment, not sure what to think, wanting to pound that brat to a pulp, to grab his grinning face and smash it on the concrete until all that remained was a red, wrecked jaw. As I moved up the bridge toward my truck, he hollered: Don't get lost in the shuffle, now.

CECIL'S TRUCK WASN'T out front when I rolled up to my house, so I figured he'd found Jack and taken him home to get clean. Light shone through the living-room windows, which meant Linnea and Nora were probably watching TV. I killed the ignition and put the truck in gear—backward slope—and hauled the e-brake tight. Then I sat listening to the engine cool down. Probably, I should have thrown Crib off the bridge.

Nora scurried around the bend when I came through the door. She didn't look happy; all the lines at the edges of her mouth, the ones that usually curled toward her eyes, were skewed down in a scowl that made her seem older than her years.

Cecil couldn't find him, she said.

He just *gave up*? I said.

73

Gone home, to wait, in case Jack goes there.

Fuck sakes.

Archer, Nora said, and pulled a stray strand of red hair from her eyes.

How's Linnea?

She's fine. No ... other bruising.

Did Cecil check the park like I told him?

Yeah, and he went back to the fort but the party was still on. Jack wouldn't be there?

No, he won't be, I said.

Should we call the police?

Not yet.

Is something wrong? she said, taking one hesitant step toward me, like a person might if their husband came through the door with a black eye. I waved her off and went out to my truck. Right then I wanted to give Cecil a backhand for good measure. About every part of me figured Jack had gone to the park—it had that loneliness a guy Jack's age needed to get over a little humiliation. It's where I'd have gone. My old man once found me cowering in the lining of a giant tractor tire, after my mom died young. He wasn't exactly gentle in the extraction of boy from rubber, but I rode his shoulders all the way to the house.

I parked as near the playground as I could get without having to try my luck fording a ditch. Light from the street-lamps hit the jungle gym and the rope swing, and the shadows and lines made it seem like walking through a jail. On the far side of the playground was the spiral slide, and even at that distance I imagined its rank stench of piss

74

and vomit. October wind blew over the field and into the playground and right through my vest. Elsewhere: revellers hooting, cop sirens wailing. Sand blanketed the base of the playground—a rudimentary form of cushioning—and in the darkness, with the wind, it looked like creatures snaking across the ground. With more light, I may have been able to search for footprints.

Jack? I called.

The playground looked like a place haunted. At its centre, where the rope swing—just a thick marine rope with knots every few feet—dangled, the shadows and lines fell in an almost-square, and in the low light it looked like a room unto itself. Standing there, I had the absurd sense of being in my living room, and it seemed fitting that I'd be searching for Jack there by myself. Sometimes, when Cecil swung by, he'd bring Jack along, and that was a dead giveaway that the old bastard had worries eating him. See, Jack would get Linnea out of the house, and Cecil'd have a moment to speak his mind, just me and him. Those days, he always packed a cut of elk meat with him, and as the kids headed up the dirt road to the gully he'd trade it for a few beer and a bit of my time. We always stayed in the kitchen; Jack was the only West to step foot in my living room, as if that place were reserved for matters unrelated to the heart.

Jack? I called again, and when he didn't answer I swore and moved toward the red spiral slide. The slide had a twisting stairwell, contained inside a tin shell, that kids climbed to get to the top. To his credit, Cecil probably stuck his head in, did a quick one-two, and pulled out. Maybe that was enough given the circumstances; Jack could have been anywhere around town. But in the darkness you could miss a kid perched on the stairwell, and Cecil should have searched a little more thoroughly.

I didn't poke my head in the slide; I booted its metal shell with a kick worthy of the NFL. Inside, Jack screamed like a boy.

Found you, I said, crouching at the door.

Go away, he said.

The slide smelled like an outhouse. I bet Jack forced himself to stay there out of some juvenile form of penance. Come on out.

You're not my dad.

He was looking for you too. I'm just a better looker.

He said nothing. It was worth a shot. I appreciate what you did, I said.

What do you mean.

You stuck up for Linnea.

Didn't do any good, he said. Crib just beat me up.

You can't win them all.

I couldn't see his face, but his voice warbled, and not just because he was in a giant tin cylinder. My dad can.

That's just dumb.

He beat *you*, Jack said, shouting—probably to fight tears.

Only after you shot me, I told him, absurdly.

He wouldn't lose.

You're missing the point.

Linnea thinks I'm a wuss.

And that, of course, was the truth behind his shame. She told me you hit the American *for her*. She's worried too.

He was silent. His boots scuffed on the stairs, landed on the soft earth. Okay, he said, and stepped into the night where I could see him. He looked pretty bad. He'd stopped crying a long time ago but blood and snot crusted his face. His lip was split, and as he breathed through his mouth I saw a missing tooth. When his fingers touched his face he winced. He smelled like blood and breath.

I laid my hand on his shoulder. He straightened under my touch.

Come on, I said.

I TOOK THE LONG WAY home. Jack didn't have much to say beyond a simple thanks, but he lowered his window as far as it'd go and leaned his forehead into the wind. I figured both him and me would benefit from a little time to cool off before facing down the women. The American kid was on my mind. I couldn't shake the thought of him—who he was, where he'd come from, what he'd done, and not only to me.

At my house, the living-room lights still glowed through the window, and as I slowed the truck to a stop, and as the engine shuddered quiet, a figure rose and silhouetted herself behind the glass. Both me and Jack looked straight at her—it was Nora; Linnea had a girl's meatless build—but I got the impression we were wishing and seeing two different things. He hopped down from the truck and marched across the grass to the front door, and I let him get some distance on me. I'm not sure why.

When I came through the door Nora had Jack at the kitchen table and with a cloth she wiped dirt and blood and whatever else from his cheeks. Her hands worked with such delicacy, in small, scrubbing motions that made Jack wince with an inhale of breath. He didn't complain, even if he scowled. Linnea sat next to him, her knees near enough to knock with his, in blue plaid boys' pyjamas. She had her elbow on the table, her cheek resting against her wrist. Jack hazarded the occasional glance at her—a quick shuffle of his head, barely enough for him to see past the swell around his eyes. Linnea's other hand lay near a knot in the wood, fingertips inches from Jack's arm. I felt so out of place in that kitchen.

I poured myself another whiskey—a gentleman's second drink—and it seemed like every *tink* of glass, every knock on the wood, every creak from my boots on the lino, was as awkward as if I'd started yelling, and I half expected to see them all with their eyes upon me. With drink in hand, I pressed myself into the corner where the counters meet—couldn't bring myself to cross the floor to the table. In hindsight, it's probably a good thing I had to find Jack: if I'd come home to a calm house after my run-in with Crib it'd have been a beeline to Cecil's place, and me and the old bastard would've gone manhunting. Cecil, in my shoes, would only have let Crib get within rifle range.

Jack touched his cheek where Nora had rubbed it clean. The skin had gone purple, veining. My face hurts, he said.

Well stop blocking punches with it, I said, and grinned over my glass.

Jack gave me the coldest stare, but I just kept grinning, and then a smile tested the tenderness in his cheeks. Not a word of sympathy, he said. Not even a word.

You know what they say about sympathy, I told him, and opened a cupboard to take out three more glasses. I splashed a bit of whiskey in two, a bit more in the third. It's in the dictionary between shit and syphilis.

Jack snorted; the women rolled their eyes. I brought the drinks over—just a smidge for Linnea and Jack and a good enough one for Nora. Linnea gave me this look like she didn't recognize me as her dad. Jack accepted the glass with his fingertip, balanced right in as if fit to a size. Don't tell Cecil, I said, passing the last to Nora.

Maybe that was the start of something. Nora finished cleaning Jack's face—why she didn't just let the boy have a shower, I'll never know—and he and Linnea turned to each other and locked us from their conversation. They sipped their splash of whiskey and cringed. It was past five in the morning, still dark, but feeling as if the very air was blood-shot. Then, almost without me noticing, Nora put her hand on my elbow, and if I weren't so goddamned bagged I'd have startled. I looked from her hand to her face—staring right at me.

You did a damned good thing tonight, she said, and, just as quick, her touch slid away. That one physical act—it made me think I'd done things right. It made me think everything was aces and spades.

THREE

Plutarch and Heraclitus:
*Fate leads those who follow it
and drags those who resist ...
Every creature is driven to pasture with a blow.*

Archer spent the afternoon telling tales of his adventures in the Marine Corps and beyond: he showed me a gimped thumb he caught in the door of a semi-trailer, many moons ago when he drove a logging truck around the Purcell Mountains; he touched a scar below his earlobe where his daughter had cracked him with a wine bottle; he rolled up his pant leg to reveal a chicken-thin calf with splatter-pattern scars in the meat, and with a wink told me to ask Gramps about that one. He'd survived two tours in Vietnam and played the part, and he talked about camaraderie, about how his buddies tortured each other to eke through the days. His voice had a twinge of reminiscence I wouldn't have expected from a veteran, though my sole comparison was Gramps, and Gramps only ever spoke about his time in the British Army when his blood-alcohol hit saturation, and even then he'd spit after every second word to curse the names of captains and colonels unencountered in the history books. Periodically, Archer sipped his orange juice and chewed the pulp and stared past my shoulder at the horizon beyond. His fingers twirled the glass round and round, like that joke about single women in a bar, and if our roles were reversed I bet he'd be thinking the same. He said he'd felt a similar companionship with Gramps, long ago, after settling in the valley. Then his lips curled up on one side in a smile that strained the malleability of his skin.

As the evening deepened, Nora shuffled outside and told Archer he had best turn in, and though he closed his eyes and exhaled a long, defeated breath, he didn't protest. I followed them through the stormdoor to the front entry. There, with the interior lights on, I could see that *all* the walls, not just the hallway, were covered with charcoal drawings like the pile I'd found in Gramps' garage years ago. None of the drawings included people—just landscapes, horizons, the valley rendered like a giant, dark pond.

Kick Cecil in the teeth for me, Archer said, and reached out to shake my hand. Nora closed in for a hug, and her arms lingered around me like a mother's.

Then I opened the front door, and Archer's arm shot out and he caught my wrist, way harder than friendly. I jerked to pull free but he'd locked on with a soldier's grip, with all his wiry, desperate strength. His handlebar cheeks cast shadows in two triangles toward his mouth. I saw the redness on his lip where the hair follicles had fallen out, a lifetime of missteps and childhood bumbles mapped by the notches on his scalp. He didn't have long to live, anyone could see that.

It was good to see you, he said, and swallowed hard.

You too, I told him, not understanding. He released me and his hands hung in the air near my arm as if the muscles had seized, and I looked at him and he looked at me and it felt like I should have said something else, that he expected me to make some kind of offer. Nora loomed over him, brow drawn in: she must've known what he wanted. Eventually, he lowered his hands to his lap and slumped his shoulders forward. Nora wheeled him out of sight.

I sat in Gramps' Ranger for a while. The radio blared power ballads from the nineties and I thought about the state of things, about Darby and Gramps and B.C.'s burning Interior. Archer had given me the name of a trucker's stop in Owenswood—a town as far west as you could get without leaving the Kootenays—where he said my mother worked. Owenswood was on evac warning, and local news cameras had already filmed the heartbeat glow reddening the sky over that slice of the Purcells. I had a momentary premonition of rolling into Owenswood just as the retreat horns blared and five thousand people crammed the highways for a French Advance.

That'd be a trip for another day: I needed to talk to Darby or squeeze answers from Gramps or, at the very least, get more shitfaced than I'd been in a very long time. It's so easy to lose your grip, or I've got a weak grip to begin with—who's to say? On the way home, hailstones pummelled my windshield with globes the size of coat buttons, and during the last stretch into town, I passed a semi-trailer that'd skipped the guardrail over a precipice. The cops had it flagged off, waiting for the wind to sweep it into the bellowing, rain-gorged gully below.

I ROLLED INTO INVERMERE at ten-thirty, well past visiting hours at the hospital, so I drove straight home. There, the tomcat mewled over and over, and even though I hated the beast more than any creature alive, I doled more food into its bowl. Puck danced in circles until I let him outside and he caught his only front leg on the sliding door's rail and faceplanted into the deck. If it fazed him, he didn't show it. He is the toughest dog I have ever known. He is like a redneck in dog form. Elsewhere in the house, water dripped from a tap, the sound incessant and tinny and menacing like the *tick-a-tick-a* wasps makes when they blunder against light bulbs. I was struck by how lonely the house seemed in Gramps' absence, by the way I expected to bump into him every time I rounded a corner.

There was one new phone message. As I stood over the answering machine, mesmerized by that red blinking light, Puck limped over and leaned his heavy body against my knees. He's the best dog, old Puck. I scratched behind his ears and he just stood there, diligently, aware in his own dog way that the devil'd come around with his handbasket. Puck is the second mastiff we Wests have kept in our employ—the first, his grandad, was by all accounts a lumbering behemoth even by mastiff standards. His name was Lucas, but I never met him: his great size killed him early—a too-big heart. There's a lesson in that, but I'm not one to push morals. Puck was past eleven and mostly unchanged even after his leg got mangled.

That must've happened a decade ago, while I was still doing my undergrad on the west coast. The vets wanted to put him down but Gramps couldn't stomach the thought. He called me long-distance from the vets' office, blubbery with guilt. He cared about that dog in a way I don't quite understand, as if they have a secret between them more intimate than lovers. The vets amputated Puck's wrecked leg at the shoulder. Watching him navigate stairs those first groggy days was an activity that could entertain a man for hours. For his part, Puck didn't seem to carry a grudge.

Anyway, he leaned against my thighs and I got the phone message playing, and man and dog listened to someone—had to be Darby, had to be—breathe on the other end. When the message cut out, Puck howled and sauntered off in pursuit of the cat. I picked up the phone and dialed the first digits of Darby's phone number, even though I knew where she'd be, who she'd be out with. The phone would just ring and ring. She and I used to spend whole days in bed together, blazing through box sets of seventies *Twilight Zone* and endless brooding seasons of *The X-Files*, and sometimes she'd text her friends, to get them to call, only so we could lie among the blankets and ignore the buzzing phone and just breathe the earthy smell of each other.

I finished dialing. After a moment of emptiness, the first ring rattled around the silence. There seemed to be a lot of space between the first ring and the second. It felt like holding my breath. Through the glass of the kitchen's sliding door, I could stare out at the road that wound behind Gramps' house—still gravel, despite Gramps' great war against road taxes. It's a steep slope, that one, and I have fond memories of piling into a wooden buggy with my idiot friends and bobsledding down it at a velocity humans are not meant to move. Somehow, none of us ever got hurt, but a wheel loosed from the buggy's axle mid-descent, and it splintered to a husk at the hill's base. For many years after, its rain-warped carcass sat beneath my buddy's tree fort like a memory, like something from a time when things were better all around.

The phone's second ring hit and I exhaled and watched poplar trees sway in neighbours' yards. Gramps never liked Darby, but I don't think Gramps would have liked any girl I could bring before him. It's the idea of girlfriends—of relationships—that Gramps mistrusts. But I suppose he'd lived long enough and worked hard enough to earn the right to hold baseless suspicions. Then on the third ring, as I admitted defeat, Darby picked up.

At first she didn't say anything—we had call display; she'd have recognized Gramps' number.

How are you doing, Alan?

About as well as, well, I said, unable to be sarcastic.

Getting anything done?

Bit of a change in plans.

Nothing too distracting, I hope.

Gramps had a heart attack.

Fuck, she said.

On our last night together, after I thought we'd rekindled our love life, I wiggled my head into the space beneath her chin and she kissed the crest of my skull. I could hear her heart beat through all the sweat and sheets and breast between me and it. Then Darby combed her fingers through my hair and pushed me sideways, breathed deeply enough to fill her chest. *Alan*, she'd said, way too throaty, like a woman fighting tears, and I roused from the dopiness she'd lured me into with warmth and sex. She was looking at me as if I was underwater, and I understood—way too late—that Darby hadn't spent our last night trying to rekindle the relationship; she'd been searching for a way to end it.

Somewhere behind me, in Gramps' dead-empty house, Puck blundered into furniture. He is not exactly the most graceful of all living creatures, but his heart is in the right place. I cleared my throat into the phone. Darby would be wearing her men's pyjamas. She'd be perched on the edge of our bed with her legs crossed and a chopped-up orange on a small, flower-painted plate.

Gramps is alright, I said. And bitchy as ever.

That's good?

I guess it's marginally better than him being dead.

She hissed into the phone. Disappointment, resentment. I don't blame her, not ever. Right then, I wished Puck would appear from around the corner and wrestle me to the ground and devour the handset whole. I wished the fires would come blazing over the mountains and end this phone call in a blaze and cackle.

I've been watching the news, she said. I'd fallen silent, was actually thinking about Missy and my run-in with her, at the hospital. If I hadn't left Invermere, that toddler might very well have been mine. Darby said something about canoes.

She said something about air pockets. The fires aren't getting better, she said.

There's the Purcells between us, I said.

I heard about trouble in the Rogers Pass, Darby said, and made a swallowing noise into the phone. Is that near you?

It's northwest.

So it doesn't trap you?

The Purcells will keep the fire away.

I'm just ... concerned, she said, sounding very uncertain.

That's a nice change, I said.

Don't be a dick.

Were you sleeping with someone else?

No, she snapped.

Did you sleep with somebody else?

Stop your fucking word games.

Then she hung up, and I slumped at the kitchen table to enjoy a moment of self-pity. Earlier, I'd left Gramps' shoebox on the table in case he came home and wanted to find it. With nothing better to do but wallow, I hauled it over and dug out the cap gun revolver. It was a damned fine toy gun, of a completely different grade than the plastic crap they produce for boys nowadays. The body looked nickel-plated, and the grip was a solid piece of white porcelain made to resemble ivory, as though it'd have been neat, as a child, to imagine an elephant had died in the making of your toy. The mechanism that operated the hammer hung loose and lifeless, missing a spring, and the door that snugged over those quarter-sized rolls of caps dangled unhinged. It needed a few bolts and a new spring and some attention to tedious work. I could've fixed it—I fancy myself a desperation handyman—but before I could mobilize to do so Puck popped his head around the corner. He'd caught Gramps' orange tom in his wide mouth and the beast sagged in his jowls like a crescent moon. It would just let itself be carried around like that. I started telling Puck to let the cat go, and then, as if in a scene from a horror movie, the cat bent up sideways—seemed to come alive—and mewled at me like a creature being gored.

I donned one of Gramps' ballcaps, grabbed a half bottle of Canadian Club—possibly the shittiest whiskey in the world— from his liquor cabinet, and went out the door. During highschool and just beyond, my buddies and I used to night-wander Invermere's asphalt streets with the scent of lake swell and vegetation on the breeze and the aftermath of cheap vodka on our breath. The streetlamps are few and far between in Invermere, and the residential roads that run through Wilder Sub lead implacably to the beach, so you can make your way there with only the incandescent spill from living rooms and porch lamps to guide you. It's something I missed about small towns—how the roads are built with people in mind, how they lack yellow lines, traffic signals, those high-pitch buzzers that sound at crosswalks so the blind can find their way. There's a quiet and a ruggedness and a rearrangement of value—guys can throw down over a debate about insulation, movies arrive in the Toby months after release, families are closely knit and gossip just one chatterbox away. The valley air tastes of nectar, and spruce, and folk have a habit of leaving things unsaid.

The Kinsmen Beach closes at night, mostly for the safety and benefit of tourists. I traced my way along the water's edge.

Dog owners often brought their bigger dogs there so the great beasts could pound up and down the waterfront. We used to do that with Puck, and he lost a leg because of it. At the far end of the navigable beachfront, probably a full kilometre from the public sand, there's a dilapidated fur-trading fort and a concrete wall that holds it above the water. Frontiersmen used it to ferry beaver pelts along the Sevenhead River in the early days of settlement. Nowadays that fort sags sideways as if under a strong wind, and the inside reeks of charcoal and marijuana.

The sand around the fort is bare of rocks, because years ago some rich Calgarian paid local highschoolers to rake it smooth, thinking to turn it into his private beach. There's also a bench there, on a raised concrete slab, erected in honour of some old, dead lobbyist who protested against the commercialization of Invermere's beaches. From that bench you can stare across the water at the mountains, a sky the colour of watery eyes.

I brushed dirt off the bench and sat down. Nearby, the remains of a small fire were half-buried, the deepest embers hinting orange. Probably everybody I grew up with had a story about that fort; first time I kissed a girl was outside it, on a Halloween night that saw us both dressed like train conductors. Then a kid shot himself with his dad's shotgun—wedged it under his jaw and fired a deer slug through his skull. I can't remember his real name, but we all called him Junior—he'd seemed happily mediocre. Not enough remained of his head for an ID, and that's probably what scared me most when I found him. The bullet had blasted him face down—or I guess, chest down—in the water, and waves broke upon the body, tussled it against the concrete retaining wall that kept the fort from sloughing into the lake. There wasn't even a lot of blood; by the time I stumbled across him, it'd drained out, seeped into the sand and swell. Just strings of tendon and meat. His clothes were slimy and dank and the cotton balled unnaturally in my fists when I took hold. Water squeaked through the gaps between my fingers and the fabric made a sound like an orange being juiced. The girl with me—Missy, incidentally—didn't get a chance to see the body. She'd stopped to pick burrs off her skirt.

Gramps found a suicide note near the corpse. It didn't say anything profound. Girl troubles, of course—why *else* does a guy that age pull the trigger? After he read it, Gramps folded it into a little square and knelt with his knuckles against his teeth. He wore his hunting vest, had yet to lose his last strands of hair, but the first of those age-splotches had crept down from the border of forehead. The note dangled from his other hand, its corner touching the ground. I know what he had to be thinking: was it worth letting anyone see the note? Did the kid's dad—an exterior painter whose own father Gramps had known in the good old days—need to read it? It's not like it'd give him closure.

What a fucking waste, Gramps said, and laid the note on the kid's chest. Then he rose, hands on his knees, and came over. He stopped only a few inches away and looked at me across his shoulder. Did your girlfriend see it?

She's not my girlfriend.

He shoved his hands in his pockets, rocked his shoulders forward.

You okay? I said.

I don't know, he told me.

Then he reached out as if to give me a hug but jerked to a stop, his whole body seizing against the action. He jutted his chin toward his Ranger. I thought he might have some advice to give; he'd fought in a war, and he was old. The truck wouldn't start right away but I could hear a *thunk* each time he torqued the key, which Gramps had taught me meant the solenoid was doing its job. Thank you solenoid, he always said.

I WOKE ON THAT BENCH with an erection and a kink in my neck so severe as to require manual realignment. Dew had slickened the seat and dampened my clothes, and each motion rubbed soggy denim or soggy cotton or soggy vinyl against my skin. I tasted whiskey and hangover at the back of my throat. The sky was cobalt, deeper than the water below it, and across the glass surface of Windermere Lake I could see the first flares of orange: fishermen on houseboats stumbling by light of oil lamp, piss-desperate, to their ships' edge; white-collar condo-dwellers uncinching the curtains of their waterfront villas; my mind imagining sparks raining down as if by precipitation, as if by embers condensed to dollops—napalm, firewater, Archimedes' flame.

I walked home. There, I loosed Puck and climbed out of my soggy clothes and showered with the last of the toiletries Gramps had relinquished to my disposal. I shaved with a throwaway razor and a salt-shaker-sized can of shaving cream and dried myself with the same face towel Gramps had given me when he showed me how to wield a razor. That was in eighth grade, when the girl whose locker was beside mine—she had too many piercings in her ear and they'd started to grow over, like a tumour, like something out of a sci-fi flick—pointed at my upper lip and told me I had a *perv 'stache*. Gramps thought she was dumber than the nine hells, but I have never let grow my facial hair since. He hooked me up with a throwaway blade and showed me the basics and laughed when I loped from the bathroom bleeding as if I'd taken a beating. He was an excellent stand-in for a father.

I climbed into Gramps' truck with my mother's address folded into the ass pocket of my jeans. Baritone Radio Man recited the latest news about the forest fire: it'd skipped the highway near the Sevenhead and outmanoeuvred the bushworkers' blockade, and a cadre of those men were digging ditches to save their lives; the eastern highway out of Owenswood had been shut down by rockslide, so if the fire breached the Purcells there'd be no way to evac save airlift. The Armed Forces were on standby and the flippant broadcasters called it Operation Infrequent Wind. I can't imagine facing that; it'd be like weathering a siege. In the sky, waterbombers rocketed westward, having drunk their glut on Lake Windermere. Valley folk watched those planes with a sense of their potential fate: the quicker those things departed and returned, the closer and the angrier the fires burned. In lineups around town, people told the same story, over and over, about a scuba diver found in full regalia in the deepest region of the forest interior—scooped up by a monsoon bucket and ferried hundreds of miles and dropped to his death upon the flame.

I stopped off at the hospital to check on Gramps. He looked better, maybe. His cheeks had filled out, or regained some colour. I could have been imagining it. Someone had bought him a bouquet of flowers but nobody had removed the tag. Gramps was propped semi-upright with his hands folded above his solar plexus—put him in a suit and he might as well have been resting in peace.

You just gonna stand there admiring me? he said, and opened one eyelid a sliver.

I see someone brought you flowers. Another grandson?

Not my fault if the ladies can't resist. They're only human.

I lowered myself to a nearby chair and he twisted onto his side, cursed when he got tangled in the monitoring wires.

No Jack yet, I said.

Don't call him that. He's your dad.

Only biologically.

Respect it, Alan, Gramps said.

I ran into Archer.

Gramps made a chewing motion, followed by an expression as if he'd gulped sour milk. How's he, then.

Dying.

Did he know where Jack is?

No, but he knows where my mom is.

A goddamned family reunion, Gramps said. He mopped a hand through his sewing-thread hair and exhaled a breath that puffed out his cheeks. With his thumbnail he picked at an adhesive disc stuck to his forearm. So where's your mom?

Owenswood.

Well, damned shame.

What's that mean?

The highway's closed, idiot. Rockslide.

I can go around the rockslide.

Probably best I die alone.

You're *actually* pouting, I said.

Gramps didn't bat an eyelash. He also didn't have eyelashes to bat. Can't wait for this whole goddamned valley to burn.

Will you cheer up, I said. Jesus.

You won't see me crying over it. Piece of shit valley.

Hey, Gramps: fuck you.

He smacked the side of his bed, cheeks flushing red. I'm dying here.

Is that what you want me to tell Jack?

He's your *dad*.

When he swallowed, his whole windpipe bobbed like an apple. He put his knuckles against his teeth and the sleeve of his hospital gown slipped down his arm. The skin was the colour of stained paper, the veins shrivelled and blue and bulging, and I noticed for the first time the same on his neck, on the jowly skin beneath his jaw, tendrilling from the temple. He looked like somebody who'd laboured for hours without rest, like he'd been shovelling dirt in the mountain heat and there was nobody at home to pat him on the shoulder. He looked lonely, I suppose. And old.

His eyes pinched shut. Call Archer, he said.

You want to see him?

Not one bit, Gramps said. He drove a logging truck.

Yeah, he told me that.

The logging roads, Gramps said again, sounding annoyed. His eyes had gone filmy, and I thought I might be about to see him cry. But frankly I'm not even convinced he had the capacity. Archer knows them. He can get you around the rockslide.

He's worse off than you.

Just tell him we'll call it even, Gramps said, and I pictured myself in his shitty truck, ambling along dirt roads his age or older. Gramps' mouth went tight-lipped like an army guy. He was frowning, or scowling, or some combination of the two. In hindsight, I should have figured it out way earlier.

And Alan, Gramps said, not looking at me. He's your grandfather too.

ARCHER AND NORA arrived after midday, in a burgundy Bonneville missing its rear bumper. When I'd called—they were Gramps' emergency contact—and explained, Archer fell silent on the line for a long time. It wasn't hard to imagine Nora nearby, watching him and knowing the weight of what was being asked. Of course he'd do it, he told me. *Of course.*

Nora got out of the car first, but Archer didn't wait for her to loop around to his side. She'd swapped her nondescript dress for a pair of jeans and a beige shirt that hung down to her thighs, but she still wore all her rings. Archer pushed the door wide open and balanced on his feet long enough for Nora to haul the wheelchair from the trunk—she only struggled with the dislodging, the first initial jerk. You could understand a lot from the way she moved: a woman who put value in destinations, maybe, a woman who didn't have the patience or time to let things happen to her—but I'm probably reading into that. When she brought the wheelchair around, Archer fell into it with a grimace. He'd dressed for the occasion, wore a heavy flannel coat over a blue T-shirt and a trucker cap pulled low on his egg-white head. His jeans were scuffed in great sweeps on the thighs and the knees and riddled with small rips and patches in the denim.

Nora wheeled him to the base of the front steps, and then I went out the door to meet them. Puck followed; Nora eyed him with a smile that faded when she returned her gaze to me. I can't deny either of them this, she said. But it's cruel of Cecil, really cruel.

I know, I said.

This will kill him.

I'm right here, Archer barked.

Nora turned toward him and raised her eyebrows and smacked the back of one hand against her palm. Archer grinned. He had everything he wanted, a blind man could see it. They both seemed so bizarrely at peace.

Gramps thinks he's dying, I said.

If he's coming to me for help, he just might be, Archer said.

He said you're my grandfather.

Archer and Nora shared a look, and Archer looped his hands behind his head, but winced when he tried to lean back—his old joints and muscles wouldn't stretch that far. I guess the cat's outta the bag, he said.

Why the hell hasn't anybody told me?

Wasn't our place, Nora said.

I was in your house.

Cecil, Archer said, and turned his hands outward as if that were answer enough.

You told me where to find my mom—your *daughter*.

Archer leaned forward in his chair, hands on his thighs. I promised that bastard grandad of yours, he said. Then he looked himself over, sized himself up. I don't have much else going for me.

He settled his hands in his lap with a *thwap*, and Puck took this as his cue to limp down the stairs and sniff him. A dollop of dog drool dropped on Archer's leg and he smeared it into his jeans, rubbed his old hands over Puck's ears and smacked his great, muscly flank. Puck leaned into him and the wheelchair tottered, but Archer didn't so much as flinch.

This guy coming with us?

Looks that way.

We had a mastiff, years back, after we left this town. Called him Dough.

With that, he let go of Puck and wheeled himself toward Gramps' truck, on his own, because Nora didn't move from the base of the steps. I went down to her. She crossed her arms. From somewhere out of sight, Puck loosed a playful bark. I'm going to Cecil, she said. I'll be there when you guys bring Jack.

If he tags along.

She laced her hands together and brought them close— almost like praying. This is all so dramatic and useless. I wish Cecil'd taken that stick out of his ass.

Maybe you can help him out with that, I said.

She stared across her knuckles at me and didn't speak for a moment. I felt that I was being measured. It's just such a fucking waste, she said, whispering the curse word.

Then Archer hollered for us to stop wasting his time, since he was dying, and to get over there and help him into the truck. And then I was heading west like a prodigal son, armed with a shoebox of memories and riding toward the horizon with its sunset glow. Archer cracked his window and stuck his elbow out, shifted to let his legs stretch across the seat. In the smoky haze everything seemed to emit an aura. Whether from the light or the escape from Cranbrook—this last grasp at the things of his past, his youth returned for one more romp—Archer had been rejuvenated. With him there, and the truck's corroded grille and the flames licking the skyline before us, it looked almost exactly how I've pictured the world in the 1970s: everything inundated with sulphur and rust like an old Polaroid photo—everything dyed orange, even the air.

Long ago, in some forgotten part of Invermere's history, the road to the gravel pits was a maintained highway, but in February 1970 it had devolved to a mess of upheaved asphalt riddled with potholes and tree trunks barely cleared aside. Jack told me about drag races there, how the American kid, Crib, bragged about his car's engine only to chase dust race after race. At the highschool, he'd become legendary not for how badly he lost but for how doggedly he kept losing, as if nothing would deter him. That's not the nicest thought to have when talking about a man who might be trailing you, but there's no point in dwelling on eventualities. Crib had also shown up at the school's parking lot, where he smoked American cigarettes—the package dressed up like the star-spangled banner, because everything we do or make needs to be broadcast as *ours*—and sat on his hood and talked in short, gruff sentences. A pair of teachers ran him off. Jack promised to keep me posted. Cecil suggested we pay Crib's car a midnight visit, to send a message, but if Crib *was* one of those guys sent to sniff out deserters, the last I wanted was to draw his eye. Better to stay hidden, to stay unobserved. Human attention is drawn first to action and second to contrast.

In winter, the switchback to the gravel pits never got plowed, so driving it was a job for four-by-fours and men with nothing left to lose. It was dark—seven p.m.—and the distinction between road and ditch was anyone's guess. I drove with one tire on the shoulder, because you could hear the gravel churn against the wheel wells, so I knew I had at least two tires on the asphalt. A couple times, my headlights caught the glint of marble eyes, but I feared to so much as touch my brakes. Deer carcasses infrequently appeared in front of me, one even fresh enough for steam to rise from the bloody tear in its flank.

You never find roadkill in groups, even if you mow down a family of beasts. I did that once—hit three deer, home after my first tour when the last thing I wanted to do was take another life. Broke all twelve legs at the knees, give or take. My ex wanted to leave them—she couldn't stand the way they didn't moan, the way they hid their suffering, their *silence*—but I am disturbed by the sight of something in pain. We didn't have a rifle with us, so I dodged their rubber-band legs and snapped their necks. It doesn't make a sound like you hear in the movies—it barely makes a sound at all. But you feel it, a *pop*, like somebody else cracking your knuckles for you. All three had dragged themselves in different directions, so I followed their slug trails in the grass. Like I've told Cecil, animals like to die alone.

That February, I had Cecil in passenger and Jack crammed in the middle of us with the stick shift between his knees, and each time I geared down he sucked a sharp breath. They were back-seat drivers, or at least whatever the equivalent is for a truck with no back seat. I'd told the two of them to shut their yaps, and they laughed at me together, like buddies, which was good to see. We were en route to a tradesmen's party. I'd been asked to be their driver, though not by either of them. In truth, driving them home was the least of my worries and the least of Nora's, but she'd ask me to go along in case Cecil needed backup. He had a history with one of the bigger contractors nobody liked but everybody tolerated—everybody but Cecil. *My hands are too rough to stroke egos*, he always said, which is a line I admire. Nora didn't know what she thought might happen, or even if the contractor would be there, but no man could have faced the look on her face and declined to lend his hand. And I owed Cecil so much—I owed him my entire way of living. Debts like that are the hardest to repay.

DAYS EARLIER, I'd met the two of them at a pond in Idlewild Park, because they'd invited me out for some skating. Idlewild

Park does not place among the ten nicest locales in the valley, but it's not so bad. Mostly, it was huge, and you could go deep enough that the road would slip from view. One time I hugged my way up a branchless pine to rescue a cat. He had a zebra coat and a tail kinked like a power cord, and as I footballed him under my arm I felt his starved muscles and meatless ribs with a glimpse of where my body would one day go.

When thawed, the pond was scummy and full of floating litter that caught in the reeds around the shore, and it smelled vaguely of piss, but winter's sanitizing cold had rendered it pure. I didn't have any blades myself, but Cecil assured me he'd be able to dig something up. He and Jack used to spend a lot of time on the ice, when the boy was younger, and Cecil thought—like all Canadian dads think, at one time or another—that perhaps his son would land in the NHL. But Jack lost interest in the ice even if Cecil kept himself sharp, sometimes looping the lake and the pond for exercise and for the feel of that mountain wind blasting on your cheeks. It'd be a good way to clear your head—in the dark with only the ice's grain moving beneath your feet. It paid off for him in other ways, too, since he figured skating was romantic. That's a hell of a thing to picture, Old Man West as a romantic, but even the rattiest onions have more than one skin.

When I arrived, they'd just climbed out of Cecil's work truck. Cecil had dressed in the heavy flannel coat he wore to the sawmill—a blue-and-black-checkered thing that weighed as much as a duvet—as well as a grey wool tuque, earflaps and all. He looked like a logger. Nora was bundled like a spaceman, hadn't bothered to come with a change of shoes because delicate movement—like bending to tie laces—made her coat squeal and rub together enough for Cecil to crack a joke about being followed by a vinyl couch. They'd driven because of laziness but also because the truck could act as a bastion of warmth should any feet go numb or any idiots crash into the deadly cobalt water.

We walked down the slope to the pond's edge. Nora's footsteps were as heavy and awkward as a mule's, until Cecil cut in front and gave her a piggyback. At the bottom, me and Cecil laced up. I saw him racing me but pretended not to notice. Not everything has to be a grab for alpha male, despite what Old Man West might think.

Nora skated in circles. I always wanted to do figure skating, she said, and immediately fell onto her ass, wrists bent to an L to cushion her landing—a good way to fracture a bone. But I kept quiet, even if it'd be the end of the world for Nora to injure herself enough to require me and Cecil to tend her wounds.

Ever play hockey? Cecil said as we set off.

Just in the street. Goalie.

The noblest position.

More like laziest.

Nora glided up to us. Does Linnea skate? she said. Jack's pretty good.

I don't know, I said, wobbling on my feet. I can keep forward momentum and I can keep my balance, but nobody should expect it to be pretty. I never took her, I said. But her mom might've.

Cecil waved to some people up the slope and they waved

back. He took the opportunity to complain about the sawmill job, and about some dumbass apprentice who nearly blinded himself by putting his face too near the welding bead. Nora mentioned the politics at her school, insisted she was not part of it. Everyone just likes to bitch about each other to me, she said.

We looped the pond.

I make a pretty decent bodyguard, I said, meaning the tradesmen's party.

You guys better not get Jack killed, Nora said. I'd get in trouble from the school.

Yes ma'am, I told her. The boy's safety is my top priority.

She let out an exaggerated sigh. I hazarded Cecil a wink. It felt good to be out there with those two. It felt like having a normal life, normal friends. The air smelled like nothing, there on the ice. Winter has a distinct scent, but you only notice it once you've gone indoors. That, to me, makes it a very human scent—a social scent. A cold cheek smells so much nicer than a warm one.

This'll be your first gravel pit, eh? Cecil said.

Been up there, looked around.

Scoping the place.

Escape routes, I said. Never know when you're gonna get shot from the forest.

Jack's a stupid boy sometimes, Cecil said.

Why, Nora said, in a long-syllable, high-pitched way that suggested she was about to make a point, did you have the gun with you to begin with?

In case of cougars.

Cougars.

Devious mountain killers, Cecil said, and gave a manly shrug.

Don't think I've forgotten about it either, West, I said.

Your leg's fine.

I still owe you.

He muttered. He was a good mutterer. You don't owe me anything.

Except a hole in the leg, Nora added.

Except that, Cecil said. But I'll make you work for that.

Not long afterward, Nora's feet got cold. Cecil figured her skates were too tight, and she agreed, but still wanted to head up, and the two of us had no chance of denying her anything she wanted.

I can wait a bit, she said. In the truck. Keys?

Cecil flipped them over. The toss was way too high, and off-centre, but Nora's mittened hand shot out and she palmed it from the air like a pop fly.

We'll just do one more lap, Cecil said, and looked to me for approval.

My feet are cold as hell, Nora said.

She turned uphill and walked to the truck with the sound of her spaceman's suit squealing as she went. She muttered something I didn't hear, but Cecil tweaked his eyebrows at me. When Nora had climbed into the truck and was out of earshot, Cecil jerked his chin in the general direction of the pond.

What'dya think, he said. Race?

You're a Canadian, I said. You skate to work.

104

Scared, then.

Of what Nora'll do to us, yeah.

Cecil craned his neck toward the truck. He puffed a big, hot breath that hung in a cloud before his face. The cab light was on but Nora wasn't visible, curled forward to loosen her skates, to warm her feet against the heaters. Insulated skates kept the heat out as easily as they kept it in.

Cecil produced a hip flask. Winner takes this, he said.

That doesn't make sense, I said. It's yours.

You in or not?

Alright.

Gimme a five-second count, Cecil said. He had a wild look in his eyes.

I counted *one*, *two*, and then pointed toward the truck. Shit, she's looking, I said, and when Cecil turned to check for himself I shoved him in the chest, hard enough to knock him over, and took off before he'd even hit the ice. I heard him scramble to his feet, the cold-metal sound of his skates carving crescents. He howled like a foreman.

Leisurely, circular skating is one thing, since I could ride out my momentum. Tear-assing across the ice is quite another. The pond was dark enough that I felt like being in a sphere of light, or a bubble. Ridges reared into my sights without warning, and only through a desperate sense of balance did I stay upright. Cecil's rhythmic gliding sounded Hollywood in its perfection. I could even hear his breath, not huffing, but chuckling.

Then he was beside me, and the ease that he kept pace seemed animalistic, as if at any moment he'd tire of the game and deem it time for me to die. He swerved inward, to dodge under a tree limb. I lifted a foot to dodge a heave in the ice. There wasn't a star in the sky, and from beneath cloud coverage the moon glowed like a low-wattage bulb.

Cecil pulled ahead, then slowed so I caught up. You're a fucker, I told him.

You're doing good, he said.

I'd punch you, if I could catch you.

I saw no way to win, unless I barrelled into him to put an end to the competition, which I wouldn't be surprised to learn was his intent all along. Somehow skating with his arms crossed, Cecil said, I'm thinking of setting a date.

I faltered a bit, accidentally, but it was a good show. Christ, I said. Where's the real Cecil West?

Fuck you.

When?

The summer. I'm just thinking.

I slowed to a stop, put my hands on my knees, took a gamble: Jack's out of school by then.

Haven't told him yet.

Not like you need his approval.

Cecil pushed his tongue to the corner of his cheek, gave me a look to say I was talking with no way to back it up. Well, I said. Okay.

Jack ever say anything, to you?

I'd let you know if he did.

He never even knew Emily—his mom, Cecil said, which might have been the first time I ever heard him mention his former wife.

How old is Jack?

Fourteen.

Just talk to him, I said.

You ever tried to talking to a fourteen-year-old?

Alright.

Kid goes from thinking you're a hero to thinking you're scum. No reason.

He sniffed, wiped his nose on his sleeve, and then shoved his hands in his pockets. We breathed a while.

I don't think he ever thought you were a hero, really, I said.

Fuck you, Archer. Jesus.

Best policy, as they say.

He waved his hand, made a sound like *ach*. Such a blast, talking to you, he said.

How's that flask?

Cecil took it out of his coat, swigged it, gave it over. I put it to my lips, almost coughed: it wasn't whiskey. I smacked him, for good measure. This is *sherry*.

Cecil loosed a belly laugh like I hadn't heard from him since that first night at the cabin. Come on, he said, taking the flask.

We got going. I thought about how things would change once he and Nora finally married, whether I'd see less of either of them. It didn't seem like there should've been a difference, but you can never predict these things, you can never predict the more tender matters of the heart. They might decide they needed a bigger house, or that they had tired of the valley—maybe Nora had family elsewhere, even out of province—and pack their things and go. *Nora West* just didn't have the same familiar ring. And it was tough to think of Cecil as a husband.

Then I lost my balance and lurched sideways, and he reached out—either to catch me or to pull me over—and his arm went around my neck, like you'd headlock someone. I hit him shoulder-first, speared him at the midsection like a rugby tackle, a desperate change of direction. There was a second where we held our balance—me double-bent, him with one skate horizontal, an arm reaching earthward—before momentum won out over us both.

I landed on him. He *oof*ed a breath against my hair. I tried to dig my skates in but my knees got tangled with Cecil's. The ice ridges bumped their way under his back, and I reached out dumbly to try and slow us down with my wrists. We plowed into the shore, through the mat of dead reeds the water had frozen around, and into a snowbank. At first, it almost didn't seem we'd stopped—just a more absolute darkness, forehead-deep in the snow. The cold tickled my cheeks and made my upper lip slick with snot and meltwater.

Cecil pushed me off him. His whole body shook with laughter. We lay against the snowbank, and it didn't even seem cold. Numbness is a lot like friendship: it helps you forget how bad things are about to get. Cecil fumbled for his flask, and I heard the tinny scrape of its cap around the thread.

Anyway, he said. I guess I'll need a best man or something.

That sounds like a proposal.

Sure is.

Is this how you proposed to Nora? I said. Anyway, I guess we'll need to get married or something?

He elbowed me, sloshed sherry on his gloved hand even as he passed it my way. I shifted in the snow and it made that crunching sound beneath us. Cecil brushed powder off his thighs. He was wearing jeans, so it'd soak right in and freeze his ass solid if we stayed much longer. Across the pond, the headlights of his truck flashed from bright to dim—Nora getting impatient. And fair enough.

THE GRAVEL PITS were big as a soccer field. One end degraded to a cliff, and, years ago, someone built a cedar fence to block it off. Since then, the fence had sagged all the way to the ground and become a tripwire that'd send a drunk somersaulting downslope. The other end of the pits was ringed by forest, and on either side by eroded hills that rednecks tried to drive their Ski-Doos up in winter. Guys found the weirdest things among the gravel—unexplainable things: beer cans from breweries that none of us had ever heard of; this black, polished volcano stone; even a set of baby teeth, arranged in a tight circle as wide as a Mason jar lid.

I knew many of the guys at that gathering, most good enough to trust your house keys to. Harold was there, and some of his workers, including the Frenchman, Philippe, who Harold had fired and then rehired and who spoke with his jaw loose so his *o*'s took on a long moaning quality. I waved but didn't join them, and Harold touched his beer to his forehead in salute. Crib was nowhere to be seen, but I refused to dip into the liquor in case he showed. Cecil told me it's better to prepare for what you expect than to expect what you've prepared for, and I agree with him wholeheartedly. As for himself, Old Man

West introduced Jack to colleagues and cohorts and guys who may someday hire him to weld their shops. I kept my distance. That was their thing, some version of father-son bonding. Not that I judge them for it. I am not keen to judge people for the ways they try to get closer to one another. Everybody's weird in some way.

The man Nora feared showing up was a guy named Morgan Lane. There were a few unspoken rules around town among the tradesmen, not about who could bid what, but about how much you could bid for. If a guy bid too low, especially a contractor like Morgan, suddenly guys had to work below their paygrade or watch outside tradesmen scoop their jobs. He was the kind of guy Cecil hated, and, by extension, the kind of guy *I* hated: a married man—Nora said she was using *married* in the loosest term—without kids, a man without anything to take responsibility for, a man who stayed behind when the rest of the world went to war. Who, I'll wager, saw a lot of lonely, worried women around town.

A car lurched up the road, tires spinning and its back end swung out in yaw. Its headlamps bobbed like a thing afloat and the noise from its muffler was like an aircraft blowing its nose. A group of guys shifted out of the way and their voices rose in that low, communal way that true rage begins. One slapped the hood. Another toed the panel. Beer splashed over the windshield, was squeegeed away by the wipers. Then it was past them, and they watched its taillights flare and dim. Now, in the glow of burning shipping flats, I could see the car for what it was—for what, it seemed, it had to be: a Ford Fairlane, all stars and stripes. Crib.

Cecil saw the car too, and he and Jack pushed their way through the gathering crowd as I tried to bury myself in it. Too much coincidence, I figured—Crib *had* to be one of those guys sent to round up deserters. A brailer. I could almost see the trajectory, past and future, like a premonition: the cat-and-mouse he'd been playing at ever since he rolled into town (*sent* into town, likely); our first encounter on the bridge, how I'd blundered headlong into that and blown my cover; the inevitable fact of our meeting in a small town, orchestrated or not. Now there'd be a scuffle. He had no jurisdiction in Canada, so he couldn't haul me away himself—especially there, at the gravel pits, among guys who'd go to bat for me—but he could get the two of us arrested, and then incite a military response. That, I guessed, would be his angle: goad me to fight, or come at me swinging. I had friends here, but a fair fight is a fair fight. Crib didn't even have to *win*.

Cecil caught my arm, leaned in. You need to disappear for a bit, he said.

What're you gonna do, old man?

These guys, they don't know what's up. If he shouts for you, they'll stick you without knowing it.

Friendly fire.

Just like we always said.

Guys had started to notice the car, to drift toward it. That's what Crib wanted: an audience.

We don't know that he's here for me, I said.

Cecil lifted his ballcap off his head and swiped a hand through his thinning hair. Part of me wished I could bear witness to whatever Cecil was about to do. I owe him for one or two other things, he said.

Nora? I said.

Yeah she'll fucking kill us all, Cecil said. He put his hand on his son's shoulder, looked down. Even you, Jack. But it's the right thing to do.

The Canadian thing to do?

That's what she'll say.

Where to, then?

I figure Jack and you climb up the hill. Get a look at us.

I'm your backup, Jack said, almost a whisper.

Cecil squeezed his shoulder like a dad, like a good dad. Next time.

Don't lie to me, West, I said. You just want to break Crib's nose.

Violence isn't always the answer to these things, he said—a true curveball that made me wonder if I didn't give him enough credit. His face bent to a smile, but it was a smile like a man would give when he has received bad news at a good time—a lonely smile. And sometimes it really is, he added with a wink. He was a good friend, Cecil West, maybe even the best of friends—or at least the best kind of friend.

Then he pushed past us, toward the car, and Jack and me shared a nod. We slipped from the back of the crowd and darted for the hills that made a valley of the gravel pits. The snow lay loose on the surface but packed beneath, and powder and dirt kicked behind us as we climbed with our hands and feet down. Jack slipped once but I caught his wrist, and he tore away. I dug my boots in, palmed handfuls of crunched snow and did my best not to go pitching downhill in a tumble.

From on top the hill we watched the crowd. Crib's car was visible through the impatient guys who wavered on their feet. It looked like Cecil had stepped into a ring of school-boys. But he didn't raise his fists, or tilt his chin, he didn't bark a few sharp words of intimidation. No: he sat down on the hood with one shoulder turned away, his hands tucked in the gut pocket of his vest. His breath plumed in the air before him. In a ring around the fire, the ice and snow had melted and the ground turned mud. Crib stood a ways off, gesturing. They were maybe sixty yards downwind, just specks and shapes, like targets, beer cans. It was an absurd thought to have right then, but I remembered how Jack had shot me at a range of thirty yards, and Cecil claimed the boy had a surgeon's eye, that it ran in the family, that it was carried in blood.

I hate him so much, Jack said, without moving.

Jack rocked back and forth on his heels—I won't call it a warm night. Leave the grudges for us old guys, I said.

You don't get it.

Maybe not, I said. Maybe I don't get it.

He blew on his hands, rubbed his knuckles in their gloves. How can you look at him?

I took my eyes off the crowd. Jack had his chin wedged in the gap of his knees, his arms encircling. His upper body rocked side to side, only his shoulders, really—like keeping time with a quiet, impatient beat, and warding off the shivers. I don't know what I was supposed to do or say on that hillside. It takes a lot of energy to hate somebody, to stay angry, I said.

Exactly, Jack said, fixed on the men below. Better to just deal with them.

He'll get what's coming for him, one of these days, I said.

Not today. It's not today. See?

Crib had lowered himself to the hood, same as Cecil. They looked relaxed, they looked like anything except two men about to fight. Crib reached across and the two of them tapped bottles, a toast. We'd all overreacted. He was far too young to be a brailer, if such a thing actually existed. Suspicion runs deep, even among friends.

It's gonna have to be you, Archer, there's no one else, Jack said, and stood up and dusted his jeans and stared long at the crowd dispersing across the gravel pits. It never occurred to me that he could have meant Cecil in the same way he meant Crib. Jack knew things I didn't, knew things none of us did. It was like he could do what he wanted; he saw the world in a different way. A berth of darkness separated us from the group, and in the glow of the campfire's blaze, that darkness seemed to be on the approach, to be creeping up the hill toward us as slow as nightfall, as slow as liquid metal.

I STEPPED OUT of the bushes that had loosely been designated for pissing in, zipping up my fly, and nearly collided with a young guy on his way in. It was Philippe, Harold's Frenchman, but the recognition didn't go both ways. Philippe grunted an *excuse me* in his nasally Quebecois and slipped on by, and in a moment I heard his piss thump tree bark. Across the gravel pits, on the far end, beyond the pallet fire and the drunks shoving around it, beyond the crowds of tradesmen grouped by profession and the few couples necking in the orange light, beyond all that, Cecil and Jack sat on the tailgate of my old Dodge. Old Man West had talked Crib down. About everybody expected a fight—especially since most guys knew what Crib had done to Jack—but Cecil just sat on that car, patted it like you'd pat a good dog, and shared a drink. It was a genius move: an information grab, but also so uninteresting that the crowd dispersed and guys forgot Crib had ever arrived. And then Crib left in such a hurry that he left his trick lighter—the one emblazoned with the American eagle—on the roof of his car and it slid off, and Jack laid claim to it.

Now I got a rare look at Cecil and Jack as they were when nobody was watching, each of them in ballcaps and hunting vests, blue jeans, each of their faces loose and their elbows on their knees. A few bushels of snow had come loose from the nearby trees, dusted their heads salt-and-pepper grey. If they noticed—on themselves or on each other—they didn't indicate. Occasionally one rubbed his shoulders or cinched his arms in against the cold, but it never lasted. Cecil leaned forward with his wrists on his thighs, held a bottle between his legs. Jack leaned back on his elbows. Their knees knocked, time to time. Their eyes said they were both having a blast. Their heads swung and bobbed at sights around the party: two dumb guys who'd smashed each other's noses; an owl, in the branches of an old conifer, curious at the lot of us; a few women that might have been good looking.

Cecil's lips moved and Jack's cheeks puffed out in a guffaw. I would have liked to know what he said, but no way I could hear them over the cackling blaze and the gruff, chuckling din. Some guys hooted as one of them shotgunned cans of beer. A couple plumbers yelled for another guy to fuck right off. Some younger kids—thirteen, maybe—had brought a jerry can along and were whipping splashes of gasoline at the fire so flames licked out in streams. Men flicked cigarette butts and empties into the blaze and the residue suds hissed and sputtered and somebody hurled a full one that exploded with a boom and a *whoomp* of air, like a rifle blast.

Another kid shoved past me, younger than Philippe. He didn't bother to offer an apology, but I didn't care to pursue it. I wandered off, put the crowd some ways behind me, but I kept watching Jack and Cecil. The old bastard finished his beer, glanced from side to side like a boy and, with a shrug to his son, rolled the empty behind him, into the box of my truck. I felt myself snort, shook my head. Jack passed his dad another drink. They were as different as a father and a son could be, maybe, but it's nice to think that blood runs deeper than that. Or such is the magic of alcohol. Cecil worried, all the time, that he wasn't the kind of dad Jack wanted, so it was nice to see that he didn't have to work so hard at it.

Then Cecil put Jack in a headlock, and Jack's ballcap fell off. Combativeness: the absolute display of affection. Right then, I wished Linnea could have come along, that I could have been sitting on the tailgate of my truck with her, just shooting shit. But we expected trouble, and I didn't care to have her see me get into trouble. Role models, as they say.

I sat down on an upturned log, almost beyond the fire's glow. People milled about, doll-like silhouettes. Paintable, maybe—if I ever decided to go back to painting people. In my own defence, Linnea never expressed a desire to go, and I figured she'd rather spend the time with Nora, since she got along better with Nora than she ever had with her mom, though I hesitate to blame her mom for that, entirely. Like anyone, my ex has a past: a gun-toting Utah reverend as a father, a gun-toting Utah prohibition activist for a mother, and a church upbringing that made me uncomfortable, even though I went every Sunday before the military shipped me to Vietnam. A hard woman to get along with, even for me. She was part of the war protests, and fair enough. I was part of the war. There were occasions when it felt like she was protesting *me*. Sometimes, when she'd come outside and find me and Linnea playing catch or wrestling on the couch, she'd call her *daddy's little soldier*.

I didn't even notice Jack and Old Man West saunter over. Cecil put his shoulder into me and smirked.

Why so glum, Mr. Party Animal?

Just thinking, Old Man. You should try it sometime.

Oh fuck you.

I grinned. You shoulda brought Nora along.

With this lot? Really?

Make people respect you a bit more. Show them your pretty lady.

I'll hit you, Cecil said, and I fully believed him. Jack'll help me.

I gave Jack an eyebrow. He swayed a little, smiled the goofy smile of a young drunk.

117

Not too worried on that front, I said.

Cecil eyed his son sideways, then gave him a shove that nearly pitched Jack wrist-first to the ground. He sat down between me and the fire, and Jack scurried to join us. He slurped on a beer and I did too, and Jack looked around as if he had misplaced his, though in reality he'd simply had enough.

Crib ain't here for you, Cecil said after a time.

No?

He's running too.

Why should I believe that?

Because he's dumb, Cecil said. And scared. You said he's got dog tags so that makes him same as you, something worse than a draft dodger. Canada won't give him amnesty if they find him.

You sound like Nora.

It's what Nora'd say.

He was trying, Old Man West. I'll give him that. I'm not sure Nora knows everything, I said.

I'm saying he isn't a threat. Hell, he probably thinks *you're* a threat.

I let that one percolate. So why the showboating?

Cecil lifted one palm in a *who-the-fuck-knows* way. He's a teenager.

Fuck him, Jack said. Cecil and I swung our heads his way. Jack set his jaw, but he didn't seem willing to offer any more. You can never know with the young. If I'm right about anything, I'm right about that.

Then a huge *ker-ack* split the air, loud as a rippling flag.

Cecil raised his shoulder. A fist of hot air *whump*ed against my cheeks and I lifted my head to stare through at the party. There, next to the bonfire, a kid writhed around on the cold earth bodywrapped in flame, wailing at me like memory. The sound came out in gurgles as he rolled over and over to extinguish himself—stop, drop, roll—and it hit my ears like the drone of wounded men in the aftermath of an airstrike. Other kids staggered nearby, dazed. If they clocked that burning boy they took no action. Someone called for water. Nobody dared get close. I bolted between Jack and Cecil and shrugged out of my jean jacket mid-stride so I could wrap him with it and put out those flames, same as I once did with my own combat vest, my own arm. I fell upon that boy and laid my coat atop him and gathered the flames to me. Gasoline, piss, the stink of fried morning sausage. My own hairless arm boiled in the heat, prickles of itch and recollection. I wrestled the kid still and he loosed a bleating mewl. I saw his eyes wet and bug-like, polished orbs in the firelight. Someone said, Jerry can. Someone else: Explosion.

It was like a nightmare. The darkness throbbed in my vision as if I'd myself suffered a concussion or gone into shock. Beneath me, the kid bucked and I patted down a flare of orange. Smoke hit my eyes, made me wind-blind, and I blinked water and saw the shadow of bodies surround me, guys my age and younger cooked char-dark in that blasted rice field. I heard a moan that sounded like my own. The sleeve of my arm was flaked away like old paint and the hairs on it had disappeared. The skin looked like grilling meat.

Move him, Cecil yelled.

I came to, or snapped out of it—whichever. Cecil'd hauled some kind of fire-resistant blanket from his truck, and he shoved by to swathe the whimpering kid in it. He spent a moment on me, touched my scarred arm with his thumb, just under the wrist, father-like. The sleeve was intact halfway to my hand, the skin pink and raw. I felt the throb then, an ache deeper than bone—my old friend. Cecil lifted the boy from the ground and carried him through the gathered crowd. Me and Jack nudged people aside, the whole crew of them gone grave-yard quiet while the kid moaned his suffering at us, so obvious it seemed baby-like, an almost-constant cooing. I should've seen it coming—those idiots winging gasoline on a fire. Christ. I've always had bad luck around fire, but that was just complacency, *again*. When you go complacent in a combat zone, people die.

THE HEADLINE SAID: *Bonfire Claims Two, One Dead.*

The *Valley Echo* had rushed the story and printed an unheard-of weekend paper, on a Sunday, barely a full day after the tragedy. I'd declined to comment and to have my picture taken. Nonetheless, my name appeared throughout the article, describing how I'd hauled the boy to my truck and driven him to the hospital where they pronounced him dead without a second's thought. It wasn't even accurate: Cecil'd done the hauling, and I just drove. I suspect he died with his head in Cecil's lap. Someone was an idiot for letting this happen, the ER doctor said to me, as if I was somehow to blame. Fuck you, I told him.

I put the paper down when Linnea came out of her bedroom. She wore her checkered boys' pyjamas, and she yawned a morning greeting. I hadn't slept—hadn't been sleeping—and my stubble had grown toward a beard. You get less and less invincible, it turns out, and not just physically. The body heals better than the mind—I know that one for fact, so does Old Man West—but even the body doesn't always heal. For some guys, fear alone keeps them going, and I don't say that with an ounce of judgment. That doesn't make them cowards; that makes them normal.

You okay, Dad? Linnea said from across the kitchen. She poured herself a glass of orange juice.

Just tired, I said, and put my elbows on the table so I could lean my chin on my knuckles.

You don't look just tired.

How do I look, then?

She sort of shrugged and sat down at the same time. Kind of shitty.

I laughed at that, had to. Thanks, I said.

No problem.

Jack teach you to talk like that?

Her fingers spun the orange juice in circles. Mostly, yeah.

She smiled, lips parted just enough to show her top teeth, her dimples. I figured in not too long she'd be able to melt hearts with that smile. Jack West was a lucky boy.

Well, I guess I'm going to have to go beat him senseless, I said.

Sure, Dad.

I'm serious.

He's got Cecil on his side, don't forget.

How's that make a difference?

Well, she said, all mischief-grin so I could see her one canine. You know?

Cecil's an old man.

I'm not sure you could take him.

I flattened my hands on the table with a slap, for effect. Like hell I couldn't.

I'm just saying, she said.

I leaned forward, put one hand to my jaw as if thinking, as if interested. Saying what?

Linnea made a show of finishing her juice, an exaggerated *ahh*.

I was shot in the leg.

She said nothing, twirled the empty glass.

It is what it is, she said, and got to her feet, made to move past me to her room, to get dressed and ready, but I reached out and caught her around the waist. She strained against me but I squeezed her into a bear hug and lifted her off the ground so she kicked wildly in the air. She was stronger than I remembered. Once, she dislocated my shoulder with a foam sword that belonged to a friend of hers—hit me at the right spot where my arm was loose, and the ball just popped from its socket. I howled and she fled for cover, but it didn't take long for her to come sleuthing back, anxious to prod the unnatural bulge under my skin.

I'm sorry I didn't take you out with me, I said, putting her down.

Kind of glad you didn't.

I guess so, I said.

Yeah.

We stood there, in the kitchen. She was as tall as my chin. A conversation can slip into awkwardness as if it is the natural state between humans. I wanted to say more, but she turned away, so like a teenager, and I watched her close the bedroom door with a gentle *click*. Sometimes, I envied the relationship Cecil had with Jack, for all its flaws. It's like they had the capacity to talk to each other, being father and son; in theory there could be no secrets between them. But some details I simply couldn't tell my daughter, some truths.

Those were grim minutes in my truck, the kid's legs kicking to spasms and the air wheezing out his throat like from an untied balloon. Jack had climbed into the bed, and I could see him in the rearview pining for glimpses of the boy. Not even Cecil knew what to do save get him to a hospital. Couldn't bandage him, couldn't do anything. He kept calling for water and Cecil pressed a cold beer to his cheek and his eyelids fluttered, so maybe it helped. I remember the way his fingers curled, unable to even clutch at himself. So does Cecil, I bet. It reminded me of the things I've seen: black flaking limbs in hospital buckets, a man's eyes bulged so wide he can't even see. You don't forget things like that. And you don't need a reminder.

After we handed the kid off, Cecil disappeared into the men's bathroom to clean up and, I bet, to kneel before the porcelain throne and *will* himself not to throw up. The whole time, Jack leaned on a lime-green wall, hands in his pockets and his eyes on the bathroom door—portrait of a diligent son.

I TOOK MY SKETCHBOOK to the public beach and then toward the fur-trading fort where Crib gave Jack a black eye. The beachfront was Crown property—could not be owned by persons—but that didn't deter those condo-dwellers from staking big signs in the sand that proclaimed ownership, threatened to prosecute trespass. There'd been an incident where a seagull tripped a bear trap some idiot had buried in the sand. It was a miracle that it hadn't been somebody's child, or dog.

With one or two notable exceptions, I had everything I wanted in those days—a daughter, friends, a job that provided me with the right mixture of freedom and exertion needed to pursue a trivial pastime. I say this as a man looking back at himself looking forward. When I was ten or eleven I watched our nearest neighbour, Mr. Halverson, in his yard, on an evening when the August light shone through the pine trees. I'd climbed one of those trees out of idle boredom. Mr. Halverson was a Bible-thumper and he worked long land-scaper hours, and at the end of a shift he'd be dropped off at the base of his front yard where the grass gave way to gravel. He'd come into his yard with a big dog and a toddler and his wife. In my mind the dog is a mastiff—a man's animal—and his wife is beautiful beyond the flexible standards of a ten-year-old boy. I picture burnt-brown bangs, a mole on her left jugular, and a habit of scrunching her nose, the kind of creamy skin you attribute to movie stars and the unattain-able girls of your teenaged years. Mr. Halverson stood on a concrete landing at the foot of his back door. His house was only one storey, army-coloured siding, inadequate lodging for his many children. The toddler slept against his shoulder. In his free hand, Mr. Halverson held a moss-coloured tennis ball. His beautiful wife lounged in a plastic lawn chair. When he tossed the tennis ball the mastiff gave lumbering pursuit, horse-like in its gait. The late-afternoon light scattered through tree branches but Mr. Halverson seemed a beacon for it, was haloed by it. Each time he pitched that ball, as the dog trotted away, he hauled his shoulders straight and adjusted the weight of the toddler in his arm and eyed his wife. A giant, sweat-stained V shadowed his chest. Dark whiskers stubbled his cheek, and the dirty remains of his work dusted his hair, but he had this look about him—iconic. He smiled at his wife and he swept his gaze across the green, inadequate house and the dog that revered him and the yard he'd sculpted, as if to say: yes, this is mine, and I am happy with it.

His was not the ideal life, no—he worked a layman's job, and rumours spread, as rumours do, about the simple, happy man with a wife too good for him. But it seemed to me, at ten years old, that what Mr. Halverson had at the foot of his back door was all any man should ever aspire to.

I don't think I'm alone in this want. Given the choice and the proper consideration—given riches and fame, a limitless credit card—I think a man will pick a dog and a daughter and a hard day's work, that tightening sensation in your shoulder blades, the scent of grime caked to your hands by sweat. We're all mostly the same. Cecil, me, Jack, Linnea, Nora, even Crib, I'd bet—we all have our Mr. Halversons. We all have moments tucked away for safekeeping: Cecil and Nora tobogganing at some big hotel's hill, their first date; Jack making desperate calls from a phone booth in Owenswood and the relief when, at last, one is answered; if I'm lucky, some soggy memory of those weeks in the British Columbia wilds when Linnea and I camped among the trees. They're like photographs from a better life, those moments, there to dig up and unfold and just lounge in the memory of. They're comforts for those times when the horizon seems grey as charcoal, when the air weighs on your tongue and tastes of metal and static and thunderstorms, when you can't shake the sensation of unavoidable things approaching as surely as a shift in the wind.

FOUR

Demanatus:
One stray note does not ruin chorus,
just as one stray act does not ruin character.
Men are the sum of their habits.

Archer had dozed off before Invermere even cleared the rearview. As we drove, his legs kicked like a dog's and he drooled on himself and dragged his chin over his denim collar. I swear Puck watched him as if to give appraisal, himself squatted in the back, his body off-centre to balance his weight over that muscly third limb.

You get guys who never escape a place like Invermere, and you get guys who escaped and came back. Two of my best friends stayed behind to shove lumber at a sawmill forty minutes south, and though their ambitions burn with less intensity and their stars circle considerably closer to the ground, they are nonetheless dreamers.

We neared Golden, The Town of Opportunity, where I

intended to stop and piss and let Puck do the same. He won't defile the inside of a vehicle—too instilled with his bizarro canine honour—but he has his own ways of making a journey unpleasant, like the range and rankness of his breath. Golden's big, punny sign swept into view as the Ranger topped one of the highway's many hills, and I marvelled at the absurdity of those slogans. Alberta: Wild Rose Country. Saskatchewan: Land of Living Skies. Ontario: Where the Women Are More Frigid Than Our Beer.

I tapped the brakes to miss a squirrel—Bambi effect—and Archer snorted awake, so much like Gramps, and I realized I didn't know the proper way to address him. Should I call him Gramps, too? Would it get confusing?

Can I look in that box, he said, dopey with sleep. His finger waggled at Gramps' shoebox and he manoeuvred himself around, shrugged the seatbelt off his chest and under his shoulder, which, I knew from CPR training, would tear the aorta from his heart.

Well it's Gramps' secret cache.

Archer took the shoebox from the seat between us. He positioned it in his lap and let his hands linger on the lid before he lifted it off. At the top was the sketch of my mom that I'd kept, and he grinned upon seeing it. I was a damned good artist, he said.

He touched the contents so gently, with so much care, that his hands trembled from the effort. The cap gun caught his attention and he hefted it to nose level, blew across it, thumbed the metal ridges—of course he'd be most interested in the gun. Jack's, he declared, which was pretty obvious to me from the get-go. Then he pinched the eagle-adorned Zippo, laid it flat in the palm of his hand and stared.

This is like being in someone else's dream. I never thought Cecil'd be the cherished-childhood type.

The things you learn, I said.

Wish I'd given him the chance, he said, and closed the lid. He set the picture on the dashboard, the revolver on the seat between us. Jack might want this.

I think Gramps gave me the box in case Jack doesn't want to come. Leverage, or something.

Jack'll come.

That's not the point.

Yep, Old Man West always was a crafty bastard, Archer said. Then, almost without pause: You got a girlfriend or anything?

I don't know, I said.

How's that the case?

We sort of hate each other.

Sounds like every marriage on the planet, he said, which was a bit cliché. Still, I gave him a one-sided smile; you humour old guys.

She's a handball player, I said.

Is that a joke?

They are terrifying to behold and overly sensitive to sarcasm.

What happened, then? he said, and sounded—finally—like a grandfather.

I'd rather not discuss it. Brief me on my dad.

He brushed his hands over his jeans, a full-bodied action, like operating a belt sander. I could see stitches along his jaw, near his ear, and a scar under his elbow, white like a patch of freezer ice, and I wondered what kind of cancer plagued him, mostly out of a primal self-cataloguing. On Gramps' side I had a misfiring heart, bad teeth, a genetic predisposition to say and do stupid things. Blissfulness, I've heard it said, is ignorant. Then Archer seemed to notice Puck's big head gooing drool over the base of the gearshift. You talk like Cecil, he said, looking at Puck. I miss talking to Cecil.

What happened?

Tunnel vision, he said, and gazed out the window at the Purcells, at the ochre, glowing ridge of them. According to Baritone Radio Man, the wildfires had split into two distinct blazes and the current regiment of troops (he called them) was incapable of stopping both. So they'd deployed the Armed Forces—protect the cities, let the country burn, which had the hipsters threatening protest and boycott. *Save our trees*, they chanted, and some sane-sounding fireman explained that the fires were nature's way of coiling the slack, nature's Great Recycling Plant. And it's not like we *want* the trees to burn, he added with a preachy drawl. They're the economy.

Meanwhile, on the CBC, a broadcaster with a graver-than-funeral-rites voice queried people on what they'd save if they could save only one thing. Photographs, one grandmotherly type said, and in the background a communal *awww*. My baseball cards, said some guy who sounded like he worked in the salt mines, who sounded like the sort of man who lived alone despite his suave charm, his decent soul, the sort of man who would sift through his librarious collection of poster-back cards—each in a protective polypropylene sleeve—and sniff their old-booky smell and remember a time when he didn't expect to die alone. My dad, said a kid.

I pulled us into an Esso station at the top of another hill and loosed Puck. Archer shouldered his door open and swung his legs over the side and looked around for his wheelchair. It was in the truck's bed, and he eyed the asphalt and the yellow line of the parking stall and the distance to the tailgate: only a few steps. What does a guy like that think? You labour so long and work so hard, and then the very act of mobility—that first of all gifts—is taken away. And not even by something you can test against the strength of your arm, but by wasting. I bet he could still do a lot of chin-ups. I bet he liked to arm-wrestle.

I brought Archer his chair and he mumbled thanks. Sitting down, he was no taller than Puck, and when he wheeled himself around he came face to face with the beast, with Puck's crazy eyes and those jowls like a pair of waterlogged socks.

I like this guy, he said, and pushed past. Puck lingered a moment and I thought maybe I was reading too much into it. After he'd done his thing on some bushes near a streetlamp, I opened the truck door and he got back in. He chose to sit in driver that time, and Archer shook his head. Puck could do what Puck wanted to do; he saw the world in a different way.

I kept stride with Archer as we approached the station. He made an alright clip, but his chest wheezed in and out, and I worried that he'd give himself a heart attack before asking for my help—a bluehair too stubborn to accept that he had limits.

Look, just let me push you, I said. You can carry the supplies.

Fuck you kid.

I got better things to do than deal with you dying.

Get used to it. I'm definitely dying.

We can strap you to Puck, I said.

Dogsled? A gimpo dogsled?

It'd be more of a chariot, I told him.

He didn't even let me get the door for him. At least, he attempted to get the door open without my help, and in a more vindictive state of mind I'd have stood by and let him struggle. Inside, he moved around like somebody his age and condition should. It occurred to me that I didn't know how old he was, but as his aluminum wheels *eek*ed along the station's dirty laminate floor—leaving, in their wake, a line of displaced grime, like contrails—I ballparked him at seventy-seven. *A good age to die*, Gramps would say, but he'd been saying that since I turned eighteen.

Baritone Radio Man had followed me inside, but he spoke of nothing interesting, droned statistics about square kilometres burned and grizzlies driven north to mate with polar bears and the shifting velocity of the wind. He mentioned something about the Rogers Pass but I only caught the tail end, hoped we wouldn't find it closed or backed up with traffic or something else, else it'd be north to the Yukon for us. I recalled Darby talking about the Rogers too, wished I'd been paying attention. Kamloops was entering evacuation standby, Radio Man said, which meant people were ready to ditch home at a moment's notice. The RCMP had begun drills for looter duty—a job that could very well be the loneliest on the planet. Imagine driving those empty streets knowing any movement meant malcontents. Even their dispatch would be a skeleton crew—the brave and the stupid and the mortally unlucky. Imagine the tinny radio silence. Imagine the taste of the air.

Gramps knew landscapers in Invermere who had signed up to combat the blazes, backhoes and all, normal working-class guys stepping up to the plate, stepping up to save B.C.'s economy (the pay was very good). Other maniacs parachuted into forward camps, armed only with a camelback full of retardant, maybe the most basic tools. Gramps himself had never done bushwork—too old, and he'd be the first to admit it—but he knew all the theory, knew enough to under-stand that the might of human ingenuity couldn't stop such destruction. Luck, he'd said. It'll come down to luck, or nature will sort itself out.

In the gas station bathroom, above the urinal, someone had scrawled: *I fucked your mom last night*. Below that, in answer: *Go home Dad, you're drunk*. At the front counter, Archer bought two Cokes.

The glass kind, he said when I came up beside him. He spun the bottle in his hand, and I figured he probably wasn't allowed to drink Coke. Far as I can tell, that's what relation-ships come to—a giant game of *what can I get away with*.

They're the best, I said, and he offered the second bottle, and I took it. A touching gesture of grandfatherliness, or I'm being cynical. Anything else you want? After this, it's Owenswood or bust. All or nothing.

Better get some water, be safe.

Survival kit's in the truck.

Right, he said.

Gramps is never unprepared.

Archer scowled into his hands at that. His wedding band *tink*ed on the Coke bottle and he struggled to twist the cap off, but I knew better than to do it for him, and in a moment it came off with a sizzle.

THE ROGERS PASS is as close to the mountains and as near to feeling wholly insignificant as you can get, short of climbing a mountain or, I don't know, flying into space. The rock faces loom so close that the less iron-willed feel claustrophobic; it seems wilder than other places in the valley, less tamed, but that could be because I am unfamiliar with the geography. Traditionally, Gramps and I headed south for camping, east for roadtrips.

The highway up the Rogers winds under a series of tunnels bored through rock croppings, overhangs, impassable walls of carbon. On all sides, the vertebrae of the world rise as high as the late-morning sun. The cliffs are steeper than death; the steel and concrete barricades reek of insufficiency—you'd be surprised how easily metal bends against the impact of a yawing car. I have a friend who once complained about the Canadian tendency to erect highways that climbed around nature's palisades, but there is no better option. You can't just go through them; humans are not dwellers of the underground and the dark.

We passed cars that'd pulled onto the shoulder, and drivers scowled as I trundled by. Archer, predictably, had dozed off, but not before he justified his sleepiness by insisting that westward travel affected him in a special way—that it had to do with magnets and poles and, I wouldn't have been surprised to hear, the refracting angle of solar wind. Baritone Radio Man had gone silent, so I fiddled with the tuning knob and hoped to snag CJ92, Calgary's Best Rock—Cowtown: Heart of the New West (not bad)—but, as far from the border as we were, my options were CBC's classics or Puck's musical pant.

We drove into a tunnel. When I was a kid, I held my breath through each of the underpasses, and wished. The Rogers is a goldmine of wish-granting tunnels, but I always thought that one spoiled wish—one breath not quite held—would thwart all previous and future wishes for that object of desire. If you couldn't hold your breath it would never come true. That's a grave game to play as a child, or even a teenager wishing, of course, for romantic success. I can remember blue-facing myself as Gramps cursed slug-moving semis; I can remember pounding my wrist on the dashboard and feeling that rush of expelled air, that rush of complete and inconsolable loss. What I can't remember are the wishes themselves: what preoccupies the mind of an eight-year-old? Right then, as I held my breath while Archer gargled beside me, I wished for things between Darby and me to have gone differently than they did. Someday, I won't remember even this. Maybe there's a lesson to be learned here: that it isn't *what* we desire that endures, but *that* we desire, that we are constantly reaching, hoping, pining, praying for the things beyond our grasp. Our desire is as perennial as the mountains.

Ahead, the highway—the very *asphalt*, the *fact* of the road— was heaved skyward, as if some beast had burst from its prison of soil and tar. It looked like a skateboard ramp, as steep as the snow-and-gravel toboggan jumps kids erect at the base of hills. This was what I'd missed Radio Man talking about in Golden, what had been meant by the mutters and glares from those shoulder-parked cars. The road had split in two. It was tectonic—one side of the highway shoved the other away with all the finality of rock.

I geared down, crawled the Ranger to the ridge's lip and killed the ignition. Archer woke up, jerked from sleep by the kicking of the truck's transmission. The crack cut through the highway and the dirt beneath it—wood-chop-esque, like it'd been hewn with an axe, like Paul Bunyan had had special occasion to come out of retirement. Why wasn't the highway closed off? What if it'd been night?

I got down from the truck. Puck scrambled after me.

You want a closer look? I said to Archer, and he gave a single nod, so I pushed him and the chair to the edge. Ridiculous—if I stomped on the asphalt the vibrations loosed tufts of dirt. There was only a short fall to the other side, a few feet, but also a chasm into the maw of the Earth, dark like the kind of place a demon would dwell.

That adds a few hours to the trek, I said. It meant doubling back to Golden, continuing north and cutting west along one highway or another, and frankly I'm not even sure you could get to Owenswood any of those ways. Gramps would have known, but Gramps always knows. That's his mutant power—to always have an answer. He doesn't deal with problems, he once told me. He deals with solutions. I wondered what he and Nora were doing right then—fighting, if history had taught me anything. *Old friends*, Nora had said, but it doesn't take a philosopher to spot a misdirection.

Archer scuffed his feet over the broken rock. This from the fire?

The drought, I said. Has to do with moisture transferring through the soil. Like a shrivelling apple, how the skin'll just slide off.

He sucked a loud breath through his nose. The sun had descended toward the Purcells and the air looked dusty, like someone had peeled out with bald tires, like the residue kicked by a drag-racer on a tinder-dry course. The sky was the shade of wood chips, the mountains red-rimmed like a water-colour. Was it actually getting hotter as we headed west, or is that my imagination?

You figure a three-foot drop? Archer said.

Give or take.

Foot and a half forward?

I'm not jumping Gramps' Ranger, I said. Thing barely has shocks.

So it has 'em? he said, and grinned up at me like a devious grandfather. You ever caught air off train tracks?

Puck leaned over the edge, planted his good leg on the vertical face as if to ease his drop to the lower plane. He sniffed it too, the muscles in his neck stretching as he dared his nose down and down. I snapped for him to quit it, and his big head swung toward me. *But why?*

Of course I have, I said.

Well, it's the same.

That's not the point, Archer. It could blow the tires, or the alignment, or we could skid over the cliffside.

He dragged his teeth over his upper lip, then grimaced. Probably unused to its smoothness—probably used to having a moustache. We're just turning around? he said.

Even if we jump it, and the truck survives, how do we bring Jack home? I said. This is a one-way trip. This is the point of no return.

All or nothing, like you said. I need to make things up to Cecil.

You're not seriously going to pout.

What if this is the biggest mistake? What if you get old and regret this? he said, and then he played the guilt card: You owe Cecil, too.

His eyes had gone watery and he rubbed the heel of his wrist into them. Puck straightened, fixed us with his big eyes, his posture as regal as an old general. Archer's teeth jawed in circles and he lifted his hat to mop a hand over his dappled scalp. Ahead of us: the blastland highway, the final voyage of Archer Cole, the fires, my dad, my mom, some triumvirate of emotion so outside my ken as to be alien. Behind us: Gramps, Nora, my thesis and future and the girlfriend drama that would haunt my waking hours. Fair enough, Archer; I did owe Gramps. He set me on the path out of Invermere—and at what point does a bullet start toward the beer can?

If we do this, you're going to tell me what I'm walking into, I said. I'm sick of this need-to-know bullshit.

Okay, he rasped.

Okay, I said, and whistled Puck to my side so I could help him over the heave. The truck, sadly, lacked the proper straps to batten down a dog, and I didn't really want to get his drool and breath all over me and I didn't want to see him launched through the windshield. So I climbed into the chasm and hoisted Puck into my arms. He was a heavy old bastard but I hugged him to my chest like a bag of soil, ferried him across, and walked with him to the shoulder. Now stay put, I said, as if I had any control over him. He seemed to nod.

Then we were in the truck and I reversed to gain velocity from a run. Archer clutched the oh-shit handle and braced himself against the bench, and I cinched my seatbelt and dropped the Ranger into gear, felt the truck buck against me, the engine grumble, the tires grab the road. Wind dragged through the open window and whisked my hair in a whirl around my ears. The highway slithered on by. What a thing to do—what if we hit another heave? What if it was a heave in the wrong direction? *Then we will find a way*, I remember thinking—and thinking that was something Archer would say—as the front tires mounted the slope and our plane of travel travelled up, up, the Ranger's nose like a breaching whale, the anticipation and adrenaline drumming in my throat as if I'd swallowed one of the engine's pistons.

And then weightlessness and butterflies like heartburn or the way your back itches when you've come down with a chest cold. We cleared that chasm, easy. Foot to clutch to combustion to torque, speed, *trajectory*. We could've cleared a chasm twice as big—right then, that surge of energy and awe, the boyishness of it.

Neither Archer nor I had bothered to secure much of the loose stuff in the cab. That I attribute to a failure of forward thought. The two Coke bottles, now empty, cartwheeled up and banged the roof and one struck my lap. Scraps of garbage shook free from the plastic bag strung between the seats. The cap gun gravitated into the air and Archer smacked his palms to a clap around it. I pinned the shoebox to the bench. Archer: wild, wild grin. Archer: chin to chest but his head still lollygagging on his neck. Me: maybe set-jawed if I'm lucky, but more likely looking as scared as the child I felt like. I couldn't scope myself in the mirror and thank God for that. I'd committed to something, had no idea what. Archer, for his part, didn't seem to care—but then again, I don't know how much Archer had to lose.

I throttled the gas so the tires hit the ground chewing, held the wheel as straight as a sailor. *Yee-haw*, I wanted to shout, to land and kick a spray of gravel and dust and turn the steering column and jack the e-brake, slide to a perfect perpendicular pause as if we'd stopped to affect a pose. Then the truck galumphed down and Puck bolted from his position, charged toward us, charged to intersect the Ranger's orbit.

So I cranked the wheel. But the rear tires—rear-wheel drive, O blessed Ford—were still bouncing on their shitty shocks, hadn't bit, hadn't caught, hadn't found purchase, and the truck beelined forward and I lost sight of Puck near my door, somewhere beneath the mirror and into my blind spot and peripherals and the places where it is easy to die. And *then* the tires caught, the steering wheel still cranked, me still lead-footing the pedal, and it's a miracle the truck didn't jackknife to a roll. Instead: massive fishtail, massive yaw. The end swung out on the driver's side and I felt like watching the whole thing from third person: me pumping the brakes and overcorrecting, Archer two-handing the oh-shit handle, skid marks scorched on the asphalt where we'd set down, the air strong with the singed-hair stench of rubber. I winced in the expectation of a *th-thump*—of mowing down the family dog.

In third person: Puck dancing around the Ranger and Archer's face contorted and me, Alan West, daring the emergency brake, daring the resilience of the truck's transmission. And then, me with my wits again, in the cab, in my own head—a *whack*, and a *yalp*, and the truck shuddered to a stall.

The butterflies turned acid in my gut. The sky seemed darker.

Puck was better than I expected but worse than I hoped. The Ranger had clubbed him as its tail swung out, knocked him ass-over-teakettle along the asphalt, but he'd somehow avoided getting run down. He was a mewling heap, though, without all the mewling, since he was the toughest dog walking. Scrapes were patched along his flank, and in places his short hair had scuffed off, breadcrumbed along the highway where'd he tumbled. He looked like an old butter-coloured couch, faded in places, foam out of seam. I put my hand on his head and he turned his snout to it. His side rose and fell quicker than relaxed, but I'm no vet, I didn't know what that meant.

His back leg bent weird.

Shit, boy, I said.

He whined, for effect.

He alright? Archer hollered from the truck. He'd pulled himself across the seats, so he could peer out the flapping driver door. I scowled at him for a good long second before turning to my dog. Maybe this was one of those things I would regret forever. Puck's bone hadn't pierced through, but beneath his skin the leg had extra rivets, crevices that warbled along the grain, and, of course, the obvious split. He tried to turn to look at the injury but I put my shoulder in the way and he settled down, licked his front shoulder, a ruddy spot there. It'd started to swell, too, that leg. But not much could be done about that.

His leg's bust, I yelled.

Splint it, Archer said, and I heard him rustle around in the truck. What's your bastard grandfather got in his survival kit? Any rope?

Will you give me a second here.

No, kid, I won't. Stop being sentimental and come help me.

If he weren't so old, and dying, I'd have stalked over and punched him in the neck. It was like he didn't even realize the part he played. I scratched Puck behind his ears and his jowls jiggled. Now stay put.

Gramps kept a length of nylon rope coiled in the bed. It was as thick as a candy cane, and though Puck was a beast of legendary might, it would suffice to hold his leg straight. I cut a few strands and snagged a skinny length of plywood that I had to snap in two on the tailgate.

This is going to hurt, I said, realizing.

I can pin him with my weight, Archer said. He ain't gonna like you.

You can't pin him, Archer, I said, which brought a grin to his lips, the idea that he'd get to wrestle the big dog. You can't even kick a soccer ball.

For a second his grin lingered and then straightened out, and I thought I'd lit a fire in his eyes, that he was summoning a great anger, but he looked down and away and put the back of his wrist to his mouth. The truth, of course, was that I'd have to hold Puck while Archer did the splinting. The mechanics couldn't work any other way.

I lifted him as gently as I could, not really sure how to gather that wounded leg, and he loosed a whine at me, an authentic, quiet one right into my ear. Then he licked me across the face, right over my mouth and nose and part of my eye and I felt his drool soaking into the shoulder of my shirt. His tail beat horizontal around my torso, and my hands felt the geography of his body, felt the bumps of his ribs that seemed notched out of joint, oddly spaced, and he whined again when I stopped to let my fingers probe.

I lowered him into the truck's back seat, which barely had enough room for him, but I didn't think it'd be fair to set him on the cold metal of the bed. Archer had the good sense to manoeuvre himself around the hood, to the driver's side, while I'd been carrying Puck—he did it without the chair, with two shaky hands and most of his chest pressed to the Ranger's body, a comical shuffling motion, if things had been more comical. Now, with Puck in sight, he grazed the wrecked leg with his thumb, and the grimace that split his face had to be genuine. Lesson learned, old man.

You're splinting it, I'll hold him.

I'm sorry, kid.

I shifted the driver's seat forward as far it would go, wedged myself in the gap between that and the rear bench, and basically lay atop Puck. His neck and head were pinned beneath my armpit like a UFC wrestler, and my arms stretched along his torso. Each hand gripped a leg. I suppose it'd worked out in my favour that he only had three legs to begin with. Archer nodded, took hold of the awkward bend, the alien look of it, and then on a three-breath count, straightened it with a motion so fluid he had to have done it before.

Puck kicked, and yelped, and then he growled and bit my face. When I say this, I mean my whole face, so galactic were his jaws. One moment I strained against him as he twisted, and the next he'd reared up and around—Jesus, how long was his neck?—and opened his mouth and encircled it around my head. His lower jaw cupped my lower jaw and his upper teeth touched somewhere toward my temple, and he used me like a human would use a piece of wood to grit against pain. At least, that's how I choose to believe it. My mouth clicked shut and I squeezed a *Puck* through my clenched lips and his canines scoured a line down my cheek. My ear was somewhere in the unclaimed space between Puck's tongue and the roof of his mouth. Deep within him I heard the low grumbling of his growl, like the way a fridge gargles at night to keep itself cool.

Then the pressure on my face lessened, and Puck's head eased down to the seat, and Archer blew a breath out his nose. I let go, tentatively, and Puck shifted enough to make himself comfortable. I touched my cheek, felt the red lines left there. Archer shimmied toward his side, and I got out of the truck and came around to help him along, my shoulder under his arm.

Should feed him some beer. Cecil still keep beer under the seat?

I never knew he did, I said.

Oh yes, he said, and sure enough: the last two-thirds of a six-pack of comfort beer. Archer handed it to me to open, his hands all a-shaking, and then he emptied it into the dog's water dish and put it on the seat next to Puck's big head. Puck lapped at it. Dogs are, by and large, big fans of beer.

That'll help, poor bugger.

I watched Puck in the rearview as I started the ignition. His flank still rose and fell in shallow heaves. I loved that dog. I think he's got broken ribs too, I said.

Archer said nothing for a long moment. He was from the army, after all. Once, in a similar situation, Darby's mother called her to let her know the family cat had passed away at twenty-two and a half, and that's how the conversation progressed: Darby's name, an overlong pause, and then her mother's voice like a ribbit through the receiver.

He's in rough shape, Archer said.

There's a shotgun at the bottom of Gramps' toolbox.

In the back?

Yeah, I said. Puck nuzzled his head against his good front leg.

Maybe go get it, in case.

Gramps' toolbox spanned the width of the truck's box, and I climbed up and fiddled to find the right key until the padlock popped with a satisfying *clunk*. The shotgun lay hidden on the lowest level, beneath shelves of tinsnips and linesman's pliers and ratchet sets (one of which I got Gramps for his birthday; it appeared unused) and other metal tools involved in the process of welding steel. Even that box smelled like Gramps, the sweetness of sawdust and oil and all those days he'd come home late and dirty and burned, in Carhartts and fire gear and one-strapping a heavy canvas bag on his shoulder. He'd given up full-time welding long before I landed on this planet, but he still did side jobs, still toyed and tarried with fire. It occurred to me, right then, that Gramps had never taught me much in the way of his profession—I know my way around a toolbox as surely as an uncollared shirt, but a blowtorch? I don't even know which end shoots the flame. You'd think a guy like Gramps would have set about setting me up as his mortal progeny.

I lifted out the first shelf, set it beside me. The truck's engine hissed, and in the passenger seat Archer shifted, tried to get me in his line of sight. From my vantage, I could see Puck's flank lift and ripple as it settled down. Lift and ripple. Probably, if I put my ear to him, I'd hear wheezing, the bubble of blood and fluids putting weight on his lungs. I retrieved the shotgun, a weapon that once may have been worth collecting, and brought it to the cab. It was too long to fit anywhere except on the floor, ominously near Puck.

How old is he? Archer asked, when I got in.

Eleven.

That's a good age for a mastiff. That's a good age to die.

You sound like Gramps, I said, and pulled off the shoulder, down the highway toward who-knows-what. I tried to picture myself lining Puck up in the irons, my finger on the trigger, the sonic *thwap* and then the far worse sound of the big dog going down. And of course I'd have to be the one to do it; that's how it always went. Dog owners leaned on their own triggers. Fathers unplugged iron lungs with stoic, unshaking hands. Captains rarely went down with the ship anymore, but always had a crucial part to play in their scuttling. I wonder if Archer would have done it, had I asked, and I wonder, in the end, if that would've been a kindness to both him and the dog.

Now, I said to Archer, feeling sober, feeling like I'd opened a hole in the world. You start talking. That was the deal.

He reached under the cab for the yoke of beer, tore one off and fought to crack it.

Been a long time since I had a beer, he said, trying to hook his thumbnail beneath, the tab *ta-tink*ing. Ahead of us, somewhere, the highway to Owenswood was closed, and I hoped Archer could make good on his claim to remember the logging roads, because soon the day would slide to twilight, the dying hour, and I preferred to dispense with the offroading before night settled. Archer grabbed a nickel from the dashboard and wedged it under the tab, finally got the beer open. His first pull was a long, slow slurp of shitty beer overdone with sentimentality. Puck breathed behind me. A layer of dust caked the windshield of Gramps' Ranger—a product of the moistureless summer, the very topsoil flinting away—so I hit the wipers to smear it clean, to get an unobstructed view of what was to come.

Alright, Archer said as he lowered the beer to his lap. Here's a story about Jack West.

In the spring of 1972 Linnea came down with a killer flu for three weeks. It would've been bad news if not for Nora: Jones & Sons worked me through the bleeding hours and Nora didn't teach until the afternoon, so with her help we could get near full sickbay coverage. She'd head over just before five a.m.—Cecil would already be a half-hour along the road to the sawmill, last and longest job he ever took as a welder—and let herself in. Sometimes I'd be heading out at the same time, and we'd do-si-do around the hallway and the cramped boot room with all my winter coats piled in the corners. She probably wished she had a daughter of her own—would come pretty close, one day—so I bet Linnea drew her there.

On rare occasions I still saw Crib, each time with a different girl riding shotgun, one time with bullet-hole stickers up and down the car's flank. He'd swapped his plates for B.C. blues, which meant he'd taken residency, but nowhere in Invermere—Cecil wasn't the first guy to damn near beat him pulpy, and I wasn't the only guy who came close to throwing him off a bridge. Far as I knew, he'd fled town to another Kootenay metropolis, but he came back, always came back, as if drawn to good old Invermere—and even though Nora called it paranoia, each time he came through town he *just happened* across the house Jones & Sons had been contracted to paint. I'd watch him inch along, dressed in his field coat and big, dark sunglasses or a gunmetal cadet's hat, this way of rolling his shoulders as his car bounced over the potholes on the town's ratty streets.

There was at least one more confrontation brewing between me and him. No way around it.

By this time I saw Nora more often than I saw Cecil. I just bumped into her around town: we'd nearly collide in grocery store aisles, buying dinner at the same time; the teachers tended to take lunch at a restaurant down the street from the highschool, where the guys at Jones & Sons grabbed coffee at ten-fifteen and three-forty-five. A couple times during the three weeks when all Linnea could eat was soda crackers and ginger ale, I slept late and was running behind and Nora even gave me her own packed lunch and a wallop on the shoulder, for prosperity. I've said it before, but any woman like that.

Spring in Invermere is muddy, and though the temperature rises enough for a man to bare his arms without discomfort, the meltwater that runs down the glaciers makes the lake icy, and the wind breezing across it renders the morning chill. Everybody wears gumboots and puts their trucks in four-wheel and avoids the gravel and dirt roads—like the one behind Cecil's place—for fear of workplace jibes. You hear stories about massive benders at the gravel pits and guys ditching cars over the cliff up there, the lawlessness of it, like the Wild West. The town fills up with more kids and fewer skiers. Lawn chairs are hauled from toolsheds, families eye their firewood and their hotdog pits, and in the evenings people host bonfires that make whole neighbourhoods smell like a chimney's smoke.

Jack found me one such evening, on a fold-out chair, roasting a hotdog with a coat hanger I'd unbent to a spit. I had a beer on the go and two empties done; Linnea was out for

the night with some of her friends, and I had no impressions
to make. Jack tossed a wave my way and vaulted over the fence
and rubbed his neck. I figured he'd evac soon as I told him
Linnea would not be home.

Linnea here? he said.

Nah, I told him. Want a hotdog?

Okay.

I straightened another wire hanger and pointed at the bag
of dogs. He skewered one widthwise, the amateur way. Then
he sat down on an upturned log beside me and we roasted our
food without talk. He'd have been sixteen at the time. Cecil'd
told me of his antics, that he'd been given the boot from all of
his classes at least once, that he had a hard time keeping any
friends, and that he'd never attended a school dance, never
mentioned any girl save Linnea.

Can I have a beer, Jack said all of a sudden.

Straight to the point, I see.

Sorry.

Nah, I said, and ripped one from the six-pack under my
chair.

Thanks, he said.

Don't tell Cecil.

He cracked it and slurped from it and I eyed the state of my
hotdog. Eventually I pulled it off the spit—golden brown—and
Jack's ripped in two and fell into the fire. I tore mine in half
and gave it over. He didn't say thanks, but he didn't need to. I
thought about giving Cecil a call, maybe have him and Nora
over for a drink. The poor bastard worked so damn hard at
the sawmill welding job.

Jack said: I think I might want to marry Linnea.

I swallowed the whole of my half-dog and nearly choked, but for all the wrong reasons. Jesus Christ Jack.

Sorry, he said immediately.

Look, you got a lot of time.

Yeah.

Yeah, I said. I emptied my beer and yanked another one free—figured I'd need it.

Sometimes I think about it though, he said, taking a sip, awkwardly.

Are we still talking about marriage? I said.

It's just thinking.

I'm Linnea's dad.

Sorry, he said. He prodded the fire with the spit, gave it some oxygen so it flared up for a second, threatened to burn off the delicate log stacking I'd built to last the evening.

Why don't you talk to your dad about this, I said, and he gave me a look that said he wasn't a fool but that I might be. What about your mom?

She's not my mom.

I mean Nora.

She's not my mom, he said, and sipped his beer again, eyeing me over the can.

Sorry, I said.

That's okay.

We watched the fire a while. Jack planted his forearms on his thighs and leaned toward the flame, hands together in the space between his knees. Occasionally he'd slurp the beer—a hesitant, quick tilt of the can that made me think he didn't particularly like the taste. It wasn't late enough for the flames to really make things glow, but I could still see them reddening Jack's cheek. It seemed possible to see in his face the sketches of the man he would become, when his features would harden and pull inward, tighten around the chin and tug his forehead up—a man more calculated and prepared for what lay ahead, but also sadder, lonelier, and aware of exactly these differences whenever he remembers the boy he was.

I'm not sure what you want, Jack, I said.

Me neither.

Don't do anything stupid.

Like what, he said, and gave me this single, affirmative nod, and it was my turn to glare at him over my beer can.

I'm serious, I told him, maybe a bit too stern. I let you get off with shooting me, but if you fuck up my daughter's life.

I won't, he said, and I believed him.

Okay.

Okay.

There's one more beer.

He nodded and polished his off. Hey, don't tell my old man.

No shit.

You want to go up to the cabin sometime?

Jack, I'm not your dad.

I mean with Linnea too, and Nora. Dad's so busy he never has the time.

I'll think about it, I said.

Nora won't take us alone, said she's afraid of bears.

Well—

Look Archer, he said, leaning forward like I'd seen Cecil do, his spitting image, blue ballcap and denim and dog-brown hair around his ears. He flashed a wide salesman's grin. But he didn't finish the sentence.

I'll think about it, I told him, and he bobbed his head and raised his beer as if toasting, goading me to do the same.

A COUPLE WEEKENDS later Jack organized the cabin trip with Cecil's blessing, and the four of us took my truck along the logging roads to Dunbar Lake. The kids crammed in the rear and Nora rode shotgun in a flannel overcoat that must have belonged to Cecil, because it drooped around her shoulders and its excess sleeve coiled in her lap like a cat. She'd cut her red hair short and donned a John Deere trucker cap that sunk all the way to her ears. As we drove she kicked one boot up on the dash, crossed her arms. If I'm allowed to make this call, I'd say she looked happy, sitting there—but hell, I was happy too. It would have been nice if Cecil had made it out.

Nora had packed enough food to last us and some liquor that Cecil may or may not have approved of parting with—the last fifth of his bottle of whiskey, one or two six-packs—and Jack tackled the gear we'd need for fish, said Cecil stashed equipment and canned things in a cellar beneath the cabin, accessible by a trap door hidden beneath the kitchen table. Jack also carried a shitty bolt-action rifle of Cecil's, on Nora's request, in case we had to scare off a bear, but both me and him knew—and kept it to ourselves—that it'd take a way bigger gun or a whole lot of providence to take one of those beasts down. I knew a guy who managed to kill a grizzly with a nine-mill Smith & Wesson—lucky bullet to the jugular as it charged, an all but impossible shot—but the best I hoped for was a loud enough bang.

The drive to Cecil's cabin lasts barely an hour if you don't miss the turnoff to the logging roads. On my own I'd never have found it, but Jack showed me the landmarks to watch for: a long-deserted eagle's nest on top a power pole; a white cross on the roadside with flowers all around it, tipped sideways with neglect; a patch of skeleton trees where a flash fire had erupted and then extinguished, almost directly opposite the turn. If you hit the General Convenience Store, you'd gone too far. *That* place, Cecil had told me, stayed open late to sell booze to minors, was owned and run by Morgan Lane, which should have said enough. You know how he is, Cecil'd said, and then shrugged his but-what-do-I-know shrug. Not the kind of guy you want to run into on a dark night.

The logging road leading to the cabin sloped down and down almost to a point in the valley where the roots of two mountains meet. You couldn't see anything through the tree cover—it was damned near to driving blind, but the road was wide and the shoulders not too deep, and evidence remained of times when trucks like my own had swerved into the ditch around a curve. It reminded me of a trip with my ex-wife, probably the last good memory I have of her, when her and me planned a two-week camping trek into the Bitterroot Mountains, bombing west down the I-90 in an Estate Wagon, before Linnea was born. My ex had the tiniest ears and freckles that dotted all the way down her neck. Not three hours through the first day of our hike, I caught my toe on a tree root and sprained my ankle so bad it swelled big as a boxing glove, and the two of us spent those weeks in a motel room in Missoula, Montana, living on trail mix and pork and beans and tap water rationed from canteens.

So that's what I was remembering, of all things, when the tree cover fell away and the road devolved to a mud pit as deep as my Ranger's wheel wells. We pitched forward and I felt Jack brace his forearm on the rear of my chair, and then I laid off the clutch, and with a kick we lurched into the open glade where Cecil's cabin stood a vigil. The glade was boggy with mud and milkweed and deer droppings and the truck's tires made a slushing sound as we rolled toward the cabin. That's spring in the Kootenay Valley—all deer shit and wet grass and the cold earth gone soft enough to dig your boots in. I parked the truck on what looked like the firmest ground, and the four of us hopped down. Almost instantly, Nora sank ankle-deep in the mud.

The cabin slumped like someone's wounded dog. Nearby, a pumpkin-coloured jeep rusted out its end of days. At the lake's edge six chopping blocks were upturned to stools, and Cecil's dinghy bobbed in the water's swell, tethered to a lightning-cracked pine that reached like a great V toward the sky. I peered through the windshield and the mud my wipers had smeared on the glass. Jack climbed out behind me and as he straightened beside the truck he gazed up at that cabin like a man looking at a place he is no longer welcome. The air was thick with the nectary scent of the mountains and a stickiness that gummed up my mouth like sap.

Jack jerked his chin toward the pine.

That caused a fire, he said. Flaming half landed on the cabin. Dad got knee-deep in rubble prying open the trap door to rescue his guns.

Took him a week to get the soot out of his fingernails, Nora said.

That's because he never washes his hands, I said.

Jack once told me how everything about the cabin sucked the bones from him: the soil-coloured chimney bucket that had never been cleaned; the poly-patched window in the loft he and the old bastard once blared a hollowpoint through; even Cecil's jeep, sure to pucker with gasoline. Cecil had taught him to drive on that jeep, on fishing trips when the two of them would spend days casting for trout and chewing whitetail meat Cecil's workmates had cured to jerky in their sheds. Jack said he intended to teach his own son how to drive there, at the cabin. He talked about guiding his son in lazy circles around the clearing and, when the boy's small palms had a feel for the clutch, could handle like a teenager, along the riverbeds with their muck and the dogwoods that drooled across the rapids like mastiffs.

We carried our gear from the Ranger's bed to the cabin, and once inside Jack climbed up to the loft and we passed him Nora's and Linnea's packs. There weren't enough beds for the four of us, so me and him would have to spend the night in the truck or on the floor. The inside of the cabin was unfinished, the walls undrywalled but packed full of fibreglass insulation and covered with sheets of frosted poly. Cecil had built all the furnishings himself—and it showed—save an out-of-place rug with a picture of a wolf and her pups.

Above the doorway, in a dirty picture frame that looked burned at one corner, was a picture of a woman far younger than me. The photograph inside was almost wholly obscured, save the outline of her hair, a big smile, a dress that could've been worn at a wedding. Jack slid from the loft with the arches of his feet cupping the ladder rails, one quick motion. He landed and brushed his hands on his thighs.

That's my mom, he said. In case you're wondering.

I was wondering, I said.

She got hit by a logging truck.

Sorry, Jack.

It's okay.

Cecil never said.

Jack's lip twitched up at the corner, as if I ought to be surprised Cecil didn't talk about the women of his past. He looked at Nora. I don't remember her, he said. Or what it's like to have a mom.

Nora worked so goddamned hard for the West men, and all I ever saw her take was shit from Jack—mean, petty shit like you'd dish out to somebody who'd been sleeping with your wife. Right then, in that cabin, as Nora sucked a deep breath and leaned against the wall, her hands in the pockets of Cecil's flannel coat, her head tilted forward and eyes downcast—right then I could have smacked Jack West if I were at all inclined toward that kind of upbringing. I bet Cecil would have, if Cecil were there and if he was observant enough to realize what'd been said.

Apologize, I said.

Both Nora's and Jack's heads snapped up. I'd even surprised myself, to tell the truth.

What? Jack said.

Apologize to Nora.

Archer, Nora said, but I jerked my head: *no*.

Jack's brow twitched and his lip curled, only a tad—that unmistakable teenaged dilemma, the gulf between his pride and his getting what he wanted—whatever that might be. It was a damned good thing Linnea hadn't come in, or else we'd probably have gone all the way to stalemate, Jack and I.

I'm sorry, he said, and without letting it linger—without letting Nora acknowledge it—he tramped out the door, close enough for me to feel the wind of his motion. Another inch and we'd have knocked shoulders. But maybe that was a confrontation for another day.

Nora and I didn't move for a few long moments. She tapped her boot heel on the cabin's floor and I gripped the back of a kitchen chair, pretended to stretch, to be unaware of her, there, red-haired and cross-armed and looking better than I'd seen her and knowing, me knowing, that I'd just done something she probably appreciated.

You didn't need to do that, she said.

It wasn't my place.

Jack's just a dumb boy.

I'm real sorry.

Thank you, Archer, she said with a finality that made me clam up and not apologize any further. I must have sounded like a goddamned Canadian. And yes, Cecil has told him to smarten up before.

I never doubted Old Man West, I said, which was, of course, a lie, and Nora tilted her forehead down so she had to stare past her eyebrows to look at me, to indicate in no uncertain terms she knew I wasn't telling her the truth. It's not even discipline I'm talking about. It's common courtesy.

He's afraid of you, I think, she said, and eased herself into a chair at the table, sideways, with one arm across her knees and the other extended along the tabletop. That's why he tries so hard.

That probably isn't true, I told her. It made sense, of course, for Jack to be wary of me—I am the father of the girl he wanted to marry.

It is. I see it, the way he acts around the house.

I see it too. It's normal. Harmless, even.

Sometimes, especially if Linnea is there, it's like he sees you in her, like he wants to get away. You intimidate him.

I doubt he wants to get away from Linnea, I said, and then I sat down, across from her, my elbows on the table and my hands clasped together. But he might be intimidated. He's just a boy.

For an instant, Nora made no noise except to *therrap* her fingers on the kitchen wood. She slid an eye my way, sideways, and her lips bent into something like a smirk, but not one that made me think I'd cracked a joke. I suddenly didn't know what to do with my hands, why I was sitting in such a ridiculous position.

She said: I'm not talking about Jack.

My gut reaction was to say, *Then who?* but I figured I'd already made enough of a fool of myself. There are a lot of things I'd say about Cecil West, and a lot of ways I'd describe him, but none of those included the words *scared* or *intimidated*. *Stubborn* and *insufferable*, for sure. *Awkward* and *thick-skulled*, maybe. But this was a man who I owed all the comfort of my current life to, and I would not believe that I caused him such distress. I still don't believe that—at least, that I didn't cause him that much distress back then.

I don't know, Nora. Me and Cecil just see things different.

That's what I mean.

I don't really know what you mean.

I love him, Archer, she said. And I just wanted you to know how you make him feel.

Has he said this to you? I said. This?

He says he doesn't *get* you.

I don't *get* him either.

She pressed her lips together, didn't seem convinced. A few strings of hair had come out from under her trucker cap and she tucked them behind her ear in a long combing motion with her fingers trailing all the way from ear to chin. She was such a good-looking woman, and so *aware*, so on-the-ball. Why Cecil hadn't married her by then is a mystery I sometimes still puzzle over. It seems to me that I should have figured Cecil out better than I did, and that I was in a position to do so—Cecil being my only real friend in the whole of the Great White North. But I didn't, or I couldn't, or I didn't care to; in the end, they all meant the same damn thing.

AFTER NORA AND I joined the kids outside, the day went about as smoothly as an event organized with ulterior motives can go. Jack fumed, his answers one-word and hostile and his hands stiff around whatever object he happened to be clutching or near. His constant gaze-shifting to Linnea was enough to make me want to throttle him. Somewhere along the line we'd engaged in a game of unspoken passive-aggression, and I suspect that, as part of the rules, Linnea was not supposed to know. I'll never figure out how, if at all, Cecil handled Jack's mind games. Possibly I'd missed out on learning some parental trick to deal with lippy teenaged boys, or possibly I was too damned soft. That could have been an accurate summary of me and Old Man West: one of us too dense to register bad attitude and the other a weak-willed pushover. Pair of stellar dads, the two of us.

Sometime through the afternoon I asked Linnea if she'd like to have a go at the rifle, and, when she displayed a bare kernel of interest, Jack leaped at the opportunity to show off his marksman's eye. He was a good shot as a kid, at least in comparison to other kids. I let them go—even if Jack and his old bastard had an inferior Canadian way of shooting that I figured I'd one day have to breed out of Linnea—and dug into the alcohol Nora had brought along, and me and her, the adults, sat on the cabin's porch and watched the kids at a good distance. They were at an age when they needed independence, I guess. Each time the rifle fired Nora or I would flinch, and then instantly grin as if we could overcome our animal tendency to startle at a loud noise. We didn't say a whole lot. Our main point of conversation was Cecil, and we'd already talked about him. We took turns swatting wasps out of the air with our ballcaps, and I told her how each one we killed now was a thousand we didn't need to kill later. Nora carried a six-pack to the water and submerged them, so they'd keep cool. When it came time to fetch one, we'd rock-paper-scissors and she'd beat me with rock, every time. It felt more like being a married couple than I'd have liked to admit.

We're going to need some fish, Nora said, later, as the sun began to descend. Linnea and Jack had been at the water-front all day, occasionally firing rounds, skipping rocks. Not enough food for the weekend.

Jack won't want to go on the water with me.

Too bad for Jack, she said, and tweaked her eyebrows at me in a way that made me wonder how much she—and I—had had to drink.

She suggested I simply show up on the beach with the fishing gear donned and in hand, not give Jack a chance to negotiate. That, she told me, was how she dealt with him at home. If he got to pitch an argument, if he could latch on to an excuse, you were lost.

So I did just that. He and Linnea had given up on the rifle by then—the sky turning toward dusk—and sat on a rock the size of a car door, their shoes off and their toes in the water. A part of me feared to find them engaged in a more private endeavour, and though exactly that would happen many moons later—and that is *the* fastest I have ever seen Jack West move—right then the two of them just twisted around to face me, and Jack, noticing the fishing gear, noticing my intent, pulled on his socks and boots and whispered not a word of protest or discontent. He'd calmed right down. That's what happens to a man when he spends quality time alone with a woman he has romantic interest in. Whatever savages the quiet beast, I guess.

We dumped the fishing gear in, untethered the boat from the V-shaped tree, and pushed off from the shore. As I moved the oars round the rowlocks, Jack's eyes tracked Linnea on the shore. His shoulders slouched when she and Nora disappeared up the footpath to the cabin. The lake at dusk smelled like vegetation, and the driftwood rotting to soil on the shore gave the air a scent of fish scales, of cadavers. In his fishing cap and hunting vest and damp-cuffed jeans, Jack looked like a kid somewhere else—lost in one thought or another, maybe the early stages of a scheme to clear me out of his way. He scratched his temple, incessantly.

Jack has always put me in situations I don't quite know how to handle. I like to think I've got one or two things worked out, like my priorities, or the general approach to the raising of my daughter, but Jack—Jack is something of a mystery, and not just to me. Anyone, even that old bastard Cecil, could see Jack's motives for the weekend cabin trip. It'd nearly worked out perfect for him: if I had to guess, I'd say he'd probably intended it to just be him and Linnea and Nora, and that, when Nora said she'd like me or Cecil to come along, Jack hadn't formulated a plan, had simply gone through with it hoping to find a fix later. So I didn't know exactly how to handle it, there on that boat, what to say: he was a good enough kid, Jack West, and he may be the closest thing to a son I'll ever have, but he isn't blood. He isn't a Cole.

I rowed us farther onto the lake and Jack pulled a pocket knife from the folds of his coat and used it to scrape dirt from his fingernails. When we were deep enough he flipped the blade closed and slipped it inside his coat and got the fishing gear ready. While he worked, I studied the landscape around the lake, ran my fingers over my stubble that had grown out in patches—never could grow a decent beard, which Cecil never ceased to ridicule me for. I like the dusk hours, especially on a lake, when you can't really distinguish individual trees from the forest, save those positioned to catch the last burning light of the day, their tips glowing orange like stove pokers.

Jack worked with a single-mindedness that bordered on suspicious, but maybe he felt as awkward as I did. It reminded me of when I first spent any real time alone with my ex-wife, on a camping trip with her family, while her folks went out for a walk and I had to mind the tents with her, the two us saying absolutely nothing and looking anywhere but at each other.

A mosquito landed on Jack's cheek and he brushed it away. When I was a kid my friends claimed they could pinch the skin where the bugs were sucking and they'd get stuck and explode, but I never could pull it off. I'd grown used to the stick-thin flashes in my peripherals, the feather landings on my cheeks and arms. The only time it pissed me off was when mosquitoes went for my hands—nothing in the world is as bad as itchy fingers—or, worse, my arm: I don't like the idea of a bug having a go at my mangled skin. And I can't even bugspray it, because it stings like an ulcer.

Jack reached under his seat for a can of bugspray and doused himself in it, offered it over. He had so many scars on his hands, even for a kid of sixteen: his knuckles were uneven from all the fights he got into at school, the hands nicked and burred from clumsy injuries working on things with his dad—he once hammered his thumb so hard with a tin mallet that it had dislocated toward the centre of his palm. At rest, that thumb curled beneath his index finger.

You ever see Crib? Jack said.

Sometimes.

He skewered a piece of bait on the hook and in one strong motion cast his line out into the lake. It hit the water with a *ploop*, beyond my field of vision. The evening had deepened to that time I call the dying hour, when everything is more or less the same shade of grey. Jack sniffled. His face was barely visible to me, but I could sense his posture, his one knee bent at an angle across the other—a very appraising pose.

I'd like another crack at him.

That'd be a waste of blood.

His hands worked gently on the reel, drew it in, quivered it—I liked watching a man fish almost as much as I liked to fish.

You weren't there, Jack said.

It doesn't matter.

How can you say that, he said, and leaned forward, almost quick enough to be hostile. After what he did? To Linnea.

Pick your battles, Jack.

I pick this one.

My old man used to tell me violence is the last act of the incompetent, which didn't quite make sense, but I got the gist. Jack scratched his temple. He wouldn't look you in the eye. Sometimes, I had a feeling like Jack knew things we didn't, that he was a collector of information but that he was too young and too inexperienced to know how to use it.

It's not worth it, I told him.

You say that now.

I'll say it then, too.

No you won't, Archer.

What does *that* mean?

Jack shrugged his shoulders forward, lowered his chin. If you get the chance, you'll get him back.

No, Jack. Because that would turn me into him. That can't happen. Me, you, even your dad—we have to be better than guys like him.

That's what Dad says.

Your dad's right.

Jack hawked into the water but the spitball didn't fly in the arc he wanted, and he had to wipe his chin with his sleeve. If you say so, he said.

We slithered across the water. Above us, an owl perched in a tree. If it had been Linnea sitting across from me, I would have drawn her eye to it. The owl's wide eyes tracked me and Jack across the lake and I could feel, if not see, Jack's gaze locked on me. It's hard for me to say what Jack wanted, even now. Then, almost like an omen, the owl swooped out of its tree and snagged some poor beast from the shore, and I watched the arc of its flight, the last jerk in its talons.

When I turned back to Jack I saw that he'd laid the fishing rod horizontal over the boat. I couldn't discern the expression on his face, but he'd tilted his head sideways, ear out, as if listening. I started to say something but he raised his hand. He pointed toward the shore, said, in a whisper: You hear that?

I held the paddles as steady as my arms would allow. Things I heard: water, the waves on the tin, distant, chirping creatures—nothing I shouldn't. But Jack had fresh ears—ears undamaged by time or the sounds of war. The boat idled in the water. Waves pushed it, nudge by nudge, toward the shore. With a delicacy I didn't know his young hands possessed, he took the rod and silently reeled in the line.

And as we neared the shore I saw two men up on a ridge above the lake.

One had his back to me, a rifle slung over his shoulder, a backwards cadet hat that made the hairs on my arms stand to. The other had a bald head that shone like an egg under the dim light, a checkered shirt, and the strap of another rifle across his chest like an ammo sling. He was a big man, even at a distance—as stocky as a logger.

Then the two men swung something out over the lake—something heavy that flailed as it splashed into the water. The waves rocked our little boat and we tried not to bang around the sides. The object bobbed to the surface, shapeless, island-like. The two men—one had to be Crib—brushed their hands on their thighs like boys. They had the posture of men who'd gotten away with something big: Jack and I were all but naked on the water, but the boat had drifted close enough to the shore, maybe, to be camouflaged by shrubs and driftwood, the drooping branches of trees.

I caught Jack's eye. He raised a finger to his lips.

The two men hovered at the edge of the ridge and peered at

the lake. They exchanged words that hit my ears as murmurs. I took the paddles in my palms and nodded to Jack, and he nodded back. Then I rowed us along the water's edge where the flora and overgrowth would keep us hidden, keep us shapeless. As we skimmed over the lake, Jack stared at the floor of the boat, and, watching him, I didn't know what needed to be said, if anything. In my mind: the limbs, the darkness, the meaty splash.

Eventually, Jack said, hushed: That look like a body to you, Archer?

We both watch too much TV.

Figure it was a deer? Shot out of season, he said, which sounded feasible.

Yeah.

Then why are we rowing away?

There are points in life, maybe, when we simultaneously learn a great truth about another person and a great truth about ourselves—not revelations so much as things we've denied up until a point. It happened with my ex-wife in the year leading to our separation, when I watched from the driver seat of our Estate Wagon as she watched two men fighting outside a bar. My ex looked mesmerized by the fight, drawn to it—she leaned forward with just her head and shoulders, an almost bird-like pose, a fierceness around her small, pretty, tightly drawn mouth—as if *that*, the fighting, the violence, the most basic one-upmanship, was the standard to test a mate. And watching her, there in my truck, one hand on the wheel and one on the palm-bald gearshift, seeing that, seeing *her*, seeing her *want* that, made me have to quell an urge to waltz right up to those two men and join in, crack some skulls and knuckles and taste the sheetmetal flavour of my own blood. And after everything I'd seen on tour?

Jack, perched there in the boat while I worked the paddles, had made me realize two things: first, that he was smarter than me, or at least would be; and, second, that I was not anything near comfortable with the idea of him marrying my daughter.

There's a heavy fine for shooting a deer out of season, I said, thinking: *fuck you, kid.*

So?

These are guys you know better than me, Jack. What do you think?

After a time, he said: Okay.

Okay, I said, and rowed.

AT THE CABIN, Jack went through the door and propped the fishing rod against the wall in the corner, but he was unable to get the balance, and the rod kept yawning sideways like a pool cue. The whole time, while he fumbled it, he glanced back and forth at Nora and Linnea. They were playing cards and had mugs of lukewarm tea on the table in front of them, no steam rising—but they'd paused mid-hand, probably registered the urgency in the way we came through the door.

What is it? Nora said when I stepped into the cabin. Jack held the fishing rod with his fists one above the other, as if to wring its neck.

The American kid, I told her. And somebody I don't know.

They threw a body in the lake, Jack said. He quivered there in the corner—fidgeted his hands and tapped his fingers to a tune playing in his head. You could see his excitement: the way his eyes stayed wider than natural, the way he couldn't keep a loose grin off his face, the way, for the life of him, he couldn't balance that fishing rod. That's how kids get around catastrophes, around danger—a blindness to it, but also this *need*, this compulsion to seek it out. I remember when my brother took a dive off a grain silo at twelve years old. His leg snapped in two places and those of us with him—a group of us—for a good few moments just stood gawking at the angles of his leg. Nothing draws a crowd like somebody getting hurt.

A deer's body, I told Nora. Probably shot it out of season.

Might not've been a deer, Jack said.

It was a deer.

Should we get out of here? Nora said, and as she did I saw Jack's shoulders droop, his thick eyebrows bend together under the brim of his fisherman's hat—as if he didn't want to hear that, as if he hadn't accounted for that as a possibility. And right then I wondered what was going on.

Did you know he'd be up here? I said to Jack.

How could I?

You came up here to have another crack at him—at Crib.

Jack held the fishing rod at an angle with one hand and with the other he picked at the hem of his vest, shifted his feet. Then he looked up, to Linnea, for support.

You dumb fucking kid, I told him. Out here—he could fucking kill us and who'd know?

My dad—

What if he's here to send me back? I said. What if he's here to send Linnea back?

Nora's hand touched my arm and I jerked away. Jack scratched his temple, over and over. I worked my hands in and out of fists, madder than I'd been in years, madder than I'd been since my last tour in Vietnam when stupid kids did stupid shit that got other kids killed. If anything happens to my daughter, Jack, it doesn't matter how bad you feel because I'll make you feel worse.

Nora put her palm flat on my shoulder then, and I turned toward her. Linnea chewed her lip and Jack went over to her, but they didn't say anything, just settled down in one another's presence. That close, Nora was a head shorter than me but it felt like looking up to her. Her mouth pinched tight and her eyes squinted a tad—the look of somebody giving you one last chance. Her hand slid off my shoulder but I felt its imprint in my shirt, that tingle.

Let's clear out, I said.

Then it seemed like everything hung without motion, the three of them at once perplexed and frantic by the turn of events. Jack tottered in place. Linnea, beside him, turned her head around as if scanning for a task. Eventually, she nudged Jack with her elbow but the two of them didn't move. Nora reached for some personal items in her immediate vicinity: a book, one of Jack's damp socks, a scarf I didn't recognize but which Linnea claimed with a nod. I'd seen this kind of putzing around among new guys in the army, this high-strung, get-it-done approach that got nothing done—like ratcheting a socket wrench in the wrong direction. It only lasted an instant, that bout of confused energy, and then the three of them set off and I went to Jack's shitty bolt-action, to check the breech and the action and to lean it on the wall nearby because I didn't know what was coming my way.

WHEN THE KNOCK CAME, Jack and Linnea were upstairs and Nora was at the sink. Jack's head popped over the edge of the loft and me and him shared a look—hell if I know what kind of expression I gave him—and he disappeared, I hoped, to get him and Linnea to the far back of the loft. Whoever was at the door—I had an idea—knocked again and I called, Hold on.

I opened the door to the man from the lake, the one I didn't know, bald as a chicken plucker and wearing a checkered flannel shirt. Wider than me and just as tall. He had a goatee that ringed his mouth like a biker, and a red, raw patch of skin on the underside of his jaw, spreading down his neck and beneath the collar of his shirt. Strapped to his back: a 30-30.

Sorry to bother, the guy said, in the husky, quick-syllabled way of a man not sorry at all. Me and my nephew been out cougar hunting, got a little lost.

I jerked my chin toward the exit to the cabin's clearing. Road'll take you to the highway.

Well, who'da thought, the guy said, but he didn't make as if to leave. Then: This's Cecil West's place, isn't it?

Yeah.

Then who the hell are you?

He sniffed as he said it, his nose jerking up and down, his eyes anywhere but looking at me—all the signs of a guy who might strike you at any moment. Behind me, I heard Nora go still at the sink, the creak in the wood as she faced the door, imagined the way she'd look right then, a couple loose sprigs of hair near her ear, arms plywood-straight at her sides, bunches of fabric in each fist. The guy thumbed his front teeth and I noticed that they had a forward tilt to them, an outward tilt, as if he kept constant pressure on them with his tongue. I couldn't see a damned thing in the darkness behind him, not even the lining of the trees.

Why don't you ask me again, I said. More politely.

The guy smiled—a wide, almost sideways twist of his mouth that pulled his lips as high as his gums. He ran his hand down his face, traced his goatee with his index and thumb. A scar cut horizontal on the cheek beneath his right eye, and he had a kink in his nose that probably indicated an old break— which meant if I hit him there, coming sideways at the bridge, it'd break again. Then he clacked his teeth together, twice in quick succession. Been in the bush too long, he said. Forgot my manners. Name's Morgan.

He extended his hand. I shook it even as I linked that name to the general store owner, and then to Crib. I'm Archer, I said. Where's your nephew?

Washing his boot in the lake. Stepped in a pile of shit. You are what you walk in, or whatever.

Amen to that.

Morgan crossed his arms, rocked forward as if innocently, but more likely so he could scope out the inside of the cabin. Pretty cold out here, he said. In the cold.

We were just going to bed.

Seems a bit early.

Early risers.

You don't look it, Morgan said, leaning on his heels. What'd you say your name was?

Archer.

That a first name or a last?

First.

What's your last?

I don't believe you said, I told him.

Morgan pinched his tongue sideways between his teeth so the veiny underside bulged like a sack of meat. I couldn't read his expression, but it doesn't take a genius to know when you might get into a fight. He had broader shoulders than me but a paunch, soft-looking deltoids, and a chest drooped with age— and no hand-to-hand training, if I was forced to make a guess.

Lane, he said, stretching it as though to make it more than one syllable. Odd I don't know you. I practically own this town.

He flashed me the kind of arrogant smile that rich people do, the kind any working man would love to smear off his face. He pretended to wipe his nose, kept looking anywhere but at me. I listened for the sound of boots in the darkness that would indicate Crib's approach through the mud.

Then Nora placed her hand on my back, right between my shoulder blades, a touch so light it bordered on accidental, and then she stood beside me in the doorway, her red hair pulled through the trucker cap's latch and half her body leaning on mine. Morgan's face went from scowl to neutral to something like a blush almost in the span of a breath. Hello Morgan, Nora said, squeezed my arm. We can probably offer you a beer.

Thank you *ma'am*, Morgan said. You are about the last person I expected to find out here.

I could say the same.

He mopped a hand over his scalp. Just, didn't expect to find you here. Aren't you with Cecil?

Nora smiled, only the corners going up, her eyes wide and round. She didn't look like somebody having a good time. I had no idea what was going on. The three of us ducked inside. There, Morgan sagged into a chair and lifted the rifle off his shoulders and leaned it on the table, and I lowered myself across from him. Out of her bag—that she'd begun to hastily pack—Nora produced three beer and rattled them onto the table.

All we got, she said.

Sucks to be my nephew, Morgan said. That's what you get for not watching where you step.

Morgan swiped his beer off the table, all flourish. He looked around for an opener, but I had no idea where Cecil'd keep one, or if he even kept one at all. Nora went to the sink and pulled on a drawer and *hmm*'d, as if surprised to find it missing. She turned back to us, flipped a stray strand of hair off her cheek, and said, Must've misplaced it.

I thought about Linnea and Jack upstairs, tucked under the fold-out cots with their arms around duffle bags—to mask their human shape, a basic camouflage trick I hoped I'd mentioned in passing. Then I thought about Crib, out in the darkness and likely to come banging on the door himself, cadet hat turned sideways, field coat packed with smokes and shells and coin. Last time we'd met, he was as wide as me, and he couldn't have gotten thinner, or weaker, and he had the same combat training and, now, a rifle.

So, with Nora at the kitchen counter and no choice apparent, I tipped the edge of my bottle's cap against the wood of Cecil's hand-built table and smacked it with the heel of my palm. A primary striking point, the heel of the palm—tougher even than knuckles. They taught me that in special tactics, among others. Strike a guy upwards with that bone, right under his nostril, and he'd be tear-blind.

I thought you were with Cecil, Morgan said.

She is, I said, and took his bottle to open.

What's your connection then, he said.

Nora pulled up a chair kitty-corner to the two of us. Put two army guys in a room and there might as well be no one else there, she said, and pressed her lips together. I could see her dimples, which were pretty nice dimples. Her knee knocked against mine and stayed there, pressing on my leg, longer than a simple tap, longer than by accident. I gulped my beer, saw Morgan do the same. I wondered what she was doing, and I just sort of wondered—at nothing, at the situation, at Nora as a whole.

Outside, a rifle blast cracked through the air and my head twisted toward the sound, my eyes searching through the open window. I expected to see the dark shape of Crib approaching. But Crib didn't show, and Morgan scowled, his pudgy face bending into a series of fleshy bulbs. Wasting my ammo on ghosts, the dumb cunt, he said, and his eyes widened and he touched his lips and looked at Nora. Pardon my French, *ma'am*.

At the same time, the floorboards in the loft creaked and I muttered about the workmanship. Jack says he caught a glimpse of Crib, and that it made him rock backward on his heels. Crib came out of the forest, not moving toward the cabin but parallel to the woods, as if stalking something across the glade. He had his rifle against the meat of his shoulder, Jack says, and under the moonlight his iron crab brooch glinted silver. Then Crib spun toward the cabin, rifle levelled, his eyes at the sights, and looked straight up at Jack in the loft window. He couldn't have seen a thing—pitch-black in there—but Jack swears he mouthed the word *bang*.

Morgan took a long pull from his beer, swished it through his teeth.

Cecil is a hard man to get along with, he said.

He's stubborn, I'll give you that.

You out here with his wife. Seems a guy'd know what was going on.

That's a lot of presumption.

It's good to be here, Ar-cher, he said, dragging on both *r*'s. He wasn't even looking at me, but at Nora. We should run into each other more often.

Too busy, the both of us.

Isn't that the truth, he said. So *much* to do, he said, and winked. Guys like us, Archer. No rest for us.

Morgan sucked his teeth without making a noise, just ran his upper lip across the enamel, over and over, like a lathe. He looked right at Nora, stared for a two-second count, and then rolled a grin in my direction. Nora's knee pressed harder against mine.

Good thing Cecil ain't here, Morgan said. Don't like hanging out with guys dumber than me.

Both his drink and mine were half-empty, Nora's less so. You almost done that beer? I said.

Yeah, about, Morgan said, and tipped it up and held it there while his Adam's apple rose and fell like a pressure gauge. When it was empty, he wiped spill off his chin with a sleeve. You guys eating for four? he added, and jerked his thumb at the plates stacked beside the sink. Or you hiding something?

He didn't wait for an answer, got up and grabbed his rifle fast enough to almost make me lunge. He went to the door and I followed, Nora walking stiffly behind, and the three of us stopped outside the cabin, in the open field where Crib would have a clear shot. I scanned those swishing trees and bushes and the angle of the moonlight, desperate to glimpse unnatural motion, the shape of a human. Jack doesn't think anyone was going to shoot anybody that night, it being Canada and all, but I have a bullet scar in my leg.

Well thanks for the beer, he said, and pushed past us— *between us*—toward the road to the highway, and as he did, blocking me, he placed his hand flat on Nora's ass. There are things I don't understand about that series of events: why he thought he had any clout to throw around, and why he thought I wouldn't pound him into the mud and deer shit; and how Nora caught my arm at the bicep, with her elbow. She'd anticipated it—my reaction? His grope? All of it?—and tangled herself against me, and Morgan vanished into the night unscathed.

We stood like that, pressed that close together, just breathing. My heart beat like a kid in love.

What the *fuck* was that about? I said down at her, suddenly aware of the position of her body against mine, our arms locked together, as if we'd been do-si-doing. She smelled like beer, and a fruity shampoo, and the gamey scent of the outdoors. And then it happened, for better or worse: I opened my mouth to ask *why*, again, and then she was kissing me, or I was kissing her. It lasted a moment, maybe, the two of us in the darkness, but maybe *that* moment was when it all began, and not years earlier at the same cabin. Maybe it began with a kiss instead of a bullet.

Above us, the loft window was empty and dark—Jack and Linnea had stayed out of sight, I guess—but, looking up at it, I felt a flutter in my gut, right at the base of my ribs, as if I was driving too fast around a curve.

FIVE

Parmenides:
*You must learn all things, / both the unshaken
heart of reality / and the notions of mortals
which lack all genuine conviction.*

For a long time, I'd hoped to roadtrip across the country with Darby in a canopied pickup that we'd drive in plotless tangents off the Number 1. We'd eat Babybel cheese and deli sandwiches and live that journey wholly off each other, so that at every rest stop or campground or Walmart parking lot we could stretch and make eyes and understand that this is *it—this* is where we were meant to be. Maybe we'd hit the Frank Slide and gaze over that tundra of deadly rock. Maybe we'd coast the hundredth meridian and blare Tragically Hip songs from shitty speakers, or drink mindlessly in mining towns whose resources had run dry. Maybe, I hoped, we could just travel—wander without plan, without destination. It would be the opposite of my manhunt across the Kootenays; there would be no target, there would be no end in sight, no shadowy father on the far side of the river with one or two truisms to tell. See, if you travel without a destination, your journey becomes the destination, becomes an endless regress of destinations. On a line, the only thing between point A and point B is another infinite series of points. Once a bullet hits your calf, its trajectory no longer matters—we never speak of the path it took to get there, unless it ricochets off something interesting on the way. And like that bullet, we start with a thousand thousand trajectories, we aim—or we're aimed—and we set out, and we end up on the far coast or in a foreign country, or we go nowhere at all. We don't exist over a span of time; we exist instantiated in the *now*. If you think like this, if you disregard the ethos of a journey, then wherever you might be or wherever you end up is the place you'd always been meant to go. Except you didn't go there; you just were there. To undertake a journey without a destination is to haul your destination with you, is to not undertake a journey at all.

The Ranger had suffered significant damage when we cowboyed across the breach in the road: the clutch seized, the engine stalled on steep climbs and kicked up a true and dirty fight upon reignition. At the onset of evening, Baritone Radio Man offered one final and cryptic warning: It's Hell out there, gents. Per his earlier soothsayings, the highway to Owenswood was landslid and impassable even to our sense of heightened bravado, so Archer took over navigation and led us by gut off the beaten path. The lumber roads carved along the mountain's face and a rhinestone moon lit the trees so pale and luminous they looked like prison-bar steel.

For an ex-marine, he did things that made no sense to my ingrained cynic: he used gnarled, devilly trees as landmarks, which might have been okay anywhere but within a forest; he got disoriented by the darkness, as if his mind muddled the concepts of ascending hills and then descending them, as if up and down and over had become camouflaged together; he spent far too much time worrying about our destination when it was the journey that mattered most. That last I attribute to the fact of his impending death. It would, like Gramps had said, be like approaching a wall. Perhaps, in general, dying men make poor navigators.

Sometimes, we came so close to the highway you could all but smell its gravel. There were no cars, nobody so careless as us. Between the trees my headlamps rolled shadows like a movie reel over the asphalt. The last canvas of night draped low overhead. You could see the edges of things—the lines that blurred in and out of one another under the wildfires' sawdust glow.

The forest was in the middle stages of rebirth. Parts of it had been consumed by a blaze in the eighties, and adolescent trees stood calf-like among the charred carcasses of their forefathers. That's the machine of the world, how past meshes with future: dig deep enough or wait long enough and you'll find the bones of a dead thing. Kids consume the legacies of their parents. People found cities over unmarked graves. Civilizations rise up from the ruins of those that trailblazed before them. Whole histories are built on the leftovers of older worlds.

The truck clipped a bump with its useless shocks and Puck loosed a whimper. I've seen that dog endure a lot, even lose a leg to yuppie stupidity, but with each muffled yalp I grew more and more certain he'd suffered a wound he would not recover from. Archer emptied a second beer into Puck's bowl and held it while the dog lapped it up with his wide flapping tongue. We had one more beer among us, and Archer spun it round and round in his ancient hands. The truck's tires spat mud and loose stones at the undercarriage, and with each ping Archer *tink*ed the beer's aluminum tab. Then he tucked it under the seat and lowered his window and sucked a strong sniff of air.

I sensed our approach to Owenswood in my gut and chest, even in my arms and hands and knuckles—like that eerie weightlessness on a swing set when you swing too high for the tensility of its chains. They say men seek, in women, someone who'll act as a mother; maybe my ignorance in this regard is why I did so poorly with Darby; I'd never even had a stand-in for a mom.

Archer rubbed his face, palms going up and down so the skin pulled taut, sagged, pulled taut. I wondered if he was in constant pain. You holding up? I said.

I'm tired, kid.

Nap.

You're not a full tank either, he said. His hands squeezed his lips like that joke about bus doors. Archer raised his window. He rubbed his hands over his arms. I saw the pink flesh on the underside of his eye socket, a quick, moist gleam in the darkness.

We descended a hill that traced the gradient of Rogers Pass, and as we got lower a fog built around us, so dense it scattered the Ranger's highbeams. I flipped them off. The fog settled below the truck's bumper, and I navigated by the curl of the trees on either roadside. It rendered the ground invisible, made it impossible to brace for water divots or potholes, road sheers, even animals that lay dormant and hidden. Gramps bragged that, one terrible winter, he got caught on the highway in a blizzard so thick he could only progress by sensing the different churn of his tires—one on the gravel shoulder, and one on the asphalt. He liked to claim that he'd driven more miles backward than I had forward.

The road looped to our right and, on the opposite side, the trees fell away to reveal a cliff. The fog poured over the edge in rivulets. Below us, a plane of darkness had settled into the bowl of the valley; it looked immaculate and thick enough to touch, and all the muddy evening shades bled into it, this great abyss. It gave me the sensation that at any moment the truck could plummet through the fog on the ground. On cue, we hit a moment of seesaw that brought the rear wheels in a fishtail toward the cliff. I slowed to a scuttle, pushed instinctively against my own seat. Archer hooked his fingers around the oh-shit handle. He scrubbed his forearm in small circles. His mouth opened and shut, mere millimetres, only visible in the darkness by profile—a cud-chewing motion. All of a sudden, the truck smelled like an old man: a non-specific liquor, wads of two-dollar bills bound in rubber bands.

Archer? I said.

He touched his face. Mind if we stop for a sec?

Not one bit. Stretch our legs.

I'll sit.

That's not what I meant, I said, and he tossed a wave of his hand.

I pulled the truck over to the cliffside and it gave an unhealthy kick as the engine wound down. It would inevitably betray me at a time of critical importance, like all those faulty vehicles that feature in the escape plans of Hollywood. Archer unhitched himself and reached out to graze Puck's flank with his fingertips. For better or worse, the dog did not stir.

Outside, the air tasted like burned toast, and motes of char weighed on my tongue like grit. I put my hand on the Ranger's dirty surface and circled to Archer's side. The fog varied from ankle-deep to shin-deep and with each step I squinted in the dark to see it billow out and creep back, as controlled and organic as breathing. I've had one or two unnatural experiences in fog—seen a friend suddenly and inexplicably suffer a foot-long gash on his calf, just standing around at the edge of a streetlamp's glare, for example—and I do not trust it.

I came around to Archer's window and he raised one hairless eyebrow at me, and I wished I could have summoned the nerve to ask him to stop doing that. Gimme a hand down, he said.

Let me grab the chair, I said, but he reached through the window and caught my arm.

Just give me your shoulder.

You sure?

Fuck the chair, he said, and leaned on the latch as he did, and the door tumbled open and he nearly came out with it. But he caught himself, and not for one second did he look sheepish. I put my shoulder under his. He looped his arm over my neck. With baby steps he descended to the living earth, and without having to say so we shuffled toward that open cliffside until we stood like some partygoers before the view. Archer sat down, leaned backward on his elbows like a kid. I joined him. It seemed we could stare endlessly into the valley, as if it were meant for that. We didn't say much. You don't always have to.

I'm sorry about your dog, he said after a time.

It's not only your fault.

Just hate to see him suffer. Anything, really.

The beer will help, I guess. How'd you know to find it?

Cecil always kept it there, for times like these.

How well do you know Gramps?

Not one bit anymore. He used to be my best friend.

He grunted as he said that, continued: It really sinks in when you say it, you know? *Used to be.*

The fog parted around my legs. It rolled on and over the cliff like a river, and I lifted and lowered my hand into it, transfixed. In the Ranger, Puck made a noise that sounded half snore, half gurgle. Archer and I sat and listened to it until he once again rumbled himself to quiet.

I can't believe I was so stupid, I said.

It's my fault, kid.

The whole thing, not just Puck. For leaving Toronto in the first place.

You don't always choose where you go, even though you think you do. You end up going one way and for the life of you all you can do is make the best of it.

What are you talking about? I said.

I don't know, he said. But there's always hope.

The air pulsed. Fog pillowed at our fingertips.

He won't make it, will he? I said. He's too old and too hurt.

We talking about the dog or your grandad?

I nudged him with my elbow. He let himself smile.

The fog heaved in and out, up and down. It was like breath on your neck, some kind of predator. Archer rubbed his arm like a man trying to ward off a chill. He hung like that, midway in a self-hug, too unsure to lower his limb to the fog. Humans are afraid of what we don't know, and we can't know very much. Here's something I don't know: whether or not Darby could've been the love of my life.

WE MET ON A CP RAIL train ride, aged twenty, somewhere during the run over the wind-blind prairies. It was my second day of the trip, en route to commence my studies in the epicentre of the centre of the universe. Vancouver through Toronto, that train; it'd twist around B.C.'s mountainous Interior and then dash east across the Land of Living Skies. Cheaper to fly, but everybody flew, and Gramps liked the idea of sending me off in a vehicle he trusted the mechanics of. So I boarded in Banff, a nearby winter-sport town where two years earlier I had, like every eighteen-year-old boy from Invermere, first legally entered a bar. That time, we limped in and out of the place aboard a buddy's refurbished GTO; this trip—with Gramps, toward my send-off from the valley—I sat in the passenger seat of his Ranger and marvelled at all the things-unsaid.

Gramps drove. Redneck radio twanged from the speakers. The whole journey, we barely spoke a word. Gramps spent a lot of time sucking his teeth and looking pensively at things in the distance; I don't suspect I gave him a lot of encouragement to embark on a heart-to-heart. Behind us, wedged between the fold-down seats, I had a hiking pack and one roly-poly suitcase shoved full of my worldly possessions: loose-fit T-shirts and jeans with the hems trampled off; an electric razor Gramps offered up as a going-away gift; a few books, my laptop. As we drove, Gramps eyed the speedometer and refused to go even a tick above ninety, said he didn't care to get pulled over, even though we both knew the RCMP didn't patrol the national park. The trees reeled by on either side and the highway curved in wide arcs designed to keep you on-road if caught in an icy skid. The mountains swelled bigger and bigger and the radio cut out and somehow our silence got quieter, if that's even possible. I wish I'd had the boullions to say anything, but that awkwardness seemed insurmountable. It still does, even in retrospect. I was leaving him to loneliness. He did such good for me, Gramps, and I know for a fact that back then—and more so as years went on—I was a poor stand-in for a son.

At the train station, Gramps carried the wheelable suitcase stiff-armed by his side. Still only passing words between us—a grunt of direction, one request for a loonie while he fished through the Ranger's cupholders for parking change. Now, as we waited by the train's closed doors and its carriages snaking off beyond sight, I felt *the tug*—that urge to just head right back where I came from. But I had Gramps there between me and retreat. He stood to my chin, or thereabouts, wore his charcoal-grey ballcap and denim vest and Gore-Tex boots. Wide-shouldered, wiry, somehow not-old. He looked like the kind of person you could ask to hold your coffee. The train doors yawned open before us and an attendant in a silly hat offered to help with the bags, but Gramps sent him skedaddling. Then he handed the suitcase my way.

Call me when you get there, Gramps said.

I shifted the bag on my shoulder. Of course, I said.

He thumbed a piece of truck debris off one strap. Here, he said, and drew a wad of money out of his gut pocket. I thought about a cheque, but this seemed more traditional.

I can't take this.

Yeah, you're supposed to say that, he said. Then he grinned.

Thanks, Gramps.

Don't spend it all on hookers.

Just some? I said, and he levelled me one in the gut—a quick one-two.

He stood there smiling at me. I couldn't think of a time when he'd been happier, and I didn't know what to say to please him or what to do with my hands or if I should meet that smile with my own. So I shifted the backpack again. The train didn't leave for another half-hour—time for a bite, or a beer.

Call me when you get there, Gramps said again.

Of course, I told him.

He nodded once. His smile flattened out. Right, he said, and we parted ways.

What remained? On that train, alone for the first time, I waited for the journey to start before I counted the money— five grand—and jammed it into the inner pocket of my coat.

The mountains chugged by and I tried not to think of the things that wouldn't come with me. It was late summer, some trees had started to ripen to their reds and golds, and the sun hit the mountains in great swaths. The railroad wound along the mountainside and you could look out the window and watch the wind thrash the conifers at eye level; when the needles shook free, they shimmied on the breeze like some strange, mossy snowdrift. I spent the first night alone in that carriage and sunk in and out of sleeplessness while the tracks trundled under me. Young, stupid, melancholy. We all know this sensation—the world widening before us, the past becoming just that. A twenty-year-old's greatest fear is that the best has come and gone.

The next day, Darby boarded the train in Edmonton and offloaded her own baggage in the same car as me. My age, short but tough-looking, in khakis and a T-shirt that hugged her triceps, hair braided through the clasp of an Eskimos ballcap, its tip thumping at her shoulder blades. She barrelled into a booth on the other side of the train, right in the union of window and chair, and kicked one foot up on the seat. She tapped a silver stud in her eyebrow, over and over with her fingernail, as if to a drumbeat. Above her toe, a very Canadian sign read: *If You Put Your Feet On the Seat, You May Be Asked to Remove Your Shoes.*

I did my best not to look at her but it wouldn't have taken a spy to see my interest. The train eased out of Edmonton, onto the prairies. The long, flat haul—where you could watch your dog run away for two weeks. That's an old line, but it still fits. The sky is different there, not just bigger but somehow deeper, as if it reaches closer to the ground, takes up more of the horizon. I looked for pillow clouds, signs of dangerous wind, but the plains rolled on, wheat fields as vast and flat as ocean.

It was Darby who broke the silence. When I think about it, that may have always been the case—Darby initiating, Darby taking that first, blind leap.

Feeling okay? she said to me, as the light started to turn char. She'd unloaded some of a large pack, had it strewn around her table: a doorstopper book about the Canadian West, an old, heavy thirty-five-millimetre camera, a deck of cards. She squinted an eye at me—that photographer's habit, even then.

Yeah, I said.

You look glum.

No, I told her. Just wondering.

She seemed to get this. She nodded like someone listening. Then she grabbed her camera and snapped a picture.

The first photo of the journey—hope it's a good one. I'm Darby.

Alan.

We shook hands—our first touch—and she motioned toward her table with her head.

I'll let you in on a little secret, she said, and raised her eyebrow—the right eyebrow, something I'd not seen anyone else ever able to do—and drew me toward her with the curl of her trigger finger. I've got some contraband.

She drew a wine bottle from the pack. It had a printer-paper label, a picture of two wrestling kittens. Homebrew.

I grinned, and so did she, and I could see all her lower teeth when she did. She unscrewed the cap, swigged it, and wiped her mouth with her wrist, like some girl from the frontier, like somebody I wanted to know.

She took one big gulp. This wine is the kind of wine that comes up and firmly shakes your hand. Oaky, with a hint of burning grassland. Come here, let's play cards.

I did, and we did, all through the evening until we had to procure some food, which I paid for with a twenty from Gramps' wad of money. I figured he'd approve of that, figured it was part of his plan. She ordered some gin-and-tonics, and I paid for that too—it seemed fair, for the wine—and we went right back to the card games. A first date, almost, though we'd have many more dates after that, and when we both got too drunk to stay awake there was a moment when I felt her hesitate, as if deciding to move to another seat, to get more space. But she didn't, and we pressed awkwardly together, not quite back to back but close, the train's metallic wall cold against my skin and the heat of her cheek on my bony shoulder. Her knees came up, knobs that fit in the palm of my hand, and her hair smelled like charcoal and fruit and pepper—what I thought all girls must have smelled like. At some point in the night her free hand reached behind and laced her fingers with mine, looped my arm around her, and I came to wakefulness as surely as a jolt of fear—and of our first absurd night on a cross-country train, there isn't a whole lot more to tell.

ON THE CLIFFSIDE I sniffed the air, that riverbed scent. The sky lay abandoned of all colour save when the flares lit up behind that distant ridge.

Spinal cancer, Archer said, breaking the silence. He touched his lower back about level with his gut. I can walk, technically, but can't feel my legs. Makes me clumsy as all hell, and I used to be a nimble bastard. There's that *used to* again. One day you wake up and your whole life is past tense.

Sorry about that, I said.

You win some but you always lose in the end, he said, and swept his hands over his jeans so that his whole upper body moved with the action, his shoulders clunking around their sockets like those old machines that grind grain to dust. He looked himself over, turned his palms in the air like a baby would, like he was seeing them for the first time. Or, maybe, like he was sick of seeing them.

You can cheat death, but you can't cheat getting old.

More of his wisdoms. I let him have them.

Then all of a sudden the clouds above the Purcells lit up with a flash of orange, bright enough to cast a glow on Archer's face, and a great thunderous *ker-ACK* swooped over the valley to ruffle our hair and push wind in our eyes. Archer unslouched, and as he did another percussion pounded toward us. The sky throbbed as if in the grip of artillery fire. It came once more, methodical as construction work, the sound as big and hollow as a gong, and it seemed the valley below us—the very darkness, the very emptiness of it—seethed like a coal furnace. Warm air gusted over my cheeks, heavy with the stink of sulphur.

I hope we find Jack before we end up in the middle of that, Archer said.

As long as we find him.

You don't sound worried.

I gave him the eyebrow. Neither do you.

I hate fire, he said. I fucking hate it.

Is that why you rub your arm?

He undid the buttons on his wrist. I couldn't see well in the low light, but he turned his forearm to the distant glow and touched the skin there, and it didn't look like skin so much as some kind of resin, like rubber pencil erasers stretched so thin they'll rip. Napalm, he said. Deadly shit.

You are a grab-bag of misfortunes, I said. Put that thing away.

He shoved me, a full-palm-to-shoulder, and let a grin widen his face ear to ear. His heart was probably in the right place, once you got past all the bullshit and posturing. Before us, the distant fires surged again and again, unleashed more deep, rollicking growls, and the mountain ridge reddened like the molten rims of some mythical forge. Archer raised his chin to it.

It's like staring into the maw of Hell, he said, and clapped me on the leg like a grandfather, and I felt the power that lingered in those hands—old-man strength, same as Gramps.

Then he let go of my leg and I hoisted him to his feet, and together we hobbled to the truck. There, Puck lay curled up tight, and he did not stir as we loaded ourselves in and buckled up and braced for whatever obstacle—otherworldly or otherwise—awaited us farther down the road in the dark.

WHEN WE FINALLY BROKE onto the highway, Archer let me know that our destination was a trucker stop on the perimeter of town—a place called the Verge—where, luck willing, we would find my mother. It perched on the apex of a hill that sloped toward the town below. I pulled into the Verge's parking lot, and as I did a pack of Harley-riding roughnecks swung out, their lone lamps like a swarm of glowflies. The last ground to a stop beside my window with his legs balanced akimbo, and he cupped a hand to his mouth to shout above the gurgle of his engine.

This ain't the place to be, he called. He wore a sleeveless leather vest that showed a lifetime of stretchmarked tattoos and peppery arm hair. Something like a bandana covered his head and came to a knot at the base of his skull. Hang-nail beard, chops the King himself could abide—exactly who you'd expect.

There's landslide, I hollered back, and he swooped his head from me to the road that lay before him. His lips puckered in what might have been a whistle—I couldn't hear. We came through the logging roads, I added.

Can you manage them on a bike? The roads?

Depends on the biker.

That split him in a grin. His canines looked more fang than tooth. Don't stay here long, he said, and torqued the throttle on his bike. It's the end of the world out here.

Where you coming from?

West of it. Caribou Bridge—we're all evacuating. Good luck.

You too, I told him, and he took off with a small spray of pebbles. I cranked my window up and put the truck back in first gear. Ahead, the Verge's porch had a view of the mountains that stood as the last bastion for Owenswood. The town below was just an inky, light-spotted sea.

I rolled the Ranger between a pair of slanted yellow lines and killed the ignition, and the truck gave one last desperate heave. I waited in the lingering smell of exhaust and dog and my own sweat. Archer was convinced we'd find my mother inside. Her name: Linnea, after the flower. On the dashboard: that picture of her at seventeen with the dog who could have been Puck before the trap got him. I felt like I could have gone inside and pulled off something noir—glance at the photo and the waitress before me, maybe a slow dissolve between the two.

You should scope it out, Archer said to me. Let her know I'm here. I'll keep Puck company.

Or you could come in with me.

He reached behind the seat, offered a hand to Puck, who lolled his sardine-tin tongue in the palm.

It's been a long time since I saw her.

Few years?

Archer wiped drool on his jeans, three passes. More like twenty-nine.

Jesus.

He rubbed his bicep, that wretched arm. What if I don't recognize her?

She'll recognize you, I said.

I've gone a bit downhill.

Your smell will give you away.

People milled around inside the Verge. Shapes skirted past the windows or the glass front door. A kid wearing a hairnet and a maroon uniform appeared from the rear of the restaurant, half dragging and half humping a bag of garbage nearly as big as him.

We didn't part ways on the best of terms, Archer said out the passenger window.

A shocking revelation, I said.

Fuck you, kid, he snapped.

Sorry, I said, and meant it. Poor timing.

Just do first contact. I need to gather my wits.

I'm not sure I can distract her that long.

He peered at me past the bulges where his eyebrows ought to have been, and I hopped down from the truck and ran my thumb along that sketch of my mother and thought about what kind of things I could possibly say.

The Verge smelled like a hockey arena—like ice skates and antiseptic and men breathing rust out their mouths. The scent of grilled eggs and grease wafted from the kitchen where a pair of boys, a fifth Archer's age, stacked dishes and pushed each other with great friendly heaves. The place looked how a diner ought to—maroon booths and bubbly cushions and linoleum tiles and tables like stethoscopes turned upside-down. It was like I'd walked into a Tom Waits song.

Not many people out and about right now, a woman said.

Turning, I looked upon my mother—name tag as confirm-ation—dressed how I'd expected a waitress in a place like that to dress: a whitish apron with finger smears not quite bleached out; a maroon top, to match the decor; short brown hair highlighted with dishwater blond. She had wrinkles enough to show her age. Beside her nose: a small mole, and even in that first moment she reached up to scratch it—a habit, maybe. One eye focused a degree off-centre and she seemed in constant struggle with it. She leaned her head sideways and reached for a notebook in the pouch of her apron and I just fumbled the picture in my hands and looked at it and away from it and crumpled it more than I'd wished.

You okay, kid?

I wanted to say, I'm fine, thanks, or, Much better now, thanks, but something about her rooted me in place. Here was my mother. She drew her brow together in a look of lunatic amazement, one eyebrow cocking up—how often did she deal with guys either doped up or liquored to speechlessness?—so she resembled Archer in about every way a daughter can. I felt myself swallow. Those moments, that sensation of seeing my biological origin, of seeing where I began—I don't even know why it stunned me as desperately as it did. It's not as if I had lived my life in resentment or longing, not like I counted this as a major destination in my journey to find my dad. But it felt like all of a sudden looking in a mirror, seeing yourself for the first time, or from a new angle, a different light, in a different hat, with mustard on your chin. It felt like being told to stop staring.

Outside, the world burned, and beyond that, almost back in time, men I hardly knew wrestled with demons that never let them sleep.

I'm here to see Miss West, I managed.

She ran her tongue along her teeth, pinched it between her canines. Something like a smile?

Miss West, she said, and crossed her arms. You're looking for Miss West.

I nodded.

And does Miss West have a first name?

Linnea.

I think you may have been misled, kid, she said. There's no Linnea West here.

I nodded.

But I'm going to bet you're looking for me.

Yes, I said. Probably so.

And that makes you my son.

I nodded again, hated myself for it—for just doing my impression of a bobble-head. I didn't know what to do with my hands. I didn't know where to look or stand or if I should show her the sketch that I was playing with like a highschool love letter.

You want something to eat? I can get one of my boys to make you something.

Boys?

Employees, she said. No long-lost half-brothers for you.

You don't have to apologize, I said, which is pretty much the stupidest thing.

Jack and I never married.

I know so little, I said.

My dad send you here?

Archer—

Yeah, my dad.

Archer's outside with my dog. He's hurt.

My dad's hurt?

No, my dog is.

Her face twisted up—an expression that meant *stupid boy*.

There's no vet, she said, and her face softened, became motherly, maybe. Left town with most of them when the evac was called. But my husband might be able to help, if he's not busy getting ready.

Ready for what?

She leaned sideways on a maroon booth, hip against plastic backing, and jerked her chin out the window, at the glow. You pick a helluva time to show up, she said.

Gramps had a heart attack.

Ah, shit.

He's okay.

I always had a soft spot for Cecil.

I'll let him know.

Too bad he's not here. Where's *my* dad, anyway?

Scared.

She smiled toward her feet, and I saw that her left canine tooth—the one she didn't pinch her tongue against—was chipped and flat. She looked like a woman who smiled often. There's hope in that, in knowing your mother is not too burdened by life, but I can't possibly explain it. Maybe it speaks toward your own future, your own prospects. It's nice to know you're not biologically destined to unhappiness.

Go bring him inside, she said. And when Colton gets back— my husband—I'll tell him that you're here, and to see if he can help your dog.

She turned to the kitchen, a set of double-hinged doors like you'd find at the front of a saloon. I couldn't summon the nerve to call out *Mom*.

Do you know where Jack is? I said, and she stopped cold.

Cecil finally calling him back, eh?

He thinks he's dying.

She wandered to the window that granted a view of the kitchen, crossed her arms. I imagined she was the kind of woman who could get people to follow orders. A second later, she poured herself a coffee from a stained carafe. It banged around on its rim, that sound like a hollow clock. It's pleasing to know that places like the Verge exist, that, somewhere, life simply goes on.

I have a soft spot for your grandad, she said to the window. I'm just not sure he deserves to see Jack again.

Shouldn't that be Jack's choice?

All Jack ever wanted was to be called home, she said, and lifted the coffee to her lips and swallowed a loud mouthful. Did Cecil tell you what he was gonna say?

No.

Ever seen Cecil apologize?

I thought about that. Gramps knows how to make amends, I said.

She watched me over the edge of her mug. Maybe he's changed, she said.

Gramps told me, about Archer coming along—he said it'd make them even. What's that mean?

I don't know.

Do you really not know, or do you just not want to tell me?

I'm sorry, I don't know.

Maybe we all skirt secrets, but right then I could feel the biggest one pressing on me like a dumbbell: that problem of Gramps and Archer, and Nora, and whoever the hell else. Jack, my mom—Archer had only begun filling me in, and there were things he wouldn't tell. There had to be. Everybody dangled secrets over my head as if expecting me to leap at them, or to get tired of leaping at them, to just sit and pant and idly wonder. Even Darby, goalkeeping for her handball team—another secret, another loose thread. At the end, she tricked me into believing that by some magic of pheromones and good luck we'd rekindled what was lost from our old, warm days. And what if Gramps just wanted to dish out one last blindsider? I wasn't supposed to be skulking across the Kootenays in a breakneck search and rescue. I had a thesis to complete. I had a woman to forget.

You think I'll be bringing Jack to Gramps just to have him bitched at? I said.

She *clunk*ed the mug down on the counter. Behind her, one of the kitchen boys flew by the window brandishing what looked like an inflatable lizard. I don't know, kid, she said. But it's probably something you should be prepared for.

ARCHER HAD MOVED to the driver seat. He was scratching Puck under the jowls. I leaned on the Ranger's hood.

I'm ready, he said.

Do you think this is gonna end happy?

Things look grim, I take it.

The whole thing. Will Gramps forgive Jack?

You mean, did you drive me out here for nothing?

Puck smacked his gums, flung his tongue around trying to catch Archer's hand. *I've killed my own dog, Archer*, I wanted to say. Instead: That, yes.

It ain't nothing, kid, Archer said, and flicked gobs of dog spit off his fingers. It's not the destination, it's the journey.

That's a stupid cliché, and I don't believe it.

It is what it is.

Another stupid cliché—maybe he'd earned the right to them. I fetched his wheelchair and he lowered himself in without my help. Fierce independence, as far as possible without surrender. He was such a classic old guy, such an army vet, so much like Gramps that for a moment I saw the whole trajectory of my mad search and rescue like a ricochet between those two men: like Gramps, Archer needed me to reconcile him with his daughter, except he didn't know how to ask; like Archer, Gramps was saddled with a guilt I couldn't comprehend, and I feared that by the end of it, through all the smokescreen and posturing, it'd leave him wheelchair-bound and terminally ill and more alone than he'd ever known—a man with nothing left to do but die. The saddest truth of all is that we either lose the ones we love, or they lose us.

Archer stretched his arms over his head and winced like before, like he'd forgotten that his gears hadn't been oiled.

Good luck in there, I said.

You're not coming?

This is your thing.

He tapped his wrists on the arms of the chair.

Two against one, right? Strength in numbers?

I think you're better off mano-a-mano.

I'm scared shitless.

That's the point.

What the hell do you mean by that?

You need to do the talking yourself, I said.

Don't give me a fucking lecture.

I winked. Trust me on this one.

He cupped his hands over his face, pulled the droopy skin low under his eyes.

You can't just send me in blind, he said, and I tilted my head, cat-like, with pleasure. Come on, kid, forewarned is forearmed.

Fuck you, Archer.

He craned back in his chair—an act of bewilderment. I watched him mesh his fingers together at his solar plexus, elbows loose at his sides like wings. He wasn't a stupid man—I'm sure the irony wasn't wasted on him.

Then Archer nodded and pressed his lips to a pucker to mask a stupid grin. Typical army guy. Maybe I had him pegged, after all. He vanished inside the Verge and I stood beside the open driver door and kneaded my fingers in the doughy skin at the base of Puck's neck. He drooled. He gurgled, nearly purred. As a pup, he used to kick nightly, gripped by dream chase, great hunts, moonlight pursuits of beasts far grander than he. But he'd grown out of that. For years he'd lain still on his dog bed—an old chair Gramps relinquished after Puck tore off one of the arms.

Puck lapsed into a slumber fuelled by Gramps' beer—all I could hope for given the circumstances, sleep being some intermediary between pain and death. I hoped the trade-off was worth it: dog for son. They had a history, Gramps and the mutt, but I only knew snippets of it. Some old painter named Sal had gifted Gramps with a mastiff puppy, decades before I was born, in payment for Gramps helping him build a house. That dog wasn't Puck, but it'd ignited Gramps' love for mastiffs. What's the point of having a small dog, he always said. He liked a beast with a certain weight to it, that could achieve a certain momentum. You can't wrestle a dachshund.

I could see Archer and my mom squirm through those first moments of reunion. His lips moved like a chastened man's and in his lap his hands picked themselves raw. She towered above him. She cut an imposing figure. Around her swirled her father's fate and she crossed her arms in a way that said she knew it. The neon *Open* sign above the Verge's front doors went dim but its contours stayed momentarily radiant in my vision. Archer rubbed his palms together in front of him. My mom nodded, once. Perhaps the corner of her mouth twitched to a lopsided smile. I couldn't fathom the courage that'd take from both of them: Archer to go prostrate and her to forgive—it is so much easier to stay angry and indignant. My mom discarded her apron. Archer laid his hands on his knees, knuckles down. They turned toward one of the booths and as they did Archer caught me watching, and even through the window I could see the wateriness of his eyes, the whites awash with the heady shades of plum.

A boy appeared before them, ferrying coffees. Archer touched the mug's handle, looked at his daughter, and in that span of seconds his posture grew straighter and his shoulders drew upright, as if all his tension-wound muscles had, after so many beleaguered years, released—as if a great burden had passed to someone else. I saw him smile. Coffee had long been banned to him too, I bet, so his grin was at least part mischief. Nora would've *tsk*ed at me for letting it happen. I bet Nora would've liked to see him as I saw him then.

Against my better judgment I left Puck and wandered a short distance down the road. Owenswood was only a few hauntings short of ghost town, and as I sloped away from the Verge I peered into the gaps between buildings and expected to see tumbleweeds barrel-roll alley to alley. It felt like the set of a spaghetti western, that resinous curl of splintered wood and self-smelted shot. Even the night seemed permeated by it. Uphill, the Verge squatted like a bunker, encased in its own orange glow. Figures darted here and there past windows, and I imagined the exchange between Archer and my mom—all that emotion. Christ, how do you overcome three decades of missing someone? How do you even get past *hello*? Archer would eventually try to extract himself to a booth and fail, and she'd see right through him—old, waxing alpha male. Their first contact, maybe: her hand on his bannister of a forearm, his shoulder against the swish of her hips. Who knows.

I put my weight on the shaft of a nearby lamppost and felt my entire body shudder. Fatigue, overspent muscles, Gramps' salvation in my white knuckles on that blasted Ranger's steering wheel—perhaps it all caught up with me. The ochre streetlight lit an orb around me and I studied my own shadow on the sidewalk. Up the street, the Verge could've been a church, the only object in sight not washed to some shade of brown. Haloed, almost. It felt good to have distance from it all: from Archer, my mom, even from Puck, bless him. It felt good to just slump there and wallow and let the tiredness wash on over me.

I CAME TO on the warm ground with my back to the lamppost. Someone stood above me, downlit so I couldn't see the face, and this person had tapped me awake: short, with hair at the shoulders. A woman, with her elbows loose and sideways and her hands in the gut pocket of her coat, the lower hem of an apron at her thighs. My mom, of course. Something metal in her ear caught a band of light, glinted like a ring.

You caused me a small ruckus, she cooed. Set Archer all a-tither.

I scrubbed my knuckles in my eyes, tried to blink away that gooey feeling of sleep. My lips had gone parched and my hands felt papery, as if the moisture had been sponged out of me.

How long was I asleep?

Her head tilted sideways and she didn't remove her hands from the coat. It was by now dark enough for the streets to be colourless and washed out. My mom turned at the hip and squinted along the road downhill; she stayed like that for a good few seconds. An hour, maybe? she said. Long enough for me to take notice. Back in my life not an hour and you already cause me shit.

My bad, I said.

Yeah, I'm not pissed off. Archer'd have left you out here for the wolves, though.

A gentleman, your old man.

He likes to think so.

She smiled down at me then—a twitch of the cheek, her lips drawing up. Her hair shone dark as lamp oil and the orange streetlight hid all traces of grey. I searched for a similarity between us, one biological clue or another: mannerisms, maybe, or a way of looking at the world.

You don't worry about me, she said. You just keep sitting there. Take your time.

Sorry, I said, dusting off. Didn't realize.

Of course not. It's just an evening stroll for me.

With her teeth, my mom torqued off a scrap of hangnail. Sorry, kid, she said with her mouth mostly closed. I default to sarcasm.

In the distance, the mountains flashed with ochre, but no thunder pounded down from them; that phenomenon, I guess, only Archer and I would share. My mom plucked the chunk of nail from her tongue and flicked it aside. She jerked her chin toward the Verge and set off. I followed.

The whole town's been evacuated, she said between breaths. Colton's here on evac duty. We're running a skeleton crew from the diner.

You said Colton was a park ranger?

I never said that.

So he's RCMP?

She reined up. She didn't look at me. Her gaze swung in a slow arc around the darkness, as if she expected an ambush. Uphill, the Verge had darkened, castle-like, and nobody milled around inside.

I think he prefers *last man standing*, she said after a time, with an emphasis at the end, like exasperation but more than that—like the way you'd say *enough* when you say, I've had *enough*.

We went the last few hundred metres in silence. I'd heard about those leftover squads of guys who, during an evacuation, defend people's homes from criminals. The tales were all severed radio contact and last-minute dashes down a highway with the raging blaze mere seconds behind. When we reached the Verge's parking lot, I caught the low growl of a diesel engine, and my mom turned to face the invisible grumble.

She nodded at the darkness. The engine got louder. It took me a moment to realize that whoever was driving was driving without lights.

That's Colton, she hollered, and when she spoke her cheek twitched up, under her eye.

Everything okay? I said.

She took the time to look at me. I don't know if it meant anything.

I won't lie to you, kid, she said, but never finished, because Colton's hazards came on—so as not to blind us, I suspect—and my mom stepped toward them even as the vehicle took shape in the dark. A jeep, with an engine that chortled the deep, hacking coughs of an aged bully. It ground to a halt beside Gramps' Ranger, and the headlights very briefly illuminated me and Owenswood behind me—a shantytown of rough brickwork and houses built squat as a child's cushion fort.

Shit, my mom said, and bolted for the jeep.

What's going on? I said.

I could barely see her, a thin outline glowing amber with the hazards. She put her hands on her hips, all deathstare and posture, and in a second the jeep's engine shuddered down and the door kicked open. A figure slid from the driver's seat, pitching for the gravel, but my mom managed to get between him and the ground. He sagged against her, and she helped him slouch around the jeep's grille. He wore straight military greys, and over his chest he'd strapped a blocky navy vest that I recognized as Kevlar. His hair was cut short and a pair of dog tags had come uprooted from inside his shirt; they tangled themselves with a tarnished brooch. He had wide shoulders and arms whose shape you could see through their sleeves: the build of a guy who could push you around. Sharp jawline, a mark of some kind under his eye—surgical scar maybe, or a patch of skin burned brass-smooth. Older than me by a generation: that fifty-something droop to his jowls, skin wrinkled the colour of hide, and facial hair turned a few too many shades of sun-bleach. A leather gunbelt hung from his waist, dark and tugging with weight, and I clocked a set of handcuffs and a pouch for pepper spray and the lethal telescopic baton the RCMP wore sidearm. This was Colton, and he was hurt.

His hand touched the centre of his chest and his teeth clicked together, and with much effort he unzipped a pouch in the centre of his vest. From it, he withdrew a metal plate, and even in the badly angled glow of headlights I could see the dent. Colton took a moment to wide-eye it, his breath strong enough to flutter his lips. Then he tossed it aside, my way, and seemed to finally notice me.

Lin, he said, and sucked wind through his teeth. Who's that?

His name's Alan West, she said. He's my son.

He looped his arm over her shoulders. Well, he called, huffing like an asthmatic. I'm your stepdad. Welcome to Owenswood, hoss.

Great to meet you, I said.

He winked. I'll bet.

What happened to you? my mom said.

Colton rubbed his hand down his chest—one tender pass. I had an altercation.

The restaurant looked empty as a prison, but all at once its doors flung open and the two boys from earlier scrambled into the open air. They rushed to Colton's side but my mom waved them off. One of them—the bigger one, with short hair and limbs too awkward for his torso—had the presence of mind to hold open the door.

Colton bared his teeth. I stood and watched, because I had no idea what in the hell I'd gotten myself into. My mom adjusted her husband's weight on her shoulders and ferried him toward the Verge's front door and left me standing outside, forgotten and unsure. I squinted at the darkness— the same way, I realized, that my mom had earlier. The air parched my mouth. Not thirst—too bitter. Fear.

The last coughs of exhaust from Colton's jeep plumed skyward. Moonlight came nailing through the cloudscreen and the gravel around me turned the colour of sludge. On the passenger seat of the jeep lay a nine-millimetre Smith & Wesson with its two radium sights aglow with phosphorescence. Along its barrel, toward the trigger, it'd been misted with thin splatters the pale light made black and innocent as ink.

At my feet lay the metal plate Colton had pried from his Kevlar. I picked it up: quarter-inch thick, steel or possibly titanium—a slug-stopper. The RCMP's crest was stamped in a lower corner, away from the dent that bowed out a circle wide as an eight ball. He'd been shot with something decent-calibre. I ran my fingers over the bulge, big and misshapen like your own hipbone.

The jeep's engine ticked cool and in its wake came the stink of diesel, a smell so gummy it stuck to the roof of my mouth. All of a sudden the whole damned parking lot reeked of it. Marked territory, Archer might say, and at the thought of it I wondered what'd become of him. Through the Verge's window, I saw my mom jab her thumb toward the kitchen, where the two boys scuttled ahead of her. She nodded once—I don't know to who—and drew her lips upward on one side—a smile, but not natural, as if it'd been tugged that way by a marionette's string. Resignation, maybe. Or irony. Then she disappeared through the kitchen's saloon-swinging doors, and I saw Archer sitting in one of the booths in the dark. He gazed across the parking lot, at the jeep and the Ranger and at me, but not at me, more like at that portion of space I happened to be occupying. His face had bottled right up: the jaw seized and the cheeks sucked in so you could see his rifle-stock cheekbones, the curve of his upper lip hardened to a point. He seemed to be shaking his head. He seemed to be saying, *It just can't be.*

Here's a story about Cecil West: In the first weeks of 1973 he sold his business for a quarter million dollars, joined up with Invermere's crew of volunteer firefighters. Firefighting was a long-time dream of his, mixed up with a healthy dose of fear, but Cecil faced down all his fears head-on, Cecil stared gift horses in the mouth, stuck his thumb in mousetraps twice. He's not one to talk about the things that scare him, but in a rare moment of bared hearts he told me a story about a time when he worked in an aircraft hangar outside London, during the Battle of Britain, where he mended Hurricane Mark I's that had been cheesed with bullet holes. There, he watched as a fellow welder's flame-retardant suit paid lip service. The wick effect, Cecil called it—where burning clothes feed off human fat like candle wax. I'd seen the same thing on napalm victims—people's flanks broiled like haunches of meat, knuckles and kneecaps sunburn-pink and glistening with the oily fluid of bone.

About the same time that Cecil styled himself a fireman, I caught Jack in Linnea's bedroom with his shirt off and his pants unbuckled, and I hauled him off her by his elbows. His spindly body weighed no more than the two-dollar sacks of soil you buy from hardware stores, but he kicked and thrashed like a boy being gored. He yelled at me to fuck right off, and to stop his flailing I bear-hugged his arms to his sides. Then I pitched him out the front door. He landed ribs-first on my lawn, made fists as he climbed to his feet. I chucked the T-shirt at his head and it wrapped full around, like a jellyfish or something.

Any other guy would beat you pulpy, I told him, and tapped my finger on his meatless chest. He smacked my hand aside, his heavy eyebrows pulled together, and his lips showed his twisted canines. We stayed like that until he stomped off fuming, but it's not like I wouldn't see him again in a day. My ability to intimidate him was slipping. It didn't help that I'd been sleeping with his dad's fiancée for half a year, and any threats I uttered would always be one part bluff. I had no idea what Jack knew. I had no idea who he'd tell, if he did.

I didn't see Nora for weeks following the spring confrontation at Dunbar, and for those weeks I was almost unapproachable. We hadn't talked about what happened between us—not at the cabin, or on the ride home, or after—and as far as I knew she was content to leave it at that, just a moment of weakness, a sudden flood of meaningless, desperate relief, and then back to Cecil, who deserved her more than I did. Still, I moped around the house like a teenager, answered every phone call with my heart in my throat, wasted hours and days drawing landscapes I couldn't care about one way or another. I sketched a two-by-three charcoal likeness of the nearby east-facing mountain, because it had a kidney-bean hole on its rocky surface that never changed colour. I returned to the road bridge where I first encountered Crib, and there I drew the marshland and the train tracks that speared into them and added the shape of a body in the reeds. At the lake, from shore level, I did a panorama of the horizon that looks just like every other body of water ever depicted in art. Those weeks between when we parted ways and when we eventually spoke—those I spent with my stomach fluttering.

Jack and Linnea spent a decreasing amount of time together, so that when I did encounter them it would only happen on the couches in my living room, or on their way out of Jack's house, or just sounds of them—voices scraping upward from the basement, from the yard. Seeing them together made me realize just how alone I was, not that I'm one to wallow in self-pity. They reminded me of me and the ex, not because they acted anything like the two of us had, but because of the sheer generic fact of their attraction. Most young love, I think, follows a predictable arc, and most of it ends the same. There is nothing remarkable about the path my marriage took; it simply falls under the category of general sadness of life. Like Jack and my daughter, I met my ex when we were still in high-school. She was older than me by three years, and a farmer's daughter, and rarely can I recall, in those early years, seeing her with hands cleaner than mine. Unlike Jack and Linnea, her father was not at all impressed with me, so our meetings were few and usually outdoors, often near the creek that ran through my parents' acreage. And unlike Jack and Linnea, it was me who eventually left her.

Occasionally, I'd see Nora across the street, in her yard, or on the sidewalk, and damned near every nerve in my body told me to orchestrate a meeting. One time she saw me in the window and waved, and I wouldn't be surprised if my own wave was as shaky as a boy's in love. There are two kinds of courage in this world, and having enough of one doesn't make up for lacking the other. It didn't help that Cecil was my best friend, but it didn't hurt as much as I wish it had. If our situations were reversed, you can bet that Cecil'd have suffered his aching heart and coveted not his neighbour's wife. You can bet that he'd still have grown old and lonely. He probably never expected to end up alone, but I doubt anyone ever expects that.

It seemed that logistics and common sense had seen an end to the mistake that happened at the cabin, and I am speaking with full conviction when I say this relieved me. Days slid into weeks slid indistinguishably into the drone of a multi-axle truck, into forest roads and guys with a simpler outlook in whose company a love-struck army vet can let his throbbing heart dull. Like all things, what passed—and dissipated—between me and Nora came to bother me less, or at least in a different way. The heart is resilient, the heart is insistent. My waves to her became less shaky. I thought about asking how she kept her crabapple tree in such good shape.

That July, 1972, Cecil took Jack on a hunting trip southeast of town, on the pretense of wanting a crack at some cougars. I would have liked to tag along, to watch out for them, stupid as that sounds, and also for the opportunity to just talk with Cecil, but no invitation was ever extended. Cecil'd been almost as absent as Nora, and only rarely did I glimpse him in his bedroom, almost hunchbacked. One time he cinched his curtains, shirt off, showing his sinewy body that made me wonder if I could still take him in a fight. I detected unease in the West household, but Jack never filled me in, since we'd stopped talking like friends—he was that age; I was in his way. Cecil and Nora rarely left the house together or even by the same door, and Jack spoke to Linnea in a hushed voice that trailed to muttering when I entered the room. The wedding never happened when Cecil said it would—go figure—and I think they were feeling the strain. If you ask me, Old Man

West had yet to recover from the death of his first wife. If that's even something you can recover from at all.

She came to my door while her boys were out hunting, one hot, soupy evening after darkness had settled over the town like a quilt. She had her red hair loose and she wore a baby-blue dress that reached her knees and she looked about as good as I can rightly remember. Except for the initial surprised greeting, we had little to say. I didn't even immediately think to invite her in, until she swooped her head up and down the street, crossed her arms under her breasts, and said that small towns love a good gossip.

I've only got beer, I said.

That's fine, she said.

Do you want one?

Yes, she said. At least.

She followed me to the kitchen. I fished two beer out of the fridge, and we sat at the table and sipped them and didn't talk. Everything was weird—her, the light, even the taste of the beer that bubbled on my tongue like soap.

I've been thinking about you, I said, and scooped my hand under hers. She seemed to chew on that one. But she must have known.

She moved her hand aside. I finished my beer and grabbed another, and another for her.

Where's Linnea? she said.

Camping with some friends. You picked a good day.

I guess I did. Pick a good day.

I've got whiskey too, I said.

I'll stick with beer.

Me too.

She twirled the bottle on the table, round and round. An attached woman, according to the rules. A no-fly zone.

Are you sure you want to be here? I said.

Why are you asking me this?

I just want to make sure it's what you want. I want whatever you want.

That's just being cowardly, she said.

How?

Makes you not guilty, makes it so you can say I just did what she wanted.

I thought it was being polite.

She leaned over the lip of her chair, stretching. The legs scraped on the laminate and the wood creaked backward and I watched the curve of her, felt the wind of her sigh breeze over my cheek, warm like the summer, like getting a thing you've wanted.

You're not guiltless in this, Archer—sometimes the hardest decisions are simply the hardest decisions.

And then, as if the conversation had not taken place, or as if it had some finality, I got up and put my hand around her waist and drew her close, and the world seemed about ready to tilt over, everything giddy, and I felt like a teenager with too many expectations and too much worry about what was at stake. I led her to the bedroom. There, a standing fan rattled at highest gear to cool the room to habitable and to keep mosquitoes from finding perch. We drifted to the bedside, and she sat on its edge, and then I sat beside her. Beneath her dress was pure softness, her breasts, her tough-but-not-perfect stomach that was perfect enough for me. One rib had been broken and healed off-kilter, made a bulge like the button of a denim coat. She shivered against the fan's wind. Her tiny hairs raised and her skin tautened to gooseflesh, and I lurched to my feet to switch the machine off. My back turned, she pulled the sheets to her chin. *I still know where you are*, I wanted to say, but couldn't find the words, didn't dare waste breath on a joke. I climbed in after her. Her searching fingers scuttled across my chest, abdomen, found purchase. It was good to see that my blood remembered where to go.

I'D QUIT PAINTING for Harold and Jones & Sons in the winter of '72, in favour of driving a logging truck for the same lumber mill Cecil made his money at. I had an air brake licence the American military had paid for, and that—alongside a few appraising grunts from Cecil, over beers—was all the managers needed to be convinced. The hours were more to my liking and the pay a whole lot better, and I learned my way around the breakneck dirt roads that wind between the mill and the highway. The steadier income meant me and Linnea moved into a house across the street from the Wests, such that I could look into Cecil's bedroom from the window in my den. Me and him joked about setting up a tin can phone. I had more weekends off in the first month than Harold had given me in three years, and I made a habit every Sunday of tucking my sketchbook under my arm and heading to the nearest outskirts of the valley. One time I sat on a little hilltop and traced the outline of clouds. Another, from my window, I drew some little black bird as he hopped around the yard and fell down a groundwater heating pipe—I had to rescue him, no small feat, even for a man of my ingenuity. If I was a competent tree climber, I figured there'd be some good vantages to be had.

Everybody who knew of my hobby thought it a waste of time, except Nora. She took an interest, sometimes asked for a slice of paper so she could try her hand at it, and the two of us would sit in my basement or in my truck or off some-where—like the gravel pits, or the cliff jumps at Twin Lakes where worried mothers had cordoned off the tallest jump, damned near eighty feet—and listen to our pencils *skitch* on the paper. I'd sketch the mountain vistas with their egg-white tips and Nora would do portraits of me—something I didn't quite like but couldn't summon the heart to deny. One time, she drew a picture of me and Jack, using two separate photos as guides. In it, the two of us are standing side by each with Cecil's old cabin in the background. It was a pretty damned good effort, if I'm anyone to judge, even though you'd have trouble identifying us at a glance. It could just as easily have been Jack and his old man. I stashed these drawings under my laundry hamper—beneath the bed is too obvious—in a camouflaged tin box, the papers rolled to tubes and the box fastened with a small silver lock flaking around the keyhole. After these sessions, we'd make love or we wouldn't. It didn't seem to matter. Either way, I was happy. I probably owe that to Cecil, too, since he got me the job. But when all the hands are dealt, I owe him a whole goddamned lot.

The house we moved into was twenty-four hundred square feet, two storeys, and built into a slope so the basement exit led to the backyard. The master bedroom was at the rear—unusual placement—and you'd have to cross the den to get from my room to Linnea's. Right away, she started bitching about a lack of privacy—she was coming seventeen that year—and it didn't take a genius to figure out she'd want to move downstairs. The basement was unfinished, the externals a mess of ripped poly and pink fibreglass insulation bulging through the tears in tufts. Floor joists and electrical feeds lay exposed overhead. Bare drywall had been screwed to the inside walls. Cecil agreed—actually, he'd strong-armed me into agreeing—to help me make the basement habitable, and during one of his early visits the two of us strolled from one end to the other, beers in hand, inspecting. He clucked his tongue at what he identified as structural faults: two inch-wide holes bored through a load-bearer; no pony wall beneath the bathtub (That'd make a hell of a splash, he guffawed); a darkening of the lumber on the floor joists, beneath my bedroom, that could have been water damage but upon touch felt dryer than bone.

Hope it's not rot, he told me, and kicked my boot. Or else you might step outta bed one night and fall right through.

On the day things started to go bad, Cecil showed up at my house in a pair of Carhartts and steeltoe boots, with his ballcap tilted low over his eyes and wearing a shirt that said *London: Done It*. It was February, the coldest damned month of all, and a Sunday, and his pounding on my front door roused me from the dopey sleep I'd slipped into. Waking, I couldn't remember the time of day. The sun had set, the sky gone the colour of antifreeze. I fumbled my hand across my bedside table in search of the lamp switch, heard loose change rattle against the wood and some of it *plump* to the carpeted floor. The room smelled like the ink from a ballpoint pen— the air sticky and heavy enough to feel the weight on your lips. Condensation whitened the inside glass of the window, meltwater pooled on the sill. Cecil pounded in a methodical four-beat loop.

Come on, Archer, I heard him say. Get your lazy ass up. You don't work that hard.

My truck was in the driveway, so Cecil wouldn't likely give up. *Determined* falls a few degrees short of describing the level of that man's persistence. Linnea wasn't home either, else she'd have answered the door. My hand found the light switch and with a click the room turned amber. Beside me, Nora groaned and rolled onto her side and I saw the shape of her breasts, the ends of her red hair teasing her nipples. Then she registered Cecil's knocking and hollering, only a few thin pieces of wood between us and his voice, and she bolted upright with blanket tucked to chin. Oh my fuck, she whispered.

My watch showed six-twenty-three in the evening. Nora was supposedly in Cranbrook—an hour and a half south—and the plan, before we dozed off, had been for me to drive her to her car to make the whole thing authentic. That's how we rolled it, some days. She parked in a place Cecil had no reason to go, or she left vague notes about shopping that'd allow her to stay missing in action all afternoon. Even though she lived across the street, we saw each other once a week if I was lucky. In fact, it probably averaged out to more like once every two.

Nora lowered the blanket level with her armpits, brushed

hair from her face. I sat on the edge of the bed and felt the fatigue in my arms and legs, the pleasant ache in my groin. Nora laid her palm flat against my back and I made myself focus on that touch even after her fingers had left. Cecil had no reason to suspect anything. He couldn't have. I opened the bedroom door wide enough to fit my face through.

Give me a goddamned second, old man, I yelled, and Cecil chuckled, loud so I could hear him.

Nora had lain flat, turned onto her side so she could see me standing naked at the door.

Just distract him, she said, hushed. I'll walk to my car.

He probably wants a drink, or to work on the basement, I said.

Or both.

Well, he's your fiancé, I said, and immediately winced.

Twenty-six-ounce flu—that was what I'd tell Cecil. He'd drag me to the City Saloon for some hair of the dog, or he'd tell me to cowboy up and haul me to the basement where we'd mount drywall as he told stories of his workmates, since he actually had workmates for the first time in a long career. Either way, Nora would make a getaway.

Then the front door whined open, and I heard Linnea's murmuring voice as she and Jack let Cecil through. His heavy boots stomped over the foyer and into the den. Nora looked up at me and I imagined all the horrible ways this could end, what, if anything, I could say to Cecil. He'd want to fight, but I wouldn't have the heart to give him even that. There was just my bedroom door between us now. I don't know why I hadn't told Nora to take cover.

223

Dad, Linnea called, as she and Jack came through the door behind him. Mr. West is here. I'm supposed to call you lazy.

UPSTAIRS, JACK AND LINNEA'S footsteps thumped around the living room and kitchen, and whenever the sound approached my bedroom door I had to swallow to loosen the tightness in my throat. Nora was trapped, and though I didn't necessarily expect it to happen, at any moment Linnea could waltz into my bedroom. It's not like the place was out of bounds.

Nearby, in the basement with me, Cecil balanced on the third step of a wooden ladder he'd commandeered from the fire station. He held an electric drill above his head, cord wrapped in a spiral down his arm, while he bored holes through floor joists for electrical feeds. Wood shavings rained in his hair and made the place smell like burned cedar. I don't know where Cecil got the drill from or where he'd learned the basics of electrical wiring, but some mysteries must remain so. Periodically, he let the drill's motor wind itself spent, and then he'd grin at me from high up. I'd set myself on a wire spool that looked like a giant bobbin. There, I faked hangover.

That door's a fire hazard, Cecil said, referring to the one in the basement that led out into my backyard. It needed a key to be unlocked, even from the inside, so you could trap yourself. There was also a couch there, probably older than me, that Cecil had said I could have, and that spewed bits of yellow foam if you even looked at it. He said it, too, was a fire hazard, because regulations had changed since its upholstering. Since he'd started working as a fireman, Cecil saw deathtraps in playgrounds, in grocery stores.

Planning to change it, I said, to placate him.

You get trapped down here, that'd be bad news.

At least you'll know where to look for me.

An optimist if there ever was, he said, and bored another hole. The drill wailed and Cecil swore and I laboured to my feet, making a show of it. I heard no more walking upstairs, wondered briefly where Jack and Linnea had gone. His place, likely, or one of the romantic haunts he took girls to kiss them. Or, at least, where he took Linnea to kiss her. Either way, it meant I could get Nora out the door. The mere thought of her being caught at my house, of the simple, silent way Cecil would take it—I don't know what could have scared me more. Cecil climbed down the ladder, scraped it along the concrete floor, and climbed right back up.

You gonna die? he said, squinting at me.

Feel like it.

Go make coffee. You're depressing me just looking at you.

You're the boss, I said, and offered a shaky salute.

In the kitchen, I started the coffee maker and then went to the bedroom. There was no light under the door, so if Nora was still hiding—if she hadn't left, and I didn't know for sure that she hadn't—then she was hiding in darkness, and good on her. Cecil fired up the drill again and I used the noise to mask the sound of the door's click. The room black and quiet, and then the bedside lamp turned on.

Can I get out of here now? Nora said. She sounded angry, but fair enough. She had her clothes on, ready to make a getaway.

I gave a nod and she crept across the room to me, and I took care not to move so Cecil wouldn't hear more than one set of feet. Bizarrely, part of me didn't want to see her go; I liked having her there. Not until she stood right in front of me did I slide sideways to let her pass. There was a moment when she hovered, then turned enough to kiss me, and I bent my head toward her, and that was when my daughter's door flung open and Linnea caught us dead in the act.

Nora sprung backward and mouthed a *fuck* and Linnea's gaze bounced from me to Nora, and her forehead bunched as if she was about to yell out. All I could do, goddamn it, was put a finger to my lips and wince a *shh* at her. She blocked the view into her room, and I feared more than anything that Jack was in the bedroom beside her. Cecil's drilling had stopped. The coffee maker lisped its excess steam into the air. Nora made fists. I searched for an exit, for an answer, but right then I had no recourse but to hope Linnea wouldn't run straight to Jack. Cecil was still downstairs for me to deal with, for me to distract and put at ease. I couldn't even try to talk it out or explain it to my daughter.

Nora's gotta leave, I said, as if it counted as an explanation. Linnea turned her hands outward, as if to say *no shit*. I need to bring Cecil his coffee.

What the fuck, Dad.

Watch your mouth, I said.

Watch *your* mouth, she hissed, and I shut up so fast my teeth clicked. Cecil's workboots scuffed along the concrete, but I couldn't tell if he was walking toward or away from the stairs. If I were a praying man, that would have been a chance for the heavens to ignore me.

We can talk about this, I said. But not now.

Linnea crossed her arms, but not as if she were about to exploit her sudden advantage. Blood runs deeper than that. She nodded to me, once—a grave jerk of her head that signalled for Nora to make her escape. I've heard it said that secrets both knit people together and drive them apart. Linnea turned to her room with a flip of her hand, and, at seeing that, a great pressure welled at the divot where my breastbone meets neck, a sudden anger—who was she to judge me, me who'd given up so much to get her there, to do good by her? It wasn't my fault Cecil couldn't make his fiancée happy, that he couldn't move forward from the things he'd lost. You can get so caught up with the past and with things you ought to have done. You can get so caught up with the things you don't have that you forget that you still have other things. We all carry regrets—that's human nature. What matters is how those regrets shape us.

I poured Cecil's coffee and took the mug to the basement and he met me on the landing, coming up—precious seconds to spare. The front door opened and closed—Nora leaving—but Cecil didn't react to it.

I thought the coffee maker might've got the better of you, he said.

Damn near, I said, and squeezed the bridge of my nose. He grinned and clapped me on the back and spilled coffee on the concrete floor.

He moved toward the stepladder where electrical wire dangled from the ceiling, passed it, to the far room with the door we couldn't open without the key and the ratbagged couch. He slurped his coffee—black, of course, because that's how real men drink it—and then waved the mug at the floor, at the room as a whole.

What you need down here is a fridge, where you can have some beers and admire the work you've done, he said.

A beer fridge.

Great minds and all that, he said. Then he seemed to notice the back door. You really need to change that lock. Or leave the door propped open.

Might as well just put all my shit on the lawn, I said.

What about your girl? What if she gets trapped down here.

Christ, old man. I'll change the damn thing.

Leave it propped open in the meantime.

You just want easy access to my manly basement.

That's right, he said, and gave me the most ridiculous grin, his whole face lighting up, like he really liked the idea. Upstairs, Linnea's footsteps creaked from her bedroom to the kitchen to the door, and I imagined her at the window with her arms over her chest, glaring across at the Wests' house, at Nora disappearing down the road. If Jack returned for her—where would he have gone?—she would tell him what she knew. Of course she would: that's not the kind of secret you keep without good reason. That's the kind of secret that drives a daughter from her father.

You look like you're somewhere else, Cecil said. He blew across his coffee.

The land of feeling-like-shit, I told him.

You look like you're thinking about stuff. Thinking hard.

Nah, I'm okay.

You ever think about the burned kid? he said.

He shows up in my dreams.

That's normal.

Like grieving, I said.

Cecil put his shoulder into a stud, one of the walls we'd built. It bowed against him and he scowled at it, a heartbeat away from lacing into whoever did the framework. Instead, he adjusted his ballcap and cleared his throat and tongued his teeth for coffee grinds.

It's easy to regret things.

I don't regret a whole lot.

How can you know that? he said, and bent down to set the mug on the floor. Takes a couple decades of misery to know for sure.

That pretty much covers everything we do, I said.

I shoulda married Nora years ago.

Probably, I said. Yeah.

Do you think it's too late?

To get married?

To not lose her, he said.

He looked soft-eyed to me, but I was still groggy, still trying to think about what I'd tell my daughter to make everything seem okay.

Not sure I'm an authority in the matter, old man.

Well you're teaching her to draw or whatever, he said, which caught me off guard, since I didn't know Nora had told him, or why she wouldn't have given me a heads-up. Aren't you?

The *aren't you* got my hackles up. Cecil shoved his hands in his pockets so the flaps of his jean jacket fanned out, and he turned to lean on the studs with his shoulder blades, his chin dipped forward, hat angled down. With one foot, he bounced himself against the wood, so he seemed to nod endlessly. He was probably stronger than me despite the difference in our ages, and you never know what'll happen to a guy when he faces the coveter of his wife. Rage, adrenaline, spite—these are the fuels that let men benchpress trucks.

I gave her some of my stuff to use, I said, and tried to sound annoyed. Told her what end to point at the paper.

He grunted. A laugh? I saw her fingers, charcoal. That's why I asked.

That stuff gets everywhere, I said, and imagined, as I did, Nora's pale skin with dark carbon smudges shading her ribs, the underside of her breasts, the plateau of her stomach, that soft line of her jaw and chin and ears. Yes, it got everywhere. Sometimes I go to piss, I said, and think my dick's about to fall off.

Cecil snorted, thank God.

I don't need to hear about how often you touch yourself, he said. Then we both went quiet. That's about as close to baring his heart as Cecil would ever get. I fell onto the derelict couch he'd so generously donated, and as I landed on the cushion yellow tufts of foam lifted into the air, as annoying and incessant as flies. Cecil springboarded off the wall and went straight to the stepladder and the wire dangling from the joists, since that's all he knew how to do, the only way he could deal with his emotions: a primal drive to work his body to redemption. There are worse ways to go about it. Take that from somebody who knows.

CECIL LEFT THROUGH the basement door, careful to make a show of being trapped while I searched my pockets for the key, then of fumbling the key in the lock in his hurry, until I eventually shoved him into the wall. He grinned earlobe to earlobe.

Just get this damned door fixed, he said. Or I'll knock it down with an axe.

I'll leave the key in. Makeshift doorknob.

In a fire that key'll superheat. You'll sear your fingerprints off.

Go home, old man, I said. He finally did so, and I pushed the door closed behind him and watched him swagger into the twilight, flipping a pair of linesman's pliers in his palm. Floorboards creaked overhead and I heard Linnea *tink*ing around the kitchen, spoons against porcelain, drawers gearing open and closed, footfalls like soft, deliberate knocks on wood. Her movements sounded so patient, so calculated. Nothing, in a fight, is more intimidating than a person whose rage you can't detect. I could imagine the look she'd give me as I emerged from the basement—her once thick (now plucked, teenager) eyebrows rising like a clothes-line, arms tight over her chest, chin jutting up so she could stare across the flare of her nostrils. Such incredulity. Such disappointment.

By the time I at last walked up those stairs and entered the kitchen, Linnea had made herself a plate of toast and filled a ceramic mug with coffee and plunked down at the table. As I topped the final stair I saw her with one cheek as full as a squirrel's and the mug held before her nose by the rim. Her hair was loose and frazzled like bedhead. That would have been the first time I ever looked at her as an adult, and I think I even realized it at the time—that some distance between us had closed and at the same time opened up, that there'd been a shift in power, a shift in the physics of our world.

She tipped the mug to her lips. Then, with a flip of her head, she flung her mess of hair over one shoulder, put the weight of her chin on her fist—portrait of an unimpressed woman.

I suppose you want me to keep this one quiet, she said, before I could so much as summon the wherewithal to drag a chair out from under the table.

Sorry you had to see that.

Me too, Dad.

What're you gonna do? I said.

What *can* I do?

She set the mug down. The kitchen didn't smell like coffee or toast. I figured she'd taken some liberties with my liquor cabinet. I figured I had Jack to thank for that sudden change, among others. Signs of things to come?

Well, you know how Jack is, she said.

Insecure.

Her voice went whispery: I'm not sure what he'd do—I don't know.

He's just a boy, I said, and she gave me a stare that said if I believed that, I had some quick learning to do. When, I wondered, had I stopped paying attention? Maybe complacency breeds itself. Maybe things change precisely because you don't pay attention to them.

Are you going to just keep doing this?

Kinda over the hump by now, I said. She tapped a fingernail against the ceramic. I hated myself a whole lot right then.

How long do you think this'll stay secret?

I don't know.

And what then?

I don't know, Linnea.

She leaned back in her chair, her shoulders bobbing, her one arm outstretched so she could twirl her mug round and round—at a bar, you can tell a single woman from a married woman by the way she handles her glass. She studied it, then me, then it again—only her eyes moving, an appraisal. Who is this man my dad has become? There, at that table: the last of my authority being stripped away. It felt like giving an apology. It felt like growing old.

This will ruin everything, for everyone, she said.

It doesn't have to.

Yeah, Cecil's not the type to hold a grudge.

Don't get sarcastic with me, I said.

I'm not sure you're in a position to be issuing demands, Dad.

I rubbed my wrist under my nose. My clothes smelled like Nora, maybe.

Isn't Cecil, like, your only friend?

Yes.

What the fuck were you thinking?

Watch your mouth, I wanted to say. Instead: I thought it'd be a one-time thing.

And then Nora would realize she loved Cecil instead? That's pretty tunnel-vision of you.

Don't patronize me.

Someone has to.

You think I'm being selfish, I said.

No, Dad. I think you're being stupid.

Don't talk to me like that.

You're not in a—

I'm still your father, I said, and slapped the table. And I wouldn't talk to you that way.

That seemed to get through. She looked at the woodgrain. I'm sorry.

Me too. You gonna tell Jack?

Yeah, she said into the back of her hand. She blinked at me—two heavy flutters of her eyelids.

Unless?

Linnea rubbed her eyes. Maybe it's not easy to blackmail a loved one.

Unless you do something for me, she said, and it was barely spoken, barely breath. She looked, and sounded, a helluva lot older than nineteen. She didn't look or sound anything like the girl I'd always known her to be.

Then I was alone at the table with her empty mug rattling on its rim and the darkness descending around me like a blanket, and then I was on the concrete steps in my slush-covered yard sketchbook in hand. On a neighbour's porch, a trio of teenagers talked in voices that carried over Invermere's shitty, black-iced streets. I didn't go far. I didn't take a coat—up the road to the gully's edge where kids killed time and played at war and adventure, and I drew aimless searching circles and lines that meandered without purpose and wondered if there was something hidden beneath my own scratching, if my mind or my subconscious would offer a way forward. I sketched until my fingers numbed with cold and I couldn't feel the charcoal between them. I sketched as if to find an answer.

I'm pregnant, Linnea said to me from that kitchen table. But I can't stick around to raise a kid with Jack. I'm sorry, Dad. You'll have to let me go.

SIX

Heraclitus:
It is hard to contend against the object of one's heart;
for whatever it wishes to have
it buys at the cost of the soul.

Archer and I crashed above the Verge in converted living quarters where, all night, the heating vents secreted cooking fumes—a smell more burned toast than pig fat—and the never-quiet freezers growled beneath the floorboards. Earlier, my mom and those two boys had gurneyed Colton through the saloon doors to the kitchen, and I glimpsed his naked chest beyond the swing, the whole wide middle of it gone blue and mushy with swell. I knew a thing or two about ballistics, how even a nine-millimetre handgun can produce over three hundred pounds of stopping power—about pressure waves in soft tissue and the theoretical risk of hydrostatic shock. Colton had taken a bigger round than from a handgun, and it was no small feat that he'd gathered the stones to flop inside his jeep and make an escape. When he saw me, he forced a grin that split his face like some slasher-flick killer. He touched his own injury, a few ribs gone plasticine soft. Breathe short, I heard my mom bark at him. Breathe slow.

Before bed, I went to check on Puck. We had one more beer to feed him, but when I opened the Ranger's door he did not stir. His great sock-like face had converged in a dog-smile, and I slid a hand on his flank to feel for breath that I knew would not come. He had his eyes closed, and I let myself believe that he'd passed away in his sleep. I touched his pancake ear, soft as puppy fuzz. A breeze whooshed over the parking lot and ruffled my hair, cooler than the world around me, and I imagined Puck's last proud howl gusting by me in its wake. He saw the world in a different way, old Puck. He could do what he wanted.

Many years ago, Gramps ran down a pregnant elk on Westside Road. I wasn't even eight yet, and he hit her while reaching for a coffee thermos. The truck *umpf*ed like a winded man and my seatbelt squeezed against me and the whole vehicle dragged forward as if against a current. The elk collapsed barely off the road, its hip and hind legs ruined. Gramps blamed himself mercilessly, called it a rookie error and a waste of life. He took the truck out of gear and fetched his shotgun from the back seat. It was the last he'd ever use that shotgun; afterward, it got buried at the bottom of his toolbox, beneath his pliers and ratchets and scrap metal deemed unweldable. I remember how he looked, the gun held barrel-to-earth and the elk in a heap at his shins: not angry, exactly, and not immediately sad—just a man who would benefit from a nap. The wounded beast knew not to look at him; Gramps couldn't have pulled the trigger if she'd been looking at him. We've never spoken about it, but that's the way of things between me and Gramps. Animals, he told me after, prefer to die alone.

When I returned to the Verge, the two teenaged boys bounced a navy ball between them, and if it lurched astray they'd gun each other with stares until one broke off to retrieve it. I thought about asking their names, but couldn't summon the nerve. Rarely, one said or did something to draw a smile from the other. After almost every bounce, they'd turn to the swinging doors.

Of my mom I saw little. She banged in and out of the kitchen for hours: once, she emerged with a string of gut and a ski needle brandished before her, fingers tipped red; another time, she yanked a first aid kit off the wall and emptied its contents on the restaurant's counter—I don't know what she wanted, or if she found it among the cluttered bandages and antiseptics with their labels aged yellow. Occasionally, Colton's murmurs slipped from among the fridge hums like parents whisper-fighting in a bedroom. I worked to catch stray words spoken too loud, recognized a few: *lawless* was one. *Gun*, another. *Die*.

Throughout, Archer had fallen uncharacteristically quiet and had deigned to withhold his infinite wisdom. Each time my mom came out of the kitchen, he straightened in his chair and his chin tilted off his chest. She never so much as winked. We didn't belong there; we'd stepped out of our depth. I wanted to voice exactly this, but Archer's silence made me hold my tongue. He knew something. There was little to do but wait, and sleep.

Puck captivated my dreams with his dumb-dog smile and graceless gait, and he howled and gave great chase and his body cast no shadow, looked more mist than flesh, weak and iridescent as memory. Gramps appeared too—younger, restored. He shoved his hands in his pockets and hunched away from me like a beaten kid. I did not approach him; he did not turn to me. When I tried to call to him I found my mouth so parched I could form no words, and he walked away until he was a dot on the visible horizon, less and less consequential despite his rejuvenation. Before I lost sight of him I felt a jerk in my chest, as if he had been removed not only from the world but from my life as a whole, and I knew with certainty that he feared this more than death, and that I did too. It meant he and I both had nowhere left to go, and no one left to go with, if we did.

I WOKE AFTER only a few hours of sleep, feeling dopier than a drunk. Condensation had formed on the inside of the window above my bed, and I dragged my palm over the moisture to smear the glass bare. Dawn tinselled the sky, and in the early-morning greys I looked downhill at Owenswood. It was an urban morass, heaped with tire treads and rusted vehicles and oil drums stacked horizontal like pontoons. I saw some collapsed rockwork. The streets hadn't even been paved and every building was square; in places, front doors opened onto dirt roads as if built in ignorance of the combustion engine.

Archer snored nearby on a fold-out cot, and I worried after bedsores and numbness and the hushed torment of the immobile. Drool pooled on his shirt, Puck-like. In the darkness, I listened for the movement of others. Below, something metal *tink*ed over and over—a fridge on uneven floor, maybe, or a loosely threaded water pipe. The smell of diner food hovered just below the threshold of detection; if I moved my head too quickly or put my nose too near the bedsheets I'd whiff that mix of fried egg and burned coffee. Archer gurgled, mumbled sounds that might have been words. The skin on his forehead drew together like the folds of a canvas vest. Even asleep, he looked like he was trying to solve a problem.

I touched my feet to the floor. The bed squealed beneath me. That you, Alan? Archer said.

Yes. Can't sleep.

Strange dreams, he rasped.

Same here. Must be the air.

His voice softened. Never sleep much, anyway.

Sleep when you're dead?

His arms rose above him, two muscly pillars in the low light. He turned his palms over and over, studied them. I wondered what he saw in them, his own hands, the scars and histories mapped like topography on those knuckles, that wrinkled skin.

I never thought I'd see him again, Archer said.

Colton?

We called him Crib. I saw the brooch—crab-shaped. Unmistakable.

He shuffled around on the cot and the sheets made a sound like you're supposed to hear inside a conch. Then he asked me to help him sit up, which I didn't expect him to do. His skin was clammy and the bones jutted from beneath it, hard and obvious as the bedsprings he lay upon. I propped him against the wall, so he could see out the window. Then he gave his thighs each a strong smack, one after the other.

Sometimes feel the pressure, he said. Makes me miss walking.

I had nothing to say to that. But he must've known, so he bounced his shoulders, not even a shrug, to loosen them up.

What's Colton's deal? I said.

He followed me here from the States. We think he was one of the guys sent to round up deserters and draft dodgers.

We?

Well, me, he said.

They're married, I offered.

He smacked his thighs again, this time hard enough that the sound came out muffled, as if he'd punched a pillow, or dough. When he raised his fists for a third strike, I cupped my hands around the wrists. It was the right thing to do. His arms went limp in my grasp, and I lowered them to his side, knuckles down. He kept watching them, one before the other, his head on a pivot left to right.

How did we end up here? he said.

Jumped a hole in the highway.

I hate him, Alan. I hate Crib so much. Why does he have to be here?

Archer, I said. What happened?

Crib happened.

Come on.

A breath, long like when he slurped his beer. He terrorized us, Archer said. He followed me everywhere, assaulted Jack. I lost everything because of Crib.

Not everything.

What do you know?

Nora?

His teeth came together with a *click*.

He took Linnea.

That might have been the root of it. I used to believe that love's the only emotion that can keep a man chasing someone for three whole decades, but now I'm not so sure. He made a case for it, old Archer Cole, I'll give him that. Every time the floorboards groaned or a door slammed or a draft cooed through a hallway he'd straighten on the bed and try his damnedest to look prim and proper as a suitor. It'd last seconds, his head craned forward and his eyes wide with anticipation. You could see how much he missed his daughter. It oozed off him. Christ, he even smelled like an old photo— like nostalgia, like *want*.

I owe him, Archer said after a time.

She's not a prisoner.

He took her. He assaulted Jack. Do me a favour?

Sure, I said.

He mopped a hand down the whole of his face, bald skull to chin—one single, slow pass. Bring me the gun, he said. The shotgun, in the truck.

No way.

I gave your grandad that shotgun, you know that? Might not mind seeing what he's done with it all these years.

242

No fucking way.

He lowered his head to show me a pale wrinkle behind the temple—an old scar. This is what he gave me, he said. Crib. Smashed me with a wine bottle, side of the head, when I wasn't looking. This is who's down there.

There's more to this story, I said.

Archer drew a deep breath, and on exhale his whole body shrivelled and seemed to recall his age: his shoulders drew down until he was hunchbacked; his head bobbed forward and the deep caverns of his eyes went dark, mole-like, and the skin of his face slackened so the pink beneath his eyelids glinted in the low light. Maybe he himself didn't know what he wanted or why he'd come, had no idea what would happen, hadn't played events over and over in his mind. Maybe, when we set out, he really did just want to repay a debt to Gramps. But I doubt that.

He looked out the window. The turquoise sky, that last glimpse of stars.

I guess I got in his way, Archer said, barely audible.

In the distance, the mountains burned an eerie jade. We'd had our brief respite, our few hours of sleep. I got the sense that Archer had business here, a past as thick as mashed potato, and that he would come no farther in my company. Of course I'd end up alone in my search for Jack—how else?

I'm old, he said. I'm old and by now I'm alone.

You're not alone yet.

Listen to me, Alan: don't leave your girl.

You've still got Nora, and Linnea.

That's not a proverb, Archer said. Don't leave your girl-friend. Cecil'd tell you the same.

I gave him a once-over: a man who'd lost it all, or nearly.

Wise men, I said, bitterly.

You'll regret it.

I'm not sure you're in a position to talk about regret.

Archer's teeth clicked shut. He cleared his throat. But you love her, right?

Darby, then, would be alone in Toronto in her dumb robot pyjamas with her laptop on the bed, late-nighting some crap television series, episode after episode after episode. That's what we used to do, even when one or both of us had to be awake for a dawn start. She'd have a mug of green tea going tepid between her palms, and she'd hold the ceramic at her lip until a moment of suspense, then slurp and gulp down her excitement. We'd fall asleep with an episode still playing, the laptop warm atop us. On the screen, some tough-guy cop dodged bullets to save the world. It's sad going to sleep, Darby mumbled to me once. I wish we could be together when we sleep.

Archer tapped his thigh again. I let him. I used to, I said.

That's something.

Enough?

Enough to keep trying, Archer told me. And who knows.

OUTSIDE, THE AIR PRICKLED with that morning damp and when I pulled a deep breath the moisture tasted like coal. My mom was perched on an upturned log, faced toward town. I had a few puzzles I thought she might help me put together, and I needed to bury my dog. The wind flung dust our way as I approached, and she put her cheek to it so the motes danced like ricochets off her skin. She wore a sheepskin coat unbut-toned, and its separate sides fanned outward at her hips. Hands in its gut pocket, elbows wide, dishwater-blond hair jostling at her shoulders. She slouched, and when she squinted I saw the wrinkles at their corners, her age more obvious in the morning light. She had boyish cheeks, a mole near her jugular that puckered at the edges where she'd scratched and scratched at it. My mother, nonetheless.

Sleep well? she said, but didn't look my way. In the distance, the sun teased the lip of the Rockies, highlighter orange. Four, maybe five in the morning.

Archer snores.

I got to watch over Colton all night. He'll probably want breakfast, too.

Fringe benefit of being shot, I guess.

Her lip pinched a half-smile, humouring me, and her hands wormed so deep in her pockets that the sheepskin reached her forearms. It didn't feel all that cold: somewhere under six degrees, since my breath churned warm fog. The light looked pale as a winter day. I smelled trees, that earthy scent of places where few people drive.

I pulled up a log. How's Colton? I said.

He won't complain.

Sounds like everyone else in the family.

My mom rocked on her log, one elongated *thu-thump*. Why'd you have to bring my dad here? she said.

I thought you'd be happier to see him, I said.

It's more mouths to feed, she said. And he's a cripple now.

He helped. The highway's fucked, and he knew the way through the logging roads.

Good for something after all, she said.

Her hand slipped from her pocket, pinched a clump of dirt that had collected on the log. Downslope in the town, a blockade of crushed cars formed a wall as high as the buildings that pinioned them. They were all ancient vehicles from the days of steel and eight cylinders, when cars still equalled sex. Prized in their day. Shadows now—of their former selves and physically in the world. My own vehicle was parked nearby, and, looking at it, I felt a clot tighten in my throat that I had to force down.

I need a shovel, I said.

My mom followed my gaze. Ah, shit, she said.

It's okay.

I forgot. Colton—

It's *okay*, I said.

She stood up and pressed her knuckles to her spine in a bid to ease some tension, and lurched out of sight around the restaurant, limbering up as she went. Her body moved like an old hiker, like someone with a set of injuries that'd only get worse, all shuffles and hollow joints and tendons stretched like O-rings. She swore. She muttered something about the time of day. I heard her foot acquaint with metal. Probably, I should've fetched the tool myself, but by the time this thought dawned she'd already returned with the shovel brandished hip-height like a musket.

She appraised me, like she had before—like a mother, maybe. You'd benefit from a shower. A shave, too.

I felt my cheek and its steel-wool stubble. Been a stressful few days, I told her.

A joke, kid. Lighten up.

I'm just trying to make Archer jealous, I said.

That's his thing. Wears his jealousy like a bib.

She crossed her arms, stared at the town. I got the impression she spent a long time staring at the town. Do you want to bring the dog now, or after?

After.

I followed her into the forest that circled the Verge. Branches draped low in our path and my mom trudged through them undeterred, and rarely did she pause to hold them for me. Pine needles cloaked the floor like playground mulch, not one among them green. The whole place smelled like the bonfires you light to burn piles of yardwork. I remember Gramps doing that: a stooped figure who shovelled chokecherries and grass into the back of an old truck, and, afterward, sat in the bonfire's glow with a rifle dismantled across his knees, his hands *clack*ing around the parts.

Ahead of me, my mom picked her way over roots and divots and I envied her footwear and her balance and her practised grace. I grew up rampaging through a gully just like that forest, lost in the freedom of it alongside a neighbourhood's worth of kids. Manhunt, tag, capture the flag: we played all those games in the gully. A few times, Gramps joined us for cops and robbers, and he outclassed us by tiers: once, he stepped wraithlike from behind a tree when all us kids had our backs turned; another time, he scaled a wide poplar and pegged us off from its branches until the forest floor was littered with foam bullets. Later, it was paintball, but the same story. Gramps: untouchable. Now, trudging behind my mom, I realized just how much I didn't belong.

We arrived in a small clearing with a circle of rocks that ringed some leftover charcoal.

Here? she said. People use it. Less likely to get dug up. And if spirits are real he'll have some company.

Thank you, I said, and she waved her hand.

It didn't take long to dig; the dry dirt came apart without resistance. Each scoop, a swell of dust scattered toward us, weightless in the breeze. I pushed the shovel's blade through clumps of brittle chaff and twigs and dead roots long buried. My mom hung nearby, and I wished she would say more, say anything, because it seemed like she was supposed to do that—she was my mother.

Jack was here, she said at last, and I stopped digging. Circles bagged her eyes, and her face had the sallowness of a person who's been up late, worrying. She chewed at a hangnail on her thumb. I assessed her, and the hole before me. I planted the shovel in the ground.

You're gonna have trouble getting to him, she said.

Do I have to ask when he was here?

Days ago.

And you didn't think to tell me. Like, maybe *when I asked about him.*

She leaned on a nearby tree, arms over her chest like some tomboy from the cornbelt. I waited for her to go on, but she just touched the crown of her skull to the bark. Her eyes ran up and down over me: that same appraisal of worth, like some continent-crossing pilgrim weighing the burden of a wounded companion.

He's gone west.

You say that like I can't go after him.

We might need you here. Owenswood's not a good place.

You keep saying that.

It's Colt's call, she said. This is an evac zone. You have any idea what that means? Criminals, kid. *Bad guys*. They shot my husband.

Jesus, are you a cop too?

Fuck off.

I stepped on the shovel, drove it deeper in the ground. Its haft wobbled.

We're having some trouble, she said, not toward me, and I didn't need to look up to know that she'd begun, again, to scan the tree line. Around us, I realized, the forest made no noise at all—not even the whistling of bugs. Humans are the only beasts who do not instinctively flee from fire.

Why do you keep looking around like that?

Why do you think?

But *why* did he get shot? Come on, Mom.

I'm not your mom.

I bit my tongue. Pettiness: Archer's daughter. What's keeping you guys here? I said.

You need to talk to Colton.

And Archer? What's his deal with Colton?

She spit the hangnail off her tongue—a single, quick *pip*. That's an old wound, she told me. Overhead, the sun inched above mountains' edge, though we couldn't see it through the trees—just a warmth that tasselled the cloudscreen. Anyway, you're about to finish up, she said. Can you find your way back here on your own?

Yes.

Can you carry him on your own?

Yes.

Okay, she said. Bury him, then talk to Colt.

I don't like the way this sounds.

She shrugged, shoved her hands in her coat pockets. Then she jerked her head, toward the Verge, toward Colton—*we'll see*, maybe, or *you don't have to*. I couldn't tell.

PUCK HADN'T BEEN DEAD long enough for rigor mortis to pass in full, but I ferried his stiff body to the hole I'd made and laid him down within. I slid my hand over his flank, touched one fuzz-soft ear, and thought about the wonderful mess I'd made. Not just Puck, but the whole batshit thing: Darby, and this foolish search, and now with Archer, who no doubt wouldn't abandon his long-lost daughter to whatever grim fate awaited. I should never have left Toronto. Darby'd labelled me a coward, and who was I to refute her: I'd fled home precisely because it was easier than facing the reality of *us*.

Puck's grave was shallower than I'd have liked, but he would not be soon dug up, though that's the circle of life, anyway, and I don't know if he'd have minded much. I figured Archer didn't need to find out that I'd buried him, and I didn't know what to say to Gramps, if I even got the opportunity to say anything. He'd call me a dumbass, and fair enough. I'd killed his dog.

The dirt rose in a lump above the campground floor. No amount of hardpacking had made it less obvious, so I toed through the remnant fire and the logs around it in a search for something that'd make the grave less obvious: a moss-specked log, or a couple cinderblocks shunted some few feet out of place. But in the end I settled for a bundle of arm-length blackened kindling that I dumped over Puck's final rest. If the fires blazed on through Owenswood, at least they'd pave his grave with fertile charcoal, and he could himself grow to become a tree, or a bastardly bush—stinging nettle, maybe.

I made my way to the Verge to collect Archer and carry on. We had, I figured, wasted enough time, and Colton's fight was not our fight. Through its front windows, I saw Colton and my mom bent over the Verge's front counter, side by side with mugs of coffee airing cool. Their lips moved and their eyebrows drew in and on more than one occasion they tapped the countertop as if it were a map and they two tent-dwelling generals. Four crossed arms, two hushed voices, the smell of old Folgers gone sour as bile. Colton wore no shirt, but cotton gauze bandoliered his chest, and even indoors, in his maimed state, he'd donned a set of aviator sunglasses. When he spotted me he lifted his lips upward and outward, something like a snarl though not quite—more like trying to loose stray gristle from his gums.

The front door bumped me on the ass as I went in, as if to say, *Go on.*

We had a moment of saying nothing as I reined up under their gazes. My mom tapped her foot to a rhythm nobody could hear, and Colton took one delicate sip from his coffee and set it down so it made not a sound. Those two had information that'd been too long withheld from me, and to tell the truth I was getting sick of it.

Colton broke the silence: I understand you just buried your dog. I'm sorry.

Thank you, I said.

I also understand you know how to handle a rifle.

Used to shoot clay pigeons, at school.

That all?

Deer hunting, maybe. Years ago. I can handle a gun. Why?

Colton hefted his mug from the counter and held it below the rim of his shades. His big palm enveloped it, mouth and handle all. Through the shades I could see his eyes half squinted.

Just feeling you out, hoss, he said, and slurped. When he spoke, he had a slight south-of-the-border drawl, his vowels too soft and stretched too long, as if he'd imbibed a whiskey—*feeelin, hawss.* He smacked of small-town county deputy, more lawman than federal cop, and I wouldn't have been surprised to see a tanned holster belted to his hip, an ancient six-shooter cradled in the leather and hide. *Last man standing,* my mom had called him.

I'm trying to find my dad, I said.

How's old Cecil?

Dying, I told him.

Colton sucked his teeth. His mouth came forward in a pucker. I'm sorry to hear that, he said. I got on with Cecil.

I looked to my mom. You said Jack was here?

A few days ago.

Three days ago, Colton said, almost cutting her off.

I don't appreciate being lied to, I said.

You're in the wrong family then, hoss.

I'm beginning to see that.

That's my boy, he said, and my mom rolled her eyes. But put the blame right here, not on Lin, he said, and he thumbed his chest, twice. No bad blood between blood, that's what I say. If she'd have told you about your dad you'd be gone after him, and that's not safe, to say the least.

I appreciate the concern, I said.

Colton touched his head, a salute, and pulled off the aviators and placed them beside his coffee. He had cheek-bones round as irrigation pipe and a line of dad-like stubble dulling grey in swaths, big marble eyes drooped in bags and that dead-tired flatness to his mouth—another sleepless night. His nose was off-centre, but not crooked like a busted one; it'd just grown the wrong way toward the sun.

Who shot you? I said.

He tongued his canines, chasing gristle.

There's a crew of guys out to loot the town. They've set up on the road west—the road that leads to Caribou Bridge, where you aim to find Jack. I was having a pleasant chat with those fine gentlemen yestereve. He let himself smile.

Must've tickled, I said.

Like banging your funny bone. You learn to like it.

I met some bikers who got through, I said. How'd they do it?

Colton rubbed his thumb down the culvert of his sternum. Probably just drove through. But they're heading the right way—out.

And Jack? I said.

Colton turned his hands up. He went the wrong way.

My mom climbed on the counter and sat with her legs draped over the edge—small-town girl. They're opportunists, she said, but not criminals yet.

Except for the one who shot me.

That's your history, she said.

My own uncle, Colton said, and rubbed himself, for emphasis. Bit of bad blood and he gets it in his head to take a potshot. See what I mean, hoss? No bad blood between blood.

So what's your plan? I said.

We're hoping the fires will flush them. Like foxes.

I said: Like foxes.

That's right. We flush them like foxes.

I can't wait that long.

Colton's mouth drew in and sucked air from the meniscus of his coffee. He cycled it out his nose, as if expecting to breathe steam, and after a few rounds of this my mom touched his elbow and his head pendulumed across his chest to look at her. She lifted her shoulders, let them fall. A nod, nigh imperceptible. They'd expected me to say exactly that. I realized, then, that I had the two of them scheming against me. That left me one ally for hundreds and hundreds of miles.

Unfortunately, Alan, Colton said—and when he said my name he did so without the cowboy drawl, without the camaraderie and wit—you're staying with us. I don't have the manpower to drive them out, but I do have the manpower to drive you out.

Adrenaline preened in my spit glands. Sorry. I can't.

Colton set his coffee down so it *clunk*ed and leaned forward on his elbows. Beneath the gauze, his muscle pressed like rope. I noticed the tips of a scar at the border of the tensors, a great scab-like line of skin that teased his collar. You don't have a choice, he said.

You gonna arrest me?

Well. Yes. It's my job to get this place evacuated.

We breathed at each other. He flattened his palm on the countertop, the fingers spread wide so the bones of his hand strained up against the skin. The nails were chewed down below the quick, and the sides of his palm—the part that'd rub raw against an axe handle, or a rifle stock—looked grained by callus and the hard tissue of scars.

This is really important, I said.

He fiddled with the aviators, eyes downcast. When he bored of that he looked once more to me, and I saw in his eyes a dangerous intelligence and remembered Archer's warning and wondered if, after all, I ought to have brought the old man the shotgun. A family of connivers, that's what I had, every last one of them with their cards clutched to their chest—first Gramps and Archer and now Colton and Linnea. If there's an honest gene in me it had to come from Jack.

Colton turned his hands out, looked at me like he was sorry.

Now you don't have to like this arrangement, he said. But you're just gonna have to live with it. Free rein of the restaurant, best I can do, until we get the all-clear. Unless, of course, you want to make a move and head east, and out. I won't stop you. But try to go west and I'll be watching.

I felt the urge to fight swim into my bloodstream. You can't watch me all the time.

If you make me chase you, then everyone's in danger.

So don't chase me.

I'm asking you not to make me chase you.

He put his sunglasses on and reached backward to his hip where, with a buckle-pop, he produced a set of handcuffs beaten matte from use. They clattered when their steel met laminate counter, and he just stared at them and waited and swallowed. The fight left me.

I appreciate your urgency, Colton said. And as soon as this blows over, I'll get you on your way. Man's word.

The room, all of a sudden, stunk of body odour and bacon grease. Colton's teeth appeared, off-colour like the sky, as though he'd been sucking on charcoal. Then he pushed away from the counter and he grimaced—it wouldn't have tickled. From there he stomped through the saloon doors to the kitchen beyond, and for a moment neither my mom nor I dared move or speak until, seconds later, Colton hollered *Lin* from the kitchen. She slid off the counter with a thud, and in one practised motion she swirled her coffee dregs and sent them, mug and all, down along the countertop in a spin.

I WENT OUT THE DOOR and crossed the gravel to Gramps' Ranger and turned the key in the ignition. The engine gurgled to life; the radio played static and dices of music, too white-noised to be recognizable. I pressed my wrists to the wheel as the truck shook, and I tried to figure how to look Gramps in the eye. *It's no problem*, he'd say, and probably mean it, but I would never know.

I reclaimed my key. The engine cooled down. Tufts of Puck's yellow hair caked the back seat and his unwashed, cheese-like smell lingered still. It would linger for a while, I knew. Gramps' shotgun was nowhere to be found, and I figured Colton had confiscated it in a judgment call I couldn't really disagree with.

Archer's grim scowl followed me around the parking lot and I paused long enough to offer him a nod meant to convey some semblance of watching each other's backs. For his part he returned it. I let myself kick bushels of gravel a while longer before I set my jaw and went upstairs to convene with the old bastard. It occurred to me that we were prisoners.

In the room above the kitchen, Archer had straightened on the bed and somehow come into possession of a hacksaw that he'd used to carve a series of lines on the cot's wooden frame. You are one sad case, I said to him, and confiscated the saw.

Downstairs, directly below us, the two boys bounced their ball in a two-beat loop, and now and then it banged on the ceiling. Colton and my mom had not re-emerged from the kitchen, and between the rhythm of the ball I listened for evidence of their presence, but found none. Even the groaning fridges had gone silent, but I didn't know what that meant, if anything, unless they'd been turned off so as to more easily monitor the old man and me. The morning was taking a long time to lighten into day.

I knelt beside Archer's cot. On cue, he lowered his voice to a murmur: What's up?

You were right, I said.

He blinked, twice. He flattened a palm to his chest. Oh my God, he breathed, and let the words press him backward. First time I heard those words in thirty years.

Archer, this is serious.

Okay, he said. He was suppressing a grin.

Colton won't let me go farther. He'll arrest me.

I waited.

He clapped his hands on his knees, his version of a shrug. We got bigger problems than that, he said. They're lying about the evacuation. The Force would never let one guy oversee an evacuated town all by his lonesome. There's always a skeleton crew. Dispatch, a mess hall, whatever. Sure Crib's got some boys here, and maybe your mom counts as radio. But there's always more than one cop.

Somewhere, the restaurant *caw*ed—old wood with growing pains, a cackle. Jesus, I said.

Exactly, kid. They're hiding something.

I should've got you the shotgun. It's not in the truck anymore.

He tapped his knuckles on his thigh. I saw him out there, messing around, he said.

And you didn't think to do anything?

I suppose I could have scowled at him. Put the fear of God in his heart.

Archer, this is fucking serious.

Anything that happens, happens, Archer said. He didn't

look at me when he said it, and I didn't know what he meant. It seemed like an odd thing to tell me. But before I could press him an engine's low ribbit came from outside, from the direction of Owenswood proper. Archer's head cocked sideways and I moved to the window's edge and peered around the side.

How'd you get the hacksaw, anyway? I said.

He nudged his chin toward the room's far corner. Found it near the closet.

But you can't walk.

I *can* walk. I just ain't a fucking gazelle.

Footsteps banged around downstairs as the sound got louder. Colton yelled something to the boys. My mom yelled something back. A lot of yelling went on, in general, in that place. At the sound of Colton's voice, Archer's spine had gone straight as lumber and his jaw clenched so tight sweat squeezed from his temple.

A dented pickup the colour of old paper bobbed into view at the rim of the Verge's parking lot. It kicked a flute of gravel skyward with its rear wheels, and the screech of spinning tires without traction wheezed into the air. Three guys hunched in the truck's bed, big checkered coats and denims all, camo ballcaps and cropped beards—guys a generation my senior. Each one held a hunting rifle upright at his side, muzzles in the air. A display, I thought, like a war banner.

What is it? Archer said.

Cavalry, I said, bitterly, and thought of Colton's wounded chest.

The truck came to a stop a good twenty metres from the restaurant. A man stepped down from the driver's side—no ballcap, white hair, dressed otherwise like the others. He shut the door and shoved his hands in his pockets, put his weight on the truck. He hawked at the ground, tapped a booted heel to the gravel, twice. The four of them exchanged words that looked no more than grunts. A few guffaws, their shoulders like a hammer drill. From my distance I couldn't tell if the man on the ground had a weapon, but he must have. Vibrations hummed through the floorboards and up my knees—stereo bass, air conditioner, great, otherworldly purr.

Colton went out to meet him. He'd once more donned his Kevlar vest, pulled himself as straight as he could beneath the bandages. He wasn't unassuming, even injured; he had square shoulders, the build of a washed-out bar fighter, and arrayed before the older man he looked like someone who could make people listen. But one good blow to his torso would do him in—and if I knew that, he knew that, and so did all those guys.

He halted paces from the driver door with his arms over his chest and his chin tilted low. In the truck's bed, those three men laid their rifles across their knees and stroked their palms along the lengths. One fingernailed the hammer. Another ran his thumb round and round the muzzle, like that trick with a wineglass.

What's going on? Archer said.

Truck full of guys. Some guns.

How many?

Three.

More in the tree line, out of sight. Probably.

Below me, in the parking lot, the older man wiped his mouth on one checkered sleeve.

What do you think this is? I said.

Some kind of grudge.

I suppose you'd know.

Archer's mouth craned open but he didn't speak. In the parking lot, Colton leaned his ear forward. The other guy spoke. This went on and the three men in the truck kept their hat brims low, kept their fists on their guns, hardly moved. The fires throbbed out of sight, the mountains aglow.

Colton returned to the house and barked an order from the doorway. If anyone moved to carry it out, I didn't feel the buzz of their footfalls through the floor. Outside, behind him, the white-haired man reclined against the driver door and his mouth yawned wide enough to swallow a fist. He banged on the truck and in it the three guys laughed so their shoulders shook like old generators. He climbed inside. With a hawk of gravel, the truck sped away.

Go check it out, Archer said, his voice low so it wouldn't carry downstairs.

He won't tell me anything.

Archer loosed the slow, phlegmy cough of a smoker. He thumped a fist to his thigh. No, he won't, he said. But you might learn something anyway.

I descended to the restaurant. Colton had donned his gunbelt and strung an RCMP two-way to his shoulder, and its spiral cord hung across his chest. He was leaning forward, wrists on the Verge's stainless steel counter, this look of immaculate fatigue. Stubble greyed his jawline and beside his nose, on each cheek, a red crescent had flared up in a waxy swath. The dark sunglasses hung folded together from his collar. On occasion his chest rose in bursts but tended to stay deflated, because it would hurt like a bastard to breathe. That he could stand at all was an impressive show of grit: years ago, when Darby broke three of my ribs, I barely had the pain threshold to sit at a computer and type.

Sorry you had to see that, he said.

They didn't look friendly.

Like I told you earlier, true gentlemen.

He scratched and cupped his ribs and tapped the tips of his teeth together without a click. With his chin to the radio's mouthpiece, he said, Josh, do you copy?

Moments passed. We waited for a voice to respond through the receiver, choked with static—*Copy, this is Josh*, or *Go ahead, Colton*. But after a few more seconds of radio silence his head bobbed forward, and in the come-down from the anticipation he just stood there and rubbed the nape of his neck. His toe counted out a beat nobody could hear. I watched his elbow draw in and out as he massaged his neck, methodical as a piston.

Do you need a hand? I said.

I need backup, hoss. But thanks.

Where's your partner?

His mouth pinched so tight the skin on his lip whitened. What's that mean?

Nothing, I snapped. Josh—your partner? I just can't imagine you have to run this on your own.

He exhaled with force. Sorry, he said without looking at me. We made some arrests a few days ago, and one of us had to take them to the detachment in Revelstoke. One of us had to stay here. Right about now it's hard to say who drew the short straw.

Shit, I said.

Yeah. Haven't heard from him. These kids—they're his kids.

In the kitchen, my mom called Colton's name and he hollered back. He rapped his knuckles on the stainless steel.

Think he's okay?

I can't exactly go looking for him.

Sorry, Colton, I said.

He waggled his fingers. Then he shoved off the counter. Listen, I know you're going to make a move.

I haven't decided anything, I said.

You will, he told me. It's my job to know these things. But it's also my job to stop you. So I will.

I'm not your enemy.

Never said you were. We're just travelling opposite ways down a one-way road, and I've got a bigger truck.

My God, I said, and I couldn't help it, I chuckled.

Colton chanced a grin. Thought you'd like that one. Made it up on the spot.

It's a good one.

He offered a closed-lip smile, a nod of appreciation. Then his gaze flicked up past my shoulder to the stairwell, and he sucked on his lower lip hard enough that it released with a *pop*. I didn't have to look behind to know what—or in this case, *who*—had caught his attention. Before I turned, I studied Colton, but he didn't need his dark sunglasses to appear blank and unreadable.

Don't you fucking get fooled by him, Archer called.

Colton touched that brass-smooth patch of skin beneath his eye. With the same finger, he scratched two hard lines near his temple. His eyes closed. A slow, centring breath trilled between his teeth. He lifted one foot and checked the sole, then the other, and a curl of dust shivered in the air, gaming with the scent of leather.

Archer, Colton said. What a genuine pleasure it is to see you again.

I got nothing to say to you.

That's a change.

You ain't worth my time.

No?

Not one second of it.

I never took you for the forgiving type, Colton said.

I ain't.

Regular man of the cloth you are, Archer Cole.

You go fuck yourself.

Never held me in a moment's thought.

Nope.

Even an iota.

Don't you listen to him, Alan. Don't you even listen to him.

Both men looked at me, as if I had to take sides or pass a judgment. But this fight was not mine.

Well I got things to see to, Colton said. Unless you've got something more to say, old man, another insult or accusation perhaps? A vague threat on my life and well-being?

Archer's jaw jutted forward in an underbite. These weren't evil men, those two, but you don't always have to be. Colton huffed. Archer repositioned himself in his wheelchair. They gunned each other with stares. For a second, I saw the glimmer of the better world that might have been, where both Archer and I got to know Colton and where he let me go on to find Jack because the two of them were buddies. In that world, my family had not been shattered thirty years gone, and I introduced those two men to Darby, now my fiancée. There'd be boyish grins, shadowboxing and fisticuffs on the shoulder, and Archer—not crippled by guilt, not riddled with cancer— would rise from his chair to shake our hands. I don't know that I could've reconciled Archer and Colton, but I could've tried. Maybe a person's fate is decided more readily by the decisions they *don't* make—maybe being predestined meant ending up precisely where you never decided to be.

Archer said, Fuck you.

Colton touched his forehead in salute. Gentlemen, he said, and went through the kitchen doors.

I watched them swing on their hinges and waited for Archer to bellow out a one-liner like *Don't let it hit your ass on the way out*, but, upstairs, Archer's lips peeled over his gums and the skin of his jowls sagged like power lines. It was not a time for jokes, even for him. I ascended to help wheel him to the bedroom, but he rolled away before I mounted the landing. I followed him, leaned on the door frame while he positioned himself at the window. His past, as ever, darkened the world around him. With one meatless hand he dragged the sleeve of his logger's coat up and bared his scarred arm, the skin off-white and scaled like layers of wax. He rubbed his palm over it, exhaled.

Leave me alone, he said.

Old man.

What?

You can't go on like this.

He didn't say anything. I moved across the room, tapped my fist into his wireframe shoulder.

Tell me what happened, I wanted to say. *You can talk to me.* Instead: This isn't gonna be easy.

His hand went up and down his arm, over and over. It probably hurt, same way he thumped on his legs. I'm sorry, he said, and rolled up his other sleeve. For a second, he compared the two arms, stretched scarecrowesque before him. The burned arm looked like one of those skinless mannequins you find in school laboratories, the muscle and gristle all candy-heart red and veined with grey capillaries. Archer turned his arms over one way, then the other. The scarring was marbled with streaks the colour of hide, and you could see dollops of white skin near his knuckles and above his elbow where the napalm had splashed at his covered face.

My good side and my bad side, he said, without irony. I'm like Two-Face, but better looking.

Not by much.

He didn't smile. He wouldn't look me in the eye. His arms smacked down on his thighs and his sleeves unravelled over his elbows, and with a grace that belied his age and condition he hoisted himself from the chair's rickety aluminum frame and stood, perfectly balanced and upright so he could peer outside at the mountains and the fires in the distance. Morning had come into swing, and its colours flared through that small window like a thousand kerosene lamps. And Archer, soldier-straight and lit in the flickering reds and golds of sunrise, stared into that light as if about to charge headlong into a fire.

―

Alan West, my grandson, was born in 1974 under circumstances that plenty of families endure but that I would nonetheless change, given the chance. Cecil wasn't fazed, or at least he didn't show it. Nora mumbled sleepy observations into my chest, told me how proud he was, Old Man West, how she'd catch him grinning at himself in the mirror, boyish with anticipation, how he cut back on his drinking, how he cleaned out his storeroom of welding scraps and busted furniture he'd once sworn to repair and a shellshocked standing fan that ventilated their house in the summer. *Making a room*, he told Nora. *This basically turns us into brothers*, he said to me, and punched my shoulder. *This makes us partners*.

Jack took a job pushing lumber at Cecil's sawmill and blew his first paycheque on a barbecue. This was September, the twilight of the year, and south of the border the Americans had a new president and fiercer-than-ever opposition to the Vietnam War. About anyone who cared to look would see that the war effort was on its way down. That was a weird thing to realize, like getting your sense of self split in two. Cecil figured the idea of losing made me bitter. That's not it: I wasn't exactly a proponent of the war, but a lot of people died in that jungle and pulling out meant they really did die for nothing. We may have seen things from different angles, me and Old Man West, but I figured he would've at least understood what a waste it'd all been.

Nora pressured my daughter to move to the Wests' home and I found myself often in an empty room, often visiting across the street enough for Cecil to suggest the possibility of pooling our resources. He was a practical man if nothing else. Sometimes at dinner we'd get talking about the war again, and Nora would let us go on for a while before laying into us. The world goes on and families go on around it, or something. More often than not Cecil and Nora spoke of the wedding, too, and I watched Linnea's smile and swoon and wondered where she'd learned to be such a good liar. Jack mucked about trying to be a dad. He did his damnedest, anyone could see it. A long time ago I thought that's all it took—a willingness to get your hands dirty, a willingness to put someone else first. Maybe I'm right about that, but I doubt it. An altruist is no use in a firefight; dead men can't pull triggers. I probably should've warned Jack that Linnea was going to leave because he could have stopped her, but Linnea wouldn't have been happy there in Invermere. At least, this is what I tell myself. Like Nora said, sometimes the toughest decisions are simply the toughest decisions.

Some evenings Cecil stayed late at the fire station and on those evenings Nora would find her way to my place. She never stayed long though, rarely past dark, and I saw her less, touched her less—some evenings we didn't speak, some evenings she wouldn't make it past the door frame, wouldn't help me fill that empty house, and I woke one night knowing our time together would draw to a close. It felt like becoming suddenly aware—truly aware—that I would eventually die. I was losing her to Cecil; their newborn grandson had unearthed the man he was before his first wife's death. Once, he even mentioned a double wedding, and Nora rolled her eyes and shoved him like a lover.

September rolled into October and the West household showed signs of tiredness. When I saw them, Cecil and Jack joked about me dodging a bullet. Outside, the autumn light cut swaths across the valley, great pale patches that made everything look like winter does in the movies. For the first time in months my thoughts turned toward my sketchbook. Ever since Cecil nearly pinned the affair on me, I hadn't been able to summon the wherewithal to put charcoal to paper. It was as if all inspiration had burned up by the lie I fed him, as if I'd exceeded the limits of what I could and couldn't use it for. On occasion, Nora fetched the charcoal to smear idle endless lines, but anybody could see that her heart wasn't in it. Her heart wasn't much into me anymore, either.

THEN ONE EVENING the front doorbell rang and I knew with militaristic certainty that it was Nora come to put her foot down. She never rang the doorbell, just let herself in. And she never used the front door, either—which meant she'd come over not caring if somebody saw her.

Hi, Archer, she said, and picked lint off her sweater. She was dressed like a teacher, all proper and done up. Can I have a cup of coffee?

I'll put on a pot.

Put a shot in it too, she said.

Yes ma'am, I said.

She came to the kitchen and sat down. The coffee dripped. We watched the pot fill to the rust-coloured line stained in the carafe's centre—enough for two good mugs. I'm not sure I was even trying to think of what I could say to her. I believe in problem solving, but I also believe in the inevitable.

The whiskey might curdle the milk, I said.

No milk, thanks, she said.

We could've just had whiskey.

She smiled, but I could tell she was humouring me. ·

How's the madhouse? I said.

Getting better, she said, and pressed her lips tight enough to show her dimples. You should visit more.

I feel out of place.

He's your grandson too.

It's hard for me to go over there, I said.

She thrummed her fingernails on the table. I swilled coffee around the mug, blew across it toward her, like a kiss. It made her lift an eyebrow and I thought maybe we'd sleep together one more time before she left me well and truly alone.

I don't like it being awkward for you, she said.

It's not.

He's your grandson too, she said again.

It's not you, I said.

I know, she said, and tapped her index along my knuckles—one, two, three, four. But you're Cecil's best friend. This isn't right.

It's not.

What's not?

No—it's not not right, I said.

She pushed her tongue against her cheek. I couldn't look at her.

You've got a daughter to think about. I have a stepson.

How is Jack?

A new dad, that's how he is.

He does okay?

He's fucking terrible at everything, she said, grinning. Christ, I'm talking like you now.

Or Cecil.

Cecil doesn't swear around me, she said. At least rarely. He's a good man.

Better than me?

I'm not sure I can answer that, or even would. Why's it always a competition?

Because of you, probably.

She sucked a breath through her teeth. I could all but hear her jaw clench. That's as good a reason as any, she said.

It is?

I mean for this to stop. Us.

So you're choosing him over me, I said. Would've been nice of you to tell me this would happen.

Archer, she snapped. The baby? Stop being so selfish.

I never get to be selfish, I said, and finished my coffee in a big gulp that dumped grinds over my teeth.

Now you're pouting.

I'm just tired, or something.

Jack can pout, but you're a few decades too old.

Sorry, I said, and spun the mug on the table so that it

warbled like a guitar chord. I just don't fucking know. There's gotta be a way. You're the last person I can talk to, Nora. Look at me. I wake up in the morning and don't even know who I am. I'm sleeping with you but I know I can't have you but I do it anyway—that's not me, that's too, that's too typical. Christ, if I lose you I really will be alone.

You can't analyze this, she said.

Yes I can.

Sometimes there are no answers, Archer. Is there even a question here? Cecil, Jack, me, and Linnea. Everybody likes you. I don't know what you're worried about.

There's always an answer, I said.

God, that's so military, she said. She brought her mug to her lips, inhaled the steam. It's not just logistic, Archer. This isn't what I wanted.

What did you want, Nora?

She laced her hands together on the table, straightened up. A strand of her red hair flopped against her eyebrow but she let it hang there, let it curl around her eye and frame it and make me look at her and realize that she was as good looking as the day we met, the day I first kissed her and slept with her and held her in my arms—god fucking damn it, there could not be a better woman on this living earth.

I wanted Cecil to be more like you, she breathed.

And now he is, I said, bitterly.

Then someone banged on the front door.

Archer? Jack called, and I yelled for him to come on in. He swung through dishevelled-looking, his hair askew and balloons under his eyes and his hands bunched to fists. He came to a hard stop when he saw us. Nora?

Just escaping the chaos for a moment, she said. You okay?

I can't find Linnea, Jack said, and I felt the world widen, felt a great pressure in my throat, the lights flicker, lose brightness.

Is she here? Jack was saying. I can't find her.

I FOUND HER at the Greyhound station at the edge of town, near the base of a large slope where the road turned from asphalt to dirt to asphalt again in the span of a hundred yards. Across the street was a one-storey party shack with a yard that opened to a great, wide marsh. The lights in the shack were dim but music blared through its thin walls and teenagers staggered outside to vomit on the floodplain. The Sevenhead cut through town near the station, and whenever the party quieted I heard the river hushing.

Linnea had her hair tied in a bun and her backpack one-strapped on her shoulder. She looked older than nineteen, but that could have been the sodium streetlights that make everybody's skin seem as washed-out and yellow. It was dark enough for her to not recognize my truck approaching, but she'd have known that I'd come looking. Both of her hands cupped her stomach, just above her pelvis. I don't know what that meant, if anything. Somewhere along the line I'd made a grave error of judgment, but pinpointing that exact moment is a futile and pointless game. It doesn't matter how something starts, or even how it progresses. What matters is how things end.

Linnea leaned on the station's brick wall as I stepped down from the truck and scratched my neck and thought about what I could possibly say. I wished I'd brought Nora. For all my wisdom and prostrating, I am useless in the face of emotion. When it comes to tender hearts, I am about as useless as Cecil. He, at least, has felt real grief. He has watched his loved ones disappear around corners and over hills. He has known what it is like to lose.

What're you doing here, Dad? she said.

I sat against the hood of my truck, crossed my arms. Could ask you the same.

I can't stay.

Why?

You know.

No, I said. Tell me.

She pulled at a strand of her hair, like it was a habit, but I'd never seen her do it before.

You think Jack'll make a good dad? she said. A good husband? He's a boy.

I chewed on that one. Across the street, somebody banged through the front door of the party shack and the night got loud with the noise of music and young people hooting. Cars zoomed by, in and out of town, and I waited for the sound of their engines growing distant. Every set of headlights could have been a bus. All conversations have expiry dates, but you rarely think of them, and when you do—when at any moment your daughter could hike her pack and leave you, forever, there's no time to manoeuvre. You just say what you have to say. Maybe it makes them truer.

I think he wants to be, I said.

I'm not staying here.

Okay, I said, almost whispering, afraid to let my voice crack. I wished I had my sketchbook, or a bottle of sherry. Problems are easier to solve when they are things.

Have you got money?

Some.

My eyes burned, like from staring into a fluorescent bulb. I pulled a wad of money from inside my coat.

Here, I said, and after a long second of me standing arm-outstretched, Linnea pushed off the wall. She came close, reluctant—my own daughter. Did she think I'd grab her? Hit her? Christ, what did people think of me?

You're not going to try and get me to stay? she said.

I'm doing my best.

That made her wince back tears. Me, too. She stuffed the money in her jeans. Then she stepped forward and pressed against my chest, and I laid my chin on her skull, cupped her shoulders in my palms. She shuddered, a long breath, but no tears soaked my shirt. Daddy's little soldier.

My door, I said, trying to say *is never closed*. But that was so obvious. I rubbed her arms, smelled the shampooey smell of her hair, like a teenager's. You can't keep a person where they don't want to be—that's what prison is for.

You gonna call me? I said.

Sure.

From where?

She rolled her shoulders, something like a shrug. I believed her.

When does your bus leave?

I'm not busing, she said, and pushed away, and I sensed the crossing of a boundary, I sensed the approach of something sinister in the darkness around that Greyhound station. I used to have a nightmare where the wall above my headboard would open into an abyss, black as the mouth of an old paint can, and from that abyss I would see a dot growing, growing, into the shape of a monster with crustacean eyes and a maw like an axe wound, and I would tug on my blankets, try to tug them over my head, but never be able to find the strength in my arms. Right then, I felt like that nightmare had never left me, like it was warm-up, an elaborate and long-winded warning. Of course she wasn't busing. Of course somebody would be giving her a ride. And I knew who it was, who'd emerge from the darkness. We had one more confrontation brewing between us—there had to be.

He came to a stop with gravel churning under his tires, his headlights beaming on me and my daughter and my chest inflated with protectiveness. I stepped into the open, slow, calm—trying to look as menacing and in control of my rage as I could get. The lights flashed from high to low, high to low. Linnea leaned against the brick wall. The Fairlane's driver door opened. A pair of army-issue boots crunched down on the gravel. It was too dark for me to see him clear, but I didn't have to guess.

It's not what you think, Dad, Linnea said, but I barely heard her, even though what she said was likely true. I don't know what happened at that beach fort, so many years ago, only what Jack told me, the story Linnea never confirmed nor denied. I don't know why Crib kept running into me, why he seemed to hound me, what could possibly have been gained. Nobody has ever made it clear.

I figured you'd be here, Crib said. He stepped around to the front of his car. The lights lit half of him. He had a cigarette pinched between his thumb and first finger, and he flicked it to the gravel, ground it under his boot. It was slow, methodical. I cracked my head over my shoulder.

I guess you're here to do the alpha-male thing, I said.

Nup, Crib said, emphasizing the *p*. That's your gig.

He shrugged out of his field coat, folded it in two, draped it on the hood of his star-spangled car. It blocked one of the lights. He wore a white muscle shirt that showed his iron crab brooch and a scar across the meat of his chest—a grizzly thing that zigzagged from his right collar and disappeared along the curve of his left pectoral. After a moment, he swiped the cadet hat off his head, placed it neatly in the bedding of his coat. He looked exactly as a military kid should.

I probably should have thrown you off that bridge, I said.

He flashed his teeth in what looked like a genuine smile. If I had a penny for the number of guys who've told me that, he said.

You're not taking my daughter anywhere.

I know, old man, he said. I'm not taking her.

I squeezed my hands as hard as I could. A couple knuckles popped. Crib's shoulders rose and fell, as if sighing, as if he hadn't been after this the entire time he'd been in the valley.

Well, he said, came toward me. I suppose there's no talking you down.

Nup, I said, emphasizing the *p*. This was one fight I couldn't avoid and sure as shit didn't want to.

CRIB GRABBED ME by the lapels and shoved. I tried to react, flung a punch that sailed wide and comical in the air. I landed on my wrists in the wet gravel. The dampness budded through my jeans. Stupid of me to watch the hands, like an amateur, like some highschool kid scrapping. Crib assumed a linebacker's hunch, arms bent at nineties like the idiots who watch karate flicks and think that's how things get done. His fists curled and uncurled. I wanted so much to hit him, to bludgeon his face until all that remained was a swollen, bruise-battered hump of flesh and snot.

I pressed my tongue against my teeth until I tasted blood, got to my feet, whipped wet dirt off my fingertips.

Do you even talk to your daughter? Crib said.

I stepped through Crib's haymaker and hammered my knuckles into the plush spot at the cusp of his nose, put my weight behind it, curled the wrist in a half-rotation so the impact crunched the cartilage like an egg. His head whiplashed back and his hand went to his face, and I growled a follow-up to his solar plexus, his winding point, close enough to his scar that I felt the shingly skin on the retract. His breath wheezed against my ear, so gentle as to be intimate, disarming. I talked to Linnea all the time, had always talked to her. Who the fuck did Crib think he was?

Dad, Linnea hollered, like she was in trouble, and I turned on instinct, and Crib latched his hand on my face, fingers gouging my eyes and cheekbones so my head bent back. His knee dug into my ribs. I flexed my gut against the impact of his knuckles, but he couldn't get the distance he needed to make it count. We staggered apart, breathing like athletes.

Stop, Linnea said. She stepped away from the wall, had what looked like a club in her hand. This is stupid.

You can't leave with him, I said. After all he's done?

What's he done?

Alan. What about your son?

Who's dad *are* you? she said.

Crib sniffled, wiped a sleeve over his bloodied nose. Juice squeezed out his left eye and his face looked like a mastiff's. His chest rose and fell with enough force to lift his shoulders. He spat, red. His tongue tested the solidity of his teeth. I felt gouges on my cheeks, from his fingernails. A slight burn, as if spending too much time in the sun.

I went at him. It wasn't even fair, not anymore. I had the hand-to-hand; he had talk, he had attitude. I scraped my knuckles along his ear. I clipped one downward across his forehead, eyebrow to chin. The nail of my thumb tore his lip and made him drool blood and mucus. Crib's left eye swelled shut and I'd been trained to exploit that, a blind spot, a free-hit zone. We meshed together, held each other like wounded men. He smelled like bile and limestone, like the dirty diesel engines of logging trucks. My fists clenched. I grit my teeth, felt the bloodlust and the high a man gets when he causes another's pain. And then the world sucked me backward and down, down, down, legs gone jelly and my head lolled sideways and the night kaleidoscoping, smashed up like fireworks and engine brakes and then: darkness.

WHEN I CAME TO, I was looking at my own boots in the gravel, at the hem of my jeans darkened with water stains and soaked through, and for a moment I forgot where I was. The Sevenhead hushed in the distance, and at the base of the Ford Fairlane Crib slumped between the headlamps. Linnea helped him up, her backpack discarded and her hair whipping around in the wind. His face was double-eyed and smeared with cartilage and snot, and the corners of his lips were torn into a raw Cheshire grin. My own face ached. The cheek below my ocular throbbed from haymakers and jabs not quite grazed. The back of my skull was warm, heavy. Liquid leaked over my neck and down my back, and I knew without touching it that I'd been struck upside the head. I dabbed my lips together and felt a pulse of blood, couldn't recall the last time I'd split my lip on my own teeth or someone else's bone.

I pushed onto my elbows. Beside me, the upper half of a wine bottle lay in the gravel, the glass as rigid as a shank. Only one person could have wielded that bottle, and the realization hurt me more than the headache behind my eyes or the bruises welting my cheeks or Crib's headlights like pinpricks. Linnea had actually struck me down. After everything I'd done, the sacrifices I'd made, all those years trying my goddamned best, she'd chosen Crib not only as her mate but also as her protector. Crib, the man who'd haunted my waking hours for the last years. Crib, who'd beaten Jack West bad enough that his confidence had never recovered. Who would soon make a getaway with my daughter.

And that was not something I could face without resistance.

I got to my knees, ignored the gravel that jutted into my shins. Crib leaned on his hood, on his coat, and his unsteady movements sent bars of headlight streaming into the darkness. I wrapped my groggy fingers around the neck of the wine bottle, dragged it toward me. I'd already missed one opportunity to deal with Crib. Cecil would never have let it come to this. Cecil would have handled the problem, would have faced it down—but me, I just hid. Wars are not won by hiding.

I stood up. Force of personality. Old-man strength. Across the road, teenagers had taken note of our fight, had poured out of the party shack to point and sip beers and wonder. There were a whole lot of witnesses now. The glass was slick against my palm, but also sticky—residual wine, dirty groundwater, blood turned muck. I should have thrown Crib off a bridge. Linnea had pulled him to his feet, and he maintained his own balance now, almost as shaky as me. The adrenaline had left me, but I slogged forward, tried to strain my grip on the bottle-neck and grit my teeth, to will myself to anger. Crib didn't even budge. He just waited. He palmed a lighter from inside his coat and struck a brief flame that I watched and wondered at with every single step. It was like he'd let me gore him, spill his guts, save my daughter—that easily.

What're you doing, Archer? Linnea said, and I nearly collapsed all over again. I let the bottle drop, let my shoulders sag. Is there anything more humiliating than having your child chastise you on a first-name basis? Yes: there is the humiliation of becoming something you have taught yourself to hate.

I don't want you to leave, I said, and as the words left my lips the world rose up, spun, and I felt gravel on my ass.

Dad, Linnea said.

I steadied myself, palm to wet earth. No more cards to play. What else have I got?

Jack. Nora.

I wish I'd told her that I hoped, more than anything else right then, that she'd be happy wherever she ended up. Instead, I said nothing, sat in a heap on the ground while the Sevenhead rushed and the partygoers trickled back inside and the dampness in my jeans spread to my ass and crotch. Linnea came toward me, toed the broken bottle away, leaned down and pressed her warm lips to my forehead. I felt her inhale the smell of me. And for a brief, absurd moment, I wished that I had showered more recently, I wished that she would remember the smell of me at a better time. I have been told that scent revives memory more vividly than any other sense.

She left without a word, climbed into the driver's side of the car. I don't know who'd ever taught her to drive. Crib balanced himself on his open door, and I forced myself to look at him, to let my nostrils bulge and shrink with the effort of breathing. He'd won, but I would not go gently.

Don't get lost in the shuffle now, old man, Crib said, and gave me a salute. Then he ducked into his star-spangled car, and I watched them round the corner out of the Greyhound station, just taillights now, and then I watched them disappear over the crest of the hill that led away from Invermere, away from all the horrible boredom of that small town, away from Jack, and Cecil, and Alan, and away from me.

I HAD NOWHERE ELSE to go. I went to the Wests'. I went to Nora.

The walk—couldn't have drove, and not just because I'd had my bell rung—seemed like it should have been one of those times when a guy gets a chance to clear his head, like it was time to wind things up, take stock, cut losses and move on. In a movie there'd have been a sad orchestra at work. I crossed the road bridge, where a few of the concrete barrier blocks had been dislodged. Highschool kids had spray-painted a penis on one of them, in yellow. Cars whirred by me and a couple times I trudged off the shoulder for fear of veering headlamps. I'd have liked to skirt the lake, to smell the cadaverous stink of it, to let the air—colder there—ease the burning scratches on my face, the dull throb at the crest of my skull. Whenever the wind changed, I caught a whiff of myself, like breath and body odour and vinegar, though the last had to be my imagination.

Invermere's main haul was empty and lit only by the spill from over-shop households, and if I looked directly at them even those dull lights flashed to sparks and lens flare, to beads like a welder's torch. Cars snailed through town, all their tumbling metal and muscle like an athlete, and as they passed I glimpsed faces and bodies, heard snippets of conversation. The sounds dopplered away, seemed to gather and hang between the buildings like an echo, like being underwater, or in a fishbowl, or not knowing which way was up. Sometimes when I passed under a streetlight it'd flicker and go out, as if I contained a charge or was one of those people who stop watches, as if something was trying to keep me hidden, or keep the path ahead of me hidden—some power beyond science that knew things I did not. Fate, karma having a go, unnamed gods of flame and darkness.

I knocked on the Wests' door. A baby cried, and I heard shuffling, worried murmurs about the time of night. Then the latch turned and Nora opened the door, and it was like a blast of warmth hit me, the relief at seeing her. She had men's pyjamas on. Her red hair sprawled at her shoulders. Her expression said I looked a whole lot worse than she did.

Jesus, Archer, she said. Behind her, Cecil lurched out of the bedroom, topless. His old, muscular chest was paler than a glass of milk, and I'd have liked to crack a joke but I couldn't get my tongue moving like I wanted it to. Jack poked his head around the corner. He was holding the baby—Alan—like you would hold a cat.

Feel a tad lightheaded, I said, and slouched forward. Nora caught me, or mostly, and Cecil got his shoulder under my arm, kick-boxer fast. He gave Nora a nod and she slid away, and by himself he half carried, half hugged me to the blinking white kitchen, and when he saw me squinting at the light he rolled the dimmer low.

Nora's hands touched my face, an ice cube on rug-burned skin. She tugged my hair up and strands of it caked together, caked to my forehead.

Look at this, she said, and prodded my skull where the wine bottle had hit. Her finger came back juicy and red and she sniffed it, then wiped it on my coat. What happened to you?

Too much wine, I said, and I imagined Cecil's face as he stood in the doorway, arms crossed, as stern as a father. He'd have grinned. He'd have chanced a grin at that.

Think he needs a hospital? Nora said.

Dunno, Cecil told her. He hates hospitals.

He does?

Well, I figured so.

You figured so?

Yes *ma'am,* he said. Let's get him out of the jacket.

They lifted my arms, four hands, and got me out of the coat. Nora *tsk*ed. He's soaked, she said.

Cecil brushed hair away from my eye, far more tender than I'd have thought he could—or would—be.

Looks like he's been in a fight, he said, and loosed a guffaw. I tested my aching face with a smile.

Don't encourage him, she told me.

Cecil grabbed aspirin from the cupboard, ran a glass of water. He held the two tablets in front of me, as if uncertain, until I plucked the pills and dropped them in my mouth. I tried to swallow them straight but the angle was all wrong. The bitterness made me think clearer—I'm sure of it.

The two of them hauled me to the shower and Cecil cracked a joke about having to undress me and liking it too much. Their bathroom's wallpaper showed outlines of dogs— bulldogs, mostly, but a couple others, like a greyhound—and on the floor, in front of the tub, there was a welcome mat like you'd put on the front steps of your house. It was a Cheshire cat, grinning, and the caption under it said *Beware of Dog, but the Cat Should Not Be Trusted, Either.*

They cleared out. The whole time, Nora had kept medical distance and let Cecil do the heavy lifting, and I wondered at the irony of him hobbling me around like a son, or a brother, while I thought of nothing but his fiancée. That has a weirdness to it I can't quite give the finger to. Somewhere during the night, Cecil'd found the good taste to don a flannel shirt. That made it easier for me to not think about him as him, made it easier to cope with betraying him so bad.

Then the door opened again, and Cecil entered with a set of his clothes bundled in his arms. I cranked the hot water and sat on the toilet lid listening to the pipes whinny and feeling the room grow breathy with steam. Cecil barely moved, standing there above me. He set the clothes on the vanity and propped himself against its rim, banged a hairbrush aside and cursed when something *ping*ed toward the drain. My shoulders ached, my back, face. I tasted vinegar, sweat.

You okay? he said eventually. I could barely see him through the steam, the low lights.

No.

At least you're honest.

I don't want to talk.

I know, he said.

To see him, I had to move my head in a slow arc or risk the room dissolving to swirls.

So why're you still here?

Learned a thing or two from you, maybe, he said. Or I'm trying to piss you off, snap you out of it.

Learned that too, I take it.

Something of the sort, yeah.

What're you gonna tell Jack?

Dunno. Not really my expertise.

You've lost people.

Not like this. Not by choice. I'm real sorry, Archer.

Not your fault.

I think it partly is.

I fucked up, man, I said.

Crib?

Linnea. Hit me with a wine bottle.

He didn't crack the joke. Why?

I searched my hands, inspected the gouges on the knuckles and the gravel burns on the palms and the dirt and grit beneath the nails. It felt like inspecting someone else for wounds, the foreignness of my own goddamned limbs. They furled to fists and unfurled and I don't even know if I was in control of the motion, that act.

Because I was going to kill him, I said.

Cecil knocked on the porcelain of the sink, for the reprieve of any sound, any distraction. That won't leave this room.

I got nothing left now, I said, damn near naming his fiancée. Not nobody.

A grandson, Cecil said.

Yeah, I guess that means something?

He made a sound, not quite a grunt, the kind of sound that accompanies a sad smile. I heard his arms cross, his foot *tap-tap-tap* the laminate floor.

You okay otherwise? Not bleeding anywhere you shouldn't be?

I patted my bicep, thought I could feel the ripple of its gnarled skin through the cotton.

What happened, anyway?

Fucking friendly fire. That's what does you in, what you never see coming.

He grunted, didn't say a word, and bless him.

I rolled up the sleeve of my shirt, bared the biceps and its scar to the steam. It felt, like it always does, as if constricting, as if the skin had gone taut.

I hate fire. Scares the almighty out of me. Couldn't do what you do.

God made firefighters so soldiers would have someone to look up to, he said, though he was just a voice, my vision so blurred and fogged.

The shape of him moved forward, opened the bathroom door. Lisps of steam funnelled out.

Cecil, I said, and he turned, but I couldn't see his face, just its outline, and I didn't know what the hell else to say. You know.

He might have nodded, and went out the door. I stood and wrestled my shirt off and the cotton glued to my skin like neoprene, and as it came over my head I caught a good look at myself in the mirror: the blueing bones around my eye, the yellowy bruises and cuts potholing my chest, beer gut and pasty flesh and scraggly hairs and muscles sagging like a man my age. My stubble was bristly with dirt and blood, and Nora had swept my hair back so she could inspect my forehead for injury. I could have been a beat-up action hero without all the good looks and bad puns. I could have been a man who'd been struck down by his daughter, who'd come very close to making a mistake he'd never set right. Sometimes, it's hard to look yourself in the eye.

I got into the shower and let the water thrum against my back, let the warmth bleed forward. When I lowered my head the heat stung gashes, so I opted against shampoo—just massaged splashes into my hair and watched the water run ochre. The streams thumping on my face put the ache to rest, too, but that could have been the painkillers.

I came out of the bathroom to a shadowy house, a lone glowing lamp in the living room with its shade like a hot-air balloon. There, Nora had curled into the couch with her feet tucked beneath her. She rested her cheek on her wrist, eyes closed, but they eased open as I tiptoed out of the hallway. I hefted my ruined clothes and she gestured at the kitchen, where I deposited them into the trash.

Cecil gone to bed? I said.

Works early. I can wake him, if you want.

That wouldn't be fair to the guys he works with, I said, and sat down on the far end of the couch so there was a full cushion between us. I tried not to look at her, because she was so good looking and because she was Cecil's fiancée and because Cecil, with one or two exceptions, had everything he wanted. Sitting there, in his house, on his couch, I understood what had to happen, eventually.

No fire burned in the room's small wood stove, inset on a brick heat sink. Not that a fire ought to have been burning but I wouldn't have complained, right then. Paintings hung on either side of it, and a tapestry. Nora had told me that one of those paintings—a panda bear stuffing its face with bamboo—was her sister's, and her sister's first, given as a gift for all the support she'd shown during the process of its creation. *I find it fascinating*, she'd told me, the first time I realized I had something she wanted, something Cecil didn't have. *The creative process, all that kind of stuff.*

Outside, a gust howled against the window and the crab-apples on Nora's frail tree jittered but didn't fall. Raindrops *tink*ed the glass, were shushed away by the wind. Nora looked at me and then at the couch we were sitting on.

If you're too cold to go home, she said.

I shouldn't stay.

She looked at the couch, and I marvelled at the gap between us. I thought that maybe her heels had come untucked and that her socked feet were closer to mine than when I first sat down.

Okay.

I just shouldn't, I said, and leaned forward, put my elbows on my knees. I turned my hands over, and over again. The knuckles showed blue and nicked like a raw piece of whittled pine, like they used to look when I was younger, fierier, when I'd lean over the steel basin in my laundry room while the ex massaged iodine in the cuts, winched gauze across my palms like ammo slings. Those were some times, just the bullshit of them. Maybe you miss the worst parts of people the most.

Your *knuckles*, Nora said, and reached to touch them. Her words were all breath. She took my nearest hand and flipped it in her palm. Her skin was cool, looked soft, and the warmth of her bled into my hand like the heat from a cup of morning coffee. Christ, she was such a good-looking woman, such a good woman—my eyes burned just trying to keep her in focus, to not get all swoony.

She slid across the couch and I smelled her—the outdoors, rainy air, that scent of no flowers or all of them, the kind of scent that attracts bees. Even clean she smelled like that, just naturally. Her fingers traced my swollen fists, the purply edges of the gashes that were like tightly pressed lips. Her pyjama sleeve was bunched above her elbow and I counted the freckles that dotted her arms, the soft, invisible hairs.

It's okay, she said.

I don't know, I told her.

I won't tell Cecil.

Fuck Cecil.

He wouldn't care anyway, she said, close enough that her breath tickled my collar, the stubble on my jaw. Outside, the drumbeat of raindrops on the road and the roof rose in tempo, rattled on the shingles and the hood of Cecil's old truck, and then eased off. The baby—Alan, my grandson—loosed a brief, high-pitched yawn, and then he, too, went silent. Somewhere on the dark highway out of town, Crib pressed against the passenger door, gathered his field coat around him—he'd be damp, he'd be cold—and tilted his cadet's hat over his eyes, kicked a boot up on the dashboard of his star-spangled car. Then he'd release a deep, relieving breath that could easily be mistaken for a sigh, for a balm against pain, and not what it truly was: contentedness, satisfaction, because he had what he wanted, what I could not have. He had my daughter. Nothing scares me more than loneliness.

Nora brushed a tear off my cheek. I don't know when I'd started to cry.

Cecil's too much of a father to care, she said. Then she clamped her hand on the nape of my neck and tugged my head to her shoulder, and I inhaled the full scent of her and squeezed my eyes and felt the moisture bloom in the cotton of her shirt. Her fingers combed through my hair, scraped along my scalp, almost like Crib's but so much different. Why are acts of affection so similar to acts of violence—or is that just me?

It's okay, she whispered, and it felt like she was telling the truth, that Linnea would be back, that I'd hear Crib's mufflerless car sputter into my driveway across the street. Me and him would shake hands; a misunderstanding after all.

I reached for Nora. My hand slipped against her belly and her elbow cinched down over it, her body twisted sideways, her fist balled in my hair and gently torqued, leveraged my chin up, my mouth open. I could taste her, almost, the earthiness and my own tears and the grit unwashed from the ridges of my gums, the crevices between teeth, places of dirt and gravel. Somewhere, a car carried my daughter over asphalt, over distance, carried her away and away and away.

What're you doing, Nora said, as if through closed lips. I felt the bulge of her ribs, the one she broke that had healed funny—her perfect inadequacies, the things that made her beautiful. The things that made her *her*.

Archer, she snapped.

Nora, I said.

He's in the next room.

Please.

Nora's shoulders lifted and fell. She gathered her hair in her fist and tugged on it, a nervous habit maybe, and I didn't take even a second to guess what must have been going through her mind. Tunnel vision, as they say. Then she got up and walked over the carpet without worry of noise, to their bedroom—hers and Cecil's—and stopped in the doorway. She leaned into the frame, arms crossed and one heel raised so only the tip of her foot touched the ground. She could see Old Man West by light of the streetlamp—the same one that illuminated my house across the street. I just watched her there, breathing, watching her fiancé. Cecil rarely slept under covers—didn't get cold at night—so she'd have seen the whole of him, the mountainous fact of him, all of him casket-like on the bed, fingers laced together on his naked stomach. I don't know how long she stayed there. I don't know if I was one sudden wake-up from finally losing her, if Cecil needed only turn over and blink sleep from his eyes and grin happily, sleepily, pat the bed where he expected her to join him, where he'd wrap his stubborn arms around her midsection and hug her close. She loved him. Anybody could see that.

But Nora turned away from that bedroom. She came to me, waited while I fumbled with my shoelaces and eventually padded along behind her with them untied. She grabbed one of Cecil's work coats from its peg and draped it over her shoulders. We took care to let the door close without a sound. We took care to dart around the ring of orange light that lit the scabby street in a circle. We used the back door that led into the still-unfinished basement, sweet with the smell of sawdust and drywall. In that room, the old couch with its foamy guts spilling from the seams was too obvious to ignore. Nora discarded her work coat.

Then she was in my arms, or I was in hers, and she tugged my shirt over my head as I kicked off those unlaced shoes. She pulled me onto the couch, or I pushed her, our noises sharp and truncated, an intake of breath or a quick release of it—the intimate voices and motions and patterns nobody knew but us. I pushed her shirt up and her breasts appeared, and I put my mouth to them. She arched toward me. I got my hand under the elastic of her pyjamas. The ends of her hair spilled over my back, tickled my neck and shoulders and the old couch coughed up more lemony foam, enough for us to quicksand into the cushions, and as I entered her it was a moment of held sound, of quiet, of anticipation and then realization and then wonder—two gasps, one the echo of the other, and I saw her whole body like a landscape, the way air tickled over it, the shimmer of her skin like lake surface, the moguls of her ribs, pale and white but made amber by the streetlamp, the oaky muscles of her neck and her jaw and the clefts that formed in the corners of her eyes, the meeting place of arm and chest, all her hidden mysteries and the mysterious way she moved, now, out of sight of daylight and prying eyes. And there was no more need, no more worry—not right then. All things would be rendered new. All weary travellers would reach their destinations of rest and reconcile. This was always the only way it would end.

AFTERWARD, WE HUDDLED together on the dying couch, sticky and cold but content to lie there and make each other's arms go numb. I kissed a freckle on her shoulder, cupped my hand over her breast. I love you, I said.

She blew a long trail of air out her nose. So does Cecil.

What's gonna happen?

I don't know, she said, and shifted so that pins and needles prickled my arm.

What do you want to happen?

I don't know that either.

She braced a wrist on my chest and got herself up on one elbow, pressed along the length of me. With her free hand she touched the wrecked skin on my bicep, shrivelled like an apple peel. Even the heat from her finger made flesh tighten, tingle—not painful, but almost.

Does it hurt?

When you touch it?

In general, she said, her voice low and growly. She put her lips to it; the warmth from her breath itched, like washing yourself.

Only around heat. But it's not pain, really.

Cecil saw a guy get lit on fire, burned real bad.

He's a braver man than me. Running into fires.

Don't say that, she said.

I like the cold, I said, flexed the muscle there and saw, for a second, the way that arm looked when it first happened— bloodied and gobbed with juice or skin and yellow and so red it could've been black, the smell like roasting pork, swear to God.

Since it happened, that is. I prefer the cold. Makes me more Canadian, right?

She scraped her fingernails through my hair. I cupped her shoulder.

I shouldn't stay, she said, and lingered one more moment before sitting up.

She slid her pants on. It shouldn't be a sexy thing but my opinion of her was so skewed. I thought she had nice knees.

It's a good thing you don't stink, she said, eyeing me sideways. Or else he might suspect.

Think he doesn't?

He doesn't want to.

Have you ever watched him cry? *Can* Old Man West cry?

He'd say he did all his crying when Emily died.

That's not fair to you, I said.

It's not about me, Archer, she said, in a way that didn't invite comment. She gathered her hair in her fist, tugged on it, strained the muscles in her neck—a bouncing motion. I trailed my fingers along the ridges of her spine, rubbed my hand in one slow, strong sweep between her shoulders. She leaned her weight on my hand. Then, about as gently as I could, I lowered her back into bed.

SEVEN

Xenophanes:
*All things are an exchange for fire,
and fire for all things.*

Here's a story about Archer Cole: In 2003 he sent me alone
to my estranged father's camp, unarmed save a ratbag jeep
that'd barely start and a box of sentimental crap meant to
bring epiphany to my progenitor's eyes. Himself, he stayed
behind with the dead and the gone—some remaining belief in
devotion and justice—and though we'd meet again before the
tumour in his spine bore him away, most of the Archer I came
to know those two days on the road would remain forever in
Owenswood, lost among the bleakness of it all.

I found my mom and Colton in the restaurant's dining
room, in a corner booth with a black coffee each. My mom had
her head rested on the cushioned back so her chin pointed
at the ceiling. Colton had wedged himself against the wall
and kicked up his feet, and as I passed the carafe I hoisted
it from its burner and shook it their way. With a grave nod,

Colton lifted his hand and made a *come hither* motion with the fingers.

Thank you, he said when I arrived.

No worries.

My mom leaned forward. How's my dad?

Pissy.

That means he's fine.

What do you need, Alan? Colton said.

Can I phone Gramps?

Colton shifted to sit normally in the booth. He laced his fingers around the mug, took a loud, exaggerated slurp. Steam wisped off his forehead and he held the mug under his nose, as if it were a fragrant espresso, or even freshly brewed. Here I thought you were going to ask me if you can leave, he said.

Not yet.

Fair enough. We ain't savages here. Lin, you want to show him, or should I?

Come on then, my mom said. She bid me follow her through the kitchen, where the two boys had vanished from and where she'd repaired her nigh-dead husband. It smelled like a hospital cafeteria. She'd earlier laid Colton on a steel island: no bloodstains à la some horror movie, but I clocked the first aid kit with its contents ransacked. That vague aura of iodine, the wrinkly smell of skin beneath a bandage.

Gramps had undergone similar patch-up; in fact, he all but made a habit of wounding himself miles from hospitals or help or even a bottle of hard liquor to use as sterilization, and though I personally never stitched him up I'd been present many of the times he'd done it himself. Once, he tore his leg calf to knee following an incident of four-wheeler-meets-log. Another time, he knifed his radial artery while slicing bread for a grilled cheese sandwich. One New Year's Eve he leaped from the Dunbar cabin's upper window and gashed his forehead on the wooden frame—a drunken misjudgment of depth. Each time, Gramps waved aside all offers of assistance and palmed the needle with a gleam of excitement in his eye. I think it reminds him of a time when the world was wilder and the potential for injury greater, when stakes were higher, and when attendance to your own wounds meant something. You could wind up scarfaced. You could wind up gangrened. His youth, I guess.

You're going to go after Jack, she said. It wasn't a question.

If I can.

Colt will arrest you. He's a good cop.

I understand.

Will he be upset? Cecil, I mean. If you can't do it.

No, but that's not the point.

Then what is the point?

The kitchen light flickered and *tick*ed in its socket and my mom and I both looked up at it. We didn't move, didn't even flinch. The light *ticka-ticka-ticka*'d like a moth and in my peripherals, in those unreliable half-visioned spaces where what we see may not even be real, I saw Gramps lying deathbed in that shitty hospital room, only Nora at his side—if she'd even still be at his side. Animals don't prefer to die alone; they just don't know any better.

Gramps never asked me for anything, I told her, and knew it to be true. Imagine: three decades of selflessness, and now, after how many moons of him not caring about time left on Earth, now that he had at his side the woman he hadn't spoken of for twenty-nine years—now the clock ticks down? Imagine, to wait so long for a woman and have her appear at your deathbed. Fear, outrage, loss, love. You can dodge a bullet so much more easily than you can dodge a heartache. That's something Archer would say.

He's always been there for me, I said.

After a moment, she nodded and took off once more through the building. A rear flight of stairs led to my mom and Colton's living quarters—separate from where Archer and I had slept, holdover from the days when the Verge had been a bed and breakfast—and we passed beneath a skylight, wedged open with a leather boot. The ceiling was low enough to touch with your elbow, not quite claustrophobic but bordering—a converted loft. Around me, the oddities of her life with Colton lay strewn through the stairwell and hallway and the floor in their living room: a wood giraffe with holes along its flank, for toothpicks or pins; volumes and volumes of great topographic encyclopedias stacked chest-high by the walls and some thrown open to pages that meant nothing to me—maps of the region with red-scrawled walking paths. I gazed at it all longer than I meant to and longer than was polite, but when I turned to her she had only crossed her arms and leaned on a wall. It might've been her go-to stance—a half-grin of exasperation-that-wasn't, as if always in the rhythms of an inside joke. Taking it in: me, this creature that'd appeared in her life. Who knows.

I smell rain, she said, and raised one index vertical.

Above us air leaked through the open skylight and I sucked a strong sniff, that riverbed scent. Sure enough. A drop appeared on the glass and I thought it must mean something: that nature's elaborate scheme had yet to unfold or that the rain gods had been appeased. It hinted at an end to things— that I could still find Jack. My mom's eyebrows v'd together and, after a moment, she darted around a corner and out of sight. The suddenness of it—of her being gone—made me think that she had, somehow, disappeared for good.

I heard her pound around in the kitchen, bang shut a cupboard door, and she returned bearing two tin cups, and she tucked them under the skylight, onto the roof, as the rain came down. It was by no means a torrent—back home, my buddies would've called it a tinkle—but we stood and listened for the drops that *ploop*ed into those tin mouths. Some stray water moistened the window and a few drops gathered around the sole of the leather boot, slid over the length of it to hang off the low-hanging laces. I don't know how long we stood there and watched it drip before my mom reached for the tins, each lined with a gulp's worth of rainwater.

I put the cup to my lips. It takes like smoke, I declared with a laugh.

That's what it is, my mom said. It's smoked water.

She swirled the liquid in her mug before skulling it like a shot of liquor. My water had specks of debris along the edges— ash or dirt, the dust of her house. She took me to their kitchen, a room with one square window and stainless steel sinks, the faint afterglow-scent of vinegar used as cleaner. I tried to take it all in: people's kitchens are portholes to their lives and oddities. Above the sink hung a sewn hen in a skirt, and the tails of plastic bags drooped from its ass. The wallpaper showed stencilled outlines of different dogs, and I clocked the unmistakable outlines of pit bulls and greyhounds, but the rest were mutts and undecipherable to my untrained eye. In the corner, an American flag was wrapped around its pole, its base dusted with disuse, and I imagined that they bust it out for occasions like Thanksgiving and the Fourth of July. The phone hung in its holster near the fridge—the old corded variety you can picture pressing to your ear as you tried to cook dinner. My mom went to it, checked for dial tone, and passed it to me in that straight-armed way people do in horror movies, as if to cryptically mutter, *It's for you.*

I'll be downstairs, she said.

Thank you.

She left me, and I faced the keypad. I dialed home and pressed the receiver to my ear and listened to the tinny rings roll out. Most likely they hadn't released Gramps from the hospital, and I'd have to call there next, but for whatever reason I dialed his home number first. It was early, but he rose early every day because he loved his mornings, that under-breath of chill before the heat. At three rings I figured I'd let it go once more.

A woman's voice: Hello?

Nora? I said. It's Alan.

Hi Alan.

How're you guys doing?

You know your grandfather, she said, but I couldn't tell if she was making a joke.

Archer's still kicking.

That's good news. Did you find Linnea?

Yes.

From her end came a small *tick*, a fingernail rapped on mouthpiece.

Gramps awake? I said.

Is the American there with Linnea?

Yes.

She paused. Crib?

Yes.

I listened to her breath, rhythmic, unhurried. How's Archer?

Still kicking, I said, very slowly.

Alan.

He asked me to bring him a gun.

Did you?

No.

Okay, she said, sounding tired, or fed up. I'll go wake Cecil.

Her footsteps droned over Gramps' echoey floor. I still wonder how much she knew of Archer's goal on that trip, what they'd talked about and if she'd deciphered, over their years together, what drove him. He'd pined for his daughter for three decades; at first, I thought it an immense act of love, of dedication unparalleled, but I realize now that it may been something else—those other, darker emotions that can sustain us. Jealousy, revenge.

Gramps manhandled the phone to his ear. The hell do you want? he said.

Thought I'd call to make sure you hadn't gone lazy.

Big words.

I can't punch you through the phone, I said. But I would.

He chuckled. Face to face, I'd have seen those spark burns on his chin rise with the hook of his smile. Things going alright?

It's not a walk in the park, that's for sure.

I don't want you out there anymore. Too dangerous.

Sympathy, Gramps? From you?

I imagined his grin, the fire that enters his eyes when he spies a fight, even a silly one. You know what they say about sympathy?

The flak you give me, I said. After all I've done for you.

He loosed something like a sigh—that comfort of sinking into a routine you know well, a place you like. He had so few people, I realized.

Gramps.

You can head home now, he said, weakly.

The receiver scratched against his chin, the stubble. He didn't know how to ask for help—I don't think he ever really learned how. Archer die yet? he said.

He's trying to help.

Gramps grunted, whatever that meant. Nora says there's an American there.

Colton, yeah.

I knew him as Crib.

There might be an altercation.

That's my boy.

He's a cop.

That's great.

Great?

Yeah, Gramps said. That law won't let him kill you, and he sure as hell can't make you uglier, so I can sleep easy now.

Fuck you, Gramps, I said, but found myself grinning—couldn't help it—even though I wanted to tell him everything that'd happened. He could help me: he had advice to give, practicalities to point out. He'd come up with an escape plan for me, and I'd agree with his assessment, and he'd tell me to leave Archer behind if I had to—and I'd agree with that too. But something held me back from bringing him in. I don't understand what. I might never understand. Who knows: that, right then, might've changed everything.

Now seriously, be careful with Crib. Especially if Archer's there. Those two don't mix.

I guessed that.

Quick on the uptake, like always. Archer figures he still owes Crib one, but that's grudge-holding even by my standards. You know?

Does he? Still owe him one?

I don't know, Alan, Gramps said, and I pictured him shaking his head and the way one of his cheeks would pinch up, not quite a dimple. I don't know how his mind works anymore. Maybe I never did.

Well, he's in a wheelchair.

He's the stubbornest person I ever knew. A wheelchair might not stop him.

Above me, on the Verge's roof, rainfall juddered like some faraway war drum. I spied a canister of boot polish tucked half inside a nearby drawer. All the stainless steel gave the kitchen a smell like the confines of a subway car—clean in a way that suggests it will be dirty soon. I wanted to ask him if he was happy to see Nora and if his chest ached or if he still expected to die soon.

Gramps, I said, and swallowed to find the words. What're you planning to say to Jack?

He's your *dad*.

Come on.

I heard him huff, pictured his mouth clack in circles. I don't know, he said. *Hello*, maybe.

It's a good start.

Oh fuck off, he said.

Nora said something and over the noise of Gramps' breath it sounded vaguely like a demand. His voice barked an answer, muffled because he'd buried the phone in his shirt. Of course they'd be fighting—how else could they begin to fit themselves together?

I lost Puck.

Whereabouts?

I cleared my throat, swallowed down a frog. Gramps didn't skip a beat: I'll miss him.

It was my fault.

No, Alan. It's my fault.

That's not true.

I fucked up. I fucked everything up. This too.

Bullshit, I said, but I don't think he even heard me. Did Nora tell you that?

I never had a good son, but I got lucky with you, he said, and his voice turned low and husky, more breath than word.

It's a voice I've rarely heard him use since: later, for some throaty lines mumbled at Nora's funeral; with Jack, after all the bullshit and bravado, for a clumsy *It's good to see you*; and to me, of course—some years after, when, once more alone, he'd tell me he didn't know how anything worked, and least of all people.

Shut up, Gramps.

No, I'm sick of this. You're the only reason I got through.

Shut up, I said into the phone, and realized with a start that I'd pinched my eyes shut. When I opened them, there at the end of the kitchen stood my mom. A breeze shifted in—maybe through the skylight—and gusted her with its campfire smells, and she turned so that her shortish hair swished over her cheek and the mole on her jugular: an expression of supreme nonchalance. Her shoulders rose and fell in one big, exasperated breath. She thought I was yelling at Gramps, that she'd been right about him and Jack.

Fair enough, Gramps said before I could recover. Say hi to your mother for me.

Then, with a *click*, he was gone.

I squeezed the phone to its holster. He says hi.

You good? she said.

Yes, I told her. I'm good.

She put her hip on the doorway and looked at me like a stranger. Colt thinks the fires are going to make a move, and I tend to believe him.

What's that mean?

I'll give you the keys to our jeep. Take it, and Colt can't pursue you. But you don't mention me.

Why now? I said.

She bared her teeth. I never loved Jack. He's an idiot, and an alcoholic. But I don't want him to die.

She shoved off the wall and ducked through the doorway and I heard her footsteps retreat downstairs. Outside, the raindrops drummed on the dry ground, their sound muted and constant as bass. The kitchen's one window was greased square-by-square with ash, but streaks of water cut culverts through the grime and I could squint through it, see the landscape in slices—the mountains like a diorama, the nearby pines as green as health, that sense of being a part of the bigness and of being bigger yourself, as a result. A nice place, in nicer times. Right then, the mountains were slate-grey cutouts lined orange—a child's sketch of Hades—and their trees had dried the colour of rusting steel. You couldn't distinguish the rainclouds from the fires' smoke overhead, and the sky just foamed, dark and stubborn as those waves that lap the coastline smooth.

ARCHER WAS STANDING near the foot of the stairwell, his weight heavy on the bannister while one of the boys hauled his chair down. He'd wrapped himself in a thin blanket that draped from his shoulders to the floor where it gathered in a pool. The boy placed the chair before him and Archer gave an old man's nod.

You walked downstairs?

Up and down again. I told you, I just can't feel my feet. Quicker to use the chair.

He hunched forward, favoured one of his legs.

308

You okay? I said.

Just achy, he said, and waved a hand through the slit of his makeshift shawl, shooing the boy away. Go on.

When the kid had left earshot, I said, I'm heading after Jack.

Archer looked like he was leaning on a crutch, or cane. He pivoted himself around, but didn't sit. I'll hang back on this one, he said.

You're cocked sideways, I told him.

Achy, he said again, with some annoyance.

Need a hand?

He waved at me, a flick of the wrist. Get out of here.

I'm taking his jeep, I said, so he can't follow. You need anything from me?

No, he snapped. Just get outta here.

Keep your head down.

I'm not a fucking baby, he said.

You sure you're okay?

Yes.

Something bothering you, old man?

Yes, he said, and shook a finger at me. You.

I half expected him to prod me in the chest. But he was old, pissed off at nothing—I let him be.

In the Verge's parking lot, Colton and my mom were arguing. I hung back and let them hash it out. Rain clung to the pebbles and the air smelled at once bone-dry and wet, as if with every breath we were using up what scarce moisture remained. An alien wind cooed from the west. When you listened, you'd hear only quiet—the emptiness of abandon.

Every living thing had fled; the animals sensed what lay hidden below the threshold of our awareness. Colton gave my mom the cold shoulder and faced me. He took off toward me at an aggressive pace, and I thought: *here we go*.

I told you you can't go until this is through, made myself pretty clear. Hoss, I don't appreciate you recruiting my wife against me.

Please, I said.

No, no more *please*. Go back inside.

Come on, Colton.

He grappled for his handcuffs. There are other people here than just you, Alan. I can't have you cavaliering off as you see fit. And I can't trust you to make the right decision. So. Go back inside.

Just let me take the risk. The wind's changing. I gotta get Jack. He'll die.

Colton licked his lips. I hate to say this, I really do. But fuck Jack.

My mom showed up beside him. Colton, she said, almost under her breath, and touched his elbow. I heard him draw breath and release it in that measured way you do to calm your nerves. Then he pushed past me and inside the Verge. My mom cocked her head toward the jeep while Colton banged around in the kitchen. She palmed me a set of two keys— one for door and one for ignition. Through the Verge's front windows I saw Archer watching us from the comfort of his wheelchair. I don't know what he must've been thinking right then, or how exactly he got downstairs.

I'll stall Colton, she said. Just go.

Thank you.

It doesn't matter, she told me.

I jogged to the jeep. The interior smelled like wet earth and Old Spice deodorant and wisps of dead foliage had dry-curled around the pedals. The back seat had an impression left by many years of a lying-down dog, and a few drool stains crusted the cushion like rust. It made me think of Puck, which I didn't want to do. In between the seats was the holster for a shotgun, and I pictured Colton with it clutched to his chest and wondered how fatiguing it'd be to carry that much paranoia all the time.

A foot crunched gravel outside the truck, and I looked in the mirror to see Colton approaching at an amble, his arms by his sides and his gait awkward and stiff. I looked for my mom but did not see her on intercept trajectory, so I put the key in the ignition and torqued it. The jeep shuddered alive beneath me and I palmed the stick. But Colton had covered the last stretch of ground in seconds—*objects in mirror* and all that jazz—and before I could lock the door he flung it open.

He clubbed me with the butt of his telescopic baton. The impact pitched me across the empty shotgun holster and before I recovered he dragged me nose-down to the gravel. Warmth blossomed on my cheek and when I touched it my fingers came away kissed red. Blood slicked onto my skin and was wicked up by the collar of my shirt. I ran my tongue over the teeth in the region of the impact but felt no chips, no damage. Pain is entertaining when it will not leave you crippled, but a true injury hurts most for the fact that you will never fully regain what it has taken away.

My mom yelled his name and he buried a hard toe in my gut. I cinched my elbows in, hoped to catch a leg or arm, something to grapple, but I'd lost track of myself and I'd lost track of him. He planted a fist in my hair, hauled me away on my ass toward the Verge, until the jeep was a good twenty feet away. There, he wedged a knee between my shoulders and torqued my arms behind my back. I heard the metallic *zip* of his handcuffs cinching in. I thought of Darby. I thought of her photographer's eye, the way she ate oranges and gave me so much shit and so much heartache, the way I missed her like a bastard.

Through the bewilderment, a woman's voice: Colton, stop it.

Back off.

My face burned and warmth inked toward my lips and I figured I'd look damned prize-worthy, scraped chin to ear. Even from my vantage, Colton didn't exactly cut a behemoth's jib, but I guess you don't always need to. He wore a nondescript grey coat flown open, no shirt beneath so his bandages showed white as teeth. My face rang with ache. Colton touched his lips to the radio and said, Does anyone copy?

Blood reached my mouth. I tasted its iron; the mineral salt of rainwater left resin on the pebbles on the ground.

I told you, hoss, you can't leave till this is through. Now you're under arrest. Should I read you your rights and make this official, or can we come to an understanding?

I pulled a long suck of air and my booted rib ached as if unhinged. Colton squatted beside me. When he did, he favoured one leg—as if it didn't quite respond like a leg should. I thought about trying to get to my feet, but it wasn't like I could take him with my hands behind my back, or at all. Where, I remember thinking, was everybody else?

Why'd you have to show up? he said.

I'm just looking for my dad.

Christ, he said. He touched that mark under his eye, and his cheekbones rose—a squint, or wince. He dragged a sleeve over his forehead, brought it down chin-level to inspect. The arm trembled in air, and he looked from it to me with a look on his face as if he'd sniffed diseased meat. You're persistent.

Desperate, more like it.

I admire a good, healthy dose of desperation, Colton said. He rested his wrists on his knees. Time to time I even find myself indulging. But stealing my jeep—that's classic. Linnea's idea, right?

Archer's.

Colton smiled—genuine humour. Right, and where'd he get the keys? Don't worry, hoss, I ain't even mad. Hell, I even wanna let you go.

My mom came out the Verge's front door and levelled the two of us with a Medusa's stare. All the afternoon light seemed to attach to her, make her radiant nonetheless. Colton, she said. He'll save Jack.

Didn't think you cared about Jack.

Come on.

Colton's mouth bowed at the corners; the lips moved but he made no sound. I just looked at him.

You're not in the wrong, I said.

I know, hoss. Neither are you. Come here, I'll take those things off.

I complied. He sheathed the handcuffs.

Then the Verge's doors banged open again and all three of us turned our attention to it. Archer wheeled himself out, hunched small and deathly and hairless and with eyes downcast. He had that same blanket draped across his lap, wore his big plaid coat that hung off him in folds. His arms moved with the deliberate care of someone in deep concentration; the skin on his knuckles whitened when he gripped each wheel. It seemed to take him hours to reach the gravel, and that just slowed him more. But he did not relent. He did not give up—which has always been his way—until he had aligned himself with Crib, there in the parking lot.

Whatever emotion we'd triggered in Colton left as soon as Archer came to a halt. His jaw chewed on nothing.

Figured we'd have one more chat before I died, Colton said.

Archer smoothed his hands down his thighs. Believe me, he said. I'd have passed this up.

They deadeyed each other. I touched the gash in my cheek, a chunk of skin shucked off like meat. Heat flushed my face—swell, worry. I wiped blood on my jeans.

So I guess we're not old enough to move on, Colton said.

Not by a thousand fucking years, Archer said. His voice came out strained, high-pitched. His Adam's apple quivered and the folds of flesh beneath his chin danced like a set of jowls. He was very afraid or very angry, or both.

He know about you? Colton said. He know what you caused?

Archer didn't respond.

Colton tilted his head my way. You could be my stepson, if times were better.

You ain't nobody's dad, Archer said. He all of a sudden had an accent, a drawl distinctly south-of-the-forty-ninth.

Better not a dad than a shitty dad.

I shoulda kilt you a long time ago.

Colton didn't rise to it. He turned back to me. His face had that look of supreme indifference cops do so well. I couldn't read him.

What do you want, Archer? he said.

I want you to have never been born.

Won't get that. What else?

Archer's chin came up, but it doddered in place.

You can't even tell me, can you? Let's lay it out: you want Linnea. You want her to pack up and bunk in with you. Well you won't get that either, Archer. She left you once, for good reason.

What'd you know? Archer said.

No, Archer. What do *you* know?

I know about family. I know about caring for people.

Name one family member who hasn't left you, Colton said, and moved toward the jeep. Halfway there he stooped and plucked the keys from the gravel, where they'd fallen when he hauled me from the driver's seat. He jingled them in his hand a moment before tossing them my way. They bounced to a halt against my leg and I watched him nod, sagely. I'm not even sure Archer registered any of that exchange.

You got a plan? Colton said.

Drive west. Find Jack. Save the day.

He snorted—an actual show of mirth. You could've been my kid, you know.

My cheek had ballooned. With my shirt, I daubed streaks of red from around my mouth. I'm Gramps' kid, I said.

You look it, he told me. More or less.

Then he turned to Linnea and his face lit with a small smile—just half the mouth. You win, he said. The kid's just desperate. Christ, aren't we all?

Archer had a weird look to him, a certain calmness that didn't make sense. Colton kicked a spray of gravel, and dust coiled where the rocks landed, and I understood, way too late, that he hadn't taken the shotgun from Gramps' truck, and why Archer had acted so strange and stiff-legged at the foot of the stairs, and why he was acting so strange now. Colton's foot barely touched down, and he'd barely regained his footing when Archer cast aside the blanket on his knees and raised from it Gramps' shotgun, now cut to a sawed-off that he'd concealed across his lap.

The blast lifted Colton off the ground and ragdolled him a few feet from the jeep's grille. He loosed one disbelieving cry, a sound more gasp than yell, and arched his back and dug in his heels. His elbows thrashed around and his mouth chewed nothing—the bewilderment. With his hands—bloody and roadrashed—he dragged himself to the jeep, until he could grab the bumper and hoist himself to a sit. The shot had torn his shirt and bandages open at the chest, and the flesh beneath lay raw and gaping like a dozen wet mouths. He sucked little breaths; his lips peeled over his gums and went lax. I saw him swallow—one exaggerated bob in his throat.

Archer had been de-chaired by the recoil. He crawled onto his gut with Gramps' mangled twenty-gauge levelled to finish what its first barrel had started. He rubbed a shoulder in his eye.

What've you done? I said, but Archer didn't acknowledge it.

My mom shook her head, managed a few tentative steps toward her husband. She didn't make a sound.

See, Colton said. His voice came out a whisper. He moistened his lips. See, old man?

Archer adjusted his grip.

Everywhere you go. I told you. Remember? I told you.

You told me nothing.

Colton's hand closed around a clump of pebbles. A smile, those teeth red and slick. He tossed one, but it landed way short of its mark. Look at you, he said. Look at you.

He threw another rock and it bounced along the gravel and Archer didn't so much as blink. He kept his eyes on Colton, who turned his head to the carnage around us.

You f-f-fucking American, Colton said.

Archer's hands caressed the sawed-off's shaft and I imagined the polished steel beneath his fingers—oily, like leather—and the smell of it, that tang of metal. His hairless brow seized tight and on his forehead two landmass blotches drew together, end to end. Colton's shoulders rose and fell in stutters. His eyes zigzagged in their sockets and to make them focus he blinked with all the muscles in his face.

Do you get off on ruining lives?

That's funny coming from you.

Colton's head sagged sideways. His chest heaved and he regarded the collection of pebbles in his hand. Perhaps he saw in them some final irony: his lip rose to approximate a smile, and then he flung them all—his last act—with whatever strength remained in him. They hailed upon Archer, who lowered his forehead to the scatter. A few *tink*ed off the shotgun's barrel. One caught him above the ear; in its wake it left a smudge of dirt, streaky like a grease stain. He hardly reacted to the impact; I don't think he once peeled his eyes off the dying man.

Colton's breath wheezed in his throat, a noise like a congested person's snore, so irregular you'd give anything to hear it stop. The wounds in his chest gurgled. He raised his hand to where his nipple should have been and flattened it there. It stayed for a brief span of time, then dropped limp into his lap. His eyes glazed over and lolled upward and he died looking at smokescreened sky.

Archer lowered his head to the sights. Wetness dewed the clefts of his eyes.

He's done, I said.

I want to watch him die.

Fuck, Archer.

I went to him and laid my hand on the shotgun. He tensed up, looked at me with the whole of his face screwed to fury, but I didn't budge. I hoisted the gun from him. He flopped muscleless on the ground with his head on his own shoulder, looking dead himself. He'd done a number on Gramps' shotgun: hacked off two feet or more and not bothered to ream the inside. The edges were barbed and uneven; he must've laid the weapon across his knees and held on with all his old-man strength and bitterness summoned. I don't mean this to sound honourable.

I put the gun down. Everyone watched. My mom, unreadable and distant, took hesitant steps toward her husband. She knelt beside him, touched the bloody hand in his lap, his cheek. Her teeth came together, her lips up, and she eased her husband's eyes closed. Then she knelt without motion, stroked Colton's knuckles. That much loss, and for no good reason—I had to look away.

Archer lay like a slug before me, half bent to fetal with the gravel drying to mineral against him. He pinched one pebble between his thumb and index and studied the contours.

Archer, I said. Why?

He looked up, blinked tears, so old and sad. I don't rightly know, he said.

I scooped him up, the whole tiny wiry mass of him, and returned him to the wheelchair. Archer didn't deserve even that show of compassion, but I just couldn't leave him lying there and I don't know, I don't know why. The wheelchair tottered while I fit him in. His arms clamped around me, and at first I didn't understand that he wasn't just holding on to keep himself upright in the chair, but because he needed someone to hold on to.

His fists beat helpless on my back, two infant pounds. He smelled like that mix of body odour and things gone stale, like something that hadn't moved around much—old, used up. His sobs growled deep in his throat and grew longer and louder until he no longer cared who saw him cry. But then again, I doubt anyone there cared to see him cry at all. His sobs came crooning out big as howls, and his whole body shook like an engine and his baby-smooth cheek brushed mine, and as his tears cooled lukewarm between us I wanted to cry, too, but I didn't know whether to do so for Archer or Colton or my mom or myself. My eyes ached, but no tears came. He'd killed a man he didn't need to, and I'd had a hand in it.

AFTERWARD, THE TWO BOYS sat knees-knocking on the dirt, looking lost in a way I can't describe. Archer withdrew to a deep layer of memory; he sagged halfway out his chair with his legs sprawled haphazard in the gravel. My mom cradled the corpse of her husband in the same place he'd fallen, next to the jeep's grille. It smelled like autumn and rainfall and faintly like the dead. I looked for gaps in the cloudscreen, some sash of colour to tell us that it'd all be alright.

My feet took me past the far side of the Verge, where the terrain sloped lazily down to what I recognized as a gully—a wilderness within a wilderness—and where a trail of tire marks in the gravel pitched off the edge and beyond, though no vehicle lay piled at the bottom. Just one more Owenswood oddity. I hadn't realized how high the Verge rose above its surroundings: from that vantage, at the apex of that slope, I could sight along the toothpick-bare trees toward the Rockies that cluttered the eastern horizon, no more welcoming than the Purcells. That way lay home, I thought, though I didn't feel any pull. That way lay the road back, but home? Home is where we go to anticipate change, where we cling to what we have come to know and be comfortable with.

Someone had had the good sense to build a balcony off the Verge's ass end, and someone else had turned it into a place where the day couldn't find you; there was a fold-out lawn chair cocked toward the skyline, an ashtray, and a wooden milk crate lined with one or two empties. I imagined the employees who took their smoke breaks there: one guy with crow's feet and a paunch wedged in the chair; a younger kid with his feet over the balcony, heels bumping wood. Normal people, people with things to talk about and stuff to lose. On weekends kids scoped the balcony for untouched nightcaps left by workers. Sometimes, in the wee hours after a private-cater or New Year's bash people sat and mused about plans and confessed loves for things you'd never think: jive dancing, handball, the bleachy smell of a newly developed photograph.

Right then, I'd have done anything for a beer or to be anywhere else. The bleeding from my cheeks had stopped, more or less, unless I picked at it. If I listened hard, I thought I could hear my mom weeping over the murdered body of her husband, and though I knew I ought to be out there helping, *somehow*, I also knew I wouldn't be able to. Regardless how things turned out, I had played a part in that man's death. The idea of sleep terrified me: every time I blinked, I saw Colton suspended mid-air with that feral energy in his eyes, the bewil-derment when he hit the ground. I saw the way he clawed at the wounds and the rocks and the jeep's grille—pure unbelieving desperation, like an animal. For all our evolutionary advan-tages, at the end, we simply don't believe, and we simply don't understand. So few of us, I think, are ever ready to die.

I sat down. Everything—even thinking—ached.

MY MOM WOKE ME.

Hey, she said, and touched my foot.

She sat on the wood with her legs crossed, her elbows on her thighs, tomboyish. She looked as if she'd been there a while. I pressed a knuckle to my spine. In the natural light her blond-streaked hair was thinner and going on grey, and her face looked taut beyond the elasticity of her skin, as if at any moment it'd shrivel up. She'd been crying, or at least rubbing her eyes. The sun had reached its peak and begun to descend—but I'm no outdoorsman, I don't know how long I was out.

Hey, I said.

I let you nap.

Are you alright? I said.

She had with her the tin first aid kit, a bottle of iodine, and a plain white shirt bundled under her arm. Your cheek's bleeding, she told me. It'd stained my collar and wicked down my chest and I thought, callously, that I would've looked as if I'd been shot. I peeled it off and tossed it over the side. She touched the damage Colton had caused, her hand cool against the swell. She handed me a damp rag to clean my face and neck with, and I pressed it to my cheek and breathed a short sigh of relief, though I knew I had no place to allow self-pity. A woman had lost her husband.

You need a few stitches, she said.

We're too tired for that, I said.

I can stitch them. Oblige me.

Okay.

Leave the shirt off for now.

I heard her rummage through the first aid kit. The tin jangled. She took the cloth from me and lifted it to inspect.

In her hand she brandished a ski needle as long and curved as a thumb. She paused to hold it up, paused again to stare for a moment at my bloodied shirt, heaped in a pile on the ground. I heard her swallow: that loud.

You sure you're okay? I said.

It's your call, she managed.

I don't suppose you've got bandages handy?

None.

She strung some gut through the needle's eye. She brushed her fingers on her dark jeans but the dust had already settled on her thighs. It'll be okay, I told her.

I felt her prod the wound, tip my cheek to the smoky light. When the needle went through it sent a tingle all down my spine, like the pressure of an electric razor. She tugged the string after it.

I'm not sure what to do, she said.

With Colton?

In general.

What's that saying about not knowing where to go? I said.

We could ask my dad, she said, bitterly. She tweaked the gut in my cheek. The skin moved—an almost pleasant sensation. I wish we hadn't stopped you guys, she continued. I wish you'd never come.

She tied off the knot with a tug and swabbed the cut with a douse of iodine and a bolt of cheesecloth.

I am truly, truly sorry, I told her.

With just her pinky—same one she'd gnawed on—she hooked a stray hair behind her ear. I saw a missing chunk of skin at the bottom of her lobe, roughly the size of a belt buckle prong. She nudged the bundled shirt my way. It's Colt's, she said. Or it used to be.

I took it. It felt heavier than a shirt. Thank you.

Reparations, she said.

There's no need.

She flicked her hand—*stupid boy*. Her feet swung out and in. When they touched the balcony, I felt the vibrations and heard the knock—more a shush, a barely-touch. She must've done that often—sat out there with Colton, or maybe the boys. You can never know people. I had no business wishing.

She draped her legs over the balcony, propped her palms on the wood. We sat drumming our heels on the wood. I don't care to see Jack, she said, after a while.

Okay.

We were kids, Alan. Doesn't matter what he tells you. We were kids. We didn't want that.

Didn't want me, I said.

Her lips pressed together in an upside-down smile. Not even a frown—she didn't regret it, and she wouldn't refute the truth. I don't know if I should admire that or hate her for it, but I suppose it's fair to say that if I didn't exist then I wouldn't have chased after Jack or brought Archer to Owenswood, and Colton wouldn't be dead. I let that sink in, the immensity of it. It is possible to feel with conviction as though someone else deserves the life you have, or still have.

What will you do about him?

Bury him here.

Great place, Owenswood.

Fuck off, kid.

Fair enough, I thought. And Archer?

With her teeth, she torqued the nail of her pinky. Nothing? she said. Let him die?

Could go to the police.

You do what you want, but I won't be around to witness.

She got up and tucked the first aid kit under her arm. Please, let me take your Ranger.

Why's it matter?

The jeep will smell like Colton.

I took the Ranger's keys from my pocket and slid them toward her and they *jinkled* across the porch slats.

Do me a favour, kid?

Yes.

Don't report it stolen, for a while at least.

I can do that.

She swept her arm in the air in the general direction of everyone else. Her voice caught in her throat. Your grand-father did everything right, you know. Archer's always been in everyone's way. It's a giant clusterfuck. You can't choose your family or the people you care about, and nobody hurts you like those people. Doesn't matter how hard they try not to—your family fucks you over. There's my advice, Alan, straight from your mom. If you care to hear me.

I believe it, I said, though I didn't, and don't.

She blinked, twice—a flutter. All that ash and dirt in the eyes, it's a wonder we didn't blubber around, the lot of us. I saw her swallow, saw her flick something off her jeans. The fingernail *scritch*ed along the denim. Nobody had caused as much loss as Archer Cole. He didn't have much longer to live—a kindness, at least. To him and everyone else. He'd outlived his own happiness.

Jack's at a campground, at Caribou Bridge, not far west. He's been waiting to be asked home. He'll be happy to see you.

She slipped the Ranger's keys in her pocket.

I hope you find whatever it is you hope you find, she said. I truly do. It just ain't here, and I'll bet it ain't at Caribou Bridge. But that's for you to figure out, not me.

Thanks for patching me up, I said, and nearly—nearly—called her mom.

My mom was staring right toward me but not at me, as if addressing an earlier version of me, as if addressing a progenitor, or a father. I'd landed in the middle of something I would never fully understand. Our time together was drawing to an end without closure, and as each second passed my hope dwindled. But then again, I don't think I had hoped for anything at all: that I'd find my mother and father amidst the fallout from their pasts, maybe, or that I'd reunite a few old lovers, or that I'd get an explanation for why things happened as they did. *Why*, not *how*: that's a simple matter of trajectory.

All I want to know is what drove you to leave, I said.

She rapped the top of the tin box. She hung her head. It was the kind of moment when you should hang your head. There are so many ways to live, she rasped. So many ways life can go. And you have to pick, Alan, somehow, even though you can never know what's right. There might not even *be* a right. But you have to choose. I chose to leave. It was just more terrifying to stay.

Does that make you a coward?

She combed her pinky once more through her hair. It parted a small channel down her temple. What's worse, to be born a coward, or to choose to turn into one?

I looked at her, my mother. She licked her lips, rattled the keys in her pocket. If she said goodbye, I didn't hear it. She didn't go inside to say goodbye to Archer, that much I know— one more thing for him to regret. I listened to her rattle around in the kitchen. A freezer lid yawned wide and closed with its vacuumy thump. She placed a few cans of who knows what on one counter or another. Then the front door opened and closed, and I would not see her again.

The wind hushed down off the Purcells, a chinook almost, and breezed over my arms, lifted the hairs like goosebumps, but I sat there and stared at nothing and wished for a beer, or sleep. Maybe eastward Gramps and Darby did the same, at their version of the sunset. Maybe my mom did, too, as she settled into the driver's seat. We can never know other people, as I've already said.

From the yellow couch, myself peppered with its sticky foam, I watch Nora shuffle away. She's naked, has one hand pressed to her lower back, her neck rolling on her shoulders to work out kinks, aches, other pains of lovemaking. The house creaks, moans, seems to take a breath. Summer light glows through the basement window, the locked basement door—it makes her skin look the colour of suede. She stops at the entrance to the rec room, hand on the door frame.

Got any aspirin? she says, and I manoeuvre to a sit, then a stance, put a hand on her hip and nudge her toward the door at the base of the stairwell.

I'm steps away, no more—swear to God, just mere steps— but she reaches that door before I do, she opens it, and there's this sound like a cat's hiss, and then a fist of darkness billows from that door and strikes her square in the face. It takes a second, less: she drops like deadweight, so fast I can't catch her and I'm only mere feet away, and her head cracks on the concrete floor. Christ, I still remember it: her naked, tensed body slackening, her red hair like tassels in the wake of her descent. It's the last day I will ever spend as Cecil's friend, and part of me knows it, even then. The sound of her head on the concrete—it's the death knell for me and Cecil. Nora moans, her legs kick. I've ducked—instinct—and let the darkness fill the basement, thick as tar. Blood pools near her face, near the cleft of her legs. Then I'm at her side, and I kick the door shut, glimpse an orange glow at the landing, through the crack at the bottom. Charcoal, heat, the dryness of air that has had its moisture burned away—these are what I taste, smell. And the house breathes, exhales, cackles. It's on fire. It's breathing fire. Around me, above me, my house is burning.

THOSE WEEKS THAT FOLLOWED Linnea's leaving blurred like slate or sheetmetal skies. My days were punctuated by different moments of hoping for her to come back. Each morning I'd check the foyer for her shoes. After burying my head in the fridge, I'd close the door half expecting to find her standing cross-armed with her weight on the wall. At the end of a long shift I'd kill the ignition and search the house's windows for signs of light. I couldn't sit in one place with a beer. In the evenings I turned on the radio just to make it sound like the place wasn't so empty. Even Nora felt it, when she swung by—a coldness. And sometimes after sleeping with her I'd rouse, groggy, and stumble to the bathroom and pause on the way to listen to Linnea's quiet old room.

But no matter how much I missed her, I can say with authority that Jack missed her more. Not that he was one to make his feelings clear. You could see it, though—the squinch in his eyes, the bags on his cheeks that never diminished. Even in the way he held the baby, as if Alan West were a relic of a better time and nothing more. None of us had even told Jack the full extent of the circumstances, because nobody stood to gain by him knowing that she'd left with Crib. The last was Cecil's call, one evening in his living room where me and him were guarding Alan. Cecil wore his denims and his ballcap and he hadn't shaved, so scraggly hair patched his cheeks and some even showed in his ears, the old, ugly bastard.

It'd be a waste of day, Old Man West said, and pressed his thumbs to his temples, himself looking tired enough to die. The boy's going through enough. He doesn't need that.

Understanding, Cecil? I said. From you?

Got something on your mind?

You know what they say about understanding? It's in the dictionary between ulcer and urethra.

Just don't tell him, Archer.

Not a word.

I'll warn Nora, he said.

She probably already figured it out.

Yeah, she's got us outmatched, he said, and got up to fetch beers, came back with four so he wouldn't need to get up again. Across the room, Alan napped on the couch and Cecil watched our grandson even as he popped off the caps.

I don't know what to tell him, Cecil said. He sounded like he had congestion in his throat. Never had to deal with this, people just leaving you.

Guess I've been on both ends, I said.

He grunted at that. His bottle *clink*ed off his lower teeth, and he swore.

What do I tell him?

Tell him he'll be okay.

I don't know if that's true.

Yeah, I said. But tell him.

Doesn't seem right.

Sometimes you gotta. People don't always like the truth.

Fucking hate it. Even not telling him. You know?

I scratched my scarred arm—acting up with any shift in the weather, even a couple of warming degrees.

I know, I said. People don't need to know the truth all the time. A waste, like you said.

He gulped from his beer, flopped his ballcap onto the table. He looked like a man coming to terms.

We gotta talk to him.

We?

Well, mostly you.

Cecil.

He sighed, actually sighed.

This is your thing, Archer. Talking to people. I'm not gentle enough.

He's your son.

I'm asking you for a favour. It's what you do.

I took the beer from the table. And what do you do, old man?

I go around looking handsome.

Do a damn shitty job of it, too, let that be said.

IT TOOK SOME TIME for me to start the conversation with Jack. I have a number of excuses for that, but foremost among them was the fear that it would break his heart all over again; he was on the mend, but I know first-hand how long it can take and how quickly that mending can unravel. So I logged endless looping hours hauling lumber and pulled out of the Wests' lives for worry that I'd bring things down around me. Cecil swung by on occasional evenings to drink beer and shoot tin cans with the same rifle Jack had long ago used to put a bullet in my calf. Nora and I waved; our interactions outside the bedroom were impersonal and strained. Things had changed, I can't say what. Our affair felt dutiful now, rote. I'm not even sure her skin warmed when pressed against mine, if our breath would have been visible in cold air.

Jack had gone to work on upgrading Cecil's firepit with stones he hijacked from distant areas of the gravel pits— chunks as large as car tires he had to split with a sledge. Most evenings I could hear him behind their house, the hammer's beat methodical, and I can imagine his breath between each heave—a gasp, really—and every swing backed by the full of his strength, all his body could muster. He was beating out his frustration. He even kept on as the weather froze over, scored a pickaxe to break the hardening earth. He dug holes to level depths and plugged them with stone, chipped them flat if need be, until he'd built a spiral pattern in the dirt, a solid floor around his cinderblock pit. Cecil said Jack would sometimes light that blaze and sit there on a chunk of firewood and stare at the flames until they settled down to coals. Cecil said he let it happen—the whole project—and didn't help unless the boy asked, and then the two of them would cart boulders around by their bottoms, knees deep and knuckles damned near dragging on the ground like gorillas. They drank beer and sat close together to make small comments.

It was Nora who sent me to him, one afternoon while we huddled beneath blankets, close enough and content enough for me to call it a rarity. The winter would soon be coming to a close, maybe that had something to do with it—high spirits for once again surviving the killing months. Jack's mindless work clanged through the bedroom window and Nora shifted against me, prodded at my feet with her toes. She stretched, pushed on my face when she caught me looking.

Go talk to him, she said.

Been putting it off.

We know, she said. It was unusual for her to mention Cecil, even in passing.

I sat up and Nora fished around under the covers for her bra. She snapped it on while my back was turned, while I dragged my jeans over the floor.

Archer, she said, and I felt the wind of her breath on my back, twigged on a note of severity, and as I turned to her she looked tireder than I'd ever seen her. I'm pregnant, she said.

The news didn't even shock me, not then. But it certainly explained things.

Does Cecil know?

Of course Cecil knows.

I didn't know what to say to that. Her shoulders slouched, forearms across her thighs, sitting like a boy. That old house of mine had patches of cold in it—places where the insulation had probably gone moist or places that were renovated and some that weren't. We never lit a fire in the wood stove for fear that the chimney smoke would raise alarms. Water pooled on the windowsill and if I squinted I thought I could glimpse my breath in clouds. My crotch ached—a sudden pang.

Who? I tried to say, but she just pressed her cheek to my chest and we settled right back into the bed and Jack hammered at his firepit—*clang, clang, clang.*

NORA COUGHS, high and wheezy. When I press my ear to her chest her heart races like an athlete's, and I fight to remember the things Old Man West has told me about smoke inhalation and skin flaking like paper, airways and scar tissue and the human weakness to fire—all his stories over all those years. The house stinks. Trails of smoke sneak around the poorly framed basement door. The air feels orange, as if from a Polaroid photo. There's the taste of sulphur, guncotton, campfires. I gather Nora in my arms and slink for the exit and try not to think about what Cecil will do.

In the distance: sirens, the pop of lumber. Nora's clothes lay heaped on the couch and for a moment I consider dressing her. Then I reach the back door and move to open it but the key is not in the lock. And the key is not in my pockets, or on the windowsill, or among the shoes and debris at the door's base. I've got no way to open it—I'm trapped. And I all but hear Old Man West giving me shit for that door.

There's a single window I could have smashed and climbed through, but no way could I take Nora with me. Smoke twists across the ceiling, blue and heavy, bar-like. Nora's skin has gone clammy and I try gently to wake her but she coos, she moans. I kiss her forehead. Where, I remember thinking, was Cecil?

I lower Nora to the floor and reach for the knob and it damn near sears my palm. Heat pulses through that wood, tightens my cheeks the way shower steam does. My arm and the ruined skin on the bicep light up like it's '62 all over again, and I smell gasoline and the stink of rubber cement and hair burning like tar and it's all I can do to swallow my gag reflex. Then I'm in the jungle, that quick, on my knees with my sleeve in dark tatters, skin and muscles pus-white and the whole world cackling like death. A radio sizzles nearby, a black hand, boots and pieces of people and the air shimmers like a highway. It tastes like engine grease, the air—makes your tongue feel fat, coated. Friendly fire, someone screamed, right before whatever hit us hit us. Friendly fucking fire.

Nora moans from the other room, but it sounds weak, somewhere else—like hearing her through the ringing in my ears, or not even hearing her at all, same as when that bomb hit us, the disorientation. And I can't move to her, I can't pull out of those sounds, those smells. It's all the things that'd gone wrong come to life, there in the basement, there before me in the orange glow: the war and my breakup and Crib and the kid we couldn't save from the fireball. It's Linnea leaving and Jack's broken heart. It's Cecil hauling ass across the street to rescue me and his fiancée from the fire.

JACK GREW UP pretty fast that winter. He had his coat flown open when I rounded the corner, the pickaxe on his shoulder and a dotted line of sweat on his forehead—no gloves, no tuque. The fire cackled, lit the spiral of rockwork at my feet. He didn't look much like a boy anymore: the shadow of facial hair grazed his cheeks, his lip, and he'd let his hair grow out long enough that he'd soon be wearing a tie-dyed shirt. He was damn near as tall as me too, and not the scrawny, big-eyed boy I'd grown used to and somehow not come to miss. When he saw me, he lifted a boot onto a piece of firewood and buried the pickaxe to its T in the earth, swiped his hands over his jeans.

Hey, he said.

Hey, Jack.

Sit down, he said, and gave a slow point to one of the chop-logs that rimmed the pit. I did so, eased myself down onto it, spread my palms toward the blaze and felt my bicep give an itch, a pang. Never liked fire, even if it kept you warm and moving. Want a beer or anything?

I'm good, thanks.

Where's Nora? he said.

What? I said, snapped my eyes to him.

He motioned past me with his chin, toward the house; the lights had gone on. There she is, he said.

He twirled his finger in a spiral, traced an invisible arc around the rocks he'd embedded in the ground. If you like what you see here, I could do the same for you.

I followed the path—for that's almost what it was, a path you could walk, stone to stone to stone—with my eyes; it filled the whole circle of light that the fire cast. Between each rock was brown earth, packed to level; in the summer he'd seed it and grow grass and it'd be a decent stand-in for a patio—it'd be the kind of place you could host a good barbecue, the kind of place other people eyed with jealousy. I can't say for certain where he'd learned to work, but it sure paid off. Inherited it from birth.

Hell, I might take you up on that, I said.

You look tired, he said.

I don't sleep much, yeah.

He nodded, a single quick jerk of his head. I hear ya, Archer.

I know you do.

They send you this way to give me a pep talk?

That transparent?

You and my dad, man. Not exactly masters of subterfuge.

Where's the old bastard, anyway?

At the fire hall not working.

Or working hard.

He's got you fooled, then.

It's mutual, I said, raised an eyebrow that made Jack shake his head. The kid?

He pointed at a window, cocked open an inch.

If he wakes, I'll hear him.

What're you gonna tell him, when he's old enough to ask?

Jack prodded at the fire, gave the flames some breath.

The truth, I guess? Or maybe I'll be married again by then, can keep it all a deep dark secret.

Or maybe Linnea'll come back, I said, and Jack's lips inched to a smile. He poked the fire again, sat down on one of the chop-blocks, knees bowed out and elbows on his thighs. He hung his head. Smoke whirled clockwise around the fire, almost in a spiral, too, and when it enveloped Jack he muttered something, some superstition to ward the billow away.

That would have been the time to say something. But maybe it feels better not to. Jack and me sat that comfortable distance and let the smoke dance circles. It was the kind of night when you might expect to see the northern lights, though they're rare enough in the valley. Jack drew a Zippo from his pocket and sparked a flame—three inches, like a carnival trick. It was the lighter he took from Crib, that time Cecil chased Crib away, and I guess Jack kept it as a trophy or maybe a reminder of what he'd lost. To be honest, I'm not sure which is more likely to be the Wests' way of doing things.

And then I noticed that Jack's rock work not only filled the firelight but snaked beyond, stretched outward and got wider and spread into the darkness—he'd laid stone over most of the whole goddamned yard. It looked meticulous as all hell—evenly spaced and levelled and I can't imagine when he'd have had time to do anything else—for instance, to be a father.

Jack stood up when he saw me notice, moved to the pickaxe and hefted it off the dirt, its head cradled in the palm of his hand, the whole thing held horizontal at his hip. His shoulders rocked back with inhalation, came forward with the weight of the axe. It's how you'd breathe if you were really tired, or really angry, or if you had something to say you'd not wanted to say for a long, long time.

I know you're fucking Nora, he said.

He moved the pickaxe to his shoulder, like I'd seen Cecil do—a stance that meant *I can't wait to see what you've got to say*.

That's a bold claim.

I haven't told my dad.

Why not?

Linnea asked me not to.

You talk to Linnea? I said.

He grimaced. She's the one who told me.

She told you?

Said someone besides her needed to know, just in case.

In case what?

His hand torqued the pickaxe in the air; it slid down and caught at his shoulder. Then he shrugged his dumb-boy shrug and gave me an ear-to-ear grin, as if to say, *She played you like a fool, old man*.

I knew she was leaving, months before she left, I told him.

His big smile wiped in a second, less. Why didn't you tell me? he said, and he squinted now—smoke in the eyes.

She didn't want me to.

I could have changed her mind.

She said she didn't think you'd make a good dad.

He made a sucking noise; wind passed over his teeth. It looked like he had something to say. Instead he pinched his eyes shut, strode out into the darkness where my eyes lost sight of him. I squinted and searched but they wouldn't adjust. The firelight heaved, glinted off the rocks as if they had a sheen on them. It was cold, but not damningly so; my breath made fog. Jack scuffled around beyond the reach of my vision. He snorted, suppressed sobs. I don't exactly feel proud about the way that transpired, let me say that.

Get back here, I called. Not like it's the first time I've heard you cry.

Then he went dead quiet, and I imagined him out there glaring in, me just this hunched old man in a sphere of light. It was the same damn thing, maybe, as all those years ago. I got lazy; I didn't scope the yard or the layout and, hell, I didn't do a very good read on Jack West.

He appeared beside me, to my blindside, and levelled a punch like I can guess Cecil had been teaching him to do for years. Right at the temple, right at the ear—that's where he hit me, and I went down with a ring in my head as if someone had fired a shotgun. I hit the rock wrist-first and Jack grabbed my coat and fell upon me. He hauled me over onto my back and I felt older than ever before. He booted a wood-chop stool aside and hauled me across the buried stone. There he was: Jack West, red and orange and uplit like something risen from the fiery earth.

This won't make you feel better, I said, but he didn't hear me, not then, not through the adrenaline and rage and the fire and me scratching over rock and dirt.

He advanced. I booted him in the shin, scrambled backward. Cold spiked up my wrist. He retaliated, drove a steeltoe to my thigh so hard the whole leg went numb. Christ, he was going to kill me—I was sure of it. That may be the closest I've ever come to dying; not any of my time in Vietnam under attack, or at the hours in a military hospital with my arm flaking like braised meat, the mutters of may-or-may-not. I should've known better than to visit Jack while he tended a fire. I never, *ever* have good luck around fire.

His boot kicked out again but I caught the leg against my chest, a textbook trap.

What're you gonna tell Alan? I said. That you killed his grandpa?

He dropped his knee to my chest and we were grappling, my hands on his coat and neck and his palm in my face. I dug for the soft part at the base of the throat. He wedged an elbow inside my arms, brought his other leg in to pin my bicep and we hung like that a moment, muscles cinched and teeth clenched and our throats throttling deep, low-key growls. And I realized I didn't even want to fight him, or that I couldn't bring myself to keep fighting him—this, the son of Cecil West—or that maybe, simply, it wasn't right. So I let go. I let him have it. And I remember his fist at his ear, the colour of the knuckles like plywood, stove elements, rust, and not much else until Nora's voice from the rear step.

Jack! she called, and I blinked through tears and blood to look at her—dressed in one of Cecil's work coats so it sagged on her shoulders. She crossed her arms, hugged the flannel tight. Really, Jack?

He breathed horse-like above me, great snorts of fog that clouded out his nostrils. His fist was still at his ear, red and wrecked with blood, and he had a handful of the front of my shirt, had it twisted for a tight grip that curled me forward off the ground. My head hung half-loose. I choked up blood, spat sideways, tasted snot, sweat, metal. Tears stung my eyes—nose shots, blinding shots—and I pinched them shut one after the other.

You don't know what he said, Jack yelled to her.

I don't think I care.

You're not my mother.

You don't have a mother.

Fuck you.

Get off him, Nora said. She sounded like Cecil, that mix of exasperation and authority.

You're fucking him, Jack said. He hadn't relaxed his grip.

Yes, Nora said, and Jack's eyes shut and his neck craned sideways and I don't know, I don't know. The poor kid. And you can tell Cecil if you want.

No I can't, he growled. Why did you?

Sorry, kid, I started to say, but he shoved me down.

Not you. I'm not surprised by you. You just take, that's all you do.

Mistakes happen, Nora said. We're good people.

He was looking at her now. He let go of my shirt and I rested my head, rested the muscles in my neck.

My dad's a good person. This'll kill him.

Then don't let him find out.

That's what I've been doing, he said. And how can

you ask that? That I lie to him while you go on—go on fucking?

It's your call, kid, I said.

Fuck you, Archer, shut the fuck up.

I'm sorry about Linnea, Nora said.

This isn't about Linnea, Jack yelled. He gestured at me, a dismissive wave of his hand. This is about you, Nora. What do you even see in him?

Jack—

Well? This nobody? This—this thief?

Nora's eyes fell to me then, and I sensed myself being appraised in a way I never had been before. It's like you need a certain kind of light to really see people, like you need to be made to evaluate and judge. We are excellent at not seeing what is motionless right there in front of us.

I see the man I once wanted your dad to be, Nora said.

Jack held me a moment longer, poised still to strike me, and then he shoved off and left me there on the stone and stormed over to Nora, fists clutched on the hem of his shirt like when he was a kid. Nora stood her ground—of course she stood her ground—until he towered above her, somehow small beneath her gaze. I didn't know what could happen, what could've happened. Neither of them moved, the firelight seemed to dim, I struggled to a sit and wiped a sleeve over my gums. Maybe that was a last chance, that evening—maybe one of us really needed to tell Jack it'd all be okay, or maybe he should have beat me to death. I can't say.

Then he pushed past her, shoulder clipped shoulder, and a minute later his shadow appeared in Alan's room and the window snapped shut. Nora leaned on the side of the house, closed her eyes, shook her head—so disappointed. I touched the shape of my nose, the state of my face, didn't immediately bring myself to look at her.

Well, I croaked.

Don't you dare crack a joke, she said. Her voice sounded like a mother's, a schoolteacher's. I had never seen her cry, never seen her weaken. She put us all to shame, every last one of us. Any woman like that deserves better than me—don't think I don't know it.

Is it even worth apologizing?

Yes, Archer. Holy fuck.

Well then, I said. I'm sorry.

She dragged hair behind her ear, first one side of her face and then the other. She looked so damn good there on the concrete step.

Don't you think you say that a bit too often? she said, and went inside and killed the light and I stayed on the stone, beaten and tired, and let myself grow cold as the coals dimmed down.

THE FIRE MADE a noise, a great ghostlike *oooh*, and something inside snapped me back into the world. I kicked the stairwell door, blind with panic. Smoke puffed between its seams and it looked as if the door was bulging, and some primal part of me knew well enough that I had to get away. By then I had to slouch-walk under the veil of smoke, and even the air below was turning to fog that parched my throat and nostrils. I went back to Nora, to our only possible exit, and I booted that door as hard as I could, and it didn't so much as budge—it was designed with a deadbolt to keep people out. A better man could have kicked it off its hinges, I believe that.

Then the door shook again, from the outside.

Archer? Cecil called.

Thank fuck, I said.

Get this door open, get the fuck out.

I don't have my key.

Then use the window.

I can't.

He paused—*why not?*

I fucking told you, he said. Then: I'll get my axe.

I didn't hear him depart, not over the crackle. Nora wheezed and her eyes fluttered open and I looked down at her: watery, but of course they were—she'd taken a blast of smoke to the face. I wanted so much to tell her everything'd be alright, even if I couldn't know whether or not it would. So I squeezed her close and thought about the things I'd say to her fiancé when he came bashing through that door. There, in that burning house, I could count the minutes that remained of my happy time in Invermere, B.C. Even friendship has an expiry date.

Wood creaked overhead and I had a sudden, terrifying fear that the floor above me would cave. Then Cecil axed the door at the latch, splintered a hole, and as the first light blazed through the split in the wood I felt the fire upstairs draw breath, felt the heat rescind like waiting lungs. I cushioned Nora's head against my bicep, adjusted her weight in my arms. Her muscles tensed, arm and collar and neck, all the way to her jaw. My other arm, cradling her legs, was soupy with blood. I wish I had been nearer her—that I'd opened the door into that first blast of smoke, that I'd been quicker, had caught her before her head bounced on the concrete. The way she went down—Christ, just like she'd taken a bullet. The house smelled like charcoal, and so did she, so would the outside world, my clothes, Cecil. The heat warmed my neck and I hazarded a look behind me, to the dark hallways and the ochre glow spilling like sunset beneath the stairway door.

Then Cecil bellowed for me to back up, and he booted that door open with a flat-footed kick, and there he was, Cecil West, some maniac Canadian, haloed by the whiteout that glowed behind him. I can still remember it—his initial, wry smile (*Warned you about that door*, I bet he was ready to say) bent toward the brim of his half-cocked ballcap, his action-movie posture, elbows flung wide, axe handle draped over his shoulder like some lumberjack supreme. Jeans: soot-stained and grime-smeared, handprints in streaks. Shirt: wet in a dark V, framed by a checkered coat. And I remember how quickly his expression changed, how it hung first in a moment of not-understanding—a temporary disconnect, a gap between expected and actual—at seeing Nora in my arms, Nora, who should have been in Cranbrook. Fiancée, best friend, fire— then he went neutral. No anger, pure neutrality. Almost as if he'd suspected it—but of course he'd suspected it. We are, if nothing else, jealous and suspicious men.

He stepped aside so I could get out, and we jogged across the street while the fire consumed my home. I laid Nora on the grass beneath her crabapple tree, saw the blood on my forearm with dread, as if she'd taken a wound. Cecil's jaw clacked in circles, like chewing cud. He crossed his arms and gripped big handfuls of his denim coat. Jack, on the driveway, watched us and the fire and us again. Beside him: Alan, held stiff beneath a firm hand.

Start the fucking truck, Cecil yelled to his son.

Nora was breathing, coughing. I knelt beside her but Cecil hip-checked me aside and, in the same action, draped his coat over her. He put his ear to her mouth, he brushed hair off her face, tugged a strand from the corner of her lips. Her skin looked clammy and wrinkled, like she'd been in a lake, like she'd almost drowned.

What happened? Cecil said.

Smoke inhalation, banged her head, I said.

Didn't catch her?

I wasn't nearby.

Fancy that.

He let his wrist hang off his knee, put his other hand to his chin—pensive.

Why's she bleeding? he said, but I could barely hear him.

Old man—

That's not my name.

He turned his head to profile, enough that I could see the scrunch of his nose and lip and I thought he must've got some smoke in his eyes, too. Cecil emptied his lungs and at least some of his stomach. His hands had squeezed to fists. He was going to beat the living shit out of me—anyone could see it.

I guess I don't have to ask what you were doing, he said. He flicked his hand at me. I hung at a distance. Jack got into the truck, Alan on his lap. They rolled down the driveway.

This how you do things? Cecil said. He pivoted so he could see my house go up in flames behind me. A guy gives you all this and you shoot him in the back. That your thing, Archer?

Say whatever you want.

He drew from his pocket a Zippo lighter, adorned with the American flag. He hefted it, didn't stand.

Found this outside your house, he said, and tossed it to me.

It had a smudgy fingerprint on it. I turned it over in my hand.

A paper burn pile, near your deck, Cecil said. Untraceable. Only a fireman's kid would know that.

Jack rolled up behind me, in the truck. He looked about as pale as the dead.

What are you going to do? I said, to Cecil.

What would you do, Captain Forgiveness.

I don't know.

You forgive Linnea yet, for leaving you here?

She didn't leave me.

Right, he said, and cupped his hands on his chest. Crib *took her*. Or maybe Crib *saved* her.

Fuck you, Cecil.

You don't see it, you blind fuck. The way people look at you. Nobody is close to you.

Your fiancée is.

He showed his gums, still didn't stand up, just knelt beside Nora, there on the cool grass.

And it turned out about as well for her as it did for your daughter.

Go fuck yourself.

Finally, he stood up. Ballcap, wrinkled jaw, eyes squinched to pearls. An enemy now—and bigger than I thought, or had noticed. Maybe you don't see your friends for what they are. Or maybe you do, and Cecil had seen me for what I was all along. He took his ballcap off and set it on the ground beside Nora, probably so it wouldn't obscure his view, so he could pin his chin to his chest and graze my haymakers off his forehead, get inside my guard.

Not so wise now, he said. No wise-man saying to tell me how to raise my son? You sure done well with your daughter.

My fists curled, almost against my will, that pulse of adrenaline in your spit glands that makes you want to chew your tongue. Cecil brought his guard up, right arm forward— a southpaw when it came to haymakers. He hadn't been in a fight since I showed up in the valley. His army training was limited. His age was a disadvantage. He still had no real scars on his wrinkly face except those burn marks on his chin, little dents lining the ridge of his jaw like a set of leftover stitches. He looked like an army vet now. I wondered how long this had been coming, if one or both of us had known all along that we would part ways on blows.

Cecil's fists fell to his sides.

I'm not gonna fight you, Archer, he said, and knelt to scoop his cap. He brushed it off, two sweeps of his palm, though it wasn't dirty. He placed it on his head, straightened it. Every time he moved I twitched, my heart thumped in my throat. I'd lost some kind of battle right then, but I don't know what. I simply don't know. The way he looked at me, looked down at me.

You think you're so wise.

I don't know what I think anymore.

He cradled Nora in his arms, murmured something to her that must have been comforting, because her fingers dug his forearm—something that hadn't happened when I held her in the same way, carried her from the fire. I still don't know what Cecil had that I didn't.

He jerked his chin toward Jack.

The boy know?

Why would he? I said.

You're all buddy-buddy, you two. I'll ask you again, Archer: does Jack know?

We breathed at each other. There'd be no more lies between us.

Old man, I said, but he brushed past me. Jack opened the passenger door and Cecil stomped toward him, each step so heavy it left divots in the earth.

Cecil! I hollered, but he didn't stop, just laid Nora in the passenger seat and did a first-class job of ignoring me. I watched him tuck her feet under his big coat, buckle her in. He skirted the truck's hood and hauled open the driver door, and when Jack didn't immediately get out he grabbed his son's coat and dragged him down with way more force than a father should. Jack staggered, nearly lost his balance. He didn't say a word. Then, with all the gentleness of a grandfather, Cecil lifted Alan under the arms—the boy giggling, happy to see Grandpa—and handed him to Jack.

JACK HADN'T BUDGED from his yard when I stopped my truck in front of him. Alan wobbled on his feet and Jack held him still with one fatherly hand on the shoulder. The fire shuddered. More red-and-white lights whirred around the curve at the end of the road. Men Cecil must've known piled onto the street.

Get in, I said.

Where's your shirt? Jack said.

On fire.

Jack lifted Alan through the passenger door and I took his small body under the arms, and he giggled. He'd been dressed in a red sweatshirt that said *Speed Demon*, had short, curled hair, eyebrows that I bet would one day lift incredulously at almost anything a person could say.

I'll get you a shirt, Jack said, and jogged to the house. Across the street, everything I owned was getting consumed, but I didn't care—maybe couldn't care. Alan hopped on my knee, put his pudgy palms on the wheel and did his damnedest to turn it. I steadied him, kept my hand on his small back, spanned almost the whole of his shoulder blades, thumb to pinky.

Jack returned with a plain grey T-shirt footballed under his arm. He handed it off.

It's mine, he said.

He climbed in and I passed Alan over to him, dropped the truck into gear and started our trek to the hospital. I know you set the fire, I said.

I know you know, I heard Jack say. He reached over, buckled Alan down in the middle seat as if that'd make any difference at all. The truck mounted the steep hill out of the subdivision. We passed the hostel full of dope smokers who gave us thousand-yard stares as we rolled on by. The streets were warped and shitty, like always. Everything made me think of Cecil.

Believe me—I had no idea you were in there, Jack said. And I'm really sorry for that.

But not for the fire itself?

He chewed on that one. Alan grabbed for the gearshift and I nudged his hands aside. Jack lowered his window, squinted at the sky, the horizons, the mountains. There was a cave on one of them, shaped like a bent tin can, and you could see it as we crested the hill. The mountains don't change, much like that town. Jack leaned his elbow on the window frame, wiped a clear smudge on the dust of the mirror. Maybe people don't change either, despite what the adage says. Maybe you just get better at seeing them.

No, Jack said, as we drove straight west toward the hospital. I'm not sorry for that.

At least you're honest.

He looked down at Alan, poked his son in the shoulder, retracted before he got noticed. The boy grinned.

You believe in God, Archer?

Yes.

Then I'll get what's coming for me.

You won't need God for that, kid. There's Cecil.

He smiled the kind of smile you wear when remembering a better time. I could spot that a mile away. Well, he said, and left it at that.

I veered us into the hospital's parking lot, killed the engine, and the three of us sat there like men soon to be hanged. Jack smacked himself in the thighs, drew breath. He undid Alan's buckle and lifted him over to me.

You can stay with me a while, I said, not understanding why I'd say that, right then, to Jack West of all people. Wherever I end up. At least until you're on your feet. If you need to.

Thanks but no thanks, Archer, he said. We looked at the emergency doors, sliding open and closed, like chewing. I'll go on up. You don't need to bear witness.

Your call, kid.

Why are you so okay with this? he said, and lifted his arms in a grand shrug.

I'm getting old, I said, as if that counted, and Jack clicked the door open and made his way high-headed through the hospital doors. Alan mashed on the truck's horn and it gave a truncated bleat, but the mouth of those doors had already shut and Jack, even if he'd heard it, wouldn't have had the chance to turn and look.

THEY CAME OUT of the hospital together, Jack in the lead and Cecil mere steps behind—almost like a hostage situation. Jack had red eyes with baggy circles beneath. Old Man West kept his hands in his pockets, his chin to his chest, took shallow steps that scuffed along the asphalt. I positioned myself between them and Alan, as absurd as that was.

Jack tells me you're taking him in, Cecil called, way earlier than was natural. Bit fucked up, I gotta say.

Won't have to if you don't give your own son the boot.

No son of mine, he said, and Jack squeezed his eyes shut.

He didn't know we were in there, Cecil.

He knew you were a *we*.

That what this is about?

Smart guy like you can see how that might factor in.

Smart guy like me can see you're about to lose the last person you're close to.

Real close, Cecil said.

I didn't want to hurt you, Dad, Jack said.

Well at least someone cares.

Nora didn't either, I said.

Cecil showed his gum, made a *tsk* sound. He spat at my feet, wiped his mouth with his sleeve. How bloody noble, he said. Then he stepped forward past Jack, reached with two hands for Alan, and I slid sideways, hip-checked his arms aside.

Cecil straightened, raised himself to height, a twinkle in his eye: G*ive me a reason*.

Archer, I swear to God, he said, and reached again and I let him, and so did Jack. Cecil hefted Alan in one arm, faced us both. And that was probably it—the end of something.

How's Nora? I said.

Miscarried, he said. Mary-Rose, we'd have called her. I understand that Rose was your idea.

I'm sorry, Cecil.

Oh I know, he said.

I took my keys from my pocket, flipped them to Jack. Go home, I told him. Cecil didn't so much as blink; Cecil didn't so much as try to stop him.

Nora'll be coming your way when she's cleared, Cecil said.

Jack did as I said, left me there with Old Man West. We squared off, us two, same as we did so long ago at his cabin. I won't say we'd come full circle, because we never really started off as enemies, we started on misunderstanding. But there was none of that here, there was just us.

You want to put this behind us? he said, shifted Alan to his other arm. Me to tell you it's okay, no problem, best of luck to ya?

He set Alan down; the boy latched on to his grandpa's jeans. Cecil rubbed his jaw, stared beyond me at who knows what. I imagined the ruins of my house. Cecil put his hands back in his pockets, probably to stop himself, but Alan pulled away, as if to come to me, and Cecil's palm shot to his shoulder.

If I ever see you again, Archer, I'll kill you.

You don't mean that.

You've taken enough from me, he said. Stay away from my grandson.

He's my grandson too.

No, he's not.

And if I don't?

I'll turn you over to the army.

You don't mean that, I said, and his chest deflated. But I'll stay away.

I heard his teeth click shut. You wrecked everything.

For what it's worth, Cecil?

Fuck off, he told me, and shoved his hands in his pockets, squeezed his eyes to beads. And I mean that.

NORA AND I LEFT INVERMERE. We'd see Jack again, briefly—a short stint with us at our new place before he left to seek greener fields. I'd offer him a wad of cash—not sure why. Some obscure sense of responsibility or duty, maybe. He wouldn't take it, of course, and I probably saw that coming. He'd cross an ocean and more countries than I can name. He was ever a wanderer, not someone you can pin down in location or intention or, let it be said, stability. Poster boy for a prodigal son, Jack West.

The town felt like it had drifted from the mainland. Our roots weren't deep enough; I'd shed no sweat in the sculpting of that place. Which is not to say that I made the decision with ease; there was blood of mine in Invermere's soil, happy years and dry summers and long, good winters—memories that you can't shake even after decades. If I didn't owe Cecil so much, if I hadn't ruined him like I did, no force could have driven me from my grandson. But I suppose we can't control everything, and sometimes events don't pan out. Nora held my hand when we last climbed into my truck, and I won't pretend that I could have done it without her. We weren't even sure where we'd end up, but if you don't know where you're going then all roads lead there.

Cecil didn't come out of his house once, at least not so that I could see him, but he may have been keeping a low profile precisely for this reason. I can't imagine how lonely his house must have been, the echo of every leaking tap, the noises of Alan's toddling that would have cried out for a mother, or even a father—how depressing it must have been to round a corner to the kitchen with that subtle expectation for company, anticipation panging in him like a hunger. I took everything from Cecil West.

When we left, not even a truck full of things between us,

it was early morning, so early I hoped Cecil would be asleep, though this strikes me as pure fantasy. We made one lap past the house—Nora asked for it—and as we crept along I listened to the road gristle under the treads. We lingered only a moment, Nora's jaw set and her hair loose and at her shoulders, nudged by the warm air breathing from the radiator. It was like she had always known it would come to this. It was like I did, too. They say it is possible to love more than one person, and I believe that because I have to.

We drove out of town, onto the long, mesmerizing stretch of highway south, through forest that would one day be scorched to husks, around treacherous curves that would inherit names like Deadman's Twist, over a bridge that a homemade biplane would demolish in what witnesses would say looked like the impact of artillery. I've kept track of that highway, of the things that happen to it, as if it's an escape route, a slug trail I left behind on the slouch to Cranbrook— the long and only way home.

We drove. The Rockies kept pace, rigid and adolescent in the lifespan of geology, their peaks white-capped like the tips of a butane flame, like the pictures of mountains you draw when you're a kid. The air smelled of forest. Trees were thick trunked and dense on the roadside, as green as health, and the sunlight glared off the rooftops and made me squint, made my eyes dry right out, made them water.

I have learned that the heart is a resilient thing. Regret, loss, grief, guilt—these are not pains the heart will suffer long, but they are pains that stay as deep as muscle memory, present in each heartbeat and pulse of blood, in every chest pang that jolts you awake, afraid. I've been on both the receiving and the giving end of these pains, so I can say this with some degree of authority: they never go away. You never forget them. You live among them as if they're camouflaged, cusping the threshold of your awareness, until something catches the light: your wife towelling bathwater from her hair, like she must have done time and again with the friend you stole her from; a father and son kicking stones along the street, so content in one another's company; even the landscape, the mere presence of it, as large as imagination and possibility, as large as forgiveness, that should—but doesn't, truly doesn't—make insignificance of the worries of men.

EIGHT

Aristotle:
All human actions have one of these seven causes:
chance, nature, compulsion, habit, reason,
passion, and desire.

For many years, Jack West had lived only a few hundred kilometres from my mom, in a town called Caribou Bridge—not even a town, more a place people drive through on their way to better things. It lay at the base of three mountains in some sort of prismatic valley hailed for its winter skies. The journey'd only last hours, me once again cowboying through the flint-dry forest with its pine needles gone coppery and stinking, unbelievably, of metal.

I set out early on the morning following Colton's death. We all slept uneasily, and in the bleeding hours with the sun barely luminant I rose and found the boys already awake—two kids who never shut their eyes. They gave me the keys no questions asked, and I dragged myself gaming with fatigue to the kitchen where I shoved two cups of day-old coffee down my throat. My cheek ached, though less than you'd think. I traced the stitches with my fingers. Residual adrenaline, maybe. Self-delusion, more likely. Archer snored on a seventies-yellow couch and I thought about waking him to say *see you later, old man*, but I didn't have the stomach to look him in the eye—I didn't have the stomach to hear him justify himself. Then I drove out of the town with the dim sun warming my shoulders.

Dust had collected on the highway as if it were a mantel-piece; behind me, the jeep's tires left two finger-streaks in their wake. I fought to keep my eyelids up and more than once considered a few winks on the roadside. The air tanged with the static of a thunderstorm, a taste way back in my throat. I passed an abandoned car, the hatch thrown open, plastic bags scattered in a panic and weighted to the earth by contents I would never know. Township billboards rusted, long in disrepair. A wooden sign said *Fresh fruit—200 metres*, but two hundred metres later there was no fruit stand to find. Everywhere: the leftovers of people's lives. On the seat beside me, Gramps' maroon box sat uncovered, the unexplained postcards fading to the colour of wheat. I twisted the radio's dial and through the broken static heard Baritone Radio Man at his post. The jeep had that diminished smell of dog, like a pile of basement coats—a temporary bed, now abandoned.

My whole body ached with fatigue and emotions I couldn't get my head around; it felt like effort to even let my blood pump. I worked my palms on the steering wheel, counted my knuckles left to right until they became too much like sheep and threatened to make my eyelids droop. Then I pulled over on the blastland roadside and killed the ignition and let the morning's drought rasp in through the window while the engine ticked cool. The hours on the road had made me thirsty, not prophetic. I'd spent so much time trying to get to Jack that I hadn't put in a moment to consider what I'd say when I got there. It wasn't like I had feelings for him—some resentment, maybe—or that I thought he'd dealt me a great wrong. It was Gramps to whom Jack owed an apology, if he'd give it, and if Gramps would receive it; I have few complaints about my upbringing. But I didn't know what to expect, now that I'd at last zeroed in on the man who could've been my father. Drunk? Resistant? In denial? Or worse: would he shuffle from his house with his shoulders slumped, with nondescript features, a defeated-looking man in grey sweatpants and a sports-team windbreaker, ready to admit that, yes, he'd been wrong—so very, very wrong—and that the last three decades had been a terrible waste? That worried me. And I also worried that the whole goddamned search and scour was some masquerade, Gramps' heavy-handed way of setting things right. It doesn't take an idiot savant to see Gramps' logic: he needed someone to look out for me, needed to hand off the burden of parenthood.

Then I restarted the jeep and set off, having figured out not a thing.

Years ago, Gramps drove us through Caribou Bridge, en route to the west coast; back then, the town was summed up by a single motel, after its namesake—the Bridge. Not much had changed; the streets spread out from the motel at its centre where the main haul looped it like a moat. Shops that keep

a town alive—the liquor store, the grocery, the post office—
dotted that strip, and I cruised around it in lazy laps. By that
time in August, the wildfires had mounted the broadside of
the not very distant mountains, and smoke sizzled into the
air above them like three great, grey-haired legs. Ash and soot
coated everything: the jeep's hood and its windshield smeared
as though by oil, the eavestroughs of local houses, the grim-
skinned faces of those few remaining kids who dared the
outdoors and whose parents had elected to hold the line.

I parked in front of a shed-sized brick building cordoned
off from the grocery store. Canada Post's red sign was nailed
lopsided to the brickwork; holes and the rusted leftovers of
concrete anchors dotted the wall where the sign had previ-
ously hung—torn off by thunderstorms, teenagers without
proper angst outlets, old Father Time. It was a long shot, both
that the office would be open—the town had evac'd—and that
they'd know Jack well enough to direct a stranger to him. I
unfolded from the jeep and stood in the dregs of daylight and
imagined, had that town been populated, that people would
have watched me with shifty sideways eyes, would have shut-
tered their windows and clutched infants to their breasts.
Across the street, in a lawn chair on the gravel parking lot of
the Bridge motel, a rockstar-haired guy older than me nursed
a beer.

They're not taking mail, he hollered.

I tugged on the hem of my shirt and gathered what
remained of my endurance.

I'm actually looking for Jack West, I called, and made my
way toward him.

Think these fires are coming? he said. I'm Trevor, by the way. Guess I run this thing behind me here.

You guess? I said. He had the squint of hangover, the early stages of beer gut. His nose curved off-centre and fatigue lines shadowed his cheekbones, dark as grease smears. But he was relaxed-looking there, had the posture of a guy just happy to talk. He'd given up fighting. My name's Alan.

Trevor patted his thighs—baggy, newly washed jeans—and swept his hands outward, to indicate everything.

Family fucked off, certain the fires would take the place, he said. But these mountains never let us down before. Hell, they could landslide any minute if they wanted to. Worst you get is the occasional mountain cat, and that's not more than an uninvited guest. I know old Jack, odd case, but he'd give you the shirt off his back. Good guy to drink beers with.

I'm his son.

That's unexpected, Trevor said. He picked at the label of his beer, but I hadn't seen him take a sip. Maybe he just liked to set an image.

I've been getting that impression.

He never mentioned any kids. I guess I never thought to ask. You look about as smart as him.

Did he evac?

A smile teased its way onto Trevor.

Not Jack, no. He's at the campground, I suspect. Unless he tried to canoe his way out. Want a beer? I bought a stash, soon as I found out everyone was leaving. Keeps me from being lonely.

No thanks, Trevor.

I'm sensing this is not a happy reunion, eh?

Misery begets, I said.

Trevor let his chin tip toward his chest—not quite a nod.

You gonna cause him trouble? he said, no hint of threat, or warning, or judgment.

I don't know, I said, honestly.

Well, head north outta town until you hit the turnoff marked by a tractor tire. That's the campground he owns. Tell him I said hello, unless you're going to kill him, in that case don't tell him I said hello.

I hope this place doesn't burn up, I said.

I still got my van. If it comes to it, I'll load up whoever's left and make for high ground.

He finally sipped his beer and pressed it, afterward, to his forehead, eyes closed and his features loose in a way of great relief. I almost reconsidered his offer, but I needed my wits, needed to be able to coerce and threaten and guilt Jack into piling into my commandeered jeep. Gramps had waited long enough.

A PADLOCKED GATE barred entry to the campground's parking lot, so I abandoned the jeep on the roadside and cleared the fence with ease. The grounds had a communal roasting-pit with slate slabs laid out in a spiral and chop-logs set in a ring around the pit. A ways off: RV hookups for American campers who liked their satellite TV, a panelboard hut that said *Hot Showers—25¢*. Opposite that, somebody had attached a log cabin to a long, flat building with rusted-out flashing. Within, I saw the dim glow of small-wattage bulbs.

Administration, it read. It had a wheelchair ramp, greening wood steps, windows gone unwashed, and shingles curling up like anxious, thirsty tongues. In the distance, where tenters would pitch camp, the residue of cookfires trailed away in a line. Overhead, and blotting the sun, columns of smoke drummed skyward, wide and twisted as barbicans, and the daylight barely pierced the cloudscreen. But for once it didn't smell like burning wood—it smelled like my childhood, like good times with Gramps. This is where I came from, I thought. And then: I could die here—all it'd take was a shift in the wind.

My palms had gone sweaty, so I wiped them on the hem of my shirt. The campground was in decent shape; I had expected rust and disrepair, the stink of garbage and of meat burned to charcoal, a dirt-and-gravel slaptogether where drunks would stagger rather than home to their wives. But Jack's campground was clean, landscaped, the trees thick with greenery and life. Quaint, I guess. Like a home. Around the administration building, he'd planted bushes; I heard the *tick-a-tick-a* of a sprinkler, some ways off, probably in disregard of water regulation—and ridiculous, either way. The whole moment, all the time it took me to take it in, was like stepping into someone else's dream: a striped canvas lawn chair had been angled at the setting sun—it looked well-sat-in; at the foot of the green-wood stairs, a football tottered in the wind; inside the house, a low orange light flared up, and then went dark. I felt like I was on the verge of a memory, or on the outside of one, looking in. A dog ought to have barked, or a bird of prey should have wheeled skyward and away. But instead I got the silence of a place devoid of woodlife, a place abandoned. Caribou Bridge was a ghost town to more than the people who'd forsaken her homes.

He came out of the cabin in a ballcap and a khaki shirt, in blue jeans faded at the thighs and scuffed boots that could've been military. Average height, my height, with a bare lip—I expected a moustache?—and sideburns peppered grey. Forty-seven, he must've been, or forty-eight. His cheekbones were visible beneath his eyes and shadowy with sleepless bags and as he approached I saw or imagined the pupils constricted to beads, the whites veiny as Christmas mints—drinking alone, here beyond the end of the world.

His right leg limped and his foot tended not to lift high above the gravel and instead churned pebbles beneath the sole. A spitting image of Gramps, if Gramps were forty years younger. He moved like a man uncertain, slipped one hand in his back pocket, the other to the nape of his neck, rubbed it in the slow-motion way of someone coming to realization. Jack West, my father—a middle-aged, tired-looking guy in boots that needed a polish.

He stopped—ridiculously—at gunfight range, and I wouldn't have been surprised to see a holster on his hip, a Peacemaker unlatched and its hammer cocked, his thick, fatherly fingers two twitches shy of a draw. We stood there, breathing at one another. I think, there in that parking lot, that I understood why he couldn't have gone before Gramps without invitation.

Is it Dad? he said, and flicked his hand, as if to dry it. Then he rubbed its knuckles.

He had a heart attack, I said after a pause. But he pulled through.

Jack's hand went to his cheek, his finger scratched the skin beside his ear.

Is he okay, though?

He thinks he's dying.

Is he though? Dying?

I shoved my hands in my pockets. He sent me to find you, to bring you back. I've got a bunch of your things.

Memory box?

Something like that.

I'd like to see it, he said. He had a gravelly voice, like someone who'd spent a few good hours crying. I could see his throat bob when he swallowed. A breeze flicked his short hair, one or two strands dancing up and down.

You gonna come see him?

Been waiting almost thirty years, of course I'll go see him. Might need a drink first, but of course I'll go see him. Want to come inside?

I gave in, and he held his ground as I approached across the gravel, until I had neared enough that he could have reached out and belted me a friendly punch on the shoulder. He turned on his heel, and almost side by side we walked the last stretch to the administration building. At the entrance, he knocked his boots against the stairs; I followed suit. The door hung loose on its hinges, but once inside I saw another, stronger, wood one that barred entry to his cabin, his small reclaimed personal space. We pushed through that, too.

The cabin was the size of a studio. Its kitchen spanned one

wall opposite his bed; at night, he'd hear the fridge's growly rumble. The oven door yawned open—the cabin was probably not the best-insulated structure this side of the Rockies, and heat is heat. On the windowsill sat a knot of parched vine, some kind of herb. His tap had a filter. Outside, there'd be a compost pile.

Aren't you going to tell me I picked a helluva time to show up? I said, to pre-empt. Jack went to the sink and filled a kettle, set it on an element.

He shrugged, a flash of goofy dad. Are you hungry? he said.

I don't really eat breakfast.

How about some eggs. With the coffee I'm making.

He brandished a pan at me, reached for the cupboard door.

I'll have some eggs, I said.

Free-range, he said, then he set about cooking, and I flopped onto the shiny leather sofa that seemed like it didn't belong.

I took it in, that cabin with its manhandled walls of pine, the kerosene lamps and the candlewax that dotted the surface of a coffee table, the sooty dust that gilded all the places beyond easy reach. What I wanted to see was a clue about his life—pictures or trinkets or the kind of baubles you can stuff inside a maroon shoebox and tuck beneath your bed. A bookshelf stood against the far wall, stocked with titles like *Firewater* and *Home-Brewing for Dummies* and *European Spirits*. On the top shelf: a bottle of plum-coloured liquid with a bloated wood cross somehow crammed inside. There was an otherworldly scent to the house. I smelled dog, but more than that: I smelled a place I knew from my childhood, like déjà vu, or like coming all of a sudden into possession of a memory—like when you wake from a dream so real you can't be sure it wasn't.

I watched Jack's shoulders, the stiffness of those neck muscles so determined not to turn his head. He smeared oil in the pan and cracked two eggs, scrambled them with swift, gladiatorial thrusts. Dishes columned up at the sink's side; flattened pizza boxes were wedged between the fridge and the counter. Thirty years separated us, and I couldn't place him. Awkward, humble, reticent in that way of shy people and dads who can't talk to their sons.

Do you have a dog? I said.

Sent him away with a buddy, he said, and scraped the eggs onto a plate. He set it down in front of me on the coffee table, pressed a thumb to the edge to kill its wobble.

Why not just take him yourself?

No licence, he said. Then he dragged a chair from the table, sat in it reverse, arms draped over the backrest like a teenager. I made the trip to Owenswood to try and get Linnea out of there, but I can't drive legally.

He paused, linked his fingers together, elbows thrown wide. His eyes moved over his knuckles, as if counting each one.

There are worse things, I said.

Let me get you some cutlery.

I ate, and he gravitated from that chair to the window, watched me or watched whatever was outside. The fires maybe, so close now you could feel the heat on your cheek like breath. We needed to get in Colton's jeep and head east, we both knew that. But I finished eating and he took the plate and rinsed it without soap and set it on a drying rack of braided tree branches. For a second, he lingered like he might attack the rest of the dishes, too, but instead he ran cold water and lowered his mouth to the stream, came up wiping his chin with his sleeve, like I'd seen Gramps do a thousand times before.

Jack lit one of the kerosene lamps, lifted it from its hook.

Tell me straight: is Dad okay?

He thinks he's dying.

The skin around Jack's eyes constricted, the muscle in one cheek tensed.

But is he?

He had a heart attack, but they defibbed him.

Can't you just tell me?

I don't know if he's actually dying, Jack. I'm not a doctor.

Well, he said, and shrugged a defeated-person's shrug. I didn't know that.

He went to the cabin door carrying the kerosene lamp. Then he seemed to notice it, made a grimace at it, a confused shake of his head.

Let's have a drink, he said, and pushed on through.

I followed him out. His yard—his space—had its own firepit with handcrafted wooden chairs and another slate spiral, this one far more carefully done, more evenly spaced and angled as if measured. There, he limped toward a padlocked shed twenty or thirty metres away. Trees broke up the mountain view; the grass had been recently mowed. Strung between a couple of trunks was a tire rubber. At its base: a pigskin, worn to a snub nose at both tips. The occasional beer can lay in the grass, some of them doublebent and hole-punched by bullets. There was a swing set; I don't know why. Jack's limp became more pronounced the closer he got to the shed, or maybe he just picked up speed. With each step, he threw the leg forward at the hip, hardly bent the knee at all. That's the kind of injury that will one day cause a leg to buckle, and I thought about asking him what had happened, and I thought about telling him, then and there, the fate that had befallen Colton and that even now he wouldn't be able to get my mom back.

It's far away to reduce vibrations, he said upon reaching the door. A fist-sized padlock barred entry, and Jack drew the key from a leather cord around his neck. Inside was a distillery, barrels with their bent-up tubes and that warm smell of fermentation like a small-town pub. He kicked off his boots, tossed me a wink, and tiptoed across the floor—concrete, and probably immaculately level—and snagged a bottle from a stand. It sloshed with translucent liquid. He offered it to me, two-handed, like a thing of great worth.

I was trying for something European, he said, but pronounced it *Euro-peen*. Really, not much more than firewater. Can't make it right.

Have you got old tin cans we can swig this from? I said from the doorway.

He squinted, lifted the corners of his mouth.

I could empty out some beans.

I'm kidding, Jack.

His eyes darted instantly to the bottle. He swirled it.

I don't mind. I could empty some beans. If you'd like that?

Let's just have a drink, I said.

We crossed the yard. Jack kicked an empty beer can and something inside it *tink-a-link*ed. He paused to stare up at the smoke, to inhale through his nose and shake his head, let his chest deflate much slower than it'd inflated. He motioned to two lawn chairs in the shade cast by the small cabin, and I dropped into one while he rummaged inside for two clean glasses. Through the open window I heard water run, the squeak of him scrubbing with a bare hand. He came out flicking water from the insides of two jam jars.

I never really saw the point of buying cups, he said, and handed one to me, threads and all.

How long you been here?

I lost count. More than a decade. But I was away.

Away where?

Europe, he said, with a certain severity.

Doing what?

As he sloshed the liquor into the jars his hands shook. The liquor tasted like liquor, and not much else. Like drinking a Christmas tree, Gramps once said of a buddy's homebrew. Jack scratched his temple incessantly; the skin was raw and waxy there and when he finished he checked his nails for blood and the bedrock of dead flesh. A breeze blew by from the east, but it didn't cool me so much as just move the heat around. If I stuck my tongue out, I tasted charcoal.

Jack refilled his glass, a finger's worth.

I didn't think Dad would send you, he said after a time.

Neither did I.

How'd you find me?

Archer, then my mom. Had a run-in with her husband.

I'm not surprised, Jack said. Then he shot the liquor in his glass and wheezed against the burn.

It's a story for the drive, I told him, and he eyed me quizzically between the whoops of his cough.

When he had cleared himself, he sat just looking at the alcohol in his glass like some kind of diviner. Then he emptied the jar onto his yard in a wide spray, and corked the bottle. The chair sagged when he dropped his weight into it. I wondered what to say to him, what kinds of stories he'd like to hear, if any.

You like football? he said.

Hockey.

I don't mind the CFL. Hope the Yanks don't buy it up?

No opinion.

How about Iraq? You're young.

They say it'll be like Vietnam again.

Is that what they say?

He looked at the bottle. I considered asking for another, but the day was still young.

Do you want to toss one around? A football?

The question hung between us and we each took a moment to regard the jagged horizon and the fires on the cusp of their descent. It looked like the mountains had sprouted hairs. I couldn't even smell smoke anymore, though the scent was stronger than ever. My teeth felt fuzz-coated, same way they do after a night of heavy drinking. I didn't know how much time we had left: all the might of human ingenuity couldn't stop those fires, and it had damn well tried. Great and powerful and so far beyond us—that's what it felt like, standing there. Diminishing. As if we were not really in control of anything, even our own existence. We had to get out of there, but something had to happen to make us go. I think we both sensed that.

Toss a football? I said.

He grinned at me like a dad. Do you throw like a girl?

By now I've probably learned to throw like a woman.

Jack rose. He swiped the bottle up in his fist and jerked his chin. Come on.

We moved across the yard toward the tire strung between the trees with bright neon rope. Shards of glass coated the yard, mortared into the dirt like fertilizer: the remnants of bottles blasted to grain. Kernels popped beneath my feet, and I got the sense that not many feet besides Jack's had walked the length of that yard. He set the moonshine on a severed tree trunk and waddled to the tire, where he bent to scoop the football. His knee hardly moved when he did so. He slapped the football, hard. His muscles went tight and he squeezed it at his chest, then his arm looped over his head and he flicked it to me and it missiled through the air. The catch jarred through my shoulder and a sudden heat waved over me and I tugged my collar.

I ran my fingers over the smooth leather and the stitches stained yellow-grey. Later, he'd tell me how some nights he spent hours in that yard with the dim household glow for light, just blasting throw after throw through that tire, as if it meant something. He was a good aim, he'd say. I threw the pigskin back and it wobbled through the air and Jack cradled it to his hip in a textbook reception. He licked his lips, lasered another one at me, and this time, favouring my arm, I fumbled the catch and it jarred into my finger. I swore, and Jack said nothing while I retrieved it. We carried this on. He wanted to offer advice on how to toss the football and I wanted to ask, but conversation was beyond us. I had so many questions about him and Archer and Gramps, and I somehow knew that if I were to get any true answer it would be from him. All paths led eventually to Jack West, even my own, though I'd managed for twenty-nine years to carve my way without his ever-present spectre. Gramps, I understood, had never let himself move on from the loss of Jack; he was too stubborn, and I worried forward to their eventual meeting. I wondered if they'd both be startled by how much damage time can do, by how men become unassuming as they grow old and how even those, like Gramps, who have held their heads high will stoop their shoulders and come to prefer the look of asphalt. Men and demons, both, can grow soft and fat and normal.

The football lanced through the air like a thing made radiant.

At last I fumbled a big one and it cartwheeled far enough for me to jog after. When I picked it up and straightened, I caught Jack with the bottle pressed to his mouth and the weight of its contents on his pursed lips, suspended and anticipating. He drew a long, burning gulp, and I thought: *It has been a long time since he kissed someone.* After, he looked from me to the bottle and me again. Then he leaped forward—with as much speed as his gimped leg allowed—and flung the bottle ass-over-teakettle into the brush that walled his yard. It went up in an arc and he himself went down to his knees and I didn't know which to track. He sagged to the grass, knuckles down, and flopped over in that awkward way that forces your knees into the air. Somewhere, the moonshine landed, never to be recovered. Jack pushed himself up. His shirt slid over his waist and revealed a beer gut and he dragged down at it over and over with one clumsy hand.

THE EVENING TRICKLED inside and made his small room colder than you'd expect from August, and he said it was because the window wouldn't close and he couldn't be fucked to fix it. The smoky smell of B.C. moseyed right in. He opened the oven and cranked it on high and I dropped once more onto the couch that seemed out of place. Jack lit the kerosene lamps and stewed up something to eat on the stove while the room grew warm. He spooned it into two ceramic mugs, said he didn't have bowls, didn't see the point. He waggled another bottle of liquor at me but I shook my head, and he set it uncorked on the floor. We ate working up the courage.

Went rabbit poaching once, he said. In England, at some abandoned satellite ground. The guy I was with had one near-sighted eye and one farsighted.

Hope you didn't let him drive.

I did, Jack said, his face upturned at last.

I took another spoonful. So this is rabbit? I said, knowing.

Nah, he said. Cheap beef.

Thanks.

He sat wrong-facing in a chair, hunched with the chairback nearly to his chin.

I feel like I'm supposed to tell you something, he said, and squinted out the window at the sky turning its edges dark.

I didn't answer him, sucked meat from between my teeth.

Hell if I know what. Didn't think it'd be you, though.

I held his gaze. Me and my dad: him with a bowl of stew under his nose, his hand jittering like he needed a drink, and me slouch-shouldered beside him, elbows on my thighs and thinking about nothing, for once. I just wanted to hear him talk. He had stories to tell, a life lived. All the world reduced to that: some few feet of distance, a man en route to tears, the smell of strong liquor.

You wanted to stay, I said.

Of course I did. He's my dad.

You told him?

Yes, Jack said. I made him cry.

His hands spasmed toward the moonshine. He breathed a deep exhale through lips shrunk to an O.

Nobody saw. He cried.

The wind rattled the window. A retch of smoke pushed past us, strong enough to bring water to our eyes.

Christ, Jack said, all breath.

It's okay.

I made a lot of mistakes, but fuck.

He took off his ballcap and ran his fingers along the rim.

His voice cracked. I can't even tell you, he said. I'm sorry ... son?

It doesn't really matter anymore.

Not to you.

No, Jack, not to me, I said, bitterly.

His spoon scraped around his mug's bottom. Well I'm not sorry.

I put my food down. And what would you *possibly* have to be sorry for? I said.

Hey, he said, and at last reached for his bottle. I'm sorry I didn't tell anyone about Archer fucking Nora, and I'm sorry Dad sent her away—

Gramps sent Nora away?

Jack pushed the heel of his palms into each eye. She wanted to stay, same as me. But Dad wouldn't have it. See, *that's* my fault, son. I shoulda let it lie.

He took a tradesman's swig.

Then this wildfire happens, and I don't have a licence, and even here at the end I can't get Linnea to accept my apology. So I figure it's karma. The world has a sense of justice. Burn something up and get burned up—fucking poetic. So I'm just waiting for it to roll on down the mountain. Been trying to die for thirty years.

And then I show up, I said.

He tossed the bottle down and it rolled along the cabin's uneven floor, spewing all the way. And then you show up, he said.

I WENT TO COLTON'S jeep to get some air and to let Jack get some composure. The wind was more constant and the smoke almost ringed us like an eye wall. The Purcells had millenniums of experience in the art of holding back fire, but I won't lie: I worried about how much time we had left. Pillars of smoke coalesced in a haze above us, thick like pillow-clouds or tar or the bubbling pitch from those old cartoons about dinosaurs. It seethed and moiled, and looking at it made me feel like I was being drawn in—like I was approaching a great and impenetrable dark.

At the jeep, I leaned on the driver window and allowed myself a moment to worry that I would end up like my father. He certainly didn't have Gramps' disposition. I don't know if Gramps had failed to impart it or if Jack had simply been away too long; perhaps, like muscle, even courage can wither if unused. My father, who Gramps so desperately wanted to see again: some over-sentimental man with receding hair and a lack of personal resolve. But I guess it didn't matter. We don't choose our family, and, like my mom said, we don't really choose who we care for.

Jack had set himself up on a chair on the porch, and he barely reacted to my return until I presented him with Gramps' maroon box. He had another bottle of moonshine open beside him. I didn't say a word.

What is it? he said, but I just held it out to him. He lifted the lid and held it in the air and just stared, until something jarred him to action and he lowered it to his lap. When he touched the contents his head shook. His knuckles went to his teeth and he toothed on them. I saw his baldness and the way the middle-aged muscles on his back had grown soft despite years of physical work. His shoulders rose with a judder, sagged the same. Why? he said. His eyes were squinty, moist. He made a low, throttling sound, a bubbly groan. Why didn't he ever get in touch?

You know how he is.

But why is he like that?

That's the question. That is the question.

Can't you call me Dad?

Not now, I said. Maybe sometime.

It seemed to satisfy him. He shut the box. The wind scattered dust against his shins and scuffed boots. He kicked at the cloud of dirt rising below him until it too sped away, shucked off toward the grassblades and whatever else awaited. Everything tanged with our sweat and the soot set adrift on the wind and the fires so dangerously close; the empty glasses of moonshine gave off a stink like pure gasoline. He got up and walked off the porch, put his hand to his mouth. Part of facing your own demons is the realization that not everyone will be able to do so.

An object set on a path will remain on that path unless outside forces act upon it—that's not even philosophy, that's just physics. Bullets more or less fly straight. People, in general, maintain course toward destiny. And even those vagabonds who journey without destination remain on that journey though the winds may blow them astray. Wandering, it turns out, is just another straight line in hindsight.

Jack squinted at the light, hand to forehead in an evening salute. He scratched his chin, that polished line of stubble. He looked noble all of a sudden, like a man from the Dirty Thirties: a coal-shoveller, maybe. Or an air force cadet, unremarkable and unassuming, a man of paramount mediocrity—exactly the kind of man who should be an unlikely hero. He stood there on the dry grass with the light spread thin across him, just *being* Jack West, and for that moment it seemed the world moved around us, and not us around it. I'd never felt that way before, and not again since—like lying on your back and watching the stars rotate, but with everything, with your very existence. Jack West: my father, but more than that. Mystery, enigma, trope. Son, lover, coward. Beginning, middle, and end.

ACKNOWLEDGMENTS

This book was four years in the making, and I am humbled by all the people who've lent a hand during its creation. I've heard it said that writing is a solitary art, and writers solitary people, but I'm not sure I believe that.

As ever, my mom, dad, and sister have been pillars of support throughout this and all projects, as have my surrogates on the older side of the Atlantic: Annabel, Greville, Corty, Thomas, and Charlie. It's impossible to quantify how much it means to know that someone's in your corner.

For reasons I can't fathom, and after almost four years, Andrew Cowan continues to offer his immaculate editorial eye, his expert wit, and his invaluable constructive cynicism. Lorna Jackson taught me to write a sentence and believed in me enough that I too believed. No small feat, either of these things.

Great swaths of this book were workshopped at the University of Victoria, during my undergrad, and the University of East Anglia, during my MA. Thanks to Giles Foden, and to my fellow students at both, especially Joshua Piercey, Armando Celayo, Ben Lyle, Anna Smith, Bernardo "Bro-1" Bueno, Hal "Soulbrother" Walling, and Trevor "Chest" Wales.

Elaine and Andrea, of Massaro's Coffee, gave me the shelter I needed to get through the last two drafts; in the darkest hours, down those darkest roads, their coffee kept me going and their abuse kept me humble.

My agent, the electric Karolina Sutton, continues to tolerate my shenanigans and to convince publishers to publish my work; she is irreplaceable as an agent and a friend. As with my previous book, I am grateful to my editors—Nick Garrison at Penguin Canada, Helen Garnons-Williams at Bloomsbury UK, and Anton Mueller at Bloomsbury US—for all their work to make this book as polished as it can be. Emma Daley is one hell of a publicist, and Steve Myers, though a drunken lunatic, is not a bad one himself. I am grateful, of course, to the rest of the staff at Bloomsbury and Penguin for their ceaseless enthusiasm.

Lastly, for being forced to read the very first draft of this book, and for not telling me to give up right there and then, a shout-out to Thrasher Gaston—man of myth, legend, and unchangeable glory.

ALSO AVAILABLE BY D. W. WILSON

ONCE YOU BREAK A KNUCKLE

Winner of the BBC National Short Story Award 2011

In the remote Kootenay Valley in western Canada, good people sometimes do bad things. Two adolescents sabotage a rope swing; a heartbroken young man chooses not to warn his best friend about an approaching car; sons challenge their fathers.

Crackling with tension and propelled by jagged, cutting dialogue, D. W. Wilson's stories reveal to us how our best intentions can be doomed to fail or injure, how our loves can fall short or mislead us. An intoxicating cocktail of adrenaline and vulnerability, doggedness and dignity, *Once You Break a Knuckle* explores the courage it takes to make it through another day.

'D. W. Wilson's stories have a wonderfully raw, vernacular energy which carries the reader through some dark and spitefully funny moments. This is a cracking read'
JON MCGREGOR

'A massive achievement'
GUARDIAN

'Wilson's world is dangerous and unpredictable, and his writing has a terrific, understated force'
THE TIMES

'Wilson's voice is distinctive, confident and completely enthralling'
GEOFF DYER